PENGUIN BOOKS

RED PLAID SHIRT

Diane Schoemperlen is the author of the acclaimed novels *Our Lady of the Lost and Found* and *In the Language of Love,* and five short story collections, including *The Man of My Dreams,* which was nominated for a Governor General's Award and Trillium Award, and *Forms of Devotion,* which won the Governor General's Award for Fiction in 1998. She lives with her son, Alexander, in Kingston, Ontario.

Diane Schoemperlen

Red
Plaid
Shirt

stories

Penguin Books

PENGUIN BOOKS
Published by the Penguin Group
Penguin Group (USA) Inc., 375 Hudson Street, New York, New York 10014, U.S.A.
Penguin Books Ltd, 80 Strand, London, WC2R 0RL, England
Penguin Books Australia Ltd, 250 Camberwell Road, Camberwell, Victoria 3124, Australia
Penguin Books Canada Ltd, 10 Alcorn Avenue, Toronto, Ontario, Canada M4V 3B2
Penguin Books India (P) Ltd, 11 Community Centre, Panchsheel Park, New Delhi - 110 017, India
Penguin Books (N.Z.) Ltd, Cnr Rosedale and Airborne Roads, Albany, Auckland, New Zealand
Penguin Books (South Africa) (Pty) Ltd, 24 Sturdee Avenue, Rosebank, Johannesburg 2196, South Africa

Penguin Books Ltd, Registered Offices: 80 Strand, London WC2R 0RL, England

First published in Canada by HarperCollins Canada 2002
Published in Penguin Books 2003

10   9   8   7   6   5   4   3   2   1

PUBLISHER'S NOTE
This is a work of fiction. Names, characters, places, and incidents either are the product
of the author's imagination or are used fictitiously, and any resemblance to actual persons,
living or dead, business establishments, events, or locales is entirely coincidental.

LIBRARY OF CONGRESS CATALOGING IN PUBLICATION DATA
Schoemperlen, Diane.
Red plaid shirt : stories / Diane Schoemperlen
p.   cm.
ISBN 0 14 20.0320 4
1. Canada—Social life and customs—Fiction.   I. Title.
PR9199.3.S267 R4 2003
813'.54—dc21   2002192496

Printed in the United States of America
Set in LinoLetter

Contents

Losing Ground (1976)

The photograph is black and white, printed on heavy cardboard. Two corners are chipped off like pieces of old paint. It is a picture of my grandfather sitting on a wagon in a field of grey grain. The wagon is pulled by two horses with hair like muffs around their ankles. One of the horses has its head down, one hoof extended. Its tail is caught flicking away flies, a small bird, the camera, and my ancestral eyes. The wind, which refuses to be photographed, is hung up in my grandfather's hair. This makes him look young and careless.

He was already in his eighties by the time I was born. Everyone called him Grandpa Blake and I never thought of him as having a first name.

The photograph was taken on the family farm near Balder, Manitoba. Around the time I was born, the farm was sold to a group of Mennonites. This was when my grandfather moved into Aunt Clara's house in Balder.

In all the farm stories my mother told me, my grandfather figured as the patriarch, undisputed and self-proclaimed, a solid and sensible man. His father, my great-grandfather, was killed by the Indians when my grandfather was six days old. They threw his body in the creek and stole all the horses. I thought this was remarkable. My grandfather stayed on the farm for another eighty years and he never stopped working. At first my mother said she respected him. When I got older and he was dead, she told me that she'd hated him.

He fathered twelve children, my mother was one of the

younger ones. They all worked on the farm. The girls wore ankle-length dresses because my grandfather said showing your ankles was shameful. I imagine their skirts bunching up between their legs, the sweat trickling down their thighs, soaking through their cotton stockings. Hot prairie summer. Kerchiefs sliding down their wet foreheads, hair curling up in the sweat. Everybody wore work boots, brown lumberjack feet laced up with twine. Everybody knew what they were supposed to do. My mother figures she was born knowing how to milk the cows, bale the hay, and slop the pigs. She says, "It's taken me fifty years to forget. Finally." Sometimes now she speaks scornfully of people who are still farmers, working the land. She thinks they're doing things the hard way.

When the mares were bred with the stallion from the farm down the road, all the girls were kept inside the farmhouse. The blinds were drawn and the curtains were closed. They were also kept inside when the sow was giving birth and when Dolly, the old horse, had to be shot. All of these things, sex and birth and death, kept mixing up together. My mother thought they must be either extremely embarrassing or dangerous, something we must all be protected from. She and Aunt Clara can laugh about it now.

I never lived in Balder. My parents and I lived in Carlisle, Ontario, but every summer we went west for three weeks.

In Ontario, I was an only child and often lonely. We had no other relatives in Carlisle. But in Balder, I became part of a huge dangling tribe, there were dozens of them. Like my grandfather, the rest of the Blakes (except my mother, who'd married late in life) all seemed to be exceptionally fertile, their respective families like elongated arms stretching off in all directions. Those who didn't live in Balder were always coming out to visit, or planning to, writing long letters to Aunt Clara which she read out loud to my mother and me when I brought them home from the post office. These other relatives were the main topic of conversation among the Balder relatives and so it seemed that we were all there together at once. The bunch of them were constantly engaged in a variety of emotional activities, all of them tangled up together, waving their arms, getting married, getting into trouble (for the males this meant Jail, for the females, Unwed Pregnancy) or heading for it, having babies, moving around the country, growing older, suffering mysterious, painful, and lingering illnesses. Back home in Ontario afterwards, I tried to keep hold of them but they always faded away. They were all much more believable in the summer.

It took us one full day of driving to get from Carlisle to Balder. My father drove the whole way as my mother had never learned how. Her jobs were to light and put out his cigarettes, to pass him unwrapped sticks of Wrigley's Spearmint gum, and to keep talking so he wouldn't fall asleep. My job was to keep quiet and busy in the back seat. In aid of this end, my mother, for weeks before we left, bought a number of small items which I was not allowed to look at yet because they were *for the trip*. I thought this suspense was spectacular. The morning we left, these things appeared on the back seat in a brown paper bag which I was at last allowed to open once we were in the car, out of the driveway, and on our way. In the bag, there might be books, games you could play by yourself, sugary pink cologne in tiny bottles shaped like bells, cars, or birds, coloured pencils, notepads printed with kittens, my name, or pansies. The contents of the surprise bag kept changing as I grew older and then, I'm not sure when, it disappeared altogether.

In Balder we always stayed at Aunt Clara's house because she was my mother's favourite sister and my mother hers. This was something they had discovered only after growing up, because Aunt Clara was fourteen years older and had left the farm to get married when my mother was only six years old. Aunt Clara was a widow now.

There were about eight hundred people living in Balder then and the favourite joke around town was that half of them were widows. The men kept dying off and the women kept living on and on. There were old women everywhere you went. Very few of them remarried—there was nothing much left to choose from.

In Balder everybody knew me. When I walked downtown to collect Aunt Clara's mail at the post office, as I did every morning except Sunday every summer, people who passed me on the sidewalk smiled and said hello. Sometimes they called me by name and sometimes they said, "You must be Clara's little niece from Ontario." Some people drove by in their cars and waved. I waved back airily with Aunt Clara's keys (the one to her post office box held apart so I wouldn't get mixed up and embarrassed when I got there) as though I'd lived in Balder all my life.

When I was walking with my mother, some woman would always stop and say to her, "Now which sister are you?" Everybody said you could tell a Blake girl a mile off and none of them ever got any older.

More often though, I walked with my father. Sometimes we went out in the evening. We were closer then than we ever would be again. We had discovered how much alike we were and so didn't talk much while we walked, just pointed out odd things to each other with no explanation. Occasionally someone would recognize him and say, "You must be Iris's husband and is this her little girl?" We were both hazily annoyed by this but we kept walking and never mentioned it. There was almost always heat lightning in the sky as it grew dark.

Aunt Clara looked after my grandfather for ten years. No one ever questioned this arrangement. Aunt Clara was his oldest child: it was as though she had inherited him. When she decided to put him in the home in Winnipeg, half the family was upset and the other half said it was about time. Aunt Clara paid no particular attention to either faction. After ten years, it seemed, he was all hers: she could do whatever she wanted with him. She took care of all the necessary arrangements, packed up his few clothes in a brand new suitcase, put the suitcase in the trunk of her new Dodge, and drove him into the city herself. The black suit he was to be buried in was in the suitcase too.

In a letter to my mother, she wrote, *He'll never come out of there alive.* I took this to mean that there was little else he could be expected to do now except die. It was an unemotional issue. Most of his children were pragmatists.

That Christmas my mother sent Aunt Clara the money to buy a new pair of drapes for the living room. Inside the card, which featured a fat red Santa Claus in pince-nez reading his list and checking it twice, she wrote, *You'll never get the tobacco smell out of those old ones.* Putting the stamp on the front and two Christmas seals on the back, she turned to me and said fiercely, "When I'm too old to look after myself, I want to die. But if I don't, you just put me in a home right off the bat. You don't owe me anything!" For a few years, I thought this was both possible and true.

When we went to visit him in the home, it was a special trip to the city. My mother, my father, Aunt Clara, myself, sometimes assorted cousins came too, we all went together, safety in numbers. I think they were still afraid of him. I neither dreaded nor looked forward to these trips. We usually went twice during the three weeks we spent in Balder. We drove the fifty miles to Winnipeg over easy-angled prairie backroads, watching the windshield sprout dust and dead bugs on the way. When I was younger, I counted Volkswagens and held my nose noisily whenever we passed a pig farm or a slough of dead water, curdling and thick around the edges like sour cream. When I got older, I drank warm Coke and read, sulky with impotent prepubescent anger at my mother because she had taken so long to get ready, saying, "I just have to put on my face before we go," dressing up for him, checking out her colour coordination and her lipstick. As though going to a lot of trouble to do something you really didn't want to do somehow made up for your reluctance.

While all these preparations went on, I waited and pouted in the garden, stealing peas and poking around in the potato hills. This brought out the garter snakes, which looked greasy but felt dry when they brushed across my bare feet. I was afraid of them but pretended not to be because I knew it annoyed my mother.

Sometimes, when I was feeling more generous, I waited on the front step, listening to the caragana seed pods bursting in the heat. The Mennonite boys drove by the house in their green pickup truck, right fender gone. There were five or six of them, they seemed to go everywhere as a group, spitting sunflower seed shells and laughing. They waved and hollered hello as they passed, which produced in me that minor secret hysteria all young girls are prone to.

On the way out of town, we always stopped at Flint's Family Store to buy a bag of peppermints for my grandfather. Flint's was the sort of place that sold everything: food, clothes, shoes, jewellery, hand-tooled genuine made-in-Canada cowhide key cases, newsprint paper in bulky pads called GIANT, and salt licks. At first I thought these last were for people. They came in different colours: blue, green, an odd red that looked like half-cooked liver. I wanted to bend down and lick one, preferably a blue one, blue being my favourite colour, but once I knew they were for cows, I was afraid I would be poisoned on the spot and die a horrible death underneath the checkout counter.

I rode in the back seat, my mother and Aunt Clara were both in the front, smiling and chatting and patting each other. They saw each other just this once a year and for three weeks they talked nonstop. After a week, they were saying the same things over and over again and nobody seemed to notice but me.

My father was silent, driving in the heat, sweating and sighing. The road ahead of us glowed. By the time we got there, the car, which was black, was coated with white dust. My father always fussed about this and bought cans of Turtle Wax before we went home.

The nursing home, called Paradise Retreat, was a flat, ochre-coloured building set down like a wafer in the middle of an asphalt parking lot. Once inside, we smiled as a group past the front desk matron. Past the first-floor cleaning lady, who was always smoking, never cleaning. She was leaning, rumpled and damp-looking, against the wall. Her cigarette, which was stuck to her lower lip, bobbed at us as we filed past. Her teeth were yellow, stuck into orange gums. She seemed to be flexing them when she smiled, which was frequently and unpredictably. Once I saw her coming through a doorway with her teeth in her hand and her fingers in her mouth, rooting around for stray bits of lunch.

My grandfather's room was at the far end of a long green hallway. Corner room, corner stone, I assume the family paid more for his corner lot. He shared the room with a man named Harold Clausen. In the room were two beds, identically tucked and folded. This precision allowed us to believe that he was being well taken care of. These people were professionals, no need to worry, no need to worry at all. My grandfather's bed was covered with a grey blanket. There were bits of lint stuck to it and a zigzag line of blue stitching was coming unravelled around the edge.

The window, there was only one, was over my grandfather's bed. Once inside the room, I stood close to the door, too shy to move farther in. From the doorway, I couldn't see out the window. I had no idea what you might or might not see through the net curtains.

My grandfather was always there in the room when we arrived. He wouldn't go down to the TV room with Harold because he couldn't see well enough. But he wouldn't admit this and he wouldn't wear the bifocals they'd fitted him with. He and Harold were nearly always angry at each other for this or some other reason. Harold called my grandfather "the old man."

"Come to see the old man, did ya? Well, good luck," Harold said. "Stubborn old goat hasn't talked to me in a week. I put his glasses on him one night when he was asleep and he wore them all morning before he even noticed." Harold thought this was a good one.

My grandfather would be sitting on the side of his bed. His slippers were red plaid, sliced open across the toes to accommodate his bulging bunions. He wore a plaid flannel shirt and baggy green workpants held up by striped suspenders. He sucked peppermints two at a time from the bag we'd left him last time. The nurses doled out the mints so they'd last from one visit to the next. He was always accusing Harold of stealing them when he was asleep.

Sometimes he figured out who we were and sometimes he didn't. When he did, he always criticized my mother. "Iris, such a skimpy dress, can't you afford to sew yourself a new one?"

When he confused her with one of his other daughters, he said, "Where's the boy with the curly blonde hair? Why didn't you bring him along?"

Once, eyeing my father, he said, "Who's this you've got tagging along with you, Iris? Where's Dan?" Dan was some phantom figure my grandfather nearly always asked about, but no one could ever identify him. We told him Dan was fine, just fine, hadn't changed a bit.

He had little to say to Aunt Clara and he never spoke directly to me. I just stood there by the door, chewing my fingernails, picking the scab on my knee, dabbing at the welling blood with a dirty Kleenex. He kept asking questions and my mother kept yelling answers into his ear, imagining that she could make him understand.

The women's ward was at the other end of the hallway. One of the women was called Old Mary. Sometimes she was docile and dim like the rest of them. Other times she rushed down the hall in her backless blue nightgown, screaming at random, at the walls, into open rooms, at her own feet. Her slippers were made of yellow terry cloth, like bags sewn shut around her ankles. Her white hair was spurting out in chunks all over her head. She ignored the nurse trotting flat-footed down the hallway behind her.

This nurse, whose name was Angela Carl, usually stopped by my grandfather's room to say hello to us. She was short and pretty with pale red hair and pastel skin. She managed to look well dressed in her white nurse's uniform. Her calves were thick and muscular and I imagined this came from chasing old people around.

Angela Carl told me they'd taken Old Mary's clothes away because she kept tearing them up and throwing them out the window or trying to flush them down the toilet. I had no idea whether Angela Carl thought this horrible or hilarious and no idea why she told *me* about it.

The next summer Angela Carl told my mother that Old Mary had started wandering at night, too, sometimes crawling into bed with one of the old men. The night she tried to get into bed with Harold he pushed her out onto the floor. Harold was very proud of this and told us about it several times that summer, and the next one too.

He said, "I can still take care of myself."

The other men were afraid of her and hollered for the night nurse to come and save them. Old Mary also stole bars of soap from everyone and hid them in the sheets at the foot of her bed.

Aunt Clara said, "She's gone mental, poor thing."

Going mental, I discovered, was something that could happen to anybody at any time. There was no cause and no cure. Some women went mental when they got pregnant too many times or too late in life. Some men went mental from drinking too much and then they tried to kill their wives with knives, axes, pitchforks, and other assorted implements. The wife was usually saved by some passing neighbour and then she was put under sedation and the husband was taken away after being successfully subdued by four burly men from the provincial hospital. Mental people were uncommonly strong.

Some people who went mental died in the hospital. No one could tell me if these people died from being mental or from some other, less interesting disease.

There were other people in and around Balder who were not exactly mental but who were "not right" either. This group seemed quite large considering the size of the town. Most of the people who weren't right were middle-aged bachelors who looked in women's bedroom windows at night. They were persistent but inept and so were always getting caught in the act.

One of these was Charlie Connor. The Connor family was as indigenous to Balder as our own and Charlie had been looking in bedroom windows for years. No one was seriously afraid of Charlie but, as Aunt Clara said, it was best not to encourage him. So she had blinds and brocade drapes on both bedroom windows and we all undressed in the dark. It was also important to leave the bathroom light off if you had to get up in the night. The rest of the townspeople seemed to regard Charlie and the others who weren't right as unfortunate but unavoidable nuisances.

Younger people who weren't right were "slow." They were mostly girls. This was seen simply as a sadness for the family involved, unless one of the "slow" teenagers began talking about marriage and babies, and then it became a serious scandal, something that someone should put a stop to before it got out of hand.

Aunt Clara, who knew a lot about such matters and so was my main source of information, seemed to be sorry for and scared of Old Mary both at once. When Angela Carl caught up with Old Mary and got hold of her arm, she would lead her back down the hall to her room. Old Mary walked along passively beside her, holding her hand. They swung their arms between them.

My grandfather paid no attention to Old Mary. All the nurses told us he was a model patient. I gathered we were meant to be proud of him for this. Actually, I thought he was rather dull.

Harold, on the other hand, seemed disappointed if Old Mary didn't make it down to their end of the hall before Angela Carl caught her. He took great delight in tormenting her, bulging out his eyes and opening his mouth wide, imitating her screams without making a sound. If she came too close, he poked his fingers into her matted hair and pulled. Sometimes he rushed down the hall behind her, nodding his head and flailing his arms in time with hers. Aunt Clara thought this was shameful but she laughed at him too.

Harold spent as little time as possible in their room, preferring to pass the hours in the TV room, where he flirted gently with the caved-in old women who were always knitting and passing out cups of hot lemon tea. Sometimes they bickered over who Harold liked best. He was impartial and said, "The days are so long for the ladies if I don't go round and perk them up a bit."

Every night Harold deposited his boots and his socks in the hall by the door. Every time he said, "Stop a horse dead in its tracks, that smell would. We'd be suffocated by morning if I left them in here." We all laughed politely.

My grandfather kept his boots by the bed and he wouldn't let the nurses move them to the rack behind the door. He always needed to know they were there, right there. Maybe he was expecting a fire in the night, preparing for an emergency exit. My mother told me about the night the farmhouse caught fire and he wouldn't let the children out till they'd all put on their underwear. My mother said her hair was singed and his moustache too.

It was an antique moustache, dark red and drooping. When I was a small child, I'd duck my head down whenever he tried to kiss me. Then my mother would poke me and push me toward him. He smelled like whiskey, tobacco, and porridge. He rubbed his moustache all over my chin and down my neck. I giggled because I thought I was supposed to, but it hurt and gave me a rash.

This was when he still lived with Aunt Clara in Balder. When we stayed there, I slept in the living room on the rollaway bed. I lay awake and listened to dry cricket calls and trains on the main line right across the street. Aunt Clara's house was on Railway Avenue. When the passenger train came through, it was all lit up, the people inside eating and reading and talking with just their heads showing. I had never been on a train then and I was so impressed by the size, the motion of them, forward, ever forward, headlong. I imagined then that the train must cross the whole country without ever stopping.

A bed creaked at the back of the house. Then fumbling feet. My grandfather did this every night. He sighed as he stood up. He banged his thigh on the bureau, found his balance, and headed for the bathroom. I could hear the palm of his hand pressed flat against the wall, sliding across one wooden door, around the loose glass knob, over a blank space of much-painted wall, stopping at the open door. Inside. Door shut. Muttering and the sound of irregular splashing into the toilet bowl. A few minutes more and he would come out, go back to bed, snuffling and readjusting himself.

The summer before he went to the home in Winnipeg he kept

falling asleep in the bathroom. Aunt Clara would get up then and lead him back to bed. They didn't speak. I kept my eyes shut and was embarrassed to be listening—I thought they both must know.

In the daytime, he fixed himself in the straight-backed chair by the stove. He smoked his pipe, burning the occasional hole in his shirt, and the steam from the kettle curled all around him. Every day at four o'clock he had one shot of whiskey, downed in one gulp right out of the shot glass. Aunt Clara gave the chair to the Indians when he went into the home the next spring.

This, the last summer that my grandfather lived in the house in Balder, was also the summer I was consumed with admiration for my cousin Lyle. He was four years older than me, the son of Uncle Maurice, my mother's youngest brother, and Aunt Fay, and he was always in trouble. That whole segment of the family, in fact, was always going through trouble of one kind or another. Their youngest daughter, Charleen, who was my age, skipped school and stole men's magazines from the drugstore. Their oldest daughter, Roxanne, who was sixteen, kept running away to Winnipeg with various young men. Until she got pregnant, and then she kept running farther away to Saskatchewan with the same young man, who nobody ever referred to by name, but only as "the father." I thought Roxanne was romantically rebellious and defended her in family discussions for years afterwards.

They all lived on a farm just outside of Balder. Lyle always said, "I'm bored with this crummy place," but he made the best of it. On the farm they had fifty head of cattle, a lethargic Saint Bernard who eventually turned vicious and had to be put down, and dozens of angry white chickens who were everywhere, pecking and shitting.

Lyle knew that I liked him and so he showed me how to catch

grasshoppers in a sealer jar. When the jar was half full, all legs and eyes and broken wings, Lyle produced the ball of string which he carried with him everywhere. He had me open the jar slowly while he reached in (I thought he was fearless) and pulled out one grasshopper, pinching it just behind the eyes. Sometimes the head popped right off but Lyle kept fishing around in the jar until he got one that held together. At this point, I was no longer expected to participate, but my presence as audience was essential.

Lyle stretched out a good length of string, looped and knotted it around the grasshopper's head. Then, standing on a bale of hay and balancing himself with one arm out, he tied the other end of the string to the clothesline. I could count the mosquito bites on his arm while he did this.

Once he had strung up a dozen or so grasshoppers, he moved the bale of hay underneath the pulley and sent the clothesline out across the yard and back and out and back. The grasshoppers flapped silently until their bodies dropped off, squirting out eggs or yellow juice. "Tobacco juice," my grandfather called it, laughing and spitting real tobacco juice across the yard. I thought it quite natural that Lyle was his favourite grandchild.

By the next summer my grandfather was in the home and I had decided that Lyle was a barbarian.

This was also the summer I had my first period. I'd been prepared for it by a short speech from my mother and a book, but neither one had mentioned that the blood would be so sudden, so red. Aunt Clara and my mother were excited, as though this were an accomplishment they could somehow take credit and responsibility for. Together, they rushed to the drugstore to get me "just what you need, dear" and would not let my father in on the excitement.

Up until this time, the drugstore, Lloyd's, had been my favourite place in Balder. I was always in there looking through the stacks of elementary and high school textbooks which were piled on a plywood table near the door. In Manitoba, you had to buy your own school books every year; in Ontario, they came with the territory.

The other books in the drugstore were Harlequin romances displayed on a revolving rack in the back corner. The women on the covers had perfect hair and there was always a dark man or a dark house lurking vaguely in the background. There were twelve new titles every month, which Aunt Clara bought, kept in a stack on her night table, read through in a rush, and then circulated among the other female relatives.

At the front of the drugstore, next to the door, were the postcards, local landmarks in black and white at five cents apiece. I bought the same ones every summer. The fire station, the new Bank of Montreal, three different views of the Anglican church where Aunt Clara sang in the choir and belonged to the Women's Auxiliary (which meant going to meetings twice a month and making aprons and pies for their annual bazaar—and every year, cross-stitching, she said, "I don't know why that Liddie MacAllister even bothers. All she ever brings is a pound cake and they're so plain . . . I just don't see it!"). There were also two postcard views of Main Street, one looking west, the other east, down a line of clean cars angle-parked on both sides of the street. For years I thought the signs said *"Angel* Parking Only," and this was one of the great mysteries of Manitoba which did not occur in Ontario.

After my mother and Aunt Clara rushed back to the house with their (my) box of Kotex wrapped in brown paper, I could think of the drugstore only as an embarrassing place where you went to buy "Sundries." I thought this was the polite adult word for Kotex.

I was angry and I said, "I bet the Queen doesn't have this!", gesturing wildly at my lower abdomen.

My mother laughed indulgently and said, "You're a woman

now." I thought this was ridiculous but didn't say so. For the first time in my life, I realized there were things about myself that were supposed to be kept hidden.

Just back from the home one day in July, Aunt Clara said, "He's losing ground." She arranged herself at the kitchen table with her mending basket and a cup of tea. She spread my green-flowered blouse, the one with the ripped armpit, in her lap. "This'll just take me a minute," she said to me.

That day, which was my birthday, my grandfather, despite the nurses' assurances, had seemed much worse. I had complained about going to see him on my birthday—it wasn't my idea of a suitable celebration. My mother said I was being selfish: "You might never see him again, you know." This was some kind of threat. I wasn't sure why it worked but it did.

He didn't recognize any of us that day and his eyes seemed to have grown more opaque, covered with a shiny scum that made me think of a raw egg oozing over a white tile floor. He was very pale, even his lips were white. My mother told me this was because your blood gets thinner when you get old. He had been in the home for almost four years.

When we got back to Balder, we had the birthday cake. As usual, we looked and looked for the candles. Aunt Clara always put them away in a safe place. This time we found them in the cupboard above the stove. They were all bent out of shape by the heat and stood at odd angles around the cake in all the customary colours: pastel pink, blue, green, and white like nurses' uniforms or bathroom walls. My father lit the candles and then, after I blew them out, my mother cut the cake.

Aunt Clara dished out the pieces as we arranged ourselves around the kitchen table in the heat. I was wearing my new short-shorts, a present from Aunt Clara, who said I had the legs to pull it off. My thighs stuck to the chair and I thought about the drive across the prairie all the way to Aunt Clara's. I was stuck to the seat then too and I kept putting my arm straight out the window, feeling the wind. My mother, when she caught me, said this was a dangerous thing to do because the force of the air would suck me right out the window. I thought this was ridiculous and said so. She said, "Don't be cheeky with me, young lady."

The birthday cake was my favourite kind: chocolate layer with boiled white icing. It was growing dark while we ate and mosquitoes made sounds like pins dropping on the window screens. Moths flickered around the outside light.

Looking out the corner windows, I saw a drunk Indian coming up the sidewalk, weaving but stepping on every crack with some determination. Step on a crack, break your mother's back. There were still some angry days when I jumped fiercely on the cracks with both feet, seeking revenge.

I looked away from the window with a curdled feeling in my stomach. Maybe if I asked for more cake, no one else would notice him. I knew that the mere sight of him would provoke instant anger in my mother and Aunt Clara. They would sigh and be disgusted and then they would compete grimly with each other for the worst Indian story, the most outraged sensibilities. I was at an age where I could not bear dissension: it made me want to throw up. I was afraid of all kinds of anger. I wanted everyone in the world to get along. I was always running around intervening in other people's, adults', arguments. I thought I could control everybody if only I worked at it.

He was still coming closer to the house. He stopped right in front, right where the lawn had been cleverly sloped, carefully landscaped to furnish the family with both aesthetic pleasure and good drainage. His back was toward me now. I could see just the edge of his white underwear above his pants. He kept tugging at the waist of his jeans, he had no belt, no hips to hold them up—

had drunk them all away, lost them in a back alley somewhere on the other side of town, or maybe in the all-night truck stop out on the highway. My mother wouldn't let me go there because she said that's where all the Indians went to drink coffee and try and sober up, which, she said, was impossible.

He lay down on the lawn, pillowing his head in one arm. I thought he might have to spend all night there. Maybe he belonged to one of the families who lived across the highway in abandoned cars with dangling headlights and no tires.

Aunt Clara came up behind me. "Bastards!" she said, so close to my ear that I jumped.

In a minute, she was gone from behind me and then she was out in the front yard too. She thrashed one arm at a swarm of mosquitoes and carried the broom in the other. Her mouth was moving but I couldn't hear what she was saying, not through that double layer of safe suburban glass. Like watching the late-night movie with the sound turned off. She poked at him with the broom. He looked up at her stupidly. It was dark now, there was heat lightning in the west, and I couldn't see the expression on his face, only the quizzical canary tilt of his head. Trying to stand up, he stumbled and Aunt Clara almost put out a hand to help him. But she caught herself in time and snatched it back. Her knuckles were white around the broom handle. He was moving away.

Aunt Clara came back into the kitchen, squeezing a sliver out of her thumb. She put the broom back in the corner. She and my mother shook their heads together. He had been some kind of threat to them, but his power did not extend to my father, who was in the living room now, reading the paper and having a drink of rum. Aunt Clara said, "There's more of them every year, they keep moving in from the reserve, we're losing ground."

When the phone rang about an hour later, Aunt Clara and my mother were at the sink, doing up the dishes. My mother was drying, Aunt Clara was washing and saying, "I'll do them, Iris, there's only a few, you go and sit down." But my mother kept hold of the tea towel on which was printed a map of Manitoba with a calendar inside it. She stood her ground and kept on drying the little plates which were painted with blue roses and a trim of gold leaves. I was moving between the kitchen and the living room, not sure whether I wanted to be with my father, who was still reading, or with Aunt Clara and my mother, who were talking about some woman I didn't know. Aunt Clara was saying, "She may be a breed but you'd never know it to look at her wash . . . so white, just beautiful." My mother was agreeing that the state of a woman's washing was very significant.

When the phone rang, we all turned and looked at it. It was nearly midnight. Drying her hands on her apron, Aunt Clara said, "Now who can that be at this hour?" I heard my father in the living room shake his paper and mutter, "Well, answer it and find out."

We watched Aunt Clara, who was listening into the receiver and nodding.

She hung up and said, "Grandpa died in his sleep, not a heart attack or anything, he just died. The night nurse found him on her rounds."

Everybody was quiet at first and then they said it was a blessing really.

We went to the nursing home once more after that. We had to gather up his things, sign some papers which would make his death official and legal.

When we went in past the front desk, the matron was flipping through papers in a manila file folder. She didn't look up but smiled automatically at the sound of our feet on the linoleum.

Harold was still there and my grandfather's bed was already being used by another old man who was asleep in a lump. Harold, who knew something about everybody, said his name was Jack Manywounds and he had been an unsuccessful rodeo cowboy. "Not much fun anymore though," Harold said.

No one said anything about Jack being an Indian. I supposed there was either something about this place or something about being old and asleep that removed all that, rendered everyone equally harmless.

When we left, Harold said he was sorry we wouldn't be coming back.

Summers at Aunt Clara's continued and there were still pilgrimages to be made. We went to the Balder Cemetery now. We went more frequently to the cemetery than we had to the home. These visits were less demanding—no conversation, no diplomacy, no peppermints.

The names on the headstones were unfamiliar at first but Aunt Clara, like Harold, knew something about everybody and I soon learned most of the names. There was one family who'd lost five children, all of them stillborn. They had five white headstones set in a row, with little sculpted lambs on top. There were also half a dozen suicides, unofficial of course, but Aunt Clara always knew what had really happened. My grandfather's grave was sealed with cement to prevent erosion and gopher holes. Aunt Clara planted peonies at the headstone.

The Indian graveyard was at the north end of the cemetery. The grass there had never been mowed and most of it had gone to seed. It looked like wheat. There were no headstones in the Indian graveyard, only the occasional white wooden cross heaved out of place by the frost. In some places, where the grass was thin, you could see that the ground had sunk down two or three inches where the bodies were.

Nobody tended the Indian graveyard and nobody ever came around. They knew that none of their dead kin would get away. They didn't have to keep making that weekly bed-check like we did, coming back for reassurance. There were no flowers on the Indian graves. I kept wanting to lie down there in the long grass where I imagined I would be hidden and ignored, sweet-smelling.

This Town

(1979)

GENERAL INFORMATION:

A lot of the people in this town have come here from other places. There is always someone new in town, there is always someone just arriving (see POPULATION).

When you meet a new person in this town, the first questions are always the same:

"Where are you from?"

"How long have you been here?"

Some people will become friends on the basis of the answers to these and other questions.

Some people will say they were just passing through on their summer holidays and they had such a good time in this town that they just never left.

"That was two years ago last summer."

Because these people didn't come to this town on purpose, they never lose that sense of just passing through and so they are always talking about leaving.

Some of these people were on their way to the coast and now they are always talking about going there for the next long weekend. Some other people were on their way to California and now they always go there for their two-week vacation in the summer. They come back with furious suntans and colour slides of the ocean.

In this town someone is always talking about leaving. Some of them do leave, but some of them don't. Most of those who do, come back in two months. Sometimes it is only when these people come back that the other people in this town notice they've been gone.

CLIMATE:

The standard saying in this town is: "If you don't like the weather, wait five minutes, it'll change." Living in this town means never knowing what to wear when you get up in the morning and then having to change your clothes four times a day anyway. This generates a lot of washing (see LAUNDROMAT). It is considered overly optimistic to go out without a jacket in July.

POPULATION:

There is room in this town for everyone. Someone is always arriving (coming to this town is easier than leaving it) but this town never gets any bigger and it never gets any smaller either.

Every other year they put a new number on the green sign on the highway. No one can ever remember what the last number was so no one ever knows if this town is gaining or losing ground.

Lorraine said, "We don't need to know anyway. Those signs are for tourists. They like to know these things" (see TOURISM).

PUBLIC HEALTH:

In this town someone always has or is just getting over a twenty-four-hour bug. All such recurring afflictions are credited to the water, which is regularly infested by some kind of parasite that comes down off the mountains with the spring runoff.

All other afflictions are credited to the altitude and the thin mountain air.

Kevin said, "We are all suffering from chronic lack of oxygen."

This can be used to explain or excuse a number of things, including the milder forms of insanity and unhappiness.

Someone in this town always has a cold (see CLIMATE) or a virus.

ACCOMMODATION:

Most of the people in this town live in rented apartments or houses. These are very hard to come by. Everybody is always complaining that their rent is too high and so they are always moving to a smaller, cheaper place. Someone is always saying, "If you hear of anything coming up for rent, let me know." A lot of people, even families with children, keep renting because they are planning to leave in the spring (see GENERAL INFORMATION).

Some couples buy a lot in the new subdivision, which is the only part of town where the streets are paved. They like to build their own houses. This keeps them very busy. They are always working hard to make the mortgage payments which are usually higher than they bargained on. They are always planning patios, babies, and vegetable gardens.

The power of a nice new $100,000 house is never underestimated. Andy and Mary said together, "Once we move in, we'll be so happy."

TOURISM:

In this town it is standard summer practice to go out for a walk on Sunday afternoon with or without the dog which you may or may not own (see PETS). You will be stopped on the average of five times and asked for directions.

Most of these tourists will want to know how to get back to the highway. Before beginning your walk, it is important to know how to get to: the golf course, the liquor store, a fast food place (there isn't one), a bathroom, a campground with hookups (it's full).

One Sunday a man in sunglasses in a big blue Buick said to Barb: "This is such a quaint little town. But what do all you people *do* here?"

ENTERTAINMENT:

In this town all roads lead to the bar. There might also be one road which leads to the pool hall. The pool hall is a recreational distraction. The bar, on the other hand, is a serious place where serious business occurs.

Connie said, "We were in the bar when Kevin told me he was leaving town and moving to the coast (see GENERAL INFORMA-TION). I was crying but nobody noticed and the beer kept coming. Pretty soon the whole table was covered with empty bottles. Leon kept lying them down on their sides and calling them 'dead soldiers'. He was comforting me" (see LOVE).

In this town there is a dance once every two months. Most of the people in this town love to dance so everybody goes and nobody ever dances with the person they came with. This is important because of course everybody needs to feel free. The small-town version of freedom means flirting with your best friend's husband or lover or both. It is likely that you will end up at the same table with three old lovers and one or two new lovers. Most of the people in this town are very civilized.

Most people in this town harbour a disproportionate fear of going home alone (see LOVE). This fear becomes especially prevalent on Saturday night.

Barb said, "I hate eating breakfast alone on Sunday. If a man is with me, I make bacon and eggs and biscuits. Sometimes, if it's a special occasion or I think we might be in love, I make strawberry crepes. If I'm alone, I have three cups of coffee and five or six cigarettes. I know that's unhealthy."

HOBBIES:

A lot of people in this town are always having dinner parties. In the summer they are always having barbecues.

Lorraine said, "I enjoy taking care of people. Everyone likes to eat, everyone tells me I'm a good cook. Maybe someday I'll become a chef. I'm happy when I'm watching someone eat."

Marshall, who is Lorraine's husband and also a realist, said, "You just like showing off. Life isn't a dinner party, Lorraine."

Lorraine and Marshall are always talking about leaving this town (see GENERAL INFORMATION) or getting a divorce (see MARRIAGE).

Most of the people in this town have, at one time or another, taken up macramé, weaving, baking bread, gardening, running, and photography. Some people still do some or all of these things. Everybody owns a 35 mm camera with multiple interchangeable lenses. Most of the people in this town do not collect stamps or coins or salt and pepper shakers. Some people collect postcards or comic books.

PETS:

Everyone in this town loves animals. If you have a dog, it will be a German shepherd, a Siberian husky, or an Alaskan malamute. If you don't have a dog, it will be because your landlady doesn't allow pets or because you are planning to leave town in the spring (see GENERAL INFORMATION) and you don't want to get tied down (see LOVE).

Some people have cats. Most people have more than one.

Barb said, "I'd be lost without them."

Someone in this town is always giving away kittens or puppies.

CHILDREN:

This town is very fertile. Someone is always pregnant. There is always someone wanting to buy your old baby carriage and your bassinette. Everybody believes in cloth diapers and breast-feeding and making your own baby food in the blender.

When the baby cries in a restaurant, the parents are embarrassed but they smile proudly.

Everybody is thankful for the daycare centre which has just been established in town. The young mothers talk about how their children will grow up and be friends and go to school together.

LAUNDROMAT:

Almost none of the people in this town own a washer and dryer. Everybody goes to the laundromat, which is always full. Some of the washing machines are always breaking down. Most people go down the street to the bar while their clothes are drying (see ENTERTAINMENT).

Mary said, "If Indians are supposed to be dirty, my mother always said they were dirty, then why do they spend so much time in the laundromat?"

LOVE:

Some of the people in this town are congenitally reluctant to form attachments because they don't want to get tied down (see PETS). Most of these people have been hurt before in some other town and now they are afraid of meaningful relationships. These things, however, do not stop most people from devoting a lot of time to looking for love (see ENTERTAINMENT), even though they don't seem to know what they will do with it when they find it. They just don't like going home alone.

A lot of people think that having sex with a person is the only way to get to know them and to decide whether love is likely or not. It is educational to drive around this town early on a Saturday morning and see whose car is parked in front of (or behind, depending on the complexities of the situation) whose house.

Kevin said, "I call it the Lending Library."

When a couple breaks up, there is always some friend waiting to comfort the wounded party.

Leon said, "There's always some woman in the bar who needs

to forget her troubles (see ENTERTAINMENT). I try not to miss these opportunities to be understanding."

When an unhealthy relationship finally ends, friends are relieved and they say, "I wanted to tell you before but I didn't."

Sex, if not love, is easy to come by in this town. Barb slept with six different men in a month and a half. This was immediately after her breakup with Bill, a carpenter she'd loved fiercely for two years and four months.

Barb's friends were all worried about her and they said:

"You'll get a reputation."

"You'll get a disease."

"You'll get hurt."

"You'll get pregnant."

"You'll get bitter and cynical."

"It's time to get serious."

MARRIAGE:

Most of the married people in this town are unhappy. Some of these unhappily married people are still giving dinner parties (see HOBBIES) and pretending to be happy.

At a dinner party at Lorraine and Marshall's house, Lorraine asked Mary, "How are you?"

Mary said, "I'm so happy it seems unnatural."

Lorraine said, "Have some more guacamole."

Some of these unhappily married people aren't pretending anymore and they are always talking to anybody who will listen about their marital problems and the merits of a trial separation.

At a dinner party at Andy and Mary's house, Mary asked Lorraine, "How are you?"

Lorraine said, "I'm miserable."

Marshall said, "I want a divorce."

Mary said, "Have some more guacamole."

There are wedding parties and sometimes there are divorce parties. Everybody always gets drunk at parties.

At wedding parties, some of the guests are talking about when their divorce date is coming up. At one wedding party, the bride said, "If we get divorced, I won't ask for a thing." Hugging her, the groom said, "That's my girl."

At divorce parties, some people are always talking about how important it is to stay friends.

DEATH:

Susan said, "When I was a child, one day my father was in the basement trying to kill himself. Of course I was too young to understand how someone I loved could be that upset. After I unloaded the gun, I called the doctor. After the doctor left, my father went upstairs to his bedroom and rested. For five years my father didn't speak to me. After five years, I asked my mother to tell me why. She said it was because he thought that I thought he was crazy."

Ed said, "Well, of course he was crazy."

Three years ago, Ed tried to kill himself with pills, not a gun. In this town one death has nothing to do with another.

Frogs

(1982)

Val's mother always told her, "You've got to kiss a lot of frogs before you find your prince."

In the hot summer, there were green frogs everywhere, looping around on people's front lawns, hopping across the sidewalk, into the street, getting run over. Val's mother chased them away from the front step with the broom, even though her grandmother, who was staying with them for the summer, said a frog coming into your house would bring you good luck.

When Val finally caught one, a tiny one no bigger than her thumbnail, she carried it into the kitchen cupped in her hands, where it fluttered and thumped away like a heart. She called the little frog Bob after her dad, who would be killed the next winter in a car crash on Highway 6 North. But nobody knew that yet. He rummaged around in his pockets and found her an empty match-box to keep it in.

Her mother, who was at the stove just starting supper, said, "That's not a frog, it's a toad. You'll get warts." She didn't though, and whatever it was, it didn't last long in the matchbox.

"What's the difference between a frog and a toad?" is a very common question.

Frogs live in or near water, are slender with smooth moist skin and long hind legs which make them excellent jumpers. Toads, on the other hand, are stocky with short legs, hop rather than jump, and have rough dry skin with warts. They live away from water, in the woods, the garden, sometimes even the cellar.

After Simon moved out, Val's mother was relieved and worried both at once—relieved because she'd never liked Simon anyway, even though she'd only met him once, but worried too because she couldn't imagine what Val was going to do next.

In a letter, Val's mother writes, *You're thirty years old now, Val. You'd better get your act together.* Val knows that what she really means to say is, *Do what I want you to do.*

Val replies faithfully in that special tone she has created for her weekly letters home. Grammatical, stable, and complacent, this voice makes everything she tells her mother sound harmless, round, and slightly empty-headed. Val writes about the weather (which is just great), the gas bill (which is ridiculous), the cat (who is thriving), and the plants (which aren't). She doesn't mention Leonard, the man she has been seeing lately, because she knows her mother will like him already and there's no sense getting her hopes up. Her mother has never demanded the truth anyway, only something digestible with the least amount of difficulty. This, Val assumes, is the natural state of families.

When Val was promoted to Loans Officer at the bank, she got her own office, which is off in one corner, with glass walls on two sides. Whenever she feels claustrophobic, she opens the curtains so she can watch the tellers chatting with the customers over the sound of the computers, passing money endlessly from hand to hand. Val was a teller for five years before the promotion. Her new salary is substantial—they obviously want to hang onto her. She feels valuable and sometimes even important.

On Friday afternoon, once the after-work payday lineups have started to subside, Val straightens up her desk and then goes into the washroom to comb her hair. She splashes cold water on her face and neck, dabs on a little perfume, and admires her new haircut, which frames her face with fine blonde curls like feathers.

It's almost time to lock up. Val is going for a beer after work with some of the other women. They do this every Friday. It usually means no supper, some dancing, and a quick buzz. They are working, always working, these women, and they like to get out on the weekend.

Annette Cosgrove is Val's favourite person at the bank. Annette is the youngest woman there, maybe twenty-two, pretty in a pale red fox-like way, and very bright. She's only been at the bank for four months but Val doesn't expect she'll stay long—the good ones never do.

After work on Friday, Val and Annette walk down to the tavern together. They get a good table, close to the dance floor but not too close, and save some chairs for the other women who'll be along shortly, once they get Marsha balanced. They order a jug of draft beer. Annette pays, Val will get the next one.

The tavern is crowded, with men mostly, just having a casual after-work drink too. The men have pushed several tables together and their chairs are sticking out at all angles as more men come to join them, pulling up empty chairs from other tables and squeezing them in somehow.

The phone up front keeps ringing and the bartender keeps calling out names over the microphone. It's the women at home with the kids who are calling. Supper's ready. The men dribble out one by one. The women on the phone must be angry but Val isn't sure why.

By the time the band starts at eight, the tavern is beginning to fill up again. Val and her friends are still wearing their clothes from work, vivid summer dresses, high-heeled sandals, no nylons. This makes them more noticeable than most of the other women in the tavern and different men keep coming to their table, one at a time, grinning.

"Do you want to dance?

Sometimes yes, sometimes no.

Marsha and Mary keep pointing out possibilities all over the tavern.

"Did you see John over there? Nice eyes."

"I think he's still married."

"No, they're split up now."

"Nice eyes."

Val knows they're trying to fix her up but she's not sure yet if she's broken.

Annette is talking about her husband, Mike, yelling into Val's right ear to make herself heard over the music. She's been married for six months. She calls him "Old Mike" and makes him sound like a dancing bear, comical but potentially dangerous. It's as though being married to him means she can finally tell other women what a fool he really is.

"Let me tell you three things," Annette says.

"Okay, what?" Val asks.

"Don't ever get married."

"And?"

"Don't even fall in love."

"And?"

"Kill the first person you fall in love with."

"Here's to you!" Val raises her glass to Annette's and they're laughing.

Across the table, Marsha and Mary, who are sisters, both twenty pounds overweight and always on a diet together, are talking about food.

Marsha says, "I don't believe in white sugar," and makes it sound like a fanatic fringe religion instead of a condiment.

Annette is still talking about Mike. She wants to sell the trailer and move to Vancouver but Old Mike won't hear of it.

Now they're all four talking about birth control, which is something they always talk about when they get together. They've all tried everything but nothing's perfect. Annette, as usual, is leading the conversation. It's as though she can't imagine a reason to remain silent, a subject that can't be companionably excavated for anyone who cares to listen. This is the sphere she functions best in—intimacy and confession. And confessions are meant to be reciprocated—otherwise what possible good can they be?

The waitress comes and clears the table, empties the ashtray, and tells Annette she can't put her feet up on the chairs like that.

Val orders another jug and feels a warm desire to give Annette what she wants—secrets, memories, probably a few tears too. Annette will accept whatever she is given, will nod, smile, encourage, support. She does not debate, question, or criticize. You can say anything to her.

By this time the odd drink is getting knocked over but the little round table is covered with blue terry cloth, elasticized so it fits tight. The spilt beer just foams up and is instantly absorbed.

It's almost last call. Everyone is dancing and clapping and singing along. The humid heat is getting to be like feathers in Val's throat.

Simon moved out on a Sunday in May. Val had never liked Sundays anyway, so later this would strike her as appropriate.

They were having, as they say, "an amicable separation," even though it had been Val's idea in the first place. It was still rather unclear to her as to why they were breaking up. Something important between them was gone, maybe it had been gone for a long time, maybe it was never there at all. They both knew this was true, they'd been talking about it for weeks—so much so that Val thought they were hardly even making sense anymore.

They spent the afternoon drinking a case of beer and gathering up Simon's things—typewriter, papers, clothes. Considering he'd lived in the apartment for a year and a half, he hadn't accumulated or contributed much.

It was not an altogether unpleasant day and they both admitted, laughing, to feeling relieved that it was all over now. They hadn't been sleeping together for weeks. Val pointed out that they hadn't been talking much either.

"We're getting along better right now than we have for months," she said. Simon had to agree.

Val made a simple supper, hamburgers and a tossed salad. She refused to think of this as their last meal together. Simon kept talking the whole time they were eating, clowning, telling jokes and silly stories. His long black hair kept falling in his eyes and his glasses were sliding down his nose. Val would automatically reach over and push them back into place.

"Wait, wait, I've got another one!" He waved the remains of his third hamburger at her. "What's red and green and goes two hundred miles an hour?"

"I don't know, what?"

"A frog in a blender!"

"Sorry I asked." She was laughing and rolling her eyes, picking bits of avocado out of the last of the salad.

When the beer was all gone, Simon put on his denim jacket, kissed Val, and said, "I still love you, I guess I'll always love you. I'd better be going now."

Val said, "I love you too. You're my best friend."

Simon got into his truck and drove away. He was going to share a house with two other recently single men. Val thought of them as "the walking wounded." Maybe he'd learn something.

Once Simon was gone, Val made herself a pot of tea, turned on the TV, settled herself in the big armchair and enjoyed herself immensely. Nothing in the room was changed—even the stereo was hers—it was almost as though Simon had never been there at all. Val went to bed right after the news and slept better than she had for weeks.

The man Val is sleeping with now is Leonard DeVries, a lawyer. She has known him for a while because he deals at the bank. He's very handsome, all the women she works with say so, with deep blue eyes and short brown hair just beginning to go grey. He has a neat beard, brown streaked with red and grey. He's growing out all multicoloured. His chin could be any shape, maybe even receding or weak.

Leonard is always taking Val to places where she's never been before. They seem to spend all their time in restaurants and movie theatres and also in Leonard's new Porsche driving to and from these places.

Leonard's favourite restaurant is The Pines out on the highway just west of town. It's expensive and you have to be dressed up to feel comfortable eating there. The menu features every kind of seafood you could possibly imagine. They all know Leonard there and he always gets a table by the window so he can keep an eye on his car while they're eating. Outside in the parking lot, people keep stopping to admire and touch it.

It is usually on these evenings spent at The Pines, two or three times a week, that Val and Leonard end up sleeping together. All that food and good service makes them both feel generous and lovable.

When they do sleep together, they sleep at Val's place. Leonard says, "This is a real home. I feel so comfortable here, I never want to leave." In the morning, he likes to putter around, watering the plants and playing with the cat, while Val puts on the coffee and gets ready for work.

At first Val thought Leonard was intelligent and very interesting. He seemed to know all kinds of things that she'd barely even thought about. He doesn't read books, only dozens of newspapers and magazines. He keeps up-to-date on everything. He is so calm that sometimes he makes Val nervous.

But already she thinks he's boring. He's always talking about himself without ever telling her anything. What she really wants to know is why he has been divorced twice, where are the wives, why did he never have children, why does he like her anyway, how much money does he really make?

Leonard is almost ten years older than Val, Simon is five years younger. She tries to make something of this, but can't.

After a few weeks of sleeping with Leonard, Val finds it is usually better to think about him than to actually be with him.

Leonard and Simon know each other, sort of, because they both belong to the tennis club. Val would like to keep them apart. If they spend too much time together, they might become like each other and then she would only be more confused.

One night over dinner at The Pines, Leonard says, "I ran into Simon downtown today, we had a few drinks together." Val finds it unsettling to think of them being together, having a good time, without her. She always thought she could control them. It has never occurred to her that they might do just as well without her.

The waitress materializes abruptly with their Greek salads and seems to be bouncing lightly on the balls of her feet, which are strapped into a complicated arrangement of blue straps and gold buckles. Val studies them—she *is* bouncing.

Leonard digs in happily. Val sucks on her imported beer.

Already they are merging, then, Simon and Leonard, trespassing on each other. Their beards will grow out the same colour, sandpaper on her chin. They will play tennis together on weekends. In later years they will adopt similar gestures, admire the same women, see the same movies, have backyard Sunday barbecues with bloody steak and pink lemonade. She will serve them vodka and tonic, frosted glasses sliding on the wooden tray, and they will smile: "Thanks, Val, you're a doll." They will start talking again as soon as her back is turned. They're sitting in plastic lawn chairs, wearing Bermuda shorts, crossing and uncrossing their hairy legs. They will touch her in all the same places, grow twin erections at the mere sight of her breasts. Boys will be boys.

The main course arrives discreetly. Leonard is having a steak, Val, prawns in garlic butter. Leonard is smearing sour cream all over his baked potato. One of the things she already hates about him is the way his jaw cracks when he's chewing.

"Did you talk about me?" she asks.

"No, I don't think we did."

This is worse, even worse. Oh, to be so civilized. Maybe they should have.

One of the good things about sleeping alone is that you can get up again after you've already gone to bed and there's nobody to ruffle the blankets and mumble, "What's the matter? Are you okay?"

Val, in her nightgown and Simon's old slippers, makes herself a cup of instant hot chocolate and a piece of brown toast. The fridge gurgles flatulently. She doesn't check to see how late it is. Early or late, there's no telling time now.

Val goes into the dark living room without turning the light on and stands by the window. She's not afraid of the dark anymore now that she understands about how you can die in the daytime too. In the half light, her feet are like puddles on the hardwood floor. She hasn't bothered to wax the floor lately and there are Rorschach wine stains on one throw rug. Simon has been gone for three months now. Leonard is out of town on business but he'll be back tomorrow.

Behind Val's apartment building, there is a small nameless creek, and by the light of the moon, which will be full soon, Val can see the water shining and moving. This makes her think she can hear it too.

Some of the things Val wants to think about are too depressing. The only way to approach them is to sneak up on them from behind. She has a sense of having made the one irrevocable mistake that will ruin the rest of her life. She tries to pass this off as some melodramatic trick of the moon, fails, and panics.

Someone is walking through the backyard of the building. Caught, guilty, Val lets the curtain fall shut. She is suspicious—of the late-night wanderer, of herself. Up to no good.

She thinks of this as her secret life.

Simon and Val had only known each other for a month when he moved into her apartment. The house he was living in had been sold and he had to move on the first of January. They didn't discuss it much (or enough, Val would think later)—it seemed only logical that he should move in with her. They had both lived with other people before.

They spent New Year's Eve alone in the apartment and celebrated with lobster and champagne at midnight. Simon ran out onto the balcony and hollered "Happy New Year!" at the street, which was gently filling up with snow.

They finished the champagne in bed. Simon brushed Val's hair away from her face and stroked her cheeks, whispering, "You're lovely, you're lovely," over and over again. He did this every night for a long time.

That May Val took a week's holiday and they rented a cabin at Hazel Lake. The cabin belonged to a fellow Simon worked with at the lumberyard. He'd taken a part-time job there to support himself for a few months while he worked on his second novel. His first had never been published, which, Simon said now, was just as well. He was having some trouble with the second one though, and hadn't accomplished much during the past month. "Writer's void," he called it. They both hoped this week away would get the ball rolling again.

The road in was soft and muddy, it had rained off and on all week. Hazel Lake, when they came in sight of it, was grey and flat-looking, metallic. It was early in the season and all the other cabins were still boarded up. There was nobody else around.

The cabin was lopsided and weather-beaten, shedding flakes of paint. Val and Simon unloaded the truck in the rain—suitcases, fishing rods, typewriter, enough food, wine, and kerosene to last out the week. Inside, one large square room served as both kitchen and living area. There were two smaller rooms, curtained off—the bedroom and a storage room full of dry wood for the fireplace. The whole place smelled like wet wool.

Val and Simon were both awake for a long time the first night, lying in bed, holding hands, listening to the rain on the tin roof. Val was thinking that they were perfect here together, the way it should always be, could too, if only.

It rained every day, which was fine. Val was sleeping in late every morning, then fishing a little, walking by the lake, hugging herself against the rain. Frogs croaked around the lake all day long, a sign of more rain. Simon was always up early, writing, the sound of his typewriter coming to Val in her half-sleep, just like the rain on the roof. In the evenings, they played cribbage and backgammon in their bathrobes, drinking white wine out of coffee cups.

On Saturday night, their last night, they were reading in bed— Simon, the pages he'd written that day, and Val, an article on divorce in an old magazine. She said, "I think you and I are the only two people I know who haven't been married at least once. I'm glad you have no ex-wives hanging around anywhere."

Which wasn't exactly what she meant to say but was as good a way as any to open the discussion, which was an ongoing one they'd been having for several weeks now—this one was only a sample—and it wasn't over yet.

Simon didn't even hesitate, he jumped right in. "I'll never get married, I'll never have kids, I've always known that."

"But you didn't know me before."

"It doesn't make any difference."

"But what about me?"

"I love you. I don't need to marry you to prove it."

"What about what I want? Doesn't that matter to you?"

"I'm sorry, I guess I'll never change."

They went on for an hour at least, back and forth, back and forth, until Val couldn't believe she was saying any of this anyway and she was sobbing and hitting Simon weakly in the chest.

Simon held her until she stopped crying, then got up and went into the other room. He came back with a towel and a pot of warm water and gently washed her face.

They began to make love, slowly, carefully. Val moved to get up for her diaphragm.

Simon said, "You don't have to."

"What if I get pregnant?"

"It doesn't matter."

But nothing came of it. Val was mostly relieved. How could they have been so foolish? They weren't talking about marriage and babies much anymore anyway. Just as well.

Simon has a new job waiting on tables part-time at the tavern, weekends mostly, filling in for the regular staff. Val already knows this before she goes down on Friday with the girls. Annette was in with her husband the night before and she told Val.

They sit in Simon's section because that's where they always sit—it's closer to the band.

Val is so glad to see Simon that at first she talks even more than Annette and dances with everyone who asks her. Simon is an extremely efficient waiter and they're all giving him big tips which embarrasses everyone, but not in a bad way. Val notices that he's wearing a new plaid shirt and he's had his beard trimmed.

While the band is taking a break, Annette tells Val that Mike is pushing her to get pregnant.

"I'd never have a baby in this God-forsaken town," Annette declares. Marsha and Mary, who already have families, don't say anything. Val envies Annette even though she knows she's unhappy.

She's watching Simon all the time but he's so busy he doesn't have time to talk to her. It's been a hard day, Marsha never did balance, and Val is very tired. She knows she should go home early but she'd rather stick around and see what happens.

When the band has finished playing, complete with two ragged encores, and the bar is closed for the night, Val expects that Simon will come and sit down with her. But he leans up against the bar instead, counting his tips and chatting with the bartender.

On her way out, Val asks him if he needs a ride home but he says, "No thanks, I've got the truck." Some young girl with dark curly hair and a pretty mauve sweater has been hanging around him all night and she's still there, waiting.

Simon is coming over for coffee. It's already quite late, Val was getting ready for bed when he called but she didn't even think of telling him not to come. She puts the kettle on and debates with herself about getting dressed again. She puts a record on and stays in her housecoat.

When Simon arrives, the cat immediately jumps into his lap and goes to sleep, purring. Val tries not to see this as significant.

They are both uncomfortable, obviously, and Val finds this disappointing. Simon tells her about his novel, which is nearly done now. He's going back out to the cabin for a week to finish it.

It's almost the end of September, there won't be anybody else around.

Val says, "What about your job at the tavern?"

"Things are pretty slow right now, they won't need me again for a couple of weeks."

Val says, "How come you never talk to me when I'm there with Annette? Why can't we be friends?" She knows that questions can be dangerous. They make you vulnerable to the answers, which are uncontrollable. She wants to offer Simon some more coffee but she wants him to leave, too. She has to go to work in the morning.

"I don't want to be your friend. Will you come to the cabin with me?"

Val gets up and refills their cups. She's trying to think of an answer, she doesn't know what she wants to say.

Simon says, "I want to get married someday."

It is not a question.

"I won't hold you to that."

"Yes, you will."

Hockey Night in Canada (1982)

We settled ourselves in our usual places, my father and I, while the singer made his way out onto the ice and the organist cranked up for "O Canada" and "The Star Spangled Banner." Saturday night and we were ready for anything, my father half sitting, half lying on the chesterfield with his first dark rum and Pepsi, and I in the swivel chair beside the picture window with a box of barbecue chips and a glass of 7Up.

My mother was ripping apart with relish a red and white polka dot dress she hadn't worn for years. There were matching red shoes, a purse, and a hat once too, but they'd already been packed or given away. Trying to interest someone in her project and her practicality, she said, "Why, this fabric is just as good as new," pulling first one sleeve, then the other, away from the body of the dress.

But the game was starting and we were already intent on the screen and each other.

"They don't stand a chance tonight," I said, shaking my head sadly but with confidence as the players skated out.

My father grinned calmly and took a drink of rum.

"Not a chance," I prodded.

"We'll see, we'll just see about that." Even when they played poorly for weeks on end, my father remained cheerfully loyal to the Chicago Black Hawks, for no particular reason I could see, except that he always had been. He must have suffered secret doubts about the team now and then—anyone would—but he never let on. I, having no similar special allegiance and wanting to keep the evening interesting, always hoped for the other team.

We were not violent fans, either one of us. We never hollered, leaped out of our chairs, or pounded ourselves in alternating fits of frustration and ecstasy. We did not jump up and down yelling, "Kill him, kill him!" Instead, we were teasing fans, pretend fans almost, feigning hostility and heartbreak, smirking and groaning gruesomely by turns, exaggerating our reactions mainly for the benefit of the other and sometimes just to get a rise out of my mother, who was by this time humming with pins in her mouth, smoothing pattern pieces onto the remains of the dress, and snipping merrily away with the pinking shears, while scraps of cloth and tissue paper drifted to the floor all around her.

The dress, I discovered, was to be reincarnated as a blouse for me, a blouse which, by the time it was finished (perfectly, seams all basted and bound, hem hand done), I would probably hate. Between periods, she took me into the bathroom for a fitting session in front of the full-length mirror. I did not breathe, complain, or look as she pinned the blouse together around me, a piece at a time, one sleeve, the other, half the front, the other half, back, collar, the cold silver pins scratching my bare skin just lightly.

By the time we got to the three-star selection after the game, my mother was off to the back bedroom with the blouse, whirring away on the Singer.

When her friend, Rita, was there, my mother at least played at watching the game. Whenever the crowd roared, my father groaned, and Rita began to shriek, my mother would look up from her stamp collection, which she was endlessly sorting and sticking and spreading all over the card table, and smile encouragement at the TV.

"Who scored?" she asked innocently, as she put another page in her album and arranged another row of stamps across it. Russia was her favourite country for collecting, the best because their stamps were bigger and grander than any, especially ours, which looked stingy and common by comparison. The Russians had hockey players, cosmonauts, fruits and vegetables, wild animals, trucks, and ballerinas, in red, blue, green, yellow, even shiny silver and gold. We had mainly the Queen in pastels. My mother's everyday fear and loathing of Communists did not enter into the matter.

"Just guess, Violet, just you guess who scored!" Rita crowed.

"Don't ask," my father muttered.

"Most goals, one team, one game," Rita recited. "Twenty-one, Montreal Canadiens, March 3, 1920, at Montreal, defeated the Quebec Bulldogs 18 to 3."

"Ancient history," said my father. "Besides, who ever heard of the Quebec Bulldogs anyway? You're making it all up, Rita. Tell me another one."

"Fewest points, one season," Rita chanted. "Thirty-one, Chicago Black Hawks, 1953–54, won 12, lost 36, tied 4."

"Not quite what I had in mind." My father rolled his big eyes and went into the kitchen to fix more drinks, one for himself and one for Rita, who took her rum with orange juice, no ice. I said nothing, not being sure yet whether I wanted to stick up for my father or fall in love with the Canadiens too.

Rita had followed the Montreal team for years. Unlike my father and me, she was a *real* fan, a serious fan who shrieked and howled and paced around the living room, calling the players by their first names, begging them to score, willing them to win with clenched fists and teeth. She did not consider her everyday dislike of those Frenchmen (as in, "I've got no use for those Frenchmen, no use at all") to be contradictory. Hockey, like stamp collecting, it seemed, was a world apart, immune to the regular prejudices of race, province, and country—although she did sometimes berate my father for siding with a Yankee team.

When the Black Hawks lost another one, Rita and I (for I'd been won over after all by her braying) took all the credit for knowing the better team right off the bat, and heaped all the blame upon my father, who was now in disgrace along with his team—a position he took rather well. When they did win, as far as he was concerned, it was all or mainly because he'd never given up on them.

After the game, my father and I usually played a few hands of poker, a penny a game, with the cards spread out on the chester-field between us. My mother and Rita were in the kitchen having coffee and maybe a cream puff. The hum of their voices came to me just vaguely, like perfume. I wanted to hear what they were saying but my father was analyzing the last power play and deal-ing me another hand. I won more often than not, piling up my pennies. For years after this I would think of myself as lucky at cards. In certain difficult situations which showed a disturbing tendency to repeat themselves, I would often be reminded of Rita's teasing warning: "Lucky at cards, unlucky at love."

Later, after Rita had gone home, I would find the ashtray full of lipstick-tipped butts which I pored over, looking for clues.

My mother had met Rita that summer at Eaton's, where Rita was working at the Cosmetics counter. Rita still worked at Eaton's, but she was in Ladies' Dresses now, having passed briefly through Lingerie and Swimwear in between.

To hear Rita tell it, you'd think their whole friendship was rooted in my mother's hair.

"I just couldn't help myself," Rita said, telling me the story. "There I was trying to convince this fat lady that all she really needed was a bottle of Cover Girl and some Midnight Blue mascara and up walked your mother with her hair."

Patting her hair fondly, my mother said, "I couldn't figure out what she was staring at."

I already knew that before Rita had come to live in Hastings, she was a hairdresser in Toronto. She'd been to hairdressing

school for two years and still took the occasional special course
in cold waves or colouring. She was about to open her own
beauty parlour just when her husband, Geoffrey, killed himself
and everything was changed. It was not long after that Rita
gave up hairdressing and moved to Hastings to stay with her
younger sister, Jeanette. Six months after that Jeanette married a
doctor and moved back to Toronto. But Rita stayed on in Hastings
anyway, bought herself a second-hand car and rented an apartment downtown in the Barclay Block above an Italian bakery
(which was the very same building my parents had lived in when
they were first married, a fact that I found significant and somehow too good to be true).

My mother always did her own hair, putting it up in pincurls
every Sunday night so that it lay in lustrous black waves all
around her face and rolled thickly down past her shoulders in
the back. But what Rita meant was the streak, a pure white streak
in front from the time she'd had ringworm when she was small.
Even I had to admit it looked splendid and daring, although there
were times when we were fighting and I wanted to hurt her and
tell her she looked like a skunk. Rita's own hair was straggly and
thin, half-dead from too many washings, a strange salmon colour,
growing out blonde, from too many experiments. Her bangs hung
down almost to her eyebrows. Sometimes she wore them swept
back with coloured barrettes, revealing the delicate blue veins in
her temples.

"Anyway," Rita said, pausing to light another cigarette with her
Zippo, "I finally got rid of the fat lady and your mother and I got
talking. Just seeing her hair gave me the itch again—I could just
picture all the things I could do with that hair. We went up to the
cafeteria for coffee—"

"And we've been friends ever since," my mother said in a
pleased and final-sounding voice, the way you might say, *And
they all lived happily ever after.*

My mother had never really had a friend of her own before. Oh, there was a neighbour lady, Mrs. Kent three doors down, who would come over once in a while to borrow things that she never returned—the angel food cake pan, the egg beater, the four-sided cheese grater. And so my mother would go over to Mrs. Kent's house occasionally too, to get the things back. But it was never what you would call a friendship, so much as a case of proximity and Mrs. Kent's kitchen being sadly ill-equipped.

I had never seriously thought of my mother as wanting or needing a friend anyway. Friends, particularly best friends, I gathered, were something you grew out of soon after you got married and had children. After that, the husband and the children became your best friends, or were supposed to.

But then she met Rita, and it was as though Rita were someone she had been just waiting for, saving herself up for all those years. They told each other old stories and secrets, made plans, remembered times before when they might have met, had just missed each other, almost met, but didn't. Rita was at least ten years younger than my mother. I suppose I thought of her as doing my mother a favour by being her friend. In the way of young girls, I just naturally imagined my mother to be the needy one of the two.

When Rita was in Cosmetics, she would bring my mother makeup samples that the salesmen had left: mascara, blusher, eyebrow pencils, and sometimes half-empty perfume testers for me. And her pale face was perfect. Once she moved to Ladies Dresses, she hardly ever wore slacks anymore, except when the weather turned cold. She was always trying out bold new accessories, big belts, coloured stockings, high-heeled boots. I could only imagine what she'd bought while she worked in Lingerie— the most elegant underwear, I supposed, and coloured girdles (I didn't know if there were such things for sure, but if there were, Rita would have several), and marvellous gauzy nightgowns.

On her day off during the week, Rita was usually there in the kitchen when I came home from school for lunch. While my mother fixed me a can of soup and a grilled cheese sandwich, Rita sipped black coffee and nibbled on fresh fruit and cottage cheese. This was the first time I knew of dieting as a permanent condition, for although Rita was quite slim and long-legged, she was always watching her weight. My mother, who was much rounder than Rita anyway, had taken up dieting too, like a new hobby which required supplies of lettuce, pink grapefruit, and detailed diet books listing menus, recipes, and calories. She'd begun to compliment me on my extreme thinness, when not so many years before she'd made me wear two crinolines to school so the teachers wouldn't think she didn't feed me. How was it that, without changing size or shape, I had graduated from grotesque to slender?

"How's school going this week?" Rita would ask, offering me a tiny cube of pineapple, which I hated.

She listened patiently, nodding and frowning mildly, while I told her about Miss Morton, the gym teacher who hated me because I was no good at basketball; and about my best friend, Mary Yurick, who was madly in love with Lorne Puhalski, captain of the hockey team and unattainable; and about everybody's enemy, Bonnie Ettinger, who'd beat up Della White on Monday in the alley behind the school.

It was easy to get carried away with such confidences in the hope that Rita would reciprocate, and I almost told her that I was in love with Lorne Puhalski too, and that Bonnie Ettinger was going around saying she'd knock my block off if she ever got the chance. But I talked myself out of it at the last minute. I wanted so much to have Rita all to myself but somehow it never was arranged.

With Rita there, my mother could listen to my problems with-out worrying too much or wanting to do something about them.

She and I probably learned more about each other from those kitchen conversations with Rita than we ever would have any other way.

Sometimes it was as though they'd forgotten all about me. One day when I came home for lunch my mother was sitting wrapped in a sheet on the high stool in the middle of the kitchen while Rita gave her a cold wave, something she'd been threatening to do for weeks. I made my own sandwich.

My mother was saying, "I was so young then, and everybody said I was pretty. We were in love but when they found out, they shipped him off to agricultural school in Winnipeg. I still think Sonny was my own true love."

"What about Ted?" Rita asked, wrapping pieces of hair in what looked like cigarette rolling papers and then winding them nimbly onto pink plastic rods.

"Oh, Ted."

Ted was my father, of course, but it was strange to hear my mother call him by his name when usually she called him "Dad" or "your Dad."

"Yes, well, Ted. That was different. I was older. I'm even older now. I didn't tell Ted about Sonny until long after we were married."

I went back to school that afternoon with a picture of my mother as another person altogether, someone I had never met and never would now. This woman, mysterious, incomplete and broken-hearted, pestered me all day long. The stink of the cold wave chemicals lingered too, bitter but promising.

At other times it was as though my mother could tell me things through Rita that she could never have expressed if we were alone.

One Saturday night after the hockey game I left my father dozing on the chesterfield and went into the kitchen.

Rita was saying, "When Geoffrey hung himself, his whole

family blamed me. They said I'd driven him to it. They kept bringing up the baby who died and then Geoffrey too, as if I'd
murdered them both with my bare hands. I had a nervous break-
down and they said it served me right. It was then that I realized I
would have to leave town." She spoke calmly, looking down at her
lap, not moving, and a sense of young tragic death wound around
her like scented bandages, permanent and disfiguring, the way
Japanese women used to bind their feet to keep them dainty. She
was doomed somehow, I could see that now, even though I'd
never noticed it before.

"You have to be strong, we all have to be strong," my mother
said without looking at me. "We're the women, we have to be
stronger than they think we are."

I could hear my father snoring lightly in the other room, no
longer harmless. The kitchen was snug with yellow light. The
window was patterned with frost like feathers or ferns and it was
just starting to snow. My mother pulled the blind down so no one
could see in. We could have been anywhere, just the three of us,
bending in together around the kitchen table, knowing things,
these sad things, that no one else knew yet.

That night Rita slept over. An odd thing for grown-ups to do, I
thought, but I liked it.

After I'd gone to bed, it reminded me of Christmas: something
special waiting all night long in the living room: the tree, the
unopened presents, Rita in my mother's new nightie wrapped up
in an old car blanket on the chesterfield.

Around the middle of December, Rita flew to Toronto to have
Christmas with her sister, Jeanette, and her doctor husband. My
mother had somehow not considered exchanging presents with
Rita and was horrified when she appeared the morning she left
with three gaily wrapped boxes, one for each of us. Even more
surprising was my father, who handed Rita a little package tied

up with curly red ribbons. She opened it on the spot, still stand-ing in the doorway, and produced a silver charm of the Montreal Canadiens' crest.

On Christmas morning we opened her presents first. She'd given my mother a white silk scarf hand-painted with an ocean scene in vivid blues and greens. My father held up a red Chicago Black Hawks jersey with the Indian head on the front and the number 21 on the back. I got a leather-covered datebook for the new year in which I immediately noted the birthdays of everyone I could think of. Rita's presents were the best ones that year.

After dinner, we called all our relatives in Manitoba and then my mother took some pictures of the tree, of my father in his new hockey sweater, and of me eating my dessert behind the chicken carcass. My friend, Mary, called and we told each other every-thing we got. I thought Rita might call later but she didn't.

Between Christmas and New Year's, my mother went out and bought a braided gold necklace to give to Rita when she got back. The silver charm was never discussed in front of me.

Not long after Rita returned from her holidays, she was moved from Ladies' Dresses into Ladies' Coats. Now when she came over she wore a knee-length black coat trimmed with grey Persian lamb at the collar and cuffs. She always hesitated before taking it off, caressing the curly lapels, picking off invisible lint, giving my mother and me just enough time to notice and admire it again. She knew a lot about mink and ermine now, how the little things were bred and raised on special farms, how vicious they were, how many tiny pelts it took to make just one coat. She lusted uncontrollably, as she put it, after one particular mink coat in her department but had resigned herself to never being able to afford it and seemed both relieved and disappointed the day it was bought by some doctor's wife.

"Just between you and me," my mother said right after Rita phoned to say she'd sold the fabulous coat, "I think mink is a waste of money. It's only for snobs. I wouldn't wear one if you gave it to me." Ten years later, my father bought her a mink jacket trimmed with ermine and she said, hugging him, "Oh, Ted, I've always wanted one."

It was an extravagant winter, with new records set for both snow and all-time-low temperatures. My father seemed to be always outside shovelling snow in the dark, piling up huge icy banks all around the house. He would come in from the cold red-cheeked and handsome, trying to put his icy hands around my neck. Rita came over less and less often. She said it was because her car wouldn't start half the time, even when she kept it plugged in.

On warmer days when Rita wasn't working, my mother often took the bus downtown to her apartment. When I came home from school at three-thirty, the house would be luxuriously empty. I curled up on the chesterfield with the record player on and wrote in the datebook Rita had given me or worked on the optimistic list my friend, Mary, and I had started: "One Thousand Things We Like." Well into its second spiral notebook, the list had passed seven hundred and was coming up quickly on eight with

cuckoo clocks
Canada
lace
my mother's hair
comfortable underwear and
having a bath without interruptions

being the most recent additions.

My mother returned just in time to start supper before my father got home from work. She was distracted then in a pleasant sort of way, all jazzed up and jingling from too much coffee or something, gabbing away gaily as she peeled the potatoes. Rita had given her some old clothes which could be made over into any number of new outfits for me. There was a reversible plaid

skirt I'd always admired and wanted to wear right away but my
mother said it was too old for me.

One Saturday afternoon when we had been out shopping
together, my mother suggested we drop in on Rita before catching the bus home. I had never been to her apartment before and
as we walked up Northern Avenue to the Barclay Block, I tried
to imagine what it would be like. Small, I supposed, since Rita
lived alone—and was, in fact, the only person I'd ever known
who did. Such an arrangement was new to me then, a future
possibility that became more and more attractive the more I
thought about it. The apartment would be quite small, yes, and
half-dark all the time, with huge exotic plants dangling in all the
windows, shedding a humid green light everywhere. The rooms
smelled of coffee and black earth. The furniture was probably
old, cleverly draped with throws in vivid geometrics. The hardwood floors gleamed and in one room (which one?) the ceiling
was painted a throbbing bloody red. I thought that Rita and I
could have coffee there just the two of us (my mother having
conveniently disappeared) and she would tell me everything I
needed to know. Why did Geoffrey hang himself, what
happened to the baby, do you go out with men sometimes, do
you think I'm pretty, do you think I'm smart? She could tell my
future like a fortune.

We climbed a steep flight of stairs up to the second floor. The
smell of baking bread rose up cheesy and moist from the Italian
bakery below. I'd forgotten that my parents had lived here once
too, until my mother said, "I always hated that smell, we lived in
3B," and pointed to a door on the left. I could not imagine
anything at all about their apartment.

My mother knocked loudly on Rita's door. Further down,
another door opened and a woman in her housecoat leaned out
into the hall, expecting somebody, I guess, or maybe just spying.
"Oh, it's you. Hi," she said and ducked back inside.

My mother knocked again, and then once more.

"Maybe she's working," I offered.

"No, she's not. She definitely told me she was off today."

"Where can she be then?" I was pretty sure I could hear a radio going inside.

"How would I know?" my mother said angrily and sailed back down the hall.

Only once did I find my father and Rita alone in the house. I came home from Mary's late one Saturday afternoon and they were drinking rum at the kitchen table, with the record player turned up loud in the living room. They seemed neither surprised nor sorry to see me. There was something funny about Rita's eyes when she looked up at me though, a lazy softness, a shining, which I just naturally assumed to be an effect of the rum. She poured me a glass of 7Up and we sat around laying bets on the playoffs, which were just starting, Montreal and St. Louis, until my mother came home from shopping. As it turned out, the Canadiens took the series four games straight that year and skated back to Montreal with the Stanley Cup.

Rita stayed for supper and then for the game. I went back to Mary's and then her father drove us downtown to the Junior A game at the arena. Rita was gone by the time I got home and I went straight to bed because I'd had one shot of rye in Lorne Puhalski's father's car in the arena parking lot and I was afraid my mother, who still liked to kiss me goodnight, would smell it.

They were arguing as they got ready for bed.

"She lost her son, Violet, and then her husband too," my father said, meaning Rita, making her sound innocent but careless, always losing things, people too. But he was defending her, and himself too, protecting her from some accusation, himself from some threat I'd missed, something unfair.

"Well, I *know* that, Ted."

"Don't forget it then."

"That's no excuse for anything, you fool."

"I didn't say it was."

"Be quiet, she'll hear you," my mother said, meaning me.

Clues

Every Friday just after lunch, Linda Anderson went out to their wheezing blue Chevy in the driveway next door and sat there honking for me—a ritual which irritated my mother marvellously and made me feel like I was going out on a heavy date. We were going grocery shopping.

Once in the car, I would admire Linda's new lilac skirt, multi-coloured sandals, or glittering earring and brooch set. She made the jewellery herself from little kits she got every week through a special mail order club in the States. She was always wearing something new and flamboyant to, as she cheerfully put it, "perk myself up a bit. I know I'm plain." Even then I could see that this was true. Linda was one of those young women I've often seen since, on buses or trains, pale and rabbity-looking with slightly buck teeth and round eyes, baby-fine hair, light brown or dirty blonde depending on how you look at things. One of those young women destined to be always unhappy, unhealthy, or alone.

In the Safeway store I pushed the cart while Linda joyfully loaded it up, tossing in items from either side, checking her list, flipping through the fistful of discount coupons we'd been duti-fully clipping from magazines and newspapers all week. This did not take on the stingy penny-pinching quality it did when I was forced to go grocery shopping with my parents on Saturday. Then, my mother led the way, my father pushed the cart, which was invariably one of those balky ones with the wheels going in all directions at once, and I lagged along uselessly behind. My mother didn't even need a list. She bought exactly the same things every week. You could count on it.

The Safeway on Saturday was full of disgruntled men and hectic children. But on Fridays the shoppers were mostly women, moving smoothly and courteously through the aisles, sure of themselves, experts in their element.

Linda dropped her purchases one by one into the cart. Kraft Dinner, cream corn, Brussels sprouts, dish soap. Gallons of milk. "Neil's a real milk-drinker."

Green beans. "Neil hates green beans but they're on sale."

Macaroni. "Neil just loves my macaroni and cheese."

I felt myself to be collecting these clues, learning everything there was to know about Neil Anderson and so, by extrapolation, about men in general. Neil, like all the other desirable men in the world, was swarthy and slim, brooding, sensitive, and hard to please.

More items were checked off the list. Tomato soup. "It always comes in handy."

Fish for Friday. "We're not Catholic, but still, it's nice."

Cheese slices. "Last night I made this new casserole with sausage and cheese slices and was it ever good."

Linda was always trying out new products, new dishes. She had a whole shelf of cookbooks in her kitchen, from which she liked to read me recipes out loud: Apple-Ham Open-Facers, Inside-Out Ravioli, Lazy Day Lasagna. She prided herself on both her cooking and her shopping. Being seven years younger, I was immensely interested in the entire procedure, confident that this was one of the inevitable things which lay in store for me—shopping and cooking for my husband and our eventual children—they would all love everything I served them.

We waited at the meat counter while the butcher in his bloody apron sliced four chops off a big chunk of pork. The vertical blade whined through the flesh, silver teeth grinding on bone.

The man in line behind us, wearing tinted glasses and a uniform of some kind, said, "That's just how it sounds when they cut the top of your head off to do an autopsy." Linda smiled and nodded, dropping the chops into the cart, which I was already pushing away. Now the butcher was spearing slabs of dripping liver with a pointed wooden stick.

On the way to the checkout stand, we had to stop at the candy counter to pick up something for Neil, licorice pipes or jujubes or a chocolate-covered cherry. "I have to get him a little treat or he'll be mad at me," Linda explained coyly, making her husband sound like a spoiled child or maybe a snake she had managed to charm, but just barely.

The Andersons had moved into the house next door on the first of July, newly married, just come to Hastings from Newberry, a dumpy little town to the north. Jobs were easier to come by then and within a week, Neil was working at the same paper mill as my father.

In the beginning Linda came over to our house several times a week. She could sit at our kitchen table all afternoon just chatting and drinking coffee with my mother. We soon knew all about her.

Her maiden name was Jessop. Her family had been in Newberry for decades. They owned both the dry goods store and the funeral parlour now, though they'd started out with nothing just like everybody else. Linda was in the middle, with two older sisters and two younger brothers. There had been one older brother, Lance, but he was dead now, beaten to death outside the Newberry bar by a jealous husband from a neighbouring town. The husband had then driven home, on a tractor no less, and killed his wife with a pitchfork. "As I see it," Linda said, "he knew he'd get caught so he figured he might as well finish the job."

Linda and Neil had been childhood sweethearts. "His family is basically no-count," she admitted. "Oh, don't tell him I said that, he'll kill me." As if I would. She was drawing me into a womanly conspiracy, lush with the promise of fat secrets and special knowledge.

But they were good at heart, the Andersons. In fact, one of Linda's brothers would soon be married to one of Neil's sisters. "It's a real family affair."

They were renting just until they could afford to buy a house in one of the new subdivisions. They planned to have three children and were getting busy on that right away. "I can't afford to wait too long," Linda confided. "Both my sisters were cut open for cancer when they weren't much older than me. So I suppose it'll get me too in a few years."

Linda's life, past, present, and future, was endlessly interesting to her, and to me too. But my mother wasn't much for socializing or sitting around gabbing all day, so, after the first few visits, she developed the habit of drifting inconspicuously back to the dishes, the dusting, or rolling up socks. Linda hardly seemed to notice her defection and I was flattered to think that it was really *my* company she sought in the first place.

Once, after Linda had finally gone home to start supper for Neil, my mother said viciously, "That girl's a feather-brain!" and threw the dishtowel across the kitchen after her. "And don't you go getting any crazy ideas, young lady." I could not have said exactly what she meant—ideas about what? men, marriage, babies, cancer?—but I knew, grudgingly, that she had a point of some kind.

Linda had other stories besides her own—a repertoire of alarming gruesome tales which, for a time, I neither doubted nor forgot. But I didn't repeat them either. There was the one about the man who murdered his son and his dog with an axe. The woman found strangled in her car beside the Number One highway. The man who chopped up his wife and kept the parts in the freezer, all packaged up and labelled.

Such things happened all the time, in California, Paris, Vancouver, Brazil, but they could happen to anyone anywhere. There was no reason to think that you would be spared. You could no longer know what to expect of people, especially men, in this crazy world. There were so many of them, all equally unpredictable. Most of the time there was no telling what they might do. According to Linda, the men were depraved savages who might run amok at any time and the women were helpless obvious victims, dying all over the place. The best and the worst of her stories were those in which the killers were *never caught*.

One afternoon Linda asked, "Did you hear about those kids?", casually stirring more sugar into her third cup of coffee. My mother was defrosting the fridge with pots of hot water.

"No," I said. My mother sat down at the table, wanting, I suppose, to hear the news in spite of herself.

Linda settled in to tell the story. "This couple took their four kids to an arts and crafts show at the community centre. When they left, two of the kids, a boy and a girl, went on ahead. But they never got home. They found them the next day, strangled, side by side, in a field not far from the centre."

"Here in Hastings?" I asked, for lack of any other response.

"Yes. Right here in Hastings."

My mother jumped up from the table, knocking her chair over backwards, and stomped out the door, muttering, "Garbage, garbage!" Which could have been either what she was going to do, put out the garbage, or her opinion of Linda, or both.

That night after supper I went through the newspaper page by page, hoping that no one would ask what I was looking for. On the second last page, I found the small headline, KIDS FOUND DEAD, above a half-inch story.

Two children found dead in a schoolyard in Caracas, Venezuela. They'd been left at home alone and discovered missing when their parents came home the next day.

I was both disappointed and relieved. Linda, in her hurry to tell us something horrible that we didn't already know, got the story all wrong. She was looking for proof that she was justified in her cheerful expectation of tragedy. After this, there were many times when I suspected her of lying, trying to make me as frightened as she was. This did not immediately make me like her any less, although it probably should have and would now.

I was soon spending more time at Linda's house than she did at ours. My mother, I could see, had succeeded in making her feel, if not exactly unwelcome, then certainly unappreciated.

The Andersons' house was just the way ours had been before we renovated. We called them war-time houses. They were single-storey squares with dugouts instead of basements, small cozy or cluttered rooms all opening off the kitchen, and wooden steps front and back.

When we were too hot and miserable to do anything else, Linda and I sat out on her front step in our shorts, watching the traffic and sipping pink lemonade. Occasionally a carload of boys would slowly cruise by, whistling as we stretched and admired our legs in the sun. We were feeling like sleepy cats and ignored them.

My legs were a deep reddish-brown, so dark by August that my mother said, "You look like a little Indian." Linda was fair-skinned but neither burned nor tanned, remaining all summer long a marbled, bluish white. "Too much sun is bad for you anyway," she said. "It'll give you cancer." I didn't believe her and continued to cultivate my colour. I couldn't help but notice that the blue veins in her thighs were beginning to bulge and break.

When it was cooler or raining, we sat inside, usually at their stylish new breakfast nook, which Neil had built himself and Linda had wallpapered in a blue and orange pattern featuring teapots and coffee mugs.

While Linda talked, polished her salt and pepper shaker collection, or fussed and cooed over Twinky, the blue budgie in his cage by the window, I took careful note of everything in the house. The teapot clock, the ceramic Aunt Jemima canisters, the hot pot holders which read "Don't Monkey With The Cook," the plastic placemats with kittens, roosters, or roses on them—she changed them once a week.

Every detail was important to me, an avenue into the esoteric intricacies of married life, a state of being which seemed to me then divinely blessed, glamorous, intimate but clean. I needed to know exactly how you achieved such a permanent and inviolable state of grace. As far as I was concerned, their perfect happiness was a foregone conclusion, stretching sanguinely out to embrace infinity. Any connection or resemblance between their marriage and that of my parents was remote, if it existed at all. It did not occur to me that either my parents had once been just like Linda and Neil or that Linda and Neil would one day be just like my parents, solidified and decidedly unromantic.

Linda, herself still quite convinced of the powerful magic of homemaking, was more than happy to answer my nosy questions. I was digging for information, especially about Neil and what it was like to live with a man.

"How do you make an omelette? What TV shows do you watch? Does Neil help with the dishes? How often do you vacuum? What time do you go to bed? Do you ever stay up all night? Which side of the bed do you sleep on?" The questions I was afraid to ask were the most important.

Their bedroom door stood proudly always open, displaying a dainty doll in the middle of the white chenille bedspread, her voluminous pink skirt spread around her in layers like a cake. At home the bedroom doors were always shut tight, a concession to privacy, shame, or not having made the bed yet.

One rainy afternoon Linda had the bright idea of rearranging the living room furniture to surprise Neil when he got home from the mill. The aqua-coloured couch and chair with arms at least a foot wide were unwieldy but simple enough once we threw our weight into it. Before moving the TV set we had first to take down the dozens of photographs in different-sized fili-gree frames which completely covered its top. This was a lengthy procedure which involved the identification of every person in every picture, who took which shot, and what the special occasion was and at whose house it was held that year. Dismantling the china cabinet where Linda kept her salt and pepper collection was even worse. She estimated the collection at two hundred pairs but it seemed more like eight or nine hundred to me, every set different, from cupids to corn cobs, from Santa and Mrs. Claus to Paul Bunyan and his blue ox, Babe. By the time Linda was finished fondling and explaining them, I was so bored, impatient, and somehow embarrassed for her that I went home, leaving her sprawled on the couch, sweat-ing and self-satisfied.

The one thing we had not touched was Neil's gun collection. Arrayed in wooden racks against the wall, the smooth metal barrels were perfectly, endlessly polished, cool to the touch even in this unbearable heat.

I did not go back for several days, and when I did, I found every-thing once again in its original position. Neil, obviously, had not been impressed. I was obscurely pleased, meanly imagining that he'd made her put it all back by herself. No one was going to push him around, least of all silly, fluffy Linda. It served her right. She could be so tiresome. Some days—mean, sulky days—I'd taken to wondering how Neil—quiet, sensitive, so-handsome Neil—could even stand her. I was beginning to understand why she had no other friends. And if I was too young for her, as my mother repeat-edly pointed out, then she was certainly too old for me.

• • •

I didn't spend all my time that summer with Linda. In fact, I never saw her on weekends and seldom in the evening.

Spending the day at home, I usually wanted to stay inside and read, but felt obligated to go out and suntan. I would spread myself out on a beach towel in the backyard, armed with baby oil, radio, and a pitcher of water to sprinkle on intermittently, believing this would speed the tanning process. I was essentially bored and uncomfortable but lying there made me feel more normal, doing exactly what I supposed all other girls my age were doing or wanting to.

On weekends I lay there by the honeysuckle hedge hoping that Neil Anderson would see me and want me and go back inside and holler at pale gabby Linda. Whenever I heard a sound from that direction, I couldn't open my eyes for fear it would or wouldn't be him.

I could not have said when I began to feel this way about Neil. It was all Linda's fault anyway, I reasoned. She had made him seem so desirable, so serious and important, so perfectly male, the only man worth having. How could I help myself? I no longer wanted to be like Linda. But I did want everything she had, including her house and her husband. Linda, I imagined, was the only obstacle which kept him from me. Now I fantasized about their divorce.

Evenings were usually spent with my best friend, Mary Yurick, who had a job in the kitchen of a nursing home downtown and so was not available to me during the day. I was not yet allowed to work and envied her mightily, foolishly brushing aside my mother's wise words: "You'll be working for the rest of your life— so what's your hurry?"

Mary and I passed the time at her house or mine, watching beauty pageants and variety shows on TV, playing Scrabble or poker, sipping lemon gin from her father's well-stocked liquor cabinet whenever her parents were out for the evening. When the night was too warm, too long, too inviting, we went out and we walked, restless and uneasily innocent.

We headed downtown, past those boring plump houses just like ours, with flowers, families, and fat dogs in the yard. Downtown where the dangerous young men were hanging in restaurant doorways, draped potently over parking meters or the hoods of hot cars, watching the bright street where something might happen to jerk them awake, something electric and clarion, like a siren. We were already aware of their power but not yet of the need to protect ourselves from it. We thought we could become part of it, did not know yet of the danger, of how they would use it over and against us, never offering a share.

We browsed through the record store which was always open late and peeked through the glass doors of the Hastings Hotel bar, longing. Once there was a fight out in front, two men thumping bloodless and silent on the sidewalk. Once a young woman lay face down on the curb, stinking. But nothing could deter us. We walked the nights on a leash that summer, Mary and I, all dressed up and tingling, daring each other to be disgusted. The summer was almost over and we had wasted it.

Some evenings I stayed home and read, not wanting to know. Alone in the hot house, I curled up on the couch in my nightgown with a new novel and just one light on, feeling safe and relieved. All the screens were open, hoping to catch a breeze, and I could hear June bugs hitting against them, falling to the ground on their backs. From all up and down the block came voices, thin music, the hum of sprinklers and lawn mowers. Once in a while I could hear someone else's phone ringing faintly.

My parents were out in the yard cutting peonies and roses just as it grew dark, their voices young and strong in the twilight. Sometimes they sat out front in the lawn chairs, citronella candles smoking in a circle around them to keep the mosquitoes away. I wondered what Linda and Neil were doing, wished I had never met them, would never be like them. Wished I could stay home here forever, here where they did not draw blood, here where you knew exactly what they expected of you, here where my father was coming in through the door and putting his arms around me for no reason. Here where I wanted to cry.

Friday night the week before school started, Linda called and invited me over.

"Neil's gone out again, I'm all alone. We could make popcorn, I'll do your hair." She was begging.

I was hard-hearted. "No, I can't. I'm going out with Mary." I wanted to hurt her. I wanted her to know that I had better things to do and was nothing like her after all. It was Friday and I was feeling frisky, thinking of what I would wear, who we might see, how late I could stay downtown without pushing my mother over the edge.

Grocery shopping that afternoon, Linda had been careless and preoccupied, missing half the items on her list, spending her money instead with desperate extravagance on T-bone steaks, fresh asparagus tips, a precious can of lobster. Her dirty blonde hair was greasy and her out-of-style pedal-pushers were held together at the waist with a big safety pin. She perked up only once, just long enough to tell me the story of a marine in Michigan who had murdered his wife and three children and then turned the gun on himself.

"It was a real bloodbath. You can imagine," she muttered with grim satisfaction, fondling a sweet-smelling cantaloupe before tossing it into the cart. "All I really want is one of those little gadgets you make melon balls with."

I was barely listening, absent-mindedly examining the onions, not thinking of anything else in particular, but not allowing myself to be interested either. Linda, I had decided, no longer needed to be listened to. Her grisly gossip was merely her way of reassuring herself that things could be and probably would be worse. Everybody needs to be certain of something.

In my smug, soon-to-be-undermined adolescent superiority, I pitied her. But I was shutting her off, cutting her out, moving glibly away. We could not do anything for each other anymore.

On the way home we took a detour downtown, cruising several times slowly past the Hastings Hotel so Linda could squint intently at the doorway, looking for clues. Neil Anderson, I knew from eavesdropping on my parents, was in trouble for drinking at work (this from my father) and sometimes stayed out all night without Linda (this from my mother, who liked to keep track of things). I was interested but only mildly surprised. Linda was one of those women who expected the worst and got it. Neil was clever, sly, and volatile, capable of anything.

Linda attempted to confide in me. "I just don't know what to do," she began and then stopped.

She tried again. "I just can't believe that Neil would—"

I was holding my breath, afraid to look at her. What did she want from me anyway? She was older, married, she wasn't supposed to have problems anymore. I would not be drawn into her miseries. I would not talk about Neil behind his back anymore. It felt now like a betrayal or a shameful admission of helplessness.

Downtown that night Mary and I hung around the Exchange Café for a while, spending our allowances on chocolate milkshakes and chips and gravy, and then we gravitated wordlessly toward the Hastings Hotel. We perched on the wooden bench out front where the winos slumped in the sunshine and sometimes slept under newspapers at night. The police would be by in half an hour or so, telling us to move along. We sat there smoking cigarettes stolen from Mary's mother and talking, mostly about how easy it would be to sneak inside and have a beer. We were all dressed up, trying to look older in earrings and, despite the cooler nights, new white tank tops selected to show off our silky suntans. But we both knew we wouldn't try it, not yet.

The boarded-up bar door opened—someone had kicked in the glass again—emitting a belch of boozy laughter and a country and western chorus.

Neil Anderson came out with his arm around the waist of a blonde woman wearing skin-tight slacks and white cowboy boots. She was quite stunning in an ornamental sort of way, smiling all-inclusively around her, proud of herself. Neil was just drunk enough to be expansive and flirtatious, not at all the way he was around the neighbourhood, not at all the way Linda made him out to be. Neither of us had the grace or good sense to look guilty.

He came right up to me and threw his other arm around my neck, kissing the top of my head. "Hiya, honey!"

Mary was impressed. Neil patted through the pockets of his black leather jacket, as if looking for matches or a gun. Exposing a gleaming buck knife strapped to his belt, he produced a mickey of rye.

"For you, ladies!" he said and swaggered away.

The bottle, of course, was a bribe, so I wouldn't tell Linda. As if I would. I probably should have been indignant or afraid, but instead I was feeling privileged and ripe with our secret, winking and wanting to go with them. I was aching for adventure and convinced now that Neil, more than anyone, knew where to find it.

Neil Anderson was the first in a long line of those handsome, charmingly doomed men who would inhabit my life for a time—those lovely lazy men who could get away with anything and I would never tell. For a few years anyway I thought I had it all figured out.

Tickets to Spain (1985)

"In the dream there was always a sound like bees, faint and far away, but then not really a sound at all, more like having water in your ears. It was the sound of thousands of people all in one place, all at once waiting."

I was telling Howard this dream this morning while he shaved. Leaning naked against the sink to get closer to the mirror, he pulled his face all out of shape and sighed. I was sitting on the edge of the tub in my housecoat, talking to his reflection, damp and steamy-looking from the shower.

"At first we weren't there and then we were, but we didn't know for sure *where* we were until they brought out the bull and every-one was cheering and jumping around in a fever. They were all strangers, men mostly, doe-eyed and handsome with oily skin."

I am always having dreams about strangers, dreams that I'm not in yet or have just left. I handed Howard a towel, one of the red ones Robin gave us for our anniversary. We've been living together for three years. The towels were mostly a joke. We'd been arguing among ourselves for days—do bulls really charge when they see red? Robin said no, I said yes. Robin said, "How would you know?"

"They were all speaking Spanish, things that aren't in the phrase book, and eating, these men. They kept passing food over to me—ice-cream cones, olives, half-eaten oranges, hot dogs dripping mustard. They do have hot dogs there, don't they?"

"I think so, Miriam," Howard said, around a mouthful of tooth-brush and mint-flavoured paste. I watched him solemnly spit, wipe his mouth, put on his glasses, and start fixing his hair. Howard has always been particular (vain) about his hair. This is one of the things I would never have suspected about him when we first met because he had a convertible then.

"It was so real—the bull shaking its head, twisting and lunging, forward and away; the picador up on his horse, tormenting and stabbing. You were making notes on a paper napkin and I was saying stupid things like: 'Oh the poor thing! Does it know it's going to die? I want to go home.' The sky was so hot it looked white."

"It won't be like that, Miriam. Don't worry—you'll love it. Everyone does—the drama," Howard said, patting my knees and heading for the bedroom to get dressed.

Howard and I have been going to Spain for a year and a half. It all started, I suppose, at that foreign film festival at The Plaza. The Spanish entry, *A Night Sky*, was melancholy and turbulent, dense with subtitles and classical guitar music. Juanita, the voluptuous overheated heroine, was falling in love all the time with swarthy political men who were everywhere in the unyielding countryside. They were all so intelligent and intense, with stomach muscles like rock.

Then my sister, Robin, went to Spain for the summer and came back brown and spiritual, with intricate symbolic stories of revolution, renaissance, and throbbing hotel rooms. This was all the proof I needed. Spain was another world, the one I should have been in all along.

It was more my dream than Howard's to begin with. But then he swallowed it whole. In the way of young couples seriously in love, we were always assimilating. Sometimes it gets confusing, this Siamese-twin trading of tokens, blue jeans, and dreams.

"At first I was sweating but then it was rain on my face." The rain in Spain falls mainly on the plain.

This summer we are really going. After so much anticipation

we are determined not to be disappointed. I have been buying travel guides and studying the phrase book, *Spanish in Three Months*. We practise and practise until we can have whole conversations like:

"I am very fond of apples. *Me gustan mucho las manzanas.*"

"I prefer pears. *Prefiero las peras.*"

"We like oranges best. *Nos gustan más las naranjas.*"

We are always collecting mementoes of Spain: castanets, rough clay pots, a stuffed bull with a spear where its heart should be, posters of flamenco dancers and the young men running the bulls through the streets of Pamplona. In this picture there are eleven bulls altogether, two white ones, and the boys are running barefoot in a pack, all in white with red scarves wound around their waists. One boy is leaping, he could be dancing. Another is doing a somersault, or he could be falling and breaking his neck. It is all so dreamy and daring. Boys will be boys.

Sometimes we buy bottles of good Spanish wine to drink with our friends. We put on the classical guitar tapes and show them our souvenirs, as if we've already been there. Sometimes I wish we had.

"For a while in the dream I was wearing a white wedding gown with a rose in my teeth, a red one, of course, which means blood. You were wearing a black tuxedo with a white carnation and smoking a fat cigar. For a while it was like a rock and roll video and I thought we were going to dance. But then we were just normal again and no one was singing."

We used to talk about getting married. Sometimes now I think we did and I just can't remember. Just as I can't remember how, according to my mother, when I was five, my sister, Robin, who was ten, tried to drown me in the bathtub. Something like that you'd think would leave a permanent mark on you, distinguishing, if not disfiguring. But it didn't, and I'm not afraid of water or my sister either.

"The matador was like a ballet dancer, or a scrap of paper blown around by the wind, and then he was riding the bull instead of killing it."

The matador knows that his chance of meeting death in the ring is one out of ten, and the odds are one to four that he will be seriously wounded. His suit is called the traje de luces, *the suit of lights.*

I was talking and passing over underwear, socks, clean shirt, suit pants to Howard in precise order, as if we were in surgery. Our bedroom is small and crowded with a matching pair of antique dressers with mirrors and, stuck in the middle like a raft, a king-size bed that seems to be spreading. The trees outside the window shed into it a greenish wavering light like that inside an aquarium. This is our morning ritual: I tell him my dreams and make the bed; he gets dressed up as a shoe salesman.

"In the end, a team of mules dragged the dead bull out of the ring on its back like a giant insect."

I handed Howard the lint brush. We imagine that shoe sales-men are notoriously neat. Would you let them fiddle with your feet if they weren't?

We went into the kitchen to have coffee. I worked hard on that room, hanging plants in the window, wicker baskets on the walls, and pots and pans from the ceiling. Shiny bottles of spices and fragrant herb teas sit on open shelves above the stove, and the cupboard doors are yellow to match the floppy old roses on the linoleum.

"The matador was a hero heaped with roses. The crowd went wild, smearing hysterical wet kisses all over each other and us."

It was one of those dreams that you think you've been having all night long and nothing will stand still and you wake up feeling scared of everything.

"Do you see?"

• • •

After Howard left for the store, I poured myself another coffee, turned on the TV, and curled up on the couch. I half-watched "The 20-Minute Workout," where all those pliable nubile women get up early to contort themselves in their skin-tight leotards, sweating just enough to make their hair curl prettily. Three more, two more, one more. Synchronize crotches.

This morning I mostly ignored them, feeling little compulsion to join them and almost no guilt. What's the point? They have no breasts and do not eat french fries. Instead I studied the phrase book. I am learning to say, among other things:

"I should like to see a bullfight. *Me gustaría ir a una corrida de toros.*"

There are other practical conversational sentences which I've memorized just in case.

"It is a beautiful day. *Hace un día hermoso.*"

"I am ashamed. *Me da vergüenza.*"

"Do it again. *Vuelva usted a hacerlo.*"

"My friend used to wear her clothes too tight. *Mi amiga usaba sus vestidos demasiado estrechos.*"

"I just want to sit in the sun and doze. *No quiero más que sentarme al sol ly dormitar.*"

From my spot on the couch, I could see right into the living room of the house across the street. An ordinary family lives there, husband, wife, half-grown twin daughters with braids who came bouncing over the day we moved in to tell us, happily, that our house was haunted. When I run into the wife at the grocery store, we chat about the neighbourhood cats digging up her flower beds and peek curiously into each other's shopping carts, as if reading tea leaves or palms.

This morning, as usual, the fat husband in his red housecoat was riding his exercise bike and looking out the window. I suppose that he could see me too, wandering around in my housecoat (blue), watering the plants and straightening the pictures, talking to myself with explosive Iberian gestures.

I was just deciding to get dressed when the phone rang. It was the travel agent. "I'm calling about the two tickets to Spain. They're ready. When can you pick them up?"

I called Howard at the store and he said he'd go tonight after work. On the phone he was friendly but careful, swallowing several times as if someone was listening or his tie was too tight. Shoe salesmen, we hypothesize, are circumspect about their private lives. On the odd occasion, at a movie or a bar, when we run into someone Howard works with, he always introduces me as his wife. Sometimes this irritates me but I smile fetchingly and try not to guzzle the sugary little cocktails they buy me. The store is an exclusive downtown boutique where summer sandals start at a hundred dollars. We can't afford to shop there.

The Spanish are a very shoe-conscious people. A high polish on the shoes is a tradition passed down from the caballero, *whose shiny boots served notice that he rode his own horse and did not walk along dusty roads with lesser men. Madrid has one street—Fuencarral—lined with shoe shops from one end to the other.*

In real life, Howard is a playwright. He has been working on the same play for nearly two years. It's even been finished a few times. We've gone out for expensive dinners to celebrate, congratulating ourselves with champagne in silver buckets. But then Howard changes his mind or the characters change their minds and they are all dissatisfied all of a sudden and Howard happily starts the rewrite. Afraid to cut the cord, babies leaving the nest, all of that. We assume that playwrights, like all artists, are supposed to struggle and squirm.

Howard's play has had various endings and titles over time—in this incarnation it is called *Tickets to Spain* and they all live almost happily ever after.

The set consists of two rooms in a small old house on a tree-lined city street.

The kitchen, stage left, is spacious and bright, very warm and wifely. Plants in the window, wicker baskets on the wall, pots and pans hang from the ceiling. Yellow cupboards, old-fashioned well-worn linoleum, round wooden table in the centre.

The bedroom, stage right, is smaller and darker. Seen through the window is a huge elm tree which casts the room in a watery greenish light. Two old-style dressers with mirrors, a king-size bed in the centre covered with a colourful handmade quilt in the Log Cabin pattern.

At first the bed was covered with a Guatemalan blanket but then my mother sent us the Log Cabin quilt which has been making its way around my family for decades, and the Guatemalan blanket got rewritten.

It is mid-May, about four in the afternoon. The kitchen is rich with sunlight and cigarette smoke hung in layers like veils.

DAVID BARNES is seated at the kitchen table, staring out the window, smoking and drinking coffee. He is wearing dark dress pants and a rumpled brown cardigan. DAVID is about thirty-five, slim, and dark-complexioned.

Sometimes DAVID is drinking beer out of a can, dressed in jeans and a sleeveless white undershirt. He is always handsome. Sometimes he has his head in his hands. He is depressed, not drunk, although at times it can be hard to tell the difference.

DENISE BARNES enters stage left. She is an attractive woman,

*about thirty, very tanned and healthy looking, dressed in a dainty
sundress, eyelet cotton, very white. She is carrying a bag of
groceries with a loaf of French bread sticking out the top.*

Sometimes a bunch of tulips sticks out of the bag. I like DENISE
best when she has blonde hair done in a perm, unruly but angelic
around her little face. When it is raining she wears a baby-blue
jacket and matching scarf.

DENISE *puts the bag on the table and looks at* DAVID *sadly.*
   Angrily.
   Lovingly.
   Guiltily.
   She puts her hand on his shoulder.
   She ignores him altogether.

DAVID: Do you still love me? (*He lights another cigarette.*)
DENISE: I don't think so, no.
DAVID: Please don't leave me, Denise.
DENISE: I can't go on this way. (*She heads for the bedroom.*) I'm
   going to live with my sister.

DAVID: Do you still love me? (*He lights another cigarette.*)
DENISE: I think so, yes.
DAVID: Please don't leave me, Denise.
DENISE: I'll never leave you, David. (*She heads for the bedroom.*)
   We can work it out. (*The telephone rings. They know it is the
   lover. Neither moves to answer it.*)

Sometimes DAVID and DENISE are married and sometimes
they're not. It doesn't seem to make much difference in the long
run. They have taken turns at being unfaithful and at being
fooled. But there is always a lover, somebody's lover, male or

female, with an unstable mind or a murderous bent, phoning, following them, ruining their lives. They have experimented with staying together, splitting up, group sex, suicide, and murder.

They've even got their tickets to Spain. I'm glad when they get to go, sorry when they don't, and depressed when the plane crashes. Or I'm just as happy when they stay home, worried when they go, and curious when they take the lover with them. Sometimes the lover is Spanish. They are learning the language:

"Do not go away until it stops raining. *No se vaya usted hasta que case de llover.*"

"See whether my umbrella is behind the door. *Mire usted a ver si mi paraguas esta detras de la puerta.*"

"Nobody likes to be deceived. *A nadie le gusta que le engañen.*"

"Lunch is ready. *El almuerzo est á servido.*"

I have grown rather fond of DAVID and DENISE and can always sympathize, no matter what happens to whom. They are nice people and I'm always relieved when Howard lets them live. I imagine how tired they must be by now of the paces he persists in putting them through.

This morning in the study, more commonly known as "Howard's room," I dusted, emptied the ashtray, gathered up coffee cups, crumb-covered plates, and a pair of socks. In Howard's room, according to law, I do not touch or remove anything else.

I also turned on the tape recorder which Howard uses when he is rewriting. This cannot, I think, strictly be considered snooping—the play, after all, is destined to become public property (someday). But I don't tell Howard I'm doing it either. It is like turning on the soap operas when you're ironing—something you do every day but wouldn't admit to just anyone. Like listening in on the people at the next table in a restaurant. Howard does this all the time but denies it.

One night at Giorgio's we took a table beside a handsome

young couple who didn't talk much and played with their pasta. Then the woman said, "Before you know it, she'll be yelling at you in public, just like I used to." The man looked pained.

DAVID *is taking* DENISE *out for Italian food, trying to break it to her gently.*
DAVID: She is a quiet and gentle woman.
DENISE: Before you know it, she'll be yelling at you in public, just like I used to. (*She reaches for a roll.*)
DAVID: You still do. (*He takes a drink of wine.*)

This morning I sat down at Howard's desk to listen.

DENISE: In the dream there was always the sound of drums, faint and far away, but then not really a sound at all, more like having water in your ears.
DAVID: I'm tired of hearing your dreams, Denise. You've never asked for mine.

Bees, it was bees, there was always the sound of bees.

This afternoon I met my sister, Robin, and her lover for lunch at The Village Green. It was one of those days when every stranger you see on the bus looks like someone you know, someone you used to know, someone you're sure you know from somewhere but you can't quite put your finger on it. Who is it, who are you, who do you remind me of?

Dwight Maguire was my lover last year, before he fell in love with Robin. We are all very civilized and (try to) find this situation amusing. I don't have a lover these days, other than Howard I mean. I suspect sometimes that he has one or is in the process of getting one, but I have no proof, am not even looking for it yet.

The Village Green is an airy, healthy-looking place filled with little glass-topped tables and many unsteady little chairs. There are aggressively healthy plants hanging everywhere and also some large leafy ones in clay floor pots that make you feel as if there is another guest at your table. The white walls are covered with posters advertising art show openings that took place five years ago in large American cities that no one here has ever been to. There are also many large photographs of vegetables—bright green broccoli big as trees, plump tomatoes precisely sliced to show off their shapely seeds.

It is the kind of place that tries to convince you that you are really somewhere else, in some more serious-minded metropolis where everyone is self-employed and artistically inclined.

We all ordered Caesar salads, flaky croissants, and the house drink, champagne and orange juice on ice, called O.J. Bubbles.

"Miriam, Dwight, Robin, how nice to see you all," said the waitress. They all know us there. They probably gossip about us after we leave, speculating about our arrangements, sleeping and otherwise. We keep showing up for lunch in various combinations of two or three, sometimes all four of us, sometimes just Howard and Dwight together. DAVID and DENISE do the same. We are all so mature. Why do I wish sometimes that we could all just make a scene, throw lettuce and forks, hate each other and get it over with?

DAVID *is sitting at the kitchen table while* DENISE *paces furiously around him.*

DENISE: How could you?

DAVID: I lost my head.

DENISE: You're losing your mind.

DAVID: You're driving me crazy.

DENISE: I've never been so embarrassed in my life.

DAVID: You've still got lettuce in your hair. (*He laughs maniacally.*)

The restaurant filled up rapidly around us. It is a popular place, drawing businessmen and bank tellers on their lunch hour, university professors and their favourite students, new mothers gracefully breast-feeding. There is always some young man alone in the corner, reading or writing in his journal. I like the look of this and think that Howard should do the same, in a tweed suit jacket with leather elbow patches. But Howard says they're probably writing grocery lists and letters to Mom asking for money.

A naturally gregarious man who delights in the intricate art of conversation, the Spaniard spends much of his time in cafés and bars. He is probably a chain-smoker and rolls his own cigarettes from his favourite cheap tobacco. He is rarely a heavy drinker.

Seated at the next table was a well-dressed young couple politely putting away vast plates of lettuce. The woman put down her fork and slipped off one diamond earring, just the way my mother does when she's getting ready to talk on the phone. By proxy for Howard, I automatically eavesdropped.

"How could you?" said the man (husband).

"I didn't want to hurt you," the woman (wife) explained.

"But you did."

"I couldn't help it."

"I'll never forgive you."

"More coffee, folks?"

I wondered why everybody seems to be conducting their crises in restaurants these days. There is something about sharing a well-prepared generous meal which arouses, all at once, a false sense of security, the illusion of normalcy, and an abstract promise of intimacy. In addition to this emotional trickery, restaurants also ensure the relative safety of hurting someone you (are supposed to) love in a public place as opposed to your own inescapable living room.

Robin nudged me. "Stop staring at those people, Miriam. It's rude."

Robin and Dwight were still talking about some party they'd been to the night before, a birthday celebration for one of his friends.

"I was having a wonderful time," Dwight said, "until you started bitching."

"I wanted to go home. You were ignoring me."

"I was not."

"You were drunk."

"I was not."

"You were disgusting."

"Maybe a little."

Before you know it, she'll be yelling at you in public.

Today, as always, Robin wore a flowing cotton dress and sandals. She has a broad peasant face, permanently tanned, and with her flaxen hair wound up in braids, she was looking like a milkmaid. On first seeing Robin, you would expect her to be the warmest, most understanding woman you have ever met.

In reality she is phlegmatic and persistently narrow-minded. She is hard on everyone, does not allow them their weaknesses, be they alcohol, excess emotions, or love. She is no good with children or small animals. She is mightily offended by television and most jokes told to her by men. She seems always on the verge of ridiculing Dwight or discarding him altogether.

I have almost always adored her and would follow her around if she'd let me. I did hate her for a few years after I found out she'd tried to drown me, but then I had to forgive her. Just as they say, blood is thicker than water. But we have never really been a close family.

All Spanish families are alike. Rich or poor, large or small, they cling together and take a profound interest in each other's lives.

Children seldom leave home until they marry. Family life centres around a large late lunch which Mother has spent most of the morning preparing.

I imagine Howard and me, poor white waifs, being hugged into the heart of a big Spanish family with clean, singing children, fat aunts always cooking for jolly uncles who are always eating and tickling us. I am learning to say:

"We are very glad that our father has come home again. *Nos alegramos mucho de que nuestro padre haya vuelto a casa.*"

"I am very like my mother. *Me parezco mucho a mi madre.*"

"She is going to marry her cousin. *Ella se va casar con su primo.*"

Robin and Dwight sulked through their salads, Robin sternly, Dwight theatrically. But by the time the coffee arrived, they were cuddling and teasing again. I was foolishly feeling left out and had to bring up the time that Dwight, drunk, had proposed to me. "But what about Howard?" I'd asked. I had never seriously considered leaving Howard for Dwight. We are the kind of couple that everyone else thinks is perfect and will stay together forever. I suppose we will. "He can come too," Dwight had said.

Robin, whose only emotional fault is jealousy (retroactive as well as concurrent), tolerated this nostalgic reverie rather well and said nothing. Neither did Dwight.

It came as no great surprise to me when Dwight fell in love with Robin. I supposed that most men would eventually. I was not in a position to put up much of a fight anyway. Howard knew about the affair by then and was talking in sad whispers, smoking in the dark till four in the morning. He had always been critical of Robin but discovered that he liked her immensely once Dwight fell in love with her.

Dwight is a widower, his wife having died two years ago of a swift and savage cancer. When I loved him, I thought of him as soft and sore, slightly infirm, as if recovering from major surgery. I pampered and petted him constantly, thinking of how much he needed me to be strong. Robin, on the other hand, spares him nothing and gives him just enough, and it looks as though he'll never leave her.

"The travel agent called this morning. Our tickets are ready," I told them.

"The Spanish are an amazing people, so intense," Robin said. Everything that Robin likes lately, including movies (films), books, and women especially, is amazing and intense.

Taking my hand in an uncharacteristic gesture, she said, "Once you've been there, you'll *know*," as if the whole country were hers to give me. Dramatically, mystically, she said, "In the searing sunshine, there is nowhere to hide. Death is no longer dark. Spain is a landscape with figures. Houses bake in the sun. It will change your life."

There can be no turning back now.

Going home on the bus, I got out the phrase book, which, I find, I have taken to carrying with me everywhere, like a lucky rabbit's foot. The man beside me edged stiffly away as I began muttering to myself like a befuddled old woman in black, counting her rosary beads.

"However difficult it may seem, you must try to do it. *Por difícil que parezca, usted debe probar a hacerlo.*"

"The more I give him, the more he wants. *Cuanto más le doy, más quiere.*"

"It is no use saying that. *No sirve de nada decir eso.*"

I was expecting to spend an agreeable evening at home, Howard in his room writing, me curled up on the couch reading or watching TV. I was in the mood for a whole series of stupid sitcoms where everyone is immaculate, articulate, and can sort out their respective but interwoven problems in half an hour, not counting commercials. The ordinary family across the street watches TV every night. They never close their curtains, having nothing, I imagine, to hide. From my spot on the couch I can see their screen clearly, colours and faces, car and cat food commercials, in their dark living room. I'm always pleased when I see that we're watching the same program.

When Howard writes in the evening, I can hear him doing the dialogue out loud, running through one speech over and over until he gets it right. DAVID and DENISE have lately shown a tendency toward interchangeable lines. It hardly seems to matter anymore who says what. In the way of young couples seriously in love, they have embraced the theory of osmosis and turned themselves into an reversible jacket. They are, as Robin would say disparagingly, joined at the hip. And of course they will look alike when they are old. But, as always, there are difficulties.

DAVID: I never *really* loved you.
DAVID: I never really *loved* you.
DAVID: I never really loved *you*. (*He lights another cigarette.*)
DENISE: I never really loved you *either*.
DENISE: I never really loved you *anyway*. (*She heads for the bedroom.*)

But tonight when Howard got home, just after six, he had company. Which is not unusual. He has lately acquired the habit of bringing strangers home for supper, as if they were bag ladies in need of a hot meal. Howard has a way with people.

Just coming out of the kitchen, it took me a minute to realize that tonight's guests were the ordinary couple from across the street. Their names, it turns out, are Cindy and Mike. We had drinks and made neighbourhood small talk, Howard insisting the whole time that they must stay for supper. Finally Mike phoned over to tell the girls to order pizza.

From childhood on, the average Spaniard has been taught to share—and share he does, quite often putting himself out in order to help the friend or stranger who stands before him. Politeness demands offering a meal to a stranger, who answers, "May it be good for you. Que aproveche."

Mike, looking even heavier up close, was wearing low-slung jeans and a greasy teeshirt which revealed a roll of hairy flesh that hypnotized me. In sandals, his stubby toes were hairy too. No wonder Howard is always washing his hands. Maybe he should have been a dentist.

Cindy, the wife, was dowdy but inoffensive in an ordinary summer dress pulled tight across the breasts. Every so often she would let her little hands flop down limply into her lap, exhausted or resigned to the inevitable. She admired everything in our living room, especially the fake fireplace decorated in a mosaic of black, red, and white tiles. I put violets where the fire should be. She also wished she had a couch just like mine, old and overstuffed, reupholstered in grey and maroon stripes. Wiggling around on the couch, nervously sipping their drinks, she and Mike talked more to each other than to either of us.

Mike experienced unpredictable moments of loquaciousness.

"We went to Europe once. It was a wonderful experience, wasn't it? So educational."

"That was before the twins, of course," Cindy explained.

Obviously Howard had already told them about the trip. Why is he always telling our secrets to strangers? (Since when was it a secret?) They are nice people, Cindy and Mike, so why do I hate them? I already know that no matter what happens, I will never like them.

I did not want them to know anything about me. I did not want them in my house, in my living room, in my bathroom snooping through my medicine chest looking for contraceptives and prescription drugs. I did not even want them living across the street from me. I was feeling vicious.

I waved the phrase book at them.

"Would you like anything to eat? *¿Quiere usted comer algo?*"

"No thanks; I am not hungry, but I should very much like a drink. *No, gracias; no tengo hambre, pero de buena gana bebería algo.*"

"Please pass me a clean plate. *Sírvase pasarme un plato limpio.*"

"I do not like stale bread. *No me gusta el pan duro.*"

They didn't laugh.

While I was in the kitchen trying to figure out what to feed these people, Howard put on a tape of Spanish guitar music. I danced briefly back into the living room, snapping my fingers and twitching my skirt, clenching a rose (wooden spoon) between my teeth. This time they laughed. Howard was showing them our souvenirs from the trip.

When a Gypsy woman grows too old and fat to dance for a living, she can be found with the blind beggars, peddling castanets, charms, flowers, and photographs.

I went back to the kitchen and Cindy trailed in behind me. "Do you need some help?" There was not much to do with leftover lasagna and garlic toast.

Howard put on a tape of his play, a scene I hadn't heard before, one that shouldn't have been written yet. Howard was getting uncannily ahead of himself. Or playing tricks on me.

DAVID *and* DENISE *have had company for supper, some new people they've just met.* DENISE *is already in bed.* DAVID *enters. They are talking in the dark.*

DAVID: Are you awake?

DENISE: Just barely.

DAVID: Nice people, aren't they?

DENISE: Nice enough.

DAVID: Why are you being so difficult?

DENISE: I'm not sure. (*She rolls over onto her back and stares at the ceiling.*)

DAVID: What are you afraid of?

DENISE: Something. Sleep.

DAVID: I don't want to go to Spain anymore.

DENISE: I don't want to go to Spain anymore.

"What a beautiful kitchen. I love those little baskets on the wall," Cindy was saying. Another drink had loosened her up. "You remind me so much of my sister, she's a poet." I was tearing lettuce while she chopped celery savagely. I did not want to remind her of anyone.

"Oh? Where does your sister live?"

"She died two years ago. Drowned." I felt instantly guilty, as if I'd killed the poor woman by not wanting to be like her.

Encouraged somehow by my silence, Cindy continued, "I have dreams. In them she is going up the stairs for a long time and when she finally gets to the top, she turns and smiles down at me. But I can hardly see her, it is like opening your eyes underwater. And when she speaks, it is in some foreign language that I don't understand. I feel like I am swimming. Sometimes there are candles. Her hair was the colour of the water when they found her and I wanted to think the fish swimming into her mouth were coming out poems, but they told me it couldn't be true."

"Supper's ready!" I hollered hysterically. I am afraid of this woman.

We had just stopped exclaiming over the sudden change in the weather—a spring thunderstorm coming up quickly from the

west, darkening the evening sky ominously—and started eating
when the lights flickered and went out. I had been looking down
at my lasagna, trying not to stare at Mike, who mashed everything on his plate together with a fork and then shaped it into a
perfectly round pile before attacking it. Like a child, for a minute
I thought I had been struck blind, punished once and for all. In
the darkness Mike chewed steadily.

Howard laughed and lit the two candles I'd set out on the table
to excuse my earlier craziness and appease my guilt. But I hadn't
gone so far as to light them. Wavering in an imperceptible breeze,
they threw long jumping shadows around the twilit kitchen.
Cindy gasped, stretched her arms out, and took first me and then
Howard by the hand, as if we were holding a seance. I thought I
would scream in the silence.

When the lights came back on a few minutes later, I thought
there should be a noise but there was nothing, only the light,
flooding.

They went home early, I went to bed, and Howard went into his
room to make notes. I forgot to ask him about the tickets. Just
before I fell asleep, I could hear him talking, into the tape
recorder or into the telephone, to some dark woman over the
ocean feeding the bulls, with a rose or a candle in her teeth.

There is never any doubt then that one has arrived in Spain.

A Simple Story

(1987)

One night in a small city a man and a woman went out to a restaurant to celebrate. On the way back, they were nearly run down by a car that went out of control and rammed into the window of an apartment building. They were lucky. They could have been killed.

DESCRIBE THE NIGHT:

The snow begins in the early afternoon, big flakes falling like shredded paper and with purpose, patiently, so that by dusk, it is drifting lackadaisically up against picket fences and unsuspecting parked cars. By the time the newspapers are delivered after supper, the wind is up and children all over the city are dawdling over their homework, peering outside every two minutes, praying that school will be closed tomorrow. Some men are already out shovelling. Others are generously offering to help with the dishes instead, feeling smug and practical because, if this keeps up all night and then the stupid snowplow comes, what's the point?

It takes this particular man, Richard, three tries to get out of his driveway in the suburbs, where there is always more snow anyway, according to a corollary of that law which causes tornadoes to hit trailer parks. He is one of those who will shovel in the morning, cursing and wiping his nose on the back of his gloves.

This evening has required so many complicated advance arrangements that they are going anyway, come hell or high water. The dangerous driving conditions only add to Richard's pleasure, making him feel calm and committed.

This particular woman, Marilyn, is waiting for him in the lane behind her downtown apartment building, turtling her chin into her expensive fur coat, sucking on the collar. She is thinking of the time when one of her ex-lovers, Jim's, ex-lovers came for the weekend.

DESCRIBE THE EX-LOVER JIM'S EX-LOVER:

Predictably pert, still on the loose, blessed with a name like Amber, Angel, or Anemone, something like that, the ex-lover Jim's ex-lover spread her perfect thighs, boots, sweater, fur coat all over the ugly couch. Marilyn is thinking of what precise pleasure it gave her when the cat jumped up on the coat and sucked its heart out. She is still congratulating herself on the way she said, "Oh, isn't that cute? He thinks it's his mother! He must be part rabbit," and stuck her head in the oven to check on the chicken.

Marilyn is thinking that if Richard shows up now, safe, not dead in a drift, she will never be nasty again. She feels relieved but eternally obligated when he finally arrives.

Once in the car, she asks stupidly, "Can you see?" and tries to peer through the blizzard by tilting her head at an impossible angle and pressing her face closer to the windshield.

When Richard answers, "Sure, I can see. No problem," she settles back into her coat and sighs, giving herself over to the experienced hands of a God who can always make the visibility better on the driver's side.

Richard didn't buy her the fur coat, although that was the sort of gesture she'd expected at first. In the beginning, she had longed fleetingly for chocolates and flowers, arriving once a week, right on schedule, just when she was feeling the most guilty, the most neglected, or the most fed up with him. They both knew that he had to buy her something: the guilt-assuaging quality of gifts is universally accepted. She took to watching movies about married men, movies with words like *confessions, secrets,* and *lies* in their titles. But they never gave her anything to go on. The only thing these various married men had in common was that they were often found alone in shopping malls at odd hours, buying gifts for their wives and their lovers both, often on the same day in the same store.

DESCRIBE THE GIFTS:

When Richard does bring her gifts, which is seldom enough, he brings her books or records which, he once explained, are more intelligent, more dignified, less likely to give credence to the inherent clichés of their situation. Marilyn makes him sign the books and then leaves them lying around for anyone to see. She doesn't read much but likes to dust them and study the authors' faces on the back jackets. She likes to hold them in her lap like kittens. She plays the records only when Richard is there, for fear of the sadness and regrettable phone calls they might elicit if played at three in the morning with a bottle of white wine. If mink has become melodramatic and embarrassing, hysteria is even worse.

So Marilyn bought the fur coat herself, with a small inheritance she received from her mother's sister, Aunt Louise.

DESCRIBE AUNT LOUISE:

The oldest in a family of fourteen, Aunt Louise was the one who never aged, bought a new bicycle at eighty, got up at six in the morning to bake blueberry pies for the kids, refused to go to the Senior Citizens' Drop-In Centre because why would she want to sit around and play cards with a bunch of old people? Aunt Louise could simultaneously make every one of her nieces, nephews, and grandchildren, Marilyn included, believe that they were her favourite.

All of the women in Marilyn's family expect to be just like Aunt Louise: growing old without illness, complaint, or other damning evidence of decline, kneeling down dead one Sunday morning in the strawberry patch, the juice like sweet blood on her hymn book and hands.

Marilyn was completely surprised when the inheritance cheque arrived. It weighed heavily on her, crazily, dead money in a bank vault, growing interest effortlessly in the dark the way potato eyes grow those waxy white roots in the bin beneath the stairs.

At that time, Marilyn had been sleeping with Richard three times a week for about six months and it was hard on her. She knew she wasn't really cut out for this sort of thing. She was always wanting what she couldn't have: she was always wanting to go grocery shopping with him on Saturday afternoon, to make him take out the garbage, to wash his socks, to wake up beside him in the morning and argue about whose turn it was to make the coffee. She was always wanting him to tell her how stupid his wife was this week, how she was always on him about something, how she didn't understand him, how she was mean to him for no reason. She was always wanting him to say that he was going to leave his wife and then she hated him for saying or not saying it. They took turns believing and not believing that he ever really would.

One day when Marilyn wasn't believing anything Richard told her anymore, she went out and bought the coat without even trying it on. She wanted him to think some other man had bought it for her, some other man who really loved her and would quite happily crawl or die for her.

He said she was silly to squander good money that way. She said it wasn't good money, it was dead money.

She wore the coat with a vengeance, modelling herself after a young woman back home, Mrs. Greene, who, when her husband, a dentist, was killed in a car accident, took the insurance money and bought herself a $50,000 Turbo-charged Porsche. She cruised all over the countryside with the sunroof open and the tape deck blaring rock and roll. The townspeople were collectively horrified, everyone keeping an eye on her now, asking each other knowingly, "Did you see Mrs. Greene today?" What did they expect her to buy: a hearse? Besides, it could have been worse: the Porsche could have been red instead of black. The more charitable among them suspected she was on the verge of a nervous breakdown, the rest thought she was glad he'd died.

All of these things happened in the small northern town where Marilyn was born and which now seems remote and symbolic, lush with significant memories, gothic.

DESCRIBE THE MEMORIES:

Street corners, weather, storefronts, furniture, meals: any of these are likely to come to Marilyn abruptly, whole and acute, when she is busy doing something else, not watching where she is going.

Waiting for the bus to work one night in front of Mac's Milk, she thinks about an old house on the corner of Cuthbert and Elm Streets, close to her parents' house. She was just a teenager, running home late from a disastrous date with a boy named Desmond who would later marry a girl she knew slightly, Celeste, and who would still later be stabbed to death in a bar fight while Celeste, pregnant with their second child, looked on. The night she thinks about was in February and snowbanks were piled up against the old house. Warm squares of window-light were yellow in the middle of the night. Marilyn stood in front of the old house, lifting and putting down her cold feet like paws, wanting to go in and pour tea from the smoky blue pot she imagined on the table, wanting to pet the cat she imagined on the chair, a grey cat, the kind with fur like a rabbit. Next morning she heard the old man who lived there, Mr. Murdoch, had died in his bed in the night.

Aunt Louise said dreaming of snowbanks was a portent of

death. But it wasn't a dream. Those snowbanks around that old house were real as pillows, real and meaningless as these ones piling up all over the city tonight.

DESCRIBE THE CITY:

This is a small, old city which prides itself on its cleanliness, friendliness, and well-laid-out street plan, as most small cities do. Richard was born and raised here. His memories are pleasant but do not tell him anything in particular. He doesn't expect them to, being, as they are, a continuum. He couldn't tell you offhand what used to be where the Royal Bank building (twelve stories, tallest in the city, an incendiary issue when the developers first moved in, but once accomplished, it was found to have disturbed nothing much and those who had voted NO in the plebiscite did their business there just like everyone else) is now, although, in fact, it was a fish and chip stand where he was always bugging his parents to take him and which still figures occasionally in his dreams.

DESCRIBE THE DREAMS:

In the dream he is a tall teenager dousing his chips with salt and vinegar. His parents are standing behind him. His mother smiles indulgently, his father hands over a five-dollar bill. Behind them, over to the left, two boys he knows from school are fighting on the sidewalk, rolling over and over through cigarette butts, chocolate bar wrappers, ketchup. He steps smoothly around them, pretends he's never seen them before, pretends the one boy, who will die the next spring in a motorcycle accident, has not reached out and grabbed him by the ankle. He shakes the boy's hand off like a puppy and thinks about fish, just walks away.

This is something that really did happen but something which Richard only remembers when he's sleeping.

He also dreams about going to the ballpark. In the station

wagon on the way there, he is socking his fist into his new leather glove, breaking it in. Sometimes after they get to the ballpark and his father parks the car, Richard turns into a grown-up and pitches a no-hitter, while the fans scream and scream, so hot and so loud that they melt.

DESCRIBE THE BALLPARK:

The ballpark is just like any other, with a green wooden fence around the field and chicken wire around the dugouts, where the junior-high kids hide in the winter after school to smoke menthol cigarettes with their mitts on. Richard knows but has never examined the implications of the fact that this ballpark, where he first made love to a sixteen-year-old girl named Eileen who later became his wife, is now the Safeway store where they do their grocery shopping on Saturday afternoons.

Richard is very comfortable in this city and everything about it is just fine with him. When the new shopping malls and suburbs go up, it seems to him that they've always been there. He believes in progress. A small businessman in a small city, he has never been accused of anything, least of all being parochial. Sometimes he feels flawless. Even his affair with Marilyn seems innocent. They're not torturing anyone, not even themselves. They're not like other cheaters. They are in love.

They are driving in the snow past City Hall, a domed limestone building with pillars and coloured floodlights, a small fountain into which tourists and townspeople alike toss coins hopefully all summer long. Tonight the floodlights colour the falling snow red, blue, and green like some curtain poised to go up on a magic show. While they wait at the corner for the light to change, Richard gazes up at the dome with a great deep satisfaction, as if he'd built it with his own two hands.

"Beautiful," he says.

They have passed this building a thousand times and every

time he says just that. It is reassuring somehow. Marilyn pats his hand on the gear shift and lovingly agrees with him. Force of habit.

Richard thinks that Marilyn doesn't know that his wife used to work there as a file clerk in the very early years of their marriage, in the happier times.

DESCRIBE THE HAPPIER TIMES:

The kitchen of Richard and Eileen's first apartment was always sun-splashed, the lemon light pouring in through frilly white curtains, running all over the black-and-white tile floor. There was no dust anywhere. Eileen was at the sink in her apron, the one with the enormous purple grapes embroidered around the hem. Her earrings sparkled and her painted fingernails flitted through the fragrant soapsuds like goldfish. She was always simmering something in a big black pot, spaghetti or chili—they weren't well off yet, they were still struggling, stirring up gallons of something spicy with hamburger and tomato sauce that would go a long way. They were tired, they'd worked all day. Gliding past each other like skaters on the shiny kitchen floor, they touched unconsciously, sweet pats and slow circular rubs across weary shoulder blades.

Over supper they talked about their friends, their jobs. She was still a file clerk, he was still a cook, frustrated and scheming, dreaming of owning his own restaurant someday. "Poor Richard," she said. On Friday nights they had a bottle of red wine and made love on the living room floor in front of the TV, which flickered like a fireplace. Richard covered himself with her apron when he went to the kitchen to get the cigarettes. Sometimes they talked about having children but Eileen never got pregnant and, as the time for it passed, this was something they stopped discussing and just accepted, going on to other futures, other things.

Marilyn knows about Eileen's job at City Hall (although she

doesn't know *how* she knows or why it seems like such a sadistic secret between them) but she doesn't know about the apron.

Marilyn alternates between trying to be more like Eileen (after all, he married her, didn't he?) and trying to be exactly the opposite. The stupid thing is: she has never met the woman, never hopes to, and yet she cannot buy a blouse without worrying that Eileen has one just like it, cannot make Richard a grilled cheese sandwich without worrying that Eileen does it better, just the way he likes it.

Once Richard said, "You sound just like my wife."

They were talking about travelling, which Marilyn hates, Eileen too. Richard loves it. What Marilyn said was: "I hate living out of a suitcase and I get constipated in strange bathrooms."

So then she said, "Well, she can't be that bad. You married her, didn't you?" Which, aside from the obvious, also meant: You'll never marry me, will you?

Now she says, "I'm starving."

Richard says, "You're wonderful, you're always hungry, healthy," and Marilyn imagines Eileen existing on clear soup and green salad, pushing the lettuce listlessly around with her fork, looking pale. Eileen is probably one of those people who says, "Oh my, I forgot to eat today." Marilyn can eat a whole medium-sized pizza by herself.

"We're almost there now," Richard assures her.

The city and the streetlights end just past the new Ford dealership. They head north on the highway, singing along with the radio, thinking about how hungry they are, about having some wine when they get there. The restaurant is a new one in the next town where, hopefully, no one will know them.

Because of the storm, there is little traffic on the highway. The headlights of the few cars which do pass them look secretive, urgent, or sinister. There is no ordinary reason to be out in this blizzard. Marilyn supposes that they must look suspicious too.

Seen through the windshield, the snow appears to be coming and going in all directions at once, even up. It is narcotic and irresistible. She cannot help staring straight into it, as into a fire, until her eyes won't focus and all the flakes are coming straight at her, the way the eyes in some pictures, the saddest, most dangerous pictures, are always looking right at you no matter what corner of the room you're hiding in. She wants to go to sleep. Richard, driving steadily, seems fortunately immune to this hypnosis.

Marilyn thinks lazily about driving one night through a snowstorm with her first lover, Luke, to the farmhouse where his best friends, Cheryl and Don, lived.

DESCRIBE THE FARMHOUSE:

Cheryl and Don had rented the farmhouse on Mapleward Road, fifteen miles north of town, for only twenty-five dollars a month as long as Don kept the place up. Luke's car was falling apart, backfiring all the way, machine-gunning through the snow. Luke was smoking a joint and turning his head every two seconds to say something to Marilyn. He was one of those people who cannot talk to you without looking at you. Marilyn was frightened, waving him away, pointing at the road, which was indistinguishable now from the deep ditches on either side. She was angry too.

"What the hell do you mean dragging me all the way out here in a blizzard?"

It was something to do with money: Luke had some for Don or Don had some for him. Either way it was stupid and probably the result of something illegal they'd cooked up between them.

The farmhouse was set back from the road on top of a hill. The car wouldn't make it up the driveway so they left it down by the mailbox and trudged up the hill toward the old house, which was glowing like a lightbulb in an empty white room.

Suddenly Marilyn wasn't mad anymore. She threw herself down in the snow and made an angel, thinking of what a pretty and innocent gesture it was, something that Luke would remember for the rest of his life. They weren't very happy together anymore and she supposed they were going to break up in a month or two but still: she wanted him to remember her fondly forever.

Don was out in the driveway shovelling. Luke grabbed up the other shovel and pounded Don on the back till the snow sprinkled off him. Don stopped for a few minutes to say hello to Marilyn, stamping his feet and slapping his leather mitts together like a seal. Then they went to work.

Inside, Marilyn and Cheryl played cribbage and listened to Janis Joplin over and over again. She was still alive then, not afraid of anything, they figured, showing few signs yet of letting them all down in the end. "Buried Alive in the Blues." The only heat in the house came from the big black woodstove and they stayed close to it, except when they had to go out back to pee in the snow. Cheryl was wearing a ridiculous outfit that looked beautiful on her: a red cotton dress over a pair of Don's long johns, a purple vest with mirrors on it, rubber boots, and a headband. Cheryl made Marilyn feel uptight and out of it in her jeans and new ski sweater.

The men came in and dried their socks and mitts on the stove, drank coffee from metal mugs, made some plans for tomorrow night, nothing special: they'd all go out for a few beers somewhere downtown.

On the way home it was still snowing but Marilyn felt calmer—you were more likely, she figured, to die going someplace else than you were heading home.

A man stood on top of a snowbank waving something at them. They stopped. He had his pant leg in his hand and there was blood dripping from the meaty inside part of his left thigh.

He struggled into the back seat and they drove off. He told them in an English accent over and over again the story of how he'd been just walking along minding his own business when a dog came running out of the trees, chewed off half his leg and kept on running. It was a black dog. It hadn't even knocked him down. He was lucky. It was only one dog. They were said to be running in packs around here. He was just walking along a deserted country road in the middle of the night in the middle of the winter's worst blizzard. Minding his own business.

Marilyn watched him out of the corner of her eye. He was sweating and talking, bleeding all over the upholstery and apologizing. It was probably ketchup. He was probably going to kill them and steal the car. He was probably going to rape her and *then* kill them and steal the car. Luke was driving wildly and trying to think of everything he knew about mad dogs and Englishmen besides that Joe Cocker album. He knew they were supposed to come out in the midday sun. The men laughed at this and Marilyn kept her eyes squeezed shut till she could hear the blood in her ears.

When they dropped the Englishman off at the hospital emergency entrance, he gave Luke a ten-dollar bill and wouldn't hear of them coming in.

Without knowing why it was his fault or what she really meant, Marilyn said to Luke, "One of these days you'll get us both killed."

By the spring, Cheryl was pregnant and she and Don had taken an apartment in the Franklin Block downtown. After Luke and Marilyn split up, she and Cheryl became good friends. Marilyn often went over to the apartment where Cheryl sat in the La-Z-Boy with her swollen feet up, eating Vanilla Wafers out of the box, watching TV all day in her housecoat. Sometimes she would get sick and come out of the bathroom wiping her mouth and groaning. In the kitchen, she cursed and slammed cupboard doors, craving Corn Flakes. But all the dishes were stacked in the sink, dirty there for days, because washing them made her even more nauseated. So Marilyn would do them, also the vacuuming and the laundry. Cheryl would sit there eating, licking her lips and her fingers, burping occasionally, cradling her stomach in her hands.

One day Don came home from work early and Marilyn was still at the sink, rinsing and wiping and putting away. Cheryl was asleep with her mouth open. Don came into the kitchen and took the dishtowel out of Marilyn's hands. He put his arms around her waist and said, "Thanks. I should have married you instead."

Now Marilyn is deciding to tell this whole story to Richard because it just might make him see that there are things about her he doesn't know yet, things he will never understand, is not meant to. He likes to say that he knows her better than anyone else ever will. Sometimes she lets this go by, other times she says, "Don't be too sure," or "Oh, you think you're so smart," which hurts him and he leaves her alone for a while. But the truth is: he is smart, he is handsome, he is a good lover, and if he hadn't gone ahead and married somebody else first, he might have been the man of her dreams.

DESCRIBE THE MAN:

Richard is wearing a brown leather bomber jacket and a multi-coloured scarf which Marilyn knit him last winter to show there were no hard feelings when he took his wife on a ski trip to Banff. She tried not to think of strangling him with the wool or poking the needles up his nose and, sure enough, the scarf turned out perfectly.

Richard owns a bar and pizza place downtown called Poor Richard's. It is not a sleazy place—it has red-and-white chequered tablecloths and tacky Italian statues with missing arms and fig leaves, yes, but the cook doesn't wander around with tomato sauce splattered all over his apron and they don't deliver. They have an extensive wine list. They feature live entertainment on weekends which always draws a good crowd.

The waitresses wear tasteful black and red uniforms and do not chew gum, their pencils, or their fingernails. Marilyn has been a waitress there for three years. She likes the uniform because it saves her clothes which will then be in good shape for occasions in her "real life"—which hasn't arrived yet, but it will. As a woman, she doesn't think of herself as a waitress *per se*. She never intended to work at the pizza place for this long. She still has a sense of waiting for something better to come along. She does enjoy the job though, working with the public, chatting with the regular customers who tell her their stories a piece or a drink at a time. Take Curtis, for instance. He owns racehorses. You'd think he was a stable boy the way he comes bow-legged into the restaurant in cowboy boots and those tight jeans. Sometimes she thinks she catches a whiff coming off him of sweat and manure, some kind of liniment. He talks to her about odds, purses, jockeys, his lonely ranch. He has been telling her the story for a week now of how his wife walked out on him five years ago.

All Marilyn's customers have something about themselves that they've always been wanting to tell. She listens and gives advice when they ask for it. They say hello to her on the street. She is always a little surprised (but proud) that they recognize her out of uniform and without a tray in her hand.

As a twenty-seven-year-old woman, she doesn't like to think of herself as aimless but sometimes, depressed, she has to admit that that's a good word for it.

DESCRIBE THE WOMAN:

Under her fur coat, Marilyn is wearing a shiny red dress she has been saving for months. It has silver buttons down the front and a black fringe at the yoke. She also has new black boots. Tonight is one of those real-life occasions she has been waiting for and she expects to feel satisfied and convinced by the time she gets home. She will not let herself consider the fact that she will be sleeping alone and Richard will be sleeping with his wife. Sometimes when they are together, she cannot enjoy herself at all for worrying toward that moment when he will look at his watch and say, "I have to get home." How does he say it? Afterwards, she can never be sure.

Because of Richard's irregular hours and his being in charge of setting up the work schedule, their rendezvous have never been difficult to arrange. Once in a blue moon, his wife decides to go to Poor Richard's with some of her girlfriends and then Marilyn gets an unexpected evening off. She sits at home in her housecoat, exploring this side of the "other woman" role, crying fitfully if she feels like it, imagining herself getting all dolled up and going down to Poor Richard's and sitting at Eileen's table, introducing herself, buying her a drink, a pizza, a dish of spumoni ice cream, imagining herself pouring a drink over Eileen's head, laughing in her face, telling her that she can have her stupid husband back, he's not that great, she never really wanted him anyway, imagining herself putting her head down on the table or in Eileen's lap (ample, she pictures it, aproned) and going to sleep. But more often lately, Marilyn ends up having a long bubble bath, reading and sipping white wine in the tub, admiring her legs as she shaves them, going to bed early and feeling obscurely pleased with herself. Then, in bed alone, she allows herself the short pleasure of fantasizing about Curtis.

DESCRIBE THE FANTASIES:

She and Curtis are at the racetrack in the clubhouse which is the exclusive area where the owners and the high rollers sit. He is wearing a white cowboy hat and rings on all his fingers. She is wearing a white dress and sunglasses. They are sipping tall frosted drinks with fruit in them. All of his horses are winning. He wants to buy her a red Porsche.

Or:

She has just impressed Curtis with a sumptuous supper and is piling the dishes in the sink. There is a saxophone on the radio. The steam from the hot water makes her hair curl prettily. Curtis comes up behind her and puts his arms around her waist. He kisses her ear and begins to turn her around slowly, gracefully . . .

The fantasies are abbreviated and unconsummated, to keep the guilt at bay. She is, after all, supposed to be dreaming of Richard and the day he will leave his wife and become forever hers. So she does. All the quirks have been worked out of this fantasy by now, everybody knows their lines and everything fits, including all of his belongings into her little apartment.

Now Richard parks the car a couple of blocks away from the restaurant—a knee-jerk kind of subterfuge. Walking away from it, they hold hands and duck their heads down in the wind.

DESCRIBE THE RESTAURANT:

Decorated in the country style, with rustic furniture, old barn wood nailed imaginatively to the walls, quilted gingham place-mats and kerosene lamps on the tables, the restaurant is called The Square Dance Room. It is empty tonight, because of the storm, they hope, not the food. Marilyn is still shaking the snow out of her dark hair, thinking that she looks artless and adorable, when the waitress fairly jumps at their table.

Richard says, "You look like a drowned rat," to Marilyn and, "Slow night, eh?" to the waitress, who is wearing a square dance dress the same gingham as the placemats. The skirt sits straight out around her on layers of starched crinoline and bumps into everything: the table, the lamp, Marilyn's arm like a cobweb, as the girl bends to put down the menus and smile sweetly at Richard. Marilyn thinks meanly of a toy clown she once had, the kind with the weighted bottom that bobs and flops drunkenly around at all angles but never falls over on its fat red lips.

They order a litre of house wine and the waitress do-si-does away.

Richard makes a toast. "Here's to our celebration."

DESCRIBE THE CELEBRATION:

Tonight is the second anniversary of their affair. They aren't sure if they should be talking about their past (they've had their ups and downs) or their future together (they don't know what to expect).

When Richard takes his wife out to celebrate their anniversary, they talk about the past year (kind of an annual report) and their hopes for the next year (kind of a prospectus) and then they talk about other things, such as the new lawn mower, the reason the car keeps backfiring, or what colour to paint the bathroom now.

At this moment, the food comes. In honour of the occasion, they have both ordered the prime rib, medium rare, with baked potato, sour cream. Marilyn likes it when they order the same meal in restaurants—it makes her feel like they are a real couple, a happy couple with no problems, not a care in the world. It makes her think of those old married couples you see waltzing together at weddings, so smoothly you'd think they were one body with two sets of legs. They dance with their eyes shut, humming.

The food, on plain white crockery plates, is so good they keep smiling at it as they dig in.

Richard says calmly, "I'm putting the house up for sale."

Marilyn thinks calmly, *He's leaving her. He's all mine now. I will be stuck with him forever.*

Richard says, "We're going to buy a new one, with a swimming pool and a bay window. We're even going to decorate it ourselves this time."

Marilyn can just imagine Eileen squinting at paint chips, caressing upholstery swatches, studying weighty wallpaper books as though they were the Dead Sea scrolls. She is sucking little mints and making little notes with a thin gold pen. Richard will let her do every little thing she wants and so he will never be able to leave her now. They will live perfectly ever after.

Over coffee and cherry cheesecake for dessert, Marilyn notices for the first time the country and western music playing in the background: "Your Cheatin' Heart," she will recall later, with satisfaction and some inverted sense of justice or triumph. For now, she supposes this is the kind of music that Curtis would like, would tap his cowboy boots to and tease her with when she tells him the story of her romance with Richard. The snow is still piling up outside, sticking to the windows in a festive Christmasy way.

They leave the restaurant and head back to the car. There is a sense between them, swinging somewhere in the vicinity of their clasped hands, hanging there like a purse, of something unsaid but settled. They step through the snow in silence, convincing themselves that it is merely companionable. They are so successful at this that soon Richard is thinking about how they will have just enough time to make love at Marilyn's before he has to go on home and Marilyn is worrying that her new black suede cowboy boots will be ruined for nothing in all this snow.

The car slides sideways toward them out of the snow slowly, so slowly, not like you might think, not like an express train or a charging wild horse. It slides sideways past them, just brushing the tail of Marilyn's fur coat which has billowed out around her at this instant in the wind. It slides into the basement window of an apartment building across the street. The glass shatters all over the sparkling snow and the hood of the car is sucked into the hole. The tail lights are red, the car is green, the snow is white, as Richard and Marilyn are running away.

DESCRIBE THE CAR:

A 1968 Chevy Biscayne Street Racer Special with Posi-traction and a 425 horsepower solid-lifter 427 cubic inch big block under the hood, the car is owned, loved, and now wrecked by a greasy teenager named Ted. He is an unlucky young man and this is just the sort of thing that happens to him. He has just been fired from his job at the gas station and has moved back in with his parents who think that all teenagers are like Ted so it's not really their fault the way he turned out. When he is not cruising in his car, which was a hunk of junk when he bought it for a song, he's working on it. Just when he gets it the way he wants it, he thinks happily of something else that should be done.

Before he hit that ice patch and drove into the window, he was on the way to pick up his girlfriend who works at the Burger King three blocks away.

DESCRIBE THE GIRLFRIEND:

Pinkie is waiting out front of the Burger King, sniffing her long blonde hair to see if the grease smell is gone. She's hoping the snow will wash it away. She has changed into her jeans and has her red uniform in a plastic bag. They are going to see a horror movie. She is thinking about getting a tattoo on her right shoulder, but she can't decide if she wants a butterfly or a unicorn. Either way, her parents will disown her but it wouldn't be the first time.

Ted is ten minutes late. Pinkie hears the sirens but is not old enough yet to be afraid for him. She is just plain mad. She stamps her little foot: if he doesn't show up in five minutes, she will break up with him. She will take a ride with Gerry, who owns a 1966 Dodge Hemi Coronet, candy apple red, and who has been hanging around the Burger King all week, drinking chocolate milkshakes and pestering her to go for a ride. He would take her anywhere, even in this snow. This stupid snow. She can hardly wait till summer.

Ted is thirteen minutes late. Pinkie guesses he got the stupid Chevy stuck in the stupid snow somewhere.

Certainly, she does not suspect that Ted has got the car stuck in an apartment building.

DESCRIBE THE APARTMENT:

In the living room of the cozy apartment, there is a floral hide-a-bed couch and two matching chairs, rust-coloured shag carpeting, glass-topped coffee and end tables with doilies, needlepoint pictures of poppies and Jesus on the walls.

Judy, the woman who lives there, is lolling around on the hide-a-bed with her lover, Hal, eating pizza and watching TV. Judy and Hal work at the Bank of Montreal, where she is the teller supervisor and he is the accountant. They have been working and sleeping together for two years. Miraculously, nobody knows this. They have ordered this extra-large deluxe pizza tonight to celebrate Hal's big raise. They feel sinful and smug because they're supposed to be dieting, each trying to lose twenty pounds by Easter. They giggle and relish their various secrets.

Judy and Hal always make love on the hide-a-bed because Judy doesn't feel right doing it in the real bed where she sleeps with her husband, Bruce. She and Bruce sold their house and moved into this apartment after their twin daughters went away to university. They needed the money to put them through, one in medicine and the other in law.

The picture window which Ted's green car comes through is right above the hide-a-bed. Glass and snow are twinkling, sprinkling everywhere and they are all screaming, including the boy in the car, but no one is really hurt. Painless pinpoints of blood well up on Hal's left arm which was in the pizza box when the car hit. One of the broken headlights springs out of its socket and dangles like an eyeball between them. Judy is getting up and tiptoeing through the glass, she is dialling the police, looking for her housecoat, and wondering what on earth she will tell her husband when he finally gets home from work at the bakery, which is where he says he is, but Judy has her doubts.

DESCRIBE THE HUSBAND:

The Man of My Dreams (1987)

I dreamed of myself in a dream, and told the dream, which was mine, as if it were another person's of whom I dreamed. Indeed, what is life when thinking of the past, but dreaming of a dream dreamt by another who seems sometimes to be oneself?

—Stopford Brooke, *Diary, June 8, 1899*

1

In the stories I read, the female characters dream in great detail of daring escapes from prisons, kitchens, and burning shopping malls; of reproduction, reincarnation, and masked terrorists tracking them through quicksand just when they are about to give birth. In these fictional dreams, the ex-husbands or -lovers are delightfully drowned in vats of warm beer or are pelted to death with wormy apples thrown by throngs of scorned women in their white negligees. These lucid dreamers wield axes, swords, scythes, and the occasional chainsaw which lops off those unfaithful legs like sugar cane. The male characters in these clever stories dream muscularly about cars, hockey, boxing, and taking their mistresses and/or their mothers out for chateaubriand and escargots.

All of this seems significant and makes good sense to me. I nod while I'm reading and often underline.

2

In the stories I write, the female characters dream about black stallions which burst into flames, carrying their young daughters to certain death in lakes a hundred feet deep; about alcoholic surgeons who keep taking them apart and putting them back together again like jigsaw puzzles, sometimes missing a piece; about bullfights at which they're wearing their wedding gowns and the matador rides the bull before he kills it and then a team of mules drags the dead bull away on its back like a giant insect and the crowd throws red roses, hysterical; about trains, catching them, missing them, chasing them; about babies, having them, losing them, selling them; about tunnels and eggs.

When they wake up in the morning, these women are gratified to remember every little detail of these dreams and tell them to their sleepy husbands or lovers who are not really interested but pretend to be as they slurp up their coffee and scratch. The women say, "Last night I dreamed you were dead," and the men say, "That's nice, honey. Where the hell are my socks?" And the women just hand those socks over without even having to think: they know where everything is, they just *know*, and they're talking about going into dream therapy and the men say, "Sure, that sounds like fun, honey. Go for it."

These male characters dream sturdily, if at all, about wrestling, drinking, baseball, skydiving, and pouring vinegar on their fish and chips when they were happy little kids. More often, though, they wake up in the morning with a simple erection and say, "Boy, I was dead the minute my head hit the pillow. I slept like a baby."

In the stories I write, I take it for granted that these men snore and roll over forty-seven times a night while these women beside them wander and moan, commit adultery, murder, and magic.

This is along the lines of my mother always saying, "When men get upset, they drink. We women, we cry."

Of course, I write fiction.

3

In real life, I dream about telephone bills, frying pans, oranges.

The dream telephone bill is ten pages long, an astronomical amount, past due, which has me calling all over town trying to track down who owes me how much for which calls. Nobody can remember phoning anybody long-distance on my phone ever in their entire lives. They tell me you have moved to a country where they don't speak English.

To dream of a telephone foretells meeting strangers who will harass and bewilder you. For a woman to dream of using one warns that she will have much jealous rivalry, but will overcome all evil influences. If she cannot hear well on the telephone, she is threatened with evil gossip and the loss of a lover. If the telephone is out of order, it portends sad news.

The dream frying pan, red, Teflon-coated, is being returned to me by the man next door and it is three times as big as the one I loaned him in the first place, which was the one my mother gave me for Christmas three weeks before she died. He grins foolishly out from under a white baseball cap as I try to make him understand that this is not the right pan, this is not *my* frying pan. I give up eventually and get busy scrambling a dozen farm-fresh eggs for brunch.

To dream of pots and pans foretells that trivial events will cause you much vexation. To see a broken or rusty one implies that you will experience keen disappointment.

Oranges, twice I have dreamed about oranges.

The first orange dream, which I had when I was pregnant with Ben, is set in Atwater, the eastern town where I grew up. I am by the water around the docks and grain elevators. My friend, Bonnie, and someone named Lynn are there too, all bundled up in big coats and plastic hats because it is cold and raining. You are at work or in the bar drinking with the boys. We three women discuss this, shaking our heads and smoking in the rain. I go walking down to the water alone and then along the shoreline, which is icy and treacherous. I am thinking about a football star I knew in high school who got a summer job on the railroad and fell from a boxcar his first day out and got both his legs cut off at the knee. I am cutting up an orange with my Swiss Army knife and throwing the slices to the seagulls. I walk back along the shoreline, being extra careful not to slip on the ice because suddenly I am pregnant. I pick my way back to where Bonnie and Lynn are still huddled together on an iron bench.

I awoke then, suddenly and fully, as if at a noise in the night: breaking glass or footsteps, but there was nothing.

The second orange dream, which didn't amount to much, is set in Hazelwood, the western town where you and I lived together. I am squeezing a whole bag of oranges to make juice for our breakfast. There are mountains out the window. You are at the kitchen table in your longjohns looking at the newspaper. I smell my orange-dipped fingers and you read me my horoscope.

To dream of eating oranges is signally bad, foretelling pervasive discontentment and the sickness of friends or relatives. A young woman is likely to lose her lover if she dreams of eating oranges. But if she dreams of seeing a fine one tossed up high, she will be discreet in choosing a husband from among her many lovers. To slip on an orange peel foretells the death of a relative.

4

In real life, I dream about my dead mother, young again in the garden there beside the peonies. Or I dream that it is my father who is dead instead.

5

In real life, I dream about grocery shopping.

My parents, both of them alive in this dream, are here to visit Ben and me in this eastern city where we have come to live. I am at the A&P buying six ears of corn despite the fact that both my parents have false teeth and will have to scrape the kernels off the cobs with a fork, which is harder than it looks. I go over to the 24-Hour Deli Counter which features fresh peaches, three-bean salad, and pickled eggs. A woman slicing meat explains that everything on her counter is twenty-four hours old or less. "This beef, for instance," she tells me, waving a knife, "this cow has been dead for less than twenty-four hours."

I go around the store picking up the ingredients for Chinese Pork: pork tenderloin, three green peppers, mushrooms. I decide I will use fresh mushrooms. My mother, who gave me the recipe, always used canned, but now I will show her how much better it is with fresh. But all the mushrooms they have are brown and shrivelling, more stems than caps. Frozen lemonade, limeade, and orange juice cans go rolling down the aisles with messages on them.

To dream of pork predicts continued prosperity whether you eat the meat, cook it, serve it, or buy it.

In the morning I dug out the recipe, one you always loved. It was written on a small blue-lined white card in my mother's neat strong hand:

CHINESE PORK

1/2 lb. pork tenderloin

2 1/2 tsp. soya sauce

2 tbsp. flour

1 tbsp. butter

1 chicken bouillon cube

1/2 cup boiling water

1 green pepper, cut in strips

1 (10 oz.) can sliced mushrooms, drained

Cut tenderloin in narrow strips. Brush strips with soya sauce, roll in flour. Melt butter in fry pan, add meat, and brown. Dissolve bouillon cube in 1/2 cup boiling water, add to fry pan with other ingredients. Cover and simmer about 15 minutes. Serve with rice. (Serves 2.)

The recipe told me nothing about either you or her. It was just something she sent me once when she was dieting, a low-calorie one-dish meal that looked good on the table, good enough to photograph, good enough to eat. We traded recipes, she and I, just as I imagine other women do, but when I went back to Atwater for the funeral, I found the ones I'd sent (Sour Cream Meatloaf, Quick Spaghetti Sauce with Clams, Chunky Chili) not even filed into the box. She had never even tried them, so I made the meatloaf for my father, who liked it very much. Of course, he would.

This was the day before the funeral. My father and I had been out all morning making the arrangements and Sonja, the woman next door, was minding Ben. When I went over to pick him up, Sonja sat me down with warm spice cake and coffee. I remembered her as cooking, always cooking, bringing over cast iron pots and crockery bowls covered with tinfoil, still steaming.

That day she was making sauerkraut soup, which I said I had never heard of but it sure did smell good. So she told me the recipe, and also one for perogies, which she'd been making twelve dozen of once a week for thirty years. These were family recipes, passed on to her by *her* mother, who was still alive but laid up these days with a bad back. Sonja had never written them down herself but performed them magically from memory, like playing the piano without sheet music. I tried to follow her directions, scribbling them on the back of an envelope: a little bit of this, a little bit of that, simmer till it looks done.

Ben hopped happily around the fragrant kitchen, eating peanut butter sandwiches and singing the "Sesame Street" theme song. Sonja and I smoked and drank coffee and talked about people I hadn't thought of for years, until finally she just wondered why my mother had never told her about Ben until he was nearly two years old.

6

In the dream about the bacon (this was years ago), you say, "I hate pork, you know I hate pork, why are you feeding me pork?"

I say, "You're lying, you asshole. You men are all alike," you being the one in real life who, every single time I made roast pork on Sunday, would say, "Oh goody, pork sandwiches for my midnight snack. They always give me the best dreams."

It makes sense to me that women should dream about food.

To dream of eating bacon is good if someone is eating with you and your hands are clean. Rancid bacon is a suggestion to see a doctor. Cooking bacon augurs a surprise or gift, which will please you very much.

The next morning I was still mad but could hardly explain myself, not sanely anyway, as I slammed around the kitchen, making lousy coffee and slapping together a cheese and tomato sandwich for your lunch, knowing full well that you hated how the bread would be soggy and pink by noon.

Either you were ignoring my mood or you were just getting used to me.

Your best dreams, your pork-induced visions, were all about work: the backhoe, the Cat, the scraper, the grader, you were operating all of them at once: knocking down trees, digging up boulders and whole mountainsides, grading steep slopes perfectly within an inch of your life so help me, loading twenty trucks a shift, unloading them all again at the other end, waking me up with your twitching as the dump truck bucked beneath you, box up, shrugging out the last of its load.

To dream of machinery foretells undertaking a project which will give great anxiety, but will finally result in good for you. If the machinery is idle or derelict, it indicates approaching family or employment problems.

I handed you your lunch and cursed you out for taking my last cigarette.

All you said was, "I'm so tired. I've been working all night."

I said nothing and glared at your hands, nicotine-stained and speckled with scabs and fresh scrapes which you liked to enumerate each evening over supper. Particularly purple and ugly were the two flat knuckles on your left hand, squashed one afternoon between a boulder and the tailgate, a story you loved to tell repeatedly in the bar, wrapping it up with, "Well, I guess that's what they mean by 'Caught between a rock and a hard place,' eh?", not mentioning how you threw up at the sound of your own bones grinding.

You were gabbing on about how in the dream you nearly rolled the truck and then the other guy just missed you with the bucket of the backhoe, until I said, gritting my teeth and spacing my words, "Can't you just be quiet for once?"

I always told you I hated to talk in the morning because, after sleeping for the last eight hours, I had nothing to talk about but my dreams and who wants to hear all that crap?

People change.

7

My best talking time was after we went to bed. We weren't having sex much anymore by then, so maybe my babbling was just a way of filling in the time. One night I remember we were talking about Italians, their industriousness, how they would come over from the old country with nothing and build up successful companies in concrete or construction. Then I told you about all the Italian women I'd worked with that one summer at the bank in Atwater. This covered lasagna (Angelina), Italian weddings (Loretta), arranged marriages (Teresa), and how some Italian women get so fat and sloppy after the first baby (Rosina) and how some Italian men fancy themselves such Romeos and like to let their chest hair show (Rosina's husband, Guido). Then I discovered you had lint in your belly button, which put me in mind of that girl I knew at the Atwater United Church who had no belly button and how we used to serve at church teas together.

And you said, "Sleep, sleep, woman, I'm begging you to let me sleep."

That night all of my dreams were accompanied by organ music.

Pleasant organ music heard in a dream is an omen of satisfying sexual prowess. To hear doleful singing with organ accompaniment denotes you are approaching a tiresome task and probable loss of friends or status. To see an organ in church warns of despairing separation of family members and death, perhaps, for some of them.

8

I dreamed I was trying to steal another woman's baby from a furniture store. Then my mother offered me $3,000 and a fancy orange sports car if only I would leave you and go live with her in a mobile home in Florida. She said, "If he really loved you, he'd marry you." We were in Sonja's kitchen, eating cabbage rolls and borscht, and the car was parked right across the street, running.

9

The reasons for our leaving each other are not especially clear. I wish you had left me for another woman. Such triangular situations are so common, so understandable. By way of compulsive comparison—myself to her, my hair to hers, my hips to hers, my cooking, my cleanliness, my clothes, my big eyes to hers—the pain would become so much more accessible, acceptable.

I wish you had left me for another woman or I wish I had left you for another man because then either or both of us could dream of revenge.

To dream of taking revenge is a sign of a weak and uncharitable nature, which will bring you trouble and loss of friends. Such a dream is a reminder that you must give consideration if you expect to get it.

10

I went to a dinner party at the home of another writer. We had a chicken, tender and meaty enough to have been a turkey, which she'd bought from the Hutterites. The other guests were writers too and one or two filmmakers. They talked about people I didn't know, movies I hadn't seen, books I hadn't read. I couldn't blame them: they all knew each other, I was new in town and not about to admit that no, I wasn't especially fond of Henry James and hadn't got around to reading Chekhov yet. Over dessert (fresh strawberries in heavy cream), they began to trade their dreams around the table like a deck of cards. They had earnest, intelligent dreams, intricate like lace or the way a prism in the window will cast colours on the backs of your hands.

"I was sitting with a group of Cossacks drinking black tea from a silver samovar. Then one of them turned into Dostoyevsky and we were debating crime and punishment until he wanted to know about Australian Rules Football and what does this word 'nuclear' mean? The windows were white with frost and a wolf howled."

"Oh, I've had that one too!"

"I was preparing Boeuf Bourguignon, sipping a good Chablis. Gurdjieff was coming for dinner. Afterwards we would play croquet and the sunset would be perfect."

"Marvellous!"

"I was having my first haircut, a child of two. Vidal Sassoon was the barber and I was reading to him from Sartre's *Being and Nothingness*."

"Wonderful!"

"I was a peacock, preening."

"Oh oh, we all know what that means!"

I felt inadequate and pushed the strawberries around in my bowl the way Ben does when he doesn't want to eat. But there was no escaping them.

So I told my recurring dream, the one where I am in bed, sweating and scared, trying to call out for my father but the sound won't come out. Everything in this dream is detailed and true; it has recast itself into every bedroom I have ever lived in. Finally, after years of this, I woke myself up one night screaming, "Dad! Dad!" and you held me and I never had the dream again.

This was so obvious as to seem shallow.

11

The puppy, I assume, dreams about cats and other dogs, raw steak maybe on a good night. She twitches and whimpers, thumps her stubby tail on the floor.

The cat, I assume, dreams about birds, mice, and other cats, a nice fresh can of tuna. She sighs.

What does Ben dream about? I like to think that he is dreaming about running, flying, cuddling, sailboats, ice cream with sprinkles, Big Bird, and lambs. I do not like to think he is dreaming about the time when he, at two months, cried all night and I whispered, hysterical at four in the morning, "Shut your fucking mouth, you little bastard!" and then laid my wet cheek against his monkey face and rocked him and watched till the streetlights went out, smelling his perfect skin.

He is too young, he will not dream about you. Oh, he may dream about your photographs, your guitar, your bald head, as I sometimes do.

To see a bald-headed man in a dream warns to guard against being cheated by someone you trust. For a young woman to dream of a bald-headed man means she must use her intelligence against listening to her next marriage offer. Bald-headed babies signify a happy home, a loving companion, and obedient children.

He is too young, he will not remember his grandmother either. For the rest of his life, he will suspect that all of the strangers in his dreams are either her or you.

12

Often I dream that I am dreaming. But still, such knowledge does not keep me from the fear.

13

When I dream about you now, you are always wearing that red shirt.

14

Two months after my mother died, my father came here to visit Ben and me. The night before he was scheduled to arrive, I dreamed that when he did, my mother was with him, wearing her pink shortie nightie and a scarf. In the dream, I thought very clearly, *Well, of course, I should have known this would happen.*

I went to pick him up at the airport, the little old-fashioned kind where the passengers still have to walk down the steps and across the tarmac in the dark windy night. I stood behind the chain-link fence and watched for him, my tall father, thinking he would be wearing that stupid hat he always wears when he has to do something official like go to the doctor or fly. But there he was, coming at me bare-headed—and alone, of course.

An East Indian family got off the plane behind him. The man, in jeans and a plaid shirt, held a sleeping child against each shoulder. The woman behind took tiny steps in her purple sari, cuddling a wide-awake fat baby whose soother fell out of its mouth and rolled across the parking lot as she passed me. I was feeling too cruel or isolated to point this out to her and the taxi they got into backed right over it.

I had two dreams about planes while my father was here. In the first, a small red and white plane had crashed in my back-yard, sending up fireworks instead of flames, and we were only surprised, not hurt or frightened. In the second, I was driving my father back out to the airport to go home but it ended up that Ben and I boarded and he stayed behind, waving. I knew it was all a mistake but there could be no turning back now.

I told my father this one at breakfast as he held Ben on his lap and fed him toast with strawberry jam, but I never told him about the fireworks.

15

During my father's visit, I had one of those dreams where you keep coming almost awake but you don't want to, so, miraculously, you are able to swim back down and pick up where you left off.

In the dream, you and my father are in the kitchen, talking about fishing. Your father, you are telling him, tied his own flies. I am making hamburgers and salad, bringing you both another beer. My dead mother, I discover, has been laid out in my new queen-size bed. I try to walk into the bedroom but see her folded hands and think I am going to throw up. I back away, then force myself forward again and then again, gagging. I never do get into the room before I wake up.

There was something in this dream about lettuce, about peeling away all those pale green leaves. Or was there? Maybe I just made it up, searching for a symbol, trying to get surreal.

16

Four months after my mother died, Ben and I went back to Atwater to visit my father. Each day he said, "Maybe we should go out to the cemetery this afternoon," until finally one day we went. I took pictures of her headstone with the lilies in the rain, something which did not strike me as an odd thing to do until after I got the prints back and could not think where to put them.

When we got back to my father's house, Ben fell asleep and I lay down too, on my parents' bed. There was thunder and lightning all afternoon. I am still afraid of storms, not the lightning so much, which is swift and can kill you instantly, but the thunder, which is unpredictable and makes you hold your breath waiting for it.

In the long dream we are driving in from the country, my mother, father, me, in a taxicab at night. I am obsessively worrying that I will have to drive in the dark, will wreck the car and kill us all. But no. It turns out that the cab driver will take us all the way to wherever we are going.

We stop at a supper club on the highway, eat steak, treat the cab driver too because he's such a nice guy. He holds my hand on the way back to the car. Then we are just travelling for a long time.

When daylight comes, I am alone in the seedy downtown section of a strange city. I walk along many slummy streets, looking for a bookstore. I even climb over a chicken-wire fence. I pass a little old lady in a green dress who says, "It's hard to get around these days," so I help her over the fence.

I go below street level into a narrow room and find it filled with colourfully dressed people and bikers. I meet a young blonde man wearing an Indian shirt, the embroidered kind with mirrors.

He says, "My name is Chris. I've fried my brain. I used to be a Hare Krishna and they killed my brain. Look into my eyes, they are dead, empty, insane."

We make love and I say, "No, your eyes are beautiful, neither dead, empty, nor insane."

A short blonde woman with a shirt just like his, dirty little hands and feet, comes over and watches us. She is his girlfriend, Kathy. She leaves.

Making love again, he says, "I'm dead, I can't feel anything."

I say, "I'll make you feel it."

He is on top, I climax, he doesn't, but says, "Still, you made me feel something, more than Kathy can."

We make love once more, I'm on top, I come twice, calling his name. He comes too and cries on me, with love and relief.

Back on the street, I'm waiting for a bus at a huge, complex intersection where eight streets converge. Behind me is a Safeway store, an A&P, and an IT&T. My watch reads 10:17 a.m. I am being blown around in the hot wind and, hanging onto a parking meter, I tell the man beside me that I wish I had a pen so I could write down the street names to find this place again.

But I've lost my purse and I panic, until I look in the pockets of the green army parka I've acquired. There I find my wallet, cigarettes, address book, and two library books: *Disturbances in the Field* by Lynne Sharon Schwartz and *Technique in Fiction*.

The bus comes and I am riding to my parents' house, thinking of how mad they're going to be that I stayed out all night. So I decide to let my mother help me choose a dress for the dance tomorrow night. This is bound to make her happy again.

It was the kind of dream that you think takes hours, the kind of dream that makes perfect sense when you first wake up and then proceeds to mystify you all day long.

17

I have never dreamed about the lilies.

> *To dream of a lily denotes coming chastisement through illness and death. For a young woman to dream of admiring or gathering lilies denotes much suffering coupled with joy. If she sees them withering, the sadness is nearer than she suspects. To dream of breathing the fragrance of lilies denotes that sorrow will purify and enhance your mental qualities.*

18

From my mother's closet, I chose a green linen suit and a white blouse and put them in a brown paper bag. I did not know beforehand that I would also have to give them her underwear: a slip, bra and panties, pantyhose. Shoes, they said, were optional. I didn't put them in because I couldn't bear to think of anyone putting them on her feet. My father at the last minute put in the emerald earrings and pendant he'd given her for Christmas three weeks earlier.

As we shuffled past the coffin, he moaned and held his arms out, leaning forward as if to kiss her. I pulled him back and led him away because I was afraid.

After the service, everyone went to Sonja's for sandwiches and dainties, dark rum and beer. Sonja gave me a huge pot of spaghetti sauce which I served with salad for supper that night to the relatives gathered in my father's house. You called long-distance with your sympathy.

That night I slept in the bed of my childhood and my feet kept bumping the borrowed crib where Ben slept at the end. He sighed and said, "Sorry." I counted the books on the shelves like sheep.

That night I dreamed of your lips, which I was always fond of.

Sweet lips in a dream signify a successful sex life and happiness in love. Thick, overly sensual, or ugly lips forecast failure in love but success in business. Sore or swollen lips denote deprivation and unhealthy desires.

At breakfast, my father said, "I had a kooky dream last night. I dreamed that your mother had left me and they said she was living with some guy on Market Street. But I said, 'No, she's dead, it can't be true, she can't be over there with him.'"

I kept on scrambling farm-fresh eggs for Ben.

19

The only childhood dream I can still remember is the one about the giant camel. I am in the school basement, wearing my black patent-leather shoes and my new tartan skirt with the gold pin. I am hiding in the bathroom, where all the toilets are short and the concrete blocks are painted pink. The camel is upstairs in the kindergarten room. His hooves come through the ceiling like shovels. I am washing my hands and there is hair on the soap.

There is never any doubt that the camel will get me.

> *To dream of a camel means you will have to work hard to overcome your obstacles. If the camel bore a burden, unexpected wealth, possibly in the form of an inheritance, will come your way. If you rode the camel, your future is bright indeed.*

20

I often dream about Lake Street in the east end of Atwater. In this dream nothing happens and I'm not in it. In this dream it is always five o'clock in the morning and raining. Cars with their headlights on pass each other all up and down the wet street, swishing and splashing to a halt, idling and waiting for the light to change. The tavern has its windows bricked up. The Chinese grocery and the pawnshop are bankrupt, vacant, the apartments upstairs condemned by the health department. Winos lounge and sleep or die in the doorways of warehouses filled with washers, dryers, fridges, stoves, dishwashers, and stereos. Bats cling and swoop. The rain stops, the sun comes up hot, and the sidewalks steam.

There is in this dream a persistent and clammy sense of danger which does not materialize and is never explained.

21

I dreamed about buying a refrigerator in the chocolate-brown colour no longer popular among major appliance purchasers (so the salesman informs me while eating a peanut butter and banana sandwich) but I just have to have the brown anyway. Then I call Annie Churchill, who I graduated from high school with and haven't seen since, although I seem to know that she is married to a dentist now and happy about it. I tell them what I've just bought, how much I love it, how much I've changed. "You're getting so domestic in your old age," he says or she says.

After a grainy digression that has to do with a party and changing my clothes, there is a slow-motion section about an enormous mound of cocaine being kneaded into a pound of raw hamburger and stashed in the fridge door behind the eggs because the cops are coming, I can hear the sirens.

To see a refrigerator in your dreams warns that your selfishness will injure someone trying to gain an honest livelihood. To place food in one brings the dreamer into disfavour.

22

I thought I was coming down with something, so I lay on the couch all afternoon, aching and feverish.

I dreamed that my friend Bonnie was running a home for retarded deformed children.

I dreamed that I went to see a lady who had advertised for someone to walk her two white sheepdogs.

I dreamed that you went to Texas and shaved off your beard for the first time in fourteen years.

I dreamed that my mother was finally teaching me how to iron a shirt properly.

Just before I woke up, I dreamed about Janet, who is married to your friend Roger now. She was always wearing blue jeans, bow-legged, flat-chested, a real tomboy, always playing in mixed softball tournaments. They had such a good relationship that she could stay out all night drinking with the girls and Roger didn't mind. In the dream I am at the ballpark with hundreds of other fans waiting for the game to start. I am alone and searching for someone to sit with. Janet is the only person I know. As I make my way toward her, she says to someone else, "I've gotta go to my feminist class. Bye now." I am carrying my new puppy in my arms and suddenly baseballs are being thrown at us. I am running away, shoulders hunched to protect the puppy, who has turned into a rabbit. The baseballs bounce off my back like ping-pong balls.

23

I have been, among other things, giving Ben his bath before bed, watching a made-for-TV movie about a compulsive gambler (female), pushing Ben's stroller up a steep street in the heat and feeling profoundly sorry for myself, when a certain sneaky word has come to me without warning:

Chimera.

It is one of those words which, for years, I've had to look up every time I come across it because I keep thinking it has something to do with water or light, shimmering.

chimera *n.* 1. (Gk Myth.) A fire-breathing monster with the head of a lion, the body of a goat, and the tail of a serpent.
2. An impossible or foolish fancy. (Gk *khimaira*, chimera, "she-goat").

The image which invariably follows is of a gorilla straddling a silver airplane wing, beating its hairy chest and roaring in at the innocent bug-eyed passengers. The airplane is flying low at night through fraying cloud cover and the eyes of this gorilla are red.

This doesn't shake me up nearly as much as it used to and I am able now to wonder maturely how this gorilla got into my head in the first place. Was it a movie or a dream? Who can I ask?

To dream of a gorilla portends a painful misunderstanding, unless the animal was very docile or definitely friendly, in which case the dream forecasts an unusual new friend.

This is like thinking of that November night in the Hazelwood Hotel, you and I drinking draft beer because we were broke, and some guy came in and said there was a dog frozen dead out front, said it was Bonnie's dog, Blitz. The entire bar emptied and outside we found that someone had let Blitz off her chain and put in her place a dead Doberman, frozen, its throat slit. So then we all got talking about that crazy guy in town for a month or two last summer, the one who always carried an empty pizza box under his arm and who chased his Doberman down Main Street with an axe that one time when the dog wouldn't mind.

So then it was last call and you and me and our friend Mike bought a case of off-sales and went over to his place for a sauna. I think of the three of us running naked in the backyard, rolling around in the snow like puppies, having heard that's how they do it in Finland. And in my drunkenness, Mike with his bulging eyes and acne-ravaged skin was starting to look pretty good to me. And I was ranting on about Remembrance Day, which has just passed, and how I was so proud of my father for what he had done in the war, fairly weeping with the intensity of my unexam-ined admiration, and Mike said, "I don't believe in war," and tried to talk me out of it, but I said, "I don't either but still . . ." and would not be swayed. So then Mike went and called his mother long-distance in Ontario at three in the morning and told her how much he loved her.

You said, "It's time to go home, I'm seeing triple and I might call my mother too, she's been dead for years," and when you tried to stand up, you knocked over the lamp, spilling kerosene all over our clothes, and I was screaming, "How stupid can one person be!"

The next morning we soaked our clothes for a while in the bathtub, then gave up and threw them away.

I don't think this was a dream but it should have been. That time I called you to check, you said you didn't remember any of it. Sometimes you're no help at all.

What I really want to know is: how did we get home without our clothes on?

24

I got my hair cut. That night I dreamed of going back to the beauty parlour, wanting to show the nice lady how good the new style looks. My mother is with me. This lady has light red hair, long red fingernails, and freckles all over her hands, what my mother called "age spots." She is talking on the phone and smoking when we go into the shop. All the chairs and dryers have been removed—all that remains is the reception desk and this French Provincial telephone.

The hairdresser recognizes me immediately, puts her hand over the mouthpiece, and asks, "Did you ever figure out how John died?"

What on earth is she talking about? Then I remember that while she cut my hair we talked about "Another World," her favourite soap opera.

I say, excitedly, "No, no, I didn't, but here's my mother." She is standing near the glass door in a red pantsuit. "She's been watching "Another World" since before I was born, she'll know." I turn to my mother and ask her how John died. She's looking right at me but can't hear me. I am yelling but still she can't hear me.

When my mother was here for Christmas three weeks before she died, I was always angry because she couldn't hear the doorbell or the telephone and the TV was turned up too loud. She might get a hearing aid, she said, someday.

When my mother went into the hospital the first time, she got my father to tape "Another World" on the VCR every day so she could catch up on the action when she got home. This last time, when the doctors were still trying to figure out how to tell her she was dying, she told my father not to bother. He told me this when he came to visit Ben and me, he told me this was how he knew that she knew. "Remember how mad she used to get when they put the ball game on instead of her show?" he asked.

Remember how when the U.S. bombed Libya and I called home to say I was watching the news all day and I was scared and she said, "Well, if you don't like it, change the channel." And the next morning I went down to the A&P and bought a case each of baby formula and cat food, praying, *Please God, let Ben live to be old.*

If you were here with me now, would I tell you all this in the morning over breakfast, fresh-ground coffee and brown toast, soft-boiled eggs?

You were always trying to figure out how to get the eggs just right at the high altitude of Hazelwood. "It's perfect, it's perfect!" you'd say before you tasted it and then you'd say, sadly, "No, no, thirty seconds more, just thirty seconds more, and it would have been perfect."

Until finally one winter morning you were satisfied, so I got out the Polaroid and snapped a shot of it: The Perfect Six-Minute Egg. We kept this picture on our bulletin board for years. I study it now: egg in the egg cup, a half-eaten piece of toast on the Blue River plate on the wicker placemat on the blue tabletop, a coffee mug with a bottle of Baileys Irish Cream beside it, also dental floss, dirty ashtray, and a pink pepper shaker which is one my mother gave me when I first left home, called carnival glass, which used to come in boxes of detergent.

25

The dreams I hate the most are those in which every person, place, and thing keeps changing into some other person, place, or thing and then back again. Even the ground seems to shift and bubble beneath my dreamy feet and occasionally it disappears altogether.

26

You become my father watching the ball game and drinking frosty beer, he becomes my mother melting, she becomes Ben eating ice cream with his fingers.

27

The coffee cup in my left hand becomes a piano and the cigarette in my right a spatula.

28

The front step of my father's house becomes a conveyor belt and then the house itself a restaurant.

29

Ben becomes a kitten even as I hold him in my arms which are turning into saxophones.

30

Waking, I open my eyes and cannot imagine for a minute where in the world you or I might be.

31

I used to dream that Ben was crying in the night. I would wake up, get out of bed, go to the kitchen, take the bottle out of the fridge, heat it to exactly the right temperature by instinct, and when I got to his room, there he was fast sleep. He'd never moved, never cried, never made a single sound.

32

Sometimes now I am pregnant in my dreams, but the pregnancy is never what the dream is about, is merely the condition I happen to be in as I board buses, go to parties, make pizza, or fly.

33

When Ben was three weeks old and I could almost sit down normally again, I had an erotic dream about Dr. Long, the one who delivered him, the handsome one who interrupted his Sunday afternoon golf game three times to come to me in the delivery room and listen to me hollering, "Do something, do something, can't you do something? What kind of doctor are you anyway? I don't want to do this anymore, I want to go home now." The one who said, "Wow, look at that, the blood squirted right across the room!" The one who handed Ben to me softly and said, "He's perfect like a flower," even though when the nurse said, "Look, look, it's a boy!" I wailed, "I don't want to look!" because after eleven hours on that table and everything going wrong— monitors, oxygen, Demerol, forceps—I thought he was going to have a big purple birthmark all over his face.

In the dream, Dr. Long was caressing me in his surgical greens, spreading me open gently on that table and burying his face in my milk-filled breasts. I awoke embarrassed and disgusted with myself.

Sometime later, in a confessional fit, I told this dream to Bonnie, who is my best friend and so I can tell her anything, disgusting or not, and she will still like me. Dr. Long had delivered her baby too. And she laughed and said, yes, yes, she'd dreamed of making love to him too. We snickered and compared details.

Sometime later still, here in this city, I was having lunch and white wine spritzers with two other women I hardly knew. I was making fun of my former self by telling them this dream and they marvelled and said, yes, yes, they'd had it too about their obstetricians and never told a single soul till now. One of these women had had four children, grown now, all delivered by the same fat, fatherly man who had also taken out her tonsils when she was six. She had dreamed of making love to him in the laundry room. We were so relieved, the three of us, to find ourselves feeling normal for a change that we laughed and laughed, hugged each other round the table, and sat there drinking all afternoon.

34

I have not slept with a man in over ten months. Every night for a week I dream of sex. I have perfunctory sex with everyone but you, including Roger who married Janet, Mike who had the sauna, David Coleman who was in my Grade Ten Health class, and the man in front of me in the checkout line at the A&P on Wednesday, buying Kraft Dinner, Oreo ice cream, and a comb. I have elaborate and extended dream sex with the man next door who borrows my frying pan and lifts weights in his front yard in his small red shorts. When I see him in the bank the next day, I blush furiously and fidget. But he does not seem to recognize me from either the street or the dream.

35

There are whole days when nothing goes through my mind but you. Then I lie down and dream all night of shopping with my mother, buying a bag of potatoes and a pair of blue high heels. What does this say about me? I wonder, I worry. Am I missing something serious in my psychological makeup? Am I missing the point? What's wrong with me anyway?

36

The night you left I dreamed about washing the kitchen floor.

In a Dark Season (1988)

You know what it's like: how when you are seeing a certain kind of man, the kind who is reliable, patient, and sensitive, the kind who is willing to do absolutely anything for you, the kind who is Nice and Boring, how you feel compelled to keep asking him over for lunch, over for dinner on Sunday, over to have coffee, a drink, a game of Scrabble, over to hook up your new stereo, over to help you wallpaper your three-year-old son's bedroom, how you have to keep driving by the bookstore where he works just to check up, not on *him*, but on your feelings for him: do you love him, do you think you will love him eventually, do you even *like* him? You do not trust your feelings for him to *stick*. Why does he love you so much? You knew damn well when you met him—you knew within the first ten minutes—that he would never hurt you. And now you have to keep reminding or convincing yourself that you will never hurt him either. The sheer weight of his *goodness* makes you want to either slap him or weep.

Sitting at your kitchen table, Nice-and-Boring assures you that the flowers he keeps sending come with no strings attached. You already know this. So why is it so hard to look at them there on the table beside your coffee cups, the newspaper, the books you are reading, your son's red and white Texaco truck, and Winnie the Pooh? Why is it so hard to see them simply for what they are: pretty, fine-scented, pink? Why is it so hard to see them without something like slug trails streaming down off the blossoms and circling your wrists like thin bracelets? Why did you cringe when you saw that poor delivery man bearing them so proudly up the driveway in a Valentine's Day snowstorm, up to his knees? You admire them extensively now in front of Nice-and-Boring who inquires intelligently about the books you are reading. You get up and make more coffee.

After he leaves, you get out your camera and take a picture of the bouquet, the cute card propped up in front. You stick it in your photo album beside all those shots of your son ripping open his presents Christmas morning, of your son with a bowl of turkey and mashed potatoes on his head, of your son sleeping sweetly.

Fifty times a day you are thinking: I will just pick up that phone, I will just call him, I will just pick up that phone and call him and I will say YES. You are creeping toward surrender.

But then you have a tuna sandwich and some salad for lunch, you wash up the dishes, do three loads of laundry, clean out the kitchen cupboards, go and get your son from daycare, make tacos for supper, read him a story about a princess or a duck, and then you make the mistake of thinking about the other one, the Brooding one who has come back to you in a dark season. You have not seen hide nor hair of Dark-and-Brooding in six months. You have been seeing Nice-and-Boring for three. You thought you had it all figured out. You thought you were over Dark-and-Brooding but now here he is again, sitting down at your kitchen table, saying, I've missed you, I've changed, you know you can trust me.

What you *do* know, within these first ten minutes, is that you are willing to do absolutely anything for him. You also know that you are going to give him another chance and he is going to hurt you again. He doesn't even ask who the nice flowers are from. It is quite possible that he doesn't even see them. You have put the cute card face down under the vase. You get up to make more coffee.

You are sitting at the kitchen table with your best friend. Your son is in bed, calling out goodnights for half an hour and then he sleeps. You and Best Friend are intelligent, well-educated women. You share a passionate interest in books, writing, language, all things literary. But all you ever talk about is men. The *same* men, Best Friend points out. She has been having similar problems.

You tell her how when Nice-and-Boring comes over, he always sits to your left at the table. Dark-and-Brooding always sits to your right. You try to find meaning in the seating arrangement. In a dark season, everything seems significant. You tell her how one night Nice-and-Boring inadvertently sits to your right because there is a Fisher-Price Piano on the other chair and how you feel a flicker of new possibilities. But you are still watching out the window behind him, trying to recognize the tail lights of the cars which pass down your dark street.

Best Friend always sits directly across from you at the table. She fondles your new books and plays with your son's Texaco truck, making engine noises in her throat. She babysits for free when you go to a poetry reading with Nice-and-Boring, also when Dark-and-Brooding takes you to see *Return of the Living Dead*. You entertain Best Friend with your black fantasy of both men showing up in your kitchen at the same time. Nice-and-Boring knows about Dark-and-Brooding but Dark-and-Brooding doesn't know about Nice-and-Boring. You want to hurt them both or you want them to hurt each other. You ask Best Friend if you are a vicious person. She says, No.

You get up to make more coffee. You realize you are spending a fortune on coffee beans these days. You try to imagine what it would be like to meet someone new.

Dark-and-Brooding bears a distinct resemblance to your son's father, who is someone you hope never to see again in your entire life. When you tell Dark-and-Brooding all about it, he says, He sounds just like me.

You can see what he means. You know you are not as concerned about this as you should be.

Your son adores Nice-and-Boring and has taken to calling him Daddy. When Dark-and-Brooding comes over, all your charming son will do is sit on your lap and whine. You put him to bed early.

You (and Best Friend, bless her) can see things in Dark-and-Brooding which other people, including your son, cannot see. You can see the things in him that he's been hoping his whole life someone would see. These are also the things he has spent his whole life trying to keep anyone from seeing. You keep thinking fondly of that one half-hour that one Saturday afternoon when he was exactly the way you knew he could be, exactly the way you wanted him to be: he was talking about something you said to him six months ago, how he knew you were right, how he knew he had lost you, how much it hurt. This is the first you have heard of his pain. Your heart goes out to him. He is saying how *you* are the only person he can really talk to, *you* are the only one who really *understands*. You are wishing you could remember what it was you said to him six months ago, just in case you have to say it again.

Dark-and-Brooding wants to know if you'd like to go skating in the park with him sometime. Downtown the next day, you just happen to pick up a pair of Lynn Nightingale figure skates. You have not skated since you were thirteen, twenty years ago.

The first afternoon he takes you over to the rink, they are watering the ice so you go back to your place for coffee instead. Dark-and-Brooding sits on your couch and reads last night's paper with his jacket on—he is looking for a job. You pretend to read the Lifestyle section, which used to be the Women's Page, but really you are watching him, the way his dark eyes move while he is reading, also his lips. He reads you the wedding announcement of a girl he dated in high school. You nod with appreciative interest, hopefully. In a dark season, everything seems significant.

The next time you are supposed to go skating, it is on an evening which turns out to be the coldest night of the winter so far. Dark-and-Brooding drops by to tell you it's too cold out for you, he's going with his brother instead. You are not the least bit insulted. Rather, you think he is being considerate and you are also relieved that you will not have to make a fool of yourself in front of him. You stay home happily enough, and warm in the terry cloth bathrobe that Nice-and-Boring gave you for Christmas. You watch television and imagine Dark-and-Brooding out there on the cold ice under the lights, chasing the puck around the rink, clapping his mittens together to keep warm, grinning with rosy apple cheeks like a little boy. Nice-and-Boring calls just to say hello. You are feeling so good that you expansively ask him out for lunch tomorrow.

At lunch you tell him you are taking up skating. He tells you he has weak ankles.

In the pursuit of happiness, you and Best Friend have temporarily abandoned great literature in favour of trading back and forth paperback books with long titles like: *Women Who Love Too Much: When You Keep Wishing and Hoping He'll Change*; *Men Who Hate Women And The Women Who Love Them: When Loving Hurts And You Don't Know Why*; *Women Men Love, Women Men Leave: Why Men Are Drawn To Women, What Makes Them Want To Stay*; and *Rapid Relief From Emotional Distress*.

Tonight you and Best Friend are putting rum in your coffee, analyzing yourselves and trying to figure Dark-and-Brooding out. You have read enough self-help books by now to know that your relationship is unhealthy but not uncommon. You are obsessed. He is inappropriate. Knowing this does not make him any less desirable, any less dangerous. You haven't heard from him in nine days. You worry that he may be sick, seriously injured, in a coma, dead. You wonder if he has lost your phone number or forgotten how to spell your last name.

You and Best Friend are trying to decide what you should do. You could go by the book and do nothing.

Or you could call him. Except sometimes his brother answers and tells you Dark-and-Brooding isn't home, even though you know damn well, you can *feel* it, he's sitting right there, shaking his head.

You could leave him a note. In which you apologize for whatever it is you've done wrong, even though you and Best Friend have been racking your brains and you can't figure out *what* you've done wrong.

You could call his mother. Who adores you and once said Dark-and-Brooding was a real asshole for the way he treated you. She regularly confesses that she doesn't understand him either. His own mother.

Flying in the face of self-help, Best Friend helps you compose the note. It takes hours. It is so good you keep a copy. You leave it on his car, tucked under the windshield wiper on the driver's side.

Dark-and-Brooding appears at your door, grinning with the note in his hand. You feel triumphant. You forgive him everything again.

You are sitting alone at the kitchen table on Friday night. Your son has been sleeping for hours. The phone does not ring. You drink coffee with and without rum. You do difficult crossword puzzles, flip through the books you should be reading, put together and take apart and put together again your son's wooden fish puzzle.

You think about calling Dark-and-Brooding but you know you shouldn't. You think about calling Nice-and-Boring but you don't know what you want to say. Best Friend is out of town. You go to bed.

You are still awake at two in the morning. The sheets are twisted around your sweaty neck. You get up and remake the bed. You check again to see if the phone is working. You drink ice water and pace around the kitchen quietly in the dark, trying not to wake your son. He turns and sighs softly in his sleep.

You read a magazine article about the lonely plight of the single parent but it doesn't tell you anything that you don't already know. You remind yourself that nobody has ever died of loneliness but you are not convinced. You put on your terry cloth bathrobe and contemplate the bouquet of flowers which is wilting now, dropping pink petals all over the table. You realize that Dark-and-Brooding wouldn't send you flowers even if you were on your deathbed. He would probably go skating with his brother instead.

You pick up the phone and cradle the humming receiver against your cheek in the dark. You will ask Nice-and-Boring to come over and hold you, just hold you, that's all you want.

You dial his number and then you are whispering into his ear. You know you can ask him because you know he will come. And he does.

Red Plaid Shirt

(1988)

RED PLAID SHIRT

that your mother bought you one summer in Banff. It is 100% pure virgin wool, itchy but flattering against your pale skin, your black hair. You got it in a store called Western Outfitters, of the sort indigenous to the region, which stocked only *real* (as opposed to designer) blue jeans, Stetson hats, and $300 hand-tooled cowboy boots with very pointy toes. There was a saddle and a stuffed deer head in the window.

Outside, the majestic mountains were sitting all around, magnanimously letting their pictures be taken by ten thousand tourists wielding Japanese cameras and eating ice cream cones. You had tricked your mother into leaving her camera in the car so she wouldn't embarrass you, who lived there and were supposed to be taking the scenery for granted by now.

You liked the red plaid shirt so much that she bought you two more just like it, one plain green, the other chocolate brown. But these two stayed shirts, never acquiring any particular significance, eventually getting left unceremoniously behind in a Salvation Army drop-box in a grocery store parking lot some-where along the way.

The red plaid shirt reminded you of your mother's gardening shirt, which was also plaid and which you rescued one winter when she was going to throw it away because the elbows were out. You picture her kneeling in the side garden where she grew only flowers—bleeding hearts, roses, peonies, poppies—and a small patch of strawberries. You picture her hair in a bright babushka, her hands in the black earth with her shirt sleeves rolled up past the elbow. The honeysuckle hedge bloomed fragrantly behind her and the sweet peas curled interminably up the white trellis. You are sorry now for the way you always sulked and whined when she asked you to help, for the way you hated the dirt under your nails and the sweat running into your eyes, the sweat dripping down her shirt front between her small breasts. You kept her old shirt in a bag in your closet for years, with a leather patch half-sewn onto the left sleeve, but now you can't find it.

You were wearing the red plaid shirt the night you met Daniel in the tavern where he was drinking beer with his buddies from the highway construction crew. You ended up living with him for the next five years. He was always calling it your "magic shirt," teasing you, saying how it was the shirt that made him fall in love with you in the first place. You would tease him back, saying how you'd better hang onto it then, in case you had to use it on somebody else. You've even worn it in that spirit a few times since, but the magic seems to have seeped out of it and you are hardly surprised.

You've gained a little weight since then or the shirt has shrunk, so you can't wear it anymore, but you can't throw or give it away either.

RED: crimson carmine cochineal cinnabar sanguine scarlet red ruby rouge my birthstone red and blood-red brick-red beet-red bleeding hearts Queen of fire god of war Mars the colour of magic my magic the colour of iron flowers and fruit the colour of meat dripping lobster cracking claws lips nipples blisters blood my blood and all power.

BLUE COTTON SWEATSHIRT

that says *Why Be Normal?* in a circle on the front. This is your comfort shirt, fleecy on the inside, soft from many washings, and three sizes too big so you can tuck your hands up inside the sleeves when they're shaking or cold. You like to sit on the couch with the curtains closed, wearing your comfort shirt, eating comfort food: vanilla ice cream, macaroni and cheese, white rice with butter and salt, white toast with CheezWhiz and peanut butter. Sometimes you even sleep in it.

This is the shirt you wore when you had the abortion three days before Christmas. They told you to be there at nine in the morning and then you didn't get into the operating room until nearly twelve-thirty. So you wore it in the waiting room with the other women also waiting, and the weight you had already gained was hidden beneath it while you pretended to read *Better Homes and Gardens* and they wouldn't let you smoke. After you came to, you put the shirt back on and waited in another waiting room for your friend, Alice, to come and pick you up because they said you weren't capable yet of going home alone. One of the other women was waiting there too, for her boyfriend, who was always late, and when he finally got there, first she yelled at him briefly and then they decided to go to McDonald's for a hamburger. At home, Alice pours you tea from the porcelain pot into white china cups like precious opaque stones.

None of this has diminished, as you feared it might, the comfort this shirt can give you when you need it. Alice always puts her arms around you whenever she sees you wearing it now. She has one just like it, only pink.

BLUE: azure aqua turquoise delft and navy-blue royal-blue
cool cerulean peacock-blue indigo ultramarine cobalt-blue
Prussian-blue cyan the sky and electric a space the colour of
the firmament and sapphire sleeping silence the sea the blues
my lover plays the saxophone cool blue he plays the blues.

PALE GREY TURTLENECK

that you bought when you were seeing Dwight, who said one
night for no apparent reason that grey is a mystical colour. You
took this judgement to heart because Dwight was more likely to
talk about hockey or carburetors and you were pleasantly
surprised to discover that he might also think about other things.
You spotted the turtleneck the very next day on sale at Maggie's
for $9.99.

You took to wearing it on Sundays because that was the day
Dwight was most likely to wander in, unannounced, on his way to
or from somewhere else. You wore it while you just happened to
put a bottle of good white wine into the fridge to chill and a
chicken, a roast, or a pan of spinach lasagna into the oven to cook
slowly just in case he showed up hungry. You suppose now that
this was pathetic, but at the time you were thinking of yourself as
patient and him as worth waiting for.

Three Sundays in a row you ended up passed out on the couch,
the wine bottle empty on the coffee table, the supper dried out,
and a black-and-white movie with violin music flickering on the
TV. In the coloured morning, the pattern of the upholstery was
imprinted on your cheek and your whole head was hurting.
When Dwight finally did show up, it was a Wednesday and you
were wearing your orange flannelette nightie with all the buttons
gone and a rip down the front, because it was three in the morning, he was drunk, and you had been in bed for hours. He just

laughed and took you in his arms when you told him to get lost. Until you said you were seeing someone else, which was a lie, but one that you both wanted to believe because it was an easy answer that let both of you gingerly off the hook.

You keep meaning to wear that turtleneck again sometime because you know it's juvenile to think it's a jinx, but then you keep forgetting to iron it.

Finally you get tough and wear it, wrinkled, grocery shopping one Saturday afternoon. You careen through the aisles like a crazed hamster, dodging toddlers, old ladies, and other carts, scooping up vegetables with both hands, eating an apple you haven't paid for, leaving the core in the dairy section. But nothing happens and no one notices your turtleneck: the colour or the wrinkles.

Sure enough, Dwight calls the next day, Sunday, at five o'clock. You say you can't talk now, you're just cooking supper: prime rib, wild rice, broccoli with Hollandaise. You have no trouble at all hanging quietly up on him while pouring the wine into the crystal goblet before setting the table for one with the Royal Albert china your mother left you in her will.

GREY: oyster pewter slate dull lead dove-grey pearl-grey brain my brains silver or simple gone into the mystic a cool grey day overcast with clouds ashes concrete the aftermath of airplanes gunmetal-grey granite and gossamer whales elephants cats in the country the colour of questions the best camouflage the opaque elegance an oyster.

WHITE EMBROIDERED BLOUSE

that you bought for $80 to wear with your red-flowered skirt to a Christmas party with Peter, who was working as a pizza cook until he could afford to play his sax full-time. You also bought a silken red belt with gold beads and tassels, a pair of red earrings with dragons on them, and ribbed red stockings which are too small but you wanted them anyway. This striking outfit involves you and Alice in a whole day of trudging around downtown in a snowstorm, holding accessories up in front of mirrors like talismans.

You spend an hour in the bathroom getting ready, drinking white wine, plucking your eyebrows, dancing like a dervish, and smiling seductively at yourself. Peter calls to say he has to work late but he'll meet you there at midnight.

By the time he arrives, you are having a complex anatomical conversation with an intern named Fernando who has spilled a glass of red wine down the front of your blouse. He is going to be a plastic surgeon. Your blouse is soaking in the bathtub and you are wearing only your white lace camisole. Fernando is feeding you green grapes and little squares of cheese, complimenting your cheekbones, and falling in love with your smooth forehead. You are having the time of your life and it's funny how you notice for the first time that Peter has an inferior bone structure.

WHITE: ivory alabaster magnolia milk the moon is full and chalk-white pure-white snow-white moonstone limestone rime and clay marble many seashells and my bones are china bones precious porcelain lace white magic white feather the immaculate conception of white lies wax white wine as a virtue.

YELLOW EVENING GOWN

that you bought for your New Year's Eve date with Fernando. It
has a plunging neckline and a dropped sash which flatteringly
accentuates your hips. You wear it with black hoop earrings,
black lace stockings with seams, and black high heels that Alice
forced you to buy even though they hurt your toes and you are so
uncoordinated that you expect you will have to spend the entire
evening sitting down with your legs crossed, calves nicely flexed.

You spend an hour in the bathroom getting ready, drinking pink
champagne, applying blusher with a fat brush according to a
diagram in a women's magazine that shows you how to make the
most of your face. You practise holding your chin up so it doesn't
sag and look double. Alice French-braids your hair and teaches
you how to waltz like a lady. Fernando calls to say he has to work
late but he'll meet you there before midnight.

You go to the club with Alice instead. They seat you at a tiny table
for two so that when you sit down, your knees touch hers. You are
in the middle of a room full of candles, fresh flowers, lounge
music, and well-groomed couples staring feverishly into each
other's eyes. The meal is sumptuous: green salad, a whole lobster,
homemade pasta, fresh asparagus, and warm buns wrapped in
white linen in a wicker basket. You eat everything and then you
get the hell out of there, leaving a message for Fernando.

You go down the street to a bar you know where they will let you
in without a ticket even though it's New Year's Eve. In the lobby
you meet Fernando in a tuxedo with his arm around a short
homely woman in black who, when you ask, "Who the hell are
you?" says, "His wife." In your black high heels you are taller than
both of them and you know your gown is gorgeous. When the

wife says, "And who the hell are *you*?" you point a long finger at Fernando's nose and say, "Ask him." You stomp away with your chin up and your dropped sash swinging.

Out of sight, you take off your high heels and walk home through the park and the snow with them in your hands, dangling. Alice follows in a cab. By the time you get there, your black lace stockings are in shreds and your feet are cut and you are laughing and crying, mostly laughing.

YELLOW: jonquil jasmine daffodil lemon and honey-coloured corn-coloured cornsilk canary crocus the egg yolk in the morning the colour of mustard bananas brass cadmium yellow is the colour of craving craven chicken cats' eyes I am faint-hearted weak-kneed lily-livered or the sun lucid luminous means caution or yield.

BLACK LEATHER JACKET

that you bought when you were seeing Ivan, who rode a red Harley-Davidson low-rider with a suicide shift, his black beard blowing in the wind. The jacket has rows of diagonal pleats at the yoke and a red leather collar and cuffs.

Ivan used to take you on weekend runs with his buddies and their old ladies to little bars in other towns where they were afraid of you: especially of Ivan's best friend, Spy, who had been hurt in a bike accident two years before and now his hands hung off his wrists at odd angles and he could not speak, could only make guttural growls, write obscene notes to the waitress on a serviette, and laugh at her like a madman, his eyes rolling back in his head, and you could see what was left of his tongue.

You would come riding up in a noisy pack with bugs in your teeth, dropping your black helmets like bowling balls on the floor, eating greasy burgers and pickled eggs, drinking draft beer by the jug, the foam running down your chin. Your legs, after the long ride, felt like a wishbone waiting to be sprung. If no one would rent you a room, you slept on picnic tables in the campground, the bikes pulled in around you like wagons, a case of beer and one sleeping bag between ten of you. In the early morning, there was dew on your jacket and your legs were numb with the weight of Ivan's head on them.

You never did get around to telling your mother you were dating a biker (she thought you said "baker"), which was just as well, since Ivan eventually got tired, sold his bike, and moved back to Manitoba to live with his mother, who was dying. He got a job in a hardware store and soon married his high school sweetheart, Betty, who was a dental hygienist. Spy was killed on the highway: drove his bike into the back of a tanker truck in broad daylight; there was nothing left of him.

You wear your leather jacket now when you need to feel tough. You wear it with your tight blue jeans and your cowboy boots. You strut slowly with your hands in your pockets. Your boots click on the concrete and you are a different person. You can handle anything and no one had better get in your way. You will take on the world if you have to. You will die young and in flames if you have to.

BLACK: ebon sable charcoal jet lamp-black blue-black bruises in a night sky ink-black soot-black the colour of my hair and burning rubber dirt the colour of infinite space speeding blackball blacklist black sheep blackberries ravens eat crow

black as the ace of spades and black is black I want my baby
back before midnight yes of course midnight that old black
dog behind me.

BROWN CASHMERE SWEATER

that you were wearing the night you told Daniel you were leaving
him. It was that week between Christmas and New Year's which
is always a wasteland. Everyone was digging up recipes called
Turkey-Grape Salad, Turkey Soufflé, and Turkey-Almond-
Noodle Bake. You kept vacuuming up tinsel and pine needles,
putting away presents one at a time from under the tree. You and
Daniel sat at the kitchen table all afternoon, drinking hot rum
toddies, munching on crackers and garlic sausage, playing Trivial
Pursuit, asking each other questions like:

What's the most mountainous country in Europe?

Which is more tender, the left or right leg of a chicken?

What race of warriors burned off their right breasts in Greek
legend?

Daniel was a poor loser and he thought that Europe was a country, maybe somewhere near Spain.

This night you have just come from a party at his friend Harold's
house. You are sitting on the new couch, a loveseat, blue with
white flowers, which was Daniel's Christmas present to you, and
you can't help thinking of the year your father got your mother a
coffee percolator when all she wanted was something personal:
earrings, a necklace, a scarf for God's sake. She spent most of the
day locked in their bedroom, crying noisily, coming out every
hour or so to baste the turkey, white-lipped, tucking more
Kleenex up her sleeve. You were on her side this time and
wondered how your father, whom you had always secretly loved

the most, could be so insensitive. It was the changing of the guard, your allegiance shifting like sand from one to the other.

You are sitting on the new couch eating cold pizza and trying to figure out why you didn't have a good time at the party. Daniel is accusing you alternately of looking down on his friends or sleeping with them. He is wearing the black leather vest you bought him for Christmas and he says you are a cheapskate.

When you tell him you are leaving (which is a decision you made months ago but it took you this long to figure out how you were going to manage it and it has nothing to do with the party, the couch, or the season), Daniel grips you by the shoulders and bangs your head against the wall until the picture hung there falls off. It is a photograph of the mountains on a pink spring morning, the ridges like ribs, the runoff like incisions or veins. There is glass flying everywhere in slices into your face, into your hands pressed over your eyes, and the front of your sweater is spotted and matted with blood.

On the way to the hospital, he says he will kill you if you tell them what he did to you. You promise him anything, you promise him that you will love him forever and that you will never leave.

The nurse takes you into the examining room. Daniel waits in the waiting room, reads magazines, buys a chocolate bar from the vending machine, then a Coke and a bag of ripple chips. You tell the nurse what happened and the police take him away in handcuffs with their guns drawn. In the car on the way to the station, he tells them he only did it because he loves you. The officer who takes down your report tells you this and he just keeps shaking his head and patting your arm. The police photographer takes pictures of your face, your broken fingers, your left breast, which has purple bruises all over it where he grabbed it and twisted and twisted.

By the time you get to the women's shelter, it is morning and the blood on your sweater has dried, doesn't show. There is no way of knowing. There, the other women hold you, brush your hair, bring you coffee and cream of mushroom soup. The woman with the broken cheekbone has two canaries in a gold cage that she carries with her everywhere like a lamp. She shows you how the doors are steel, six inches thick, and the windows are bullet-proof. She shows you where you will sleep, in a room on the third floor with six other women, some of them lying now fully dressed on their little iron cots with their hands behind their heads, staring at the ceiling as if it were full of stars or clouds that drift slowly westward in the shape of camels, horses, or bears. She shows you how the canaries will sit on your finger if you hold very still and pretend you are a tree or a roof or another bird.

> BROWN: ochre cinnamon coffee copper caramel the colour of my Christmas cake chocolate mocha walnut chestnuts raw sienna my suntan burnt umber burning toast fried fricasseed sautéed grilled I baste the turkey the colour of stupid cows smart horses brown bears brown shirt brown sugar apple brown betty brunette the colour of thought and sepia the colour of old photographs the old earth and wood.

GREEN SATIN QUILTED JACKET

in the Oriental style with mandarin collar and four red frogs down the front. This jacket is older than you are. It belonged to your mother, who bought it when she was the same age you are now. In the black-and-white photos from that time, the jacket is grey but shiny and your mother is pale but smooth-skinned, smiling with her hand on her hip or your father's thigh.

You were always pestering her to let you wear it to play dress-up, with her red high heels and that white hat with the feathers and the little veil that covered your whole face. You wanted to wear it to a Hallowe'en party at school where all the other girls would be witches, ghosts, or princesses and you would be the only mandarin, with your eyes, you imagined, painted up slanty and two sticks through a bun in your hair. But she would never let you. She would just keep on cooking supper, bringing carrots, potatoes, cabbages up from the root cellar, taking peas, beans, broccoli out of the freezer in labelled dated parcels, humming, looking out through the slats of the Venetian blind at the black garden and the leafless rose bushes. Each year, at least one of them would be winter-killed no matter how hard she had tried to protect them. And she would dig it up in the spring by the dead roots and the thorns would get tangled in her hair, leave long bloody scratches all down her arms. And the green jacket stayed where it was, in the cedar chest with the handmade lace doilies, her grey linen wedding suit, and the picture of your father as a small boy with blonde ringlets.

After the funeral, you go through her clothes while your father is outside shovelling snow. You lay them out in piles on the bed: one for the Salvation Army, one for the second-hand store, one for yourself because your father wants you to take something home with you. You will take the green satin jacket, also a white mohair cardigan with multicoloured squares on the front, a black and white striped shirt you sent her for her birthday last year that she never wore, an imitation pearl necklace for Alice, and a dozen unopened packages of pantyhose. There is a fourth pile for your father's friend, Jack's, new wife, Frances, whom your mother never liked, but your father says Jack and Frances have fallen on hard times on the farm since Jack got the emphysema, and Frances will be glad of some new clothes.

Jack and Frances drop by the next day with your Aunt Jeanne. You serve tea and the shortbread cookies Aunt Jeanne has brought. She makes them just the way your mother did, whipped, with a sliver of maraschino cherry on top. Jack, looking weather-beaten or embarrassed, sits on the edge of the couch with his baseball cap in his lap and marvels at how grown-up you've got to be. Frances is genuinely grateful for the two green garbage bags of clothes, which you carry out to the truck for her.

After they leave, you reminisce fondly with your father and Aunt Jeanne about taking the toboggan out to Jack's farm when you were small, tying it to the back of the car, your father driving slowly down the country lane, towing you on your stomach, clutching the front of the toboggan which curled like a wooden wave. You tell him for the first time how frightened you were of the black tires spinning the snow into your face, and he says he had no idea, he thought you were having fun. This was when Jack's first wife, Winnifred, was still alive. Your Aunt Jeanne, who knows everything, tells you that when Winnifred was killed in that car accident, it was Jack, driving drunk, who caused it. And now when he gets drunk, he beats Frances up, locks her out of the house in her bare feet, and she has to sleep in the barn, in the hay with the horses.

You are leaving in the morning. Aunt Jeanne helps you pack. You are anxious to get home but worried about leaving your father alone. Aunt Jeanne says she'll watch out for him.

The green satin jacket hangs in your front hall closet now, between your black leather jacket and your raincoat. You can still smell the cedar from the chest and the satin is always cool on your cheek like clean sheets or glass.

One day you think you will wear it downtown, where you are meeting a new man for lunch. You study yourself in the full-length mirror on the back of the bathroom door and you decide it makes you look like a different person: someone unconventional, unusual, and unconcerned. This new man, whom you met recently at an outdoor jazz festival, is a free spirit who eats health food, plays the dulcimer, paints well, writes well, sings well, and has just completed an independent study of eastern religions. He doesn't smoke, drink, or do drugs. He is pure and peaceful, perfect. He is teaching you how to garden, how to turn the black soil, how to plant the seeds, how to water them, weed them, watch them turn into lettuce, carrots, peas, beans, radishes, and pumpkins, how to get the kinks out of your back by stretching your brown arms right up to the sun. You haven't even told Alice about him yet because he is too good to be true. He is bound to love this green jacket, and you in it too.

You get in your car, drive around the block, go back inside because you forgot your cigarettes, and you leave the green jacket on the back of a kitchen chair because who are you trying to kid? More than anything, you want to be transparent. More than anything, you want to hold his hands across the table and then you will tell him you love him and it will all come true.

GREEN: viridian verdigris chlorophyll grass leafy jade mossy verdant apple-green pea-green lime-green sage-green sea-green bottle-green emeralds avocadoes olives all leaves the

colour of Venus hope and jealousy the colour of mould mildew
envy poison and pain and snakes the colour of everything that
grows in my garden fertile nourishing sturdy sane and strong.

Stranger Than Fiction (1988)

Any number of people will tell you that truth is stranger than fiction. They will usually tell you this as a preface to the story of how their Aunt Maude was frightened by a bald albino juggler at the East Azilda Fall Fair when she was six months pregnant (the juggler, himself frightened by a disoriented cow that had wandered into the ring, lost control of five airborne bowling pins, and one of them hit poor old Maude square in the back of the head) and later she gave birth to a bald brown-eyed baby, Donalda, who was allergic to milk and her hair grew in so blonde it looked white and now she's unhappily married to a man who owns a bowling alley in downtown Orlando.

Or they will tell it to you as an afterword to the story of how Rita Moreno appeared to their best friend, Leona's, first cousin, Fritz, in a dream, doing the Chiquita Banana routine and feeding the fruit off her hat to a donkey, and sure enough, the next day, Fritz, who was an unemployed actor, got his big TV break doing a commercial for Fruit of the Loom underwear and he was the grapes.

Oh sure, lots of people will tell you, and with very little provocation too, that truth is stranger than fiction. But I, now I have got *the proof*.

I was writing a story about a woman named Sheila. Apropos of nothing, the name Sheila, I discovered, is an Irish form of Cecilia, from the Latin, meaning "blind." In the story, Sheila was thirty-two years old, slim, attractive, and intelligent with blue eyes and

straight blonde waist-length hair. (I often give my fictional characters blue eyes and blonde hair because I have brown eyes and
brown hair and I don't want anyone to think my work is autobio-
graphical. Also, my hair is naturally curly, short.)

Sheila was married to a handsome brown-haired man named
Roger, a bank manager, and they lived in a ranch-style bungalow
in Tuxedo Park. Sheila amused herself by taking aerobics one
afternoon a week, doing volunteer work at the senior citizens'
home, and having long lunches a lot with her friends. She and
Roger got along well enough, although every once in a while
Sheila would remember that they hadn't had a meaningful
conversation in four years. They lived an easy life, gliding gracefully and politely around each other like ice dancers.

So then I made Sheila unhappy in her heart of hearts: because
what's a good story without a little angst?

The thing was, Sheila wanted to be someone else. Sheila
wanted to be a country and western singer. She knew all the
words to all the best songs, which she practised by singing along
with the CD player while Roger was away all day at the bank. She
had a special secret wardrobe stashed in the back of her walk-in
closet off the master bathroom. On the cover of her first album,
she wanted to see a picture of herself astride a white horse in her
chaps in the wind. Having never been much bothered by either
self-doubt or self-examination, it did not even occur to her that
she might very well be crazy or untalented.

Then she met a man named Carlos in a specialty record store
called Country Cousins. Carlos bore a startling resemblance to
Johnny Cash in his younger days. Of course they hit it off right
away because they were both looking for that old Patsy Cline
album with "I Fall To Pieces" on it. They went for a beer at The
Hitching Post, a nearby country bar where, as it turned out,
Carlos's band, The Red Rock Ramblers, was playing. They were
only in town for the week, having just spent two months on the

road, and now they were heading home to Saskatoon. Feeling gently homesick, Carlos talked a lot about the prairies, which Sheila had never seen, about the way they'll change colour in a thunderstorm or a dangerous wind, the way they'll make you think of things you've never thought before because you can see them forever and they have no limits. So by the time he got around to also telling her he had a wife and three kids out there, it was too late to turn back now, because he already had his hand on her thigh and his tongue in her ear.

I was having a bit of a time of it in my own life right then. Three and a half weeks earlier I had fallen in love with a man named Nathan who was from Winnipeg and also married. This was in July and it was hot, humid, and hazy; it was hard to concentrate. I was downtown Friday night having a drink at The Red Herring, which is an outdoor patio bar with a magnolia tree, orange poppies, handsome waiters, and blue metal tables sprouting red and white umbrellas advertising Alfa Romeo, Noilly Prat, and OV. The regular clientele consists largely of writers, painters, and jazz piano players who are just taking a little break in the sun. Nobody ever really gets drunk at The Red Herring: they just relax, recharge, have pleasant informed conversations about postmodernism, Chinese astrology, and free trade. They are intense and innocent.

Nathan was drinking alone and so was I, leaning against the stand-up bar inside. I'm not even sure now how we first got talking but, lo and behold, the next thing you know, he's telling me that he's a writer too! Well, you can just imagine my joy at discovering we had the whole world in common. He wrote poetry, mind you, whereas I write fiction, but I was willing, for the most part, to overlook this minor discrepancy. He was in town for a weekend workshop at the university. He was dynamic, sensitive, intelligent, funny, clean-shaven, tall, fairly well off, very supportive, unhappy in his marriage, and he'd even read my books. So what else could I do? (Caught now in the act of recollection, I recognize how flimsy all this sounds, but at the time it was compelling.)

We found a table on the patio and drank a bottle of expensive white wine while talking about our favourite writers, books, and movies, our favourite foods, colours, and seasons, and the worst reviews our respective books had ever received. We congratulated ourselves on being so much alike and ordered another bottle of wine.

He did not talk about his wife, except to say that she wasn't fond of wine, and her name was never mentioned. (I already knew from Sheila that a married man who does not call his wife by her name is pretty well ripe for the picking.) So it was easy enough, sad to say, to keep forgetting about her.

I forgot about her as we walked back to my house arm in arm at midnight, singing a slow country song, and he was the slide guitar. I did remember her as he undressed me in the living room, but I forgot about her again as he took me in his arms and his skin was so cool. I remembered her when he sighed in his sleep, but I forgot about her again in the morning when we had a shower, some coffee, and he read to me from *The Norton Anthology of English Literature.*

Then I read him the story of Sheila so far and he said he really loved it. I took this to mean that he loved me too.

Afterwards, he told me about his teacher one summer at a writers' workshop years ago in Edmonton and this teacher was a big influence on him, always telling him, "Life ain't art." I wasn't sure how to apply this apparent truism to my own life/work but I agreed eagerly, as if it were something I'd known all along.

It was shortly after this that Carlos in the story began to look less like Johnny Cash and more like the young George Gordon, Lord Byron. He admitted that when he retired from the music business, he might take up writing. Sheila recalled, but did not relate, the story she'd heard of a writer and a doctor chatting at a cocktail party and the doctor said, "When I retire and have nothing else to do, I think I'll take up writing," so the writer said, "That's a good idea! When I retire and have nothing else to do, I think I'll take up brain surgery."

Carlos told Sheila that everybody has a book in them somewhere just waiting to be written and Sheila wondered, briefly, where the book in her might be right now: lodged behind some major organ perhaps, her liver, her lungs? She had this recurring dull ache, sometimes in her left breast, sometimes in her right. It worried her occasionally, usually late at night, and then she would lie in bed beside Roger, feeling her breasts through her pink cotton nightie, looking for lumps, holding her breath. Roger, who, she was convinced, could have slept through Armageddon, sighed dreamily and draped his left arm straight across her breasts by accident, so that she lay there pinned and pleading with God. She had come to think of this pain as her "heartache" but now she wondered if it might just be a book trying to get out.

I told Nathan this pink cotton nightie of mine had once belonged to my mother who was dead now, of lung cancer, though she'd never smoked a day in her life. He said he understood my not liking to sleep in the nude and I was relieved, as this is a point some men get funny about, as if it were an insult to intimacy or their masculinity. I told him that I might like to write a book about my mother someday, as she had led an interesting life, and he assured me that everybody has a story worth telling and I'd have no trouble finding a market for that sort of human interest thing.

I told him how my first boyfriend had convinced himself that he would die young, tragically, in great pain, and alone. His name was Cornell and he suffered from migraines and whole days during which he could not climb out from under this escalating burden of impending doom. I felt guilty for dumping him but I could not let go of my own romantic fantasy of growing old beside my one true love and we would bring each other freshly fluffed pillows and cups of weak tea as the time drew near.

Sheila touched her breasts and felt nothing. Roger in the morning was always cheerful and animated, so she never told him about the pain and the sad certainty of something that would come to her at five in the morning when the earth shifts imperceptibly on its axis and everything changes or begins to be the same all over again. When she told this to Carlos between sets at the bar, he said how his six-year-old daughter often woke screaming from nightmares in which she was afraid of everything and then he would lie beside her all night while she sighed and foundered feverishly.

At five in the morning on Sunday, Nathan got up to catch a plane and I kissed him quietly goodbye without asking how old his children were.

I am comfortable enough with the derivative aspects of Sheila's story in relation to my own. I am accustomed by now to this habit fiction has of assuming the guise of reality. I am no longer surprised to go out one night for New York steak with baked potato (medium rare, sour cream, and bacon bits) and the next day my characters are enjoying the very same meal (well done, mind you, hold the bacon bits, yes, I'll have the cheesecake please). I no longer find it unsettling to see the woman beside me in a bookstore leafing through a paperback called *How To Live With A Schizophrenic* and when I get home, the next thing you know, there's a schizophrenic in my story and that book is really coming in handy.

So the whole time I was putting Sheila through her paces, I was also thinking, with some other side of my brain, about Nathan. I wasn't seriously expecting a letter or anything as incriminating as that. I did hope that he might get very drunk sometime and call me up in the middle of the night, begging and reciting love poems. I knew this wasn't something he ever could or would (considering his wife, his kids, the prairies, and all) do sober. This just shows you how little I wanted, how little it would have taken, how very little I was asking for.

But then again, in a different mood (more confident, more optimistic, very nearly jaunty), I was also thinking: Well, why not? Why couldn't he, after sleeping with me just that one weekend, go back to his bungalow in Winnipeg, pack up his word processor, leave his wife, his kids, the dog, and the algae-eater, and come back to me with tears in his eyes and a lump of love in his throat? I would pick him up at the airport, of course (all good romantic fantasies should incorporate at least one airport scene or maybe a bus station at midnight, or rain, high winds, a blizzard, a taxi at the very least, with a surly, silent driver and the meter running), where we would float across the mezzanine and fall into each other's well-dressed tingling arms while all around us dark-skinned foreign families wept on each other and tried to catch their luggage on that stupid whirligig.

Well? Why not?

Stranger things have happened. Which is another of those truisms that people will present you with just before they tell you about the time they picked up a hitchhiker on the highway halfway between Thunder Bay and Winnipeg and he turned out to be from Wabigoon where their friends, the Jacobsens, used to live and he didn't really know them but he'd heard of them and he'd seen the same flying saucer they'd seen in 1975, August 17, 11:38 p.m.

Many of these stranger things are duly documented in the weekly tabloids which I buy occasionally at the A&P when I think no one is noticing. I take solace from the headlines, tell them to my friends, and we all laugh, comforted to know that:

MICHAEL JACKSON WAS THE ELEPHANT MAN IN HIS PAST
   LIFE
FLEA CIRCUS GOES WILD WITH HUNGER AND ATTACKS
   TRAINER
MARRIAGE LASTS FOUR HOURS — GROOM WANTED TO WEAR
   THE WEDDING GOWN
TERRIFIED TELEPHONE OPERATOR CLAIMS, MY HUSBAND
   TRAINED ROACHES TO ATTACK ME
HUBBY WHO GAVE KIDNEY TO WIFE WANTS IT BACK IN
   DIVORCE BATTLE
MEN FIGHT DUEL FOR GIRL'S LOVE WITH SAUSAGES.

So yes, stranger things have happened in the past. And the
future, on a good day, extends eternally with the promise of more.

About the time I got Sheila to the point in the story where she
was actually going to get up on stage at The Hitching Post (Roger
thought she was at a Tupperware party) and sing "I Fall To
Pieces" (she had her satin shirt on, her fringed buckskin jacket,
her cowboy boots, and everything), I accidentally thought of a girl
named Sheila Shirley Harkness who was in my Grade Nine
History class. She was not a friend of mine. In fact, I avoided her,
because the one time we did have lunch together in the cafeteria,
she ate half my french fries right off my plate and told me the
story of how her Uncle Norman had killed himself by slamming
his head in the car door. Sheila Shirley Harkness was older than
the rest of us because she'd failed Grade Eight twice. Her mother
was that woman who walked around the neighbourhood in her
curlers and a mangy fur coat, twirling a baton, singing to herself,
and waving her free hand like a flag. My mother said she should
be ashamed of herself, acting like that in public, as if this bizarre
behaviour were something we all secretly wanted to exhibit but
we knew better.

Sheila Shirley Harkness was so fat that she had to sit in a special desk. And she smelled, although this was something we girls never discussed among ourselves because maybe we were afraid that we smelled too.

Sheila Shirley Harkness gave birth to a six-pound baby boy eight days before final exams. She was one of those girls sometimes written up in the tabloids who say they never knew they were pregnant: she thought she had something wrong with her, cancer, gas, or a blocked intestine. When the baby's head came out in the bathroom at three in the afternoon, she thought she was dying, turning inside out before her very own horrified eyes. She dropped out of school then, out of sight, and kept the baby, Brian, at home. There was surprisingly little speculation as to who the father might be. It was not unimportant; rather, it was unimaginable. Immaculate conception seemed more likely than Sheila in bed with a boy, any boy, moaning.

This first Sheila (or this *second* Sheila, according to your perspective on such matters as fact/fiction, life/lies, and the boundaries or dependencies like veils hung between them) has receded fairly fuzzily into my memory now and so was probably not quite the girl I remembered anyway, was probably less frightening, less doomed, might well be working at this very minute as a high-level executive for a major advertising firm, living in a harbourfront condo with an original Matisse in the loft, brass end tables, and a marble Jacuzzi, rather than lying around all day in her underwear (yellowed or grey, the elastic shot), eating maple walnut ice cream and watching "I Love Lucy" reruns while her mother bangs her head against the wall in the basement and her illegitimate children run rampant through the neighbourhood in their dirty diapers, as we all, in the grip of our mutually hard-hearted, shiny-haired adolescence, assumed she would end up.

Either way, the first Sheila was not at all like the second, like *my* Sheila, as I had come to think of her. *My* Sheila was, among other things, friendly, cheerful, clever, clear-skinned, well-educated, long-legged, ambitious, and sweet-smelling. Her last name was Gustafson and her middle name was Mary, although neither of these names actually appeared in the story. Her parents, for the sake of simplicity, were either dead or living on Ellesmere Island and so didn't bother her much anymore.

Being a fictional character, my Sheila was not obliged to explain herself to anyone or to divulge her darkest fondest secrets to total strangers. Unlike myself (with my disarming or disturbing tendency to spill my guts, to tell the worst about myself to anyone who will listen), unlike myself (me having yet to accurately determine the difference between revealing and defending yourself), unlike myself (me having only recently figured out that most people don't tell the truth about themselves, not even *to* themselves, because they don't know it, like it, or remember it), Sheila knew when to keep her mouth shut.

Nevertheless, my Sheila started to subtly change. She started feeling sluggish all the time. She wore the same old dress three days in a row. She bought a baton. She ate two cheeseburgers, a large fries, and an order of chili and toast at one sitting in a greasy spoon in a bad neighbourhood. For a minute there, she questioned the meaning of life, if there even was one, if there even *should* be one. She sniffed her armpits in public. She was on the verge of a transformation, threatening to rewrite her whole life, not to mention the story. I was having none of this.

It is for fear of exactly this sort of thing that I try never to call my fictional characters by the names of people I have really known, even just in passing. So I tried to change her name in the middle of the story. First I tried to call her Janet, then Beth, then Brenda, Delores, and Laura.

But no. None of the new names would do.

Janet was too responsible.

Beth was too timid and kept threatening to die of scarlet fever.
Brenda was too easily satisfied.

Delores was the name of my friend, Susan's, Irish setter bitch and her hair was red.

Laura was the woman who came to demonstrate a talented but over-priced vacuum cleaner all over my living room for an hour and a half one Wednesday afternoon and she was sorry she'd never heard of me but she didn't get much time to read anymore what with this new job and her two-year-old twins, not to mention her husband, Hal, and did I know Danielle Steel personally, and when I said I didn't have $2,000 to spend on anything, let alone a stupid vacuum cleaner, she said, "Now that's funny, I thought all writers were rich."

So Sheila stayed Sheila and I struggled to keep her on the right track, would not give her permission to gain weight, pick her nose, or stay in bed with her head covered up till three in the afternoon. I would not allow her, much as she tried, to dream about babies born in bathtubs, buses, or a 747 cruising over Greenland at an altitude of 22,000 feet. Against my better judgement, I did allow her one nightmare about her mother having joined a marching band, playing the bagpipes with a sound like a cat being squeezed, and the parade stretched from one end of the country to the other, but at the very last minute her mother turned into Tammy Wynette and everything worked out all right.

Sheila got a little surly with me sometimes but that was understandable, considering her situation, her frustration, and human nature being what it is.

One Friday afternoon, when I'd manoeuvred Sheila around to the place in her life where she either had to shit or get off the pot, I decided to go down to The Red Herring for a drink instead. Sheila had been a big hit at The Hitching Post. Carlos had professed his love and offered her a job with the band. She hadn't vacuumed the house all week and Roger hadn't even noticed. Two things remained unclear: what was Carlos going to do about his family back in Saskatoon and why was Roger so dense? Now Sheila either had to pack up her buckskin and join the band (Carlos was waiting outside in a cab with the meter running, off to the airport any minute now) or go home and cook a tuna casserole for Roger (who was stuck in rush-hour traffic at the bridge, fuming, sweating, and listening to the stock market report on the car radio). To the naked eye, this would seem like a simple choice, but Sheila didn't know what she wanted to do and neither did I. I wanted to make her live happily ever after (if only because I thought this would bode well for Nathan and me), but happy endings have fallen out of favour these days—modern (or should I say, postmodern?) readers being what they are (that is, intelligent, discerning, and slightly cynical), they find them just too hard to believe, too much to hope for, fake. Could I really hope to convince any of *them* that stranger things have happened?

I was tense and thought a drink or two might do the trick. Going to The Red Herring in the afternoon is not like going down to, say, The Sunset Hotel, where they have table dancing, four shows a day, and the regulars, in the manner of serious drinkers, gaze deeply into their glasses of draft between mouthfuls, dredging there for answers or hope because they don't know where else to look. Some woman in gold glitter high heels and pink short-shorts is dancing by herself and the old guy in the back booth is sleeping with his head on his arms, having just wet himself or thrown up under the table.

The Red Herring, on the other hand, is a classy place, and having a drink or even two or three there in the afternoon, especially on a Friday, is an acceptable enough thing for a real writer, even a female one, to do. I imagined that as I sat there sipping, my writer's block would be hanging off me with a certain attractive, highly intelligent sheen.

I mean, what can you expect of writers anyway when they are prone to sitting around all day with their heads full of events that never happened to people who never existed while conducting conversations that never took place in carefully decorated rooms that will never be built?

Besides, it was at The Red Herring where I first met Nathan, so that was another good enough reason to go there. If I am fortunate enough to get the same table (toward the back, to the left), I can imagine that he is sitting across from me, we are drinking dry white wine and smiling, holding hands and making plans. In this fantasy, his wife is not, as you might expect, dead, confined to a sanatorium, or cheerfully giving him a divorce—she has simply vanished, vaporized, dropped off the face of the earth like rain. She might even be alive and well on another planet, having assumed a whole new identity with the papers to prove it, living out her life like a pseudonym.

So I fix my eyes on the empty chair and construct long loving conversations with Nathan, who is always wearing the same navy teeshirt and white cotton pants because that's all I ever knew him in. Sometimes I get carried away and catch myself nodding and moving my lips, smiling away to beat the band. I can only hope that the other patrons, on seeing this, take me for one of those independent strong-minded women who is always inordinately pleased with her own company. But then I remember that Ann Landers column where someone complained about always being told to smile and Ann reminded her that people who walk around smiling all the time for no reason are often followed by unsmiling men in white coats.

No such luck that day though—the only empty table was one to the right just beneath the magnolia tree. Our table was occupied by four cheerful young women in straw hats and lacy sundresses.

They were eating elaborate beautiful salads and toasting the glorious day with Perrier and lime. I had no reason to resent, dislike, or envy them, but I did anyway.

I ordered a peach schnapps with orange juice, which is called a Fuzzy Navel, so of course the waiter and I had a chummy little chuckle over that. Then I sat back to nurse my drink and read an article in *Harper's Magazine* called "The Credible Word" by John Berger.

At the very beginning, he said: *Today the discredit of words is very great.*

And in the middle: *A scarf may demand more space than a cloud.*

And finally: *The pages burning were like ideal pages being written.*

I took this to be a validation of sorts and flipped through the rest of the magazine feeling lighthearted, encouraged, and close to inspired. (It is, I have frequently found, much easier to feel inspired in a nice restaurant, facing up to all that good cutlery, fine china, fresh pasta, and crisp lettuce, than it is in my office, facing up finally to the typewriter and all that blank paper.)

Skimming next through the "Harper's Index," I could not help but feel secure and confirmed in the knowledge that the number of brands of bottled water sold in the United States is 535, the number of fish per day that a Vermonter may shoot in season is 10, the price of an order of sushi at Dodger Stadium is only $4.50, and the number of Soviets in Petrozavodsk who were crushed to death in liquor store lineups last year was 3.

I felt myself to be having, after all, one of those dizzying days in which everything can be connected, all ideas can be conjugated and then consumed whole, sense and significance are dropped into your lap like gifts, and the very cast and camber of the air on your cheek is meaningful.

Stranger things, yes.

I ordered another drink and an appetizer, the liver pâté and some French bread.

I eavesdropped intermittently on the couple at the next table who were talking about their old dog, Shep, who was going blind, poor thing, about their new vacuum cleaner, and a misguided woman named Lisa who was looking for trouble and she was sure going to get it this time, couldn't she see that guy was no damn good?

I felt a tap on my right shoulder. I was feeling so happy and self-absorbed that I thought, without wonder, that it must be Nathan or God. It was a woman in a pale pink pantsuit, carrying one small grocery bag and a white wicker purse. She looked to be in her sixties. She said, "Please may I join you? There's nowhere to sit."

What could I do? I nodded as she took the chair beside me. She ordered a screwdriver and some escargots in mushroom caps. She said, "I like a long lunch with my friends."

I could see right away there was something *good* about her, something motherly and kind. A pair of bifocals lay on her chest, hung from a golden chain, and she'd put a blue rinse in her white waved hair. I thought of my own mother once saying that sometimes all she really wanted was a place to lay her head but why was it so hard to put it down there in the first place? This was after my father had left her for a younger woman.

I was glad enough for the company of a stranger. As opposed to family and friends, strangers will believe anything you tell them and they are less likely to ask you what's wrong right when you thought you were doing just fine. They will not tell you that you look tired on a day when you thought you felt terrific. A stranger will tell you any story as if it were true. Often I have envied total strangers on the street: just the inscrutable look of them makes it obvious that their lives are better than mine, more normal, more simple, and perfect, yes, perfect . . . perfect strangers.

"Hello," the woman said, "my name is Sheila."

I, rendered helpless in the face of coincidence, said, "Hello." It was the kind of thing that if you put it in a story, nobody would believe it. I recovered myself quickly enough because, after all, what possible harm could there be in exchanging pleasantries on a pleasant afternoon with a kind woman who happened to be, through no fault of her own, named Sheila?

It made little difference that I'm no good at small talk because this third Sheila (or was she, chronologically speaking, because of her age rather than her advent, the *first* Sheila?) proved to be exceedingly talkative. In the course of the conversation, I had to tell her very little about myself, virtually nothing in fact, except to say once, when her momentum was interrupted by the arrival of dessert (chocolate almond cheesecake) and her story was stalled, that I was a writer, single, no children, said to be successful.

She told me with detailed delight about a recent trip to the mountains she'd made with her younger sister, Serena, who had the glaucoma, and how you see things differently, more clearly, more brilliantly, bright, when you have to describe and explain them to somebody else, the blind or a child.

She confided that one of the hardest things about getting older was the feeling that your body was turning on you, falling to pieces one thing at a time, and also the hair, which got thinner and thinner and she never ever wanted to become one of those sad old ladies that you can see through to their pathetic pink scalp. In high school, she said, she had been much envied for her hair which was long and lustrous, a deep burnished red, and when she marched in the school parade twirling her silver baton, her hair swung and bounced, beautiful in the sun.

She talked about her children, three of them, two boys and a girl, who were all grown-up now and living in other cities. She understood that but still, she missed them.

Mostly she talked about her husband, Victor, who had died

tragically in a car crash in a snowstorm in December 1963, four days after they'd bought their first home, a brick bungalow on Addison Street downtown. She still lived in that house and every day she thought about her Victor, wondered if he'd have liked the new wallpaper in the bedroom, the beige shag carpet in the front room, the placemats, the blue towels, the new tuna casserole recipe, the microwave.

No, she'd never remarried. Things were different in those days: a new husband had never occurred to her. With her Victor gone, she just figured she'd had all she was ever going to get of or from love, for better or worse. She was satisfied, she said. She'd lived a lovely life, she said. For some things, yes, she agreed, yes, it was too late now. It was too late now to turn back. It was too late now to turn her back on what she had created: three children, the house, those long-felt heart-held memories of her Victor who, like all the young dead, had never aged, never betrayed her, never ever broke her heart again. Why would she want to change anything after all?

Why indeed? Why did I find all this so hard to believe: me with my constant chronic longing, my searching, my secret sadness at those moments when I should have been happy, me with this annoying ache always stuck in my heart or my head? "Why create trouble where there isn't any?" I'd asked myself often, asked myself now.

"Now I have this pain," she said unexpectedly. "This funny pain, *here*," she said, pressing the palm of her hand to her breast, which was draped with a silk scarf dramatically patterned with bright large tigers in various predatory poses.

My own hand twitched with wanting to reach across and touch her but I was afraid there would be nothing there . . .

. . . no woman

. . . no breast

. . . no scarf

. . . no tigers

. . . just air

. . . the palpable eloquent air pushing down from the swollen storm clouds which were gathering above us.

The patio was emptying quickly under the threat of rain. All around us, women were scooping up their purses and packages like prizes, gaily preparing to just disappear.

I walked slowly back to my car in the underground parkade where I'd left it.

I was tired suddenly and rested my head for a minute on my arms wrapped round the steering wheel. I thought of a morning not long ago when a navy blue Oldsmobile had pulled up suddenly in front of my house while I sat at the breakfast table in my nightie, hovering over my third cup of black coffee. The driver, a stranger, a bearded young man in a plaid shirt, sat there for a full five minutes with his head like this on the wheel. Then he drove slowly away, leaving me alone again, alone again to speculate in the dappled moted sunlight.

I hesitated as I left the parkade, not sure which way I wanted to turn, which route home I wanted to take. A man in a baseball cap in a brown van behind me leaned so hard on his horn that my eyes filled in an instant with angry insulted tears.

I turned left into the rush hour traffic and drove on.

Sometimes on my way home from The Red Herring these days, I can imagine a car (red with black interior, air scoop, chrome, shining) running the red light at 100 mph, rocketing through the intersection, hitting my car on the driver's side so that I am flung up and over, flying, then finally coming down face first on the asphalt, so mutilated that no one will be able to identify me. I can imagine this so clearly that unconsciously I brace myself for the impact, for the sound of ripping metal and breaking glass, as I roll through each intersection.

Sometimes I imagine that I am one of the poor pedestrians in the crosswalk at the time. I am mowed down right alongside the rest of them . . .

  . . . strangers

  . . . young woman, Wendy, pushing baby in stroller, pulling toddler in harness, has a headache and hates the way her hair looks like straw in this heat

  . . . bank teller, Jane, on lunch, carrying roast beef on rye with pickle and cheese in small white bag while worrying about vari- cose veins, humming sad song about cheating and hearts

  . . . old man, Ed, with white cane and dog, wishing he was dead or his wife was still alive or his children, at least, would call

  . . . businessman, Martin, with briefcase, nice teeth, green tie, has not a thought in his head, no reason to suspect that anyone else has either

  . . . stranger things have happened.

Sometimes I imagine that I am the driver of the car, with the radio on and my foot to the floor, and the bodies scatter from me like pages or petals, unleashed. Or then they are not bodies at all but balloons, of all colours, full of wonder, words, and hot air, bobbing up and away, bouncing off asphalt, the rooftops, the pain, and a cloud.

       *

Railroading or: Twelve Small Stories with the Word *Train* in the Title (1988)

LOVE TRAIN

For a long time after Lesley and Cliff broke up, Cliff was always sending her things.

Flowers.

Red roses by the dramatic dozen.

Delicate frilly carnations dyed turquoise at the edges (which reminded Lesley of a tradition they'd observed at her elementary school on Mother's Day when each child had to wear a carnation, red if your mother was alive, white if she was dead—there were only two kids in the whole school whose mothers were dead— and what then, she wondered, was turquoise meant to signify?).

A single white orchid nestled in tissue paper in a gold box, as if they had a big date for a formal dance.

Cards. Funny cards:

I thought you'd like to know that I've decided to start dating seals again, and . . . oh yes, my umbilical cord has grown back!

Sentimental cards:

I love wearing the smile . . . you put on my face!

Funny sentimental cards:

You You You You You You You You You You You You . . . These are a few of my favourite things!

Apology cards:

Please forgive me . . . my mouth is bigger than my brain!

and:

I'm sorry, I was wrong . . . Well, not as wrong as you, but sorrier!

Pretty picture cards to say:

Happy Thanksgiving!
Happy Hallowe'en!
I'm just thinking of you!
I'm always thinking of you!
I'm still thinking of you!

Letters. Mostly letters.

Often Cliff would call during the day and leave a message on Lesley's answering machine, apologizing for having bothered her with another card or letter when she'd already told him, in no uncertain terms, that she needed some space. Then he would call right back and leave another message to apologize for having left the first one when she'd already told him to leave her alone.

He did not send the letters through the mail in the conventional way, but delivered them by hand in the middle of the night. Lesley never did catch him in the act, but she could just picture him parking his car halfway down the block, sneaking up her driveway in the dark or the rain, depositing another

white envelope in her black mailbox. Where she would find it
first thing in the morning.

At first it gave Lesley the creeps to think of Cliff tippy-toeing
around out there while she was inside sleeping, but then she got
used to hearing from him in this way. She took to checking the
mailbox every morning before she put the coffee on. Waiting in
her housecoat and slippers for the toast to pop and the eggs to
poach, she would study the envelope first. Sometimes he put her
full name on it, first and last; sometimes her first name only;
once, just her initials.

Inside, the letters were always neatly typewritten on expensive
bond paper. They began with phrases like "Well no . . ." or "And
yes . . ." or "But maybe . . .", as if Cliff were picking up a conversation (one-sided though it might be) right in the middle where
they'd left off, or as if he still thought he could still read her mind.

One of the first letters was dense with scholarly historical
quotes on the nature of war. Cliff had set these erudite excerpts
carefully off from the rest of the text, single-spaced and indented:

> In quarrels between countries, as well as those between indi-
> viduals, when they have risen to a certain height, the first
> cause of dissension is no longer remembered, the minds of
> the parties being wholly engaged in recollecting and resent-
> ing the mutual expressions of their dislike. When feuds have
> reached that fatal point, all considerations of reason and
> equity vanish; a blind fury governs, or rather, confounds all
> things. A people no longer regards their interest, but rather
> the gratification of their wrath. (John Dickson).

And later in the letter he wrote:

> The strange thing about this crisis of August 1939 was that the
> object between Germany and Poland was not clearly defined,

and could not therefore be expressed as a concrete demand.
It was a part of Hitler's nature to avoid putting things in a
concrete form; to him, differences of opinion were questions
of power, and tests of one's nerves and strength. (Ernst von
Weizsäcker).

Lesley could not imagine that Cliff actually had a repertoire of
such pedantic passages floating around inside his head, just
waiting for an opportunity to be called up. But she couldn't imagine that he had really gone to the library and looked them up in
order to quote them at her either.

Still, this letter made her mad enough to call him. When she
said on the phone, "I don't take kindly to being compared to
Hitler, thank you very much," Cliff said, "Don't be ridiculous.
That's not what I meant. You just don't understand."

And she said, "Well no . . . I guess not."

He apologized for making her mad, which was exactly the
opposite, he said, of what he was intending to do. But the more he
apologized, the madder she got. The more he assured her that he
loved her even though she was crabby, cantankerous, strangled
and worried, hard, cynical and detached, mercenary, unsympathetic, callous, and sarcastic—the more he assured her that he
loved her in spite of her *self*—the madder she got. Until finally
she hung up on him and all day she was still mad, also feeling
guilty, sorry, sad, simple-minded, and defeated. She promised
herself that she would send the next letter back unopened, but of
course there was little real chance of that. She tried several times
that afternoon to compose a letter in answer to his repeated
requests for one. But she got no further than saying:

What it all comes down to is this: in the process of getting to
know you, I realized that you were not the right person for me.

It should have been simple.

In the next letter, two mornings later, Cliff turned around and blamed himself for everything, saying:

At least understand that all of this was only the result of my relentless devotion to you.

Lesley took a bath after breakfast and contemplated the incongruous conjunction of these two words.

Relentless.

Devotion.

After she'd dried her hair and cleaned the tub, she looked up *relentless* in the thesaurus. Much as she'd suspected, it was not an adjective that should be allowed to have much to do with love:

relentless, *adj*. unyielding, unrelenting, implacable, unsparing; inexorable, remorseless, unflagging, dogged; undeviating, unswerving, persistent, persevering, undaunted; rigid, stern, strict, harsh, grim, austere; merciless, ruthless, unmerciful, pitiless, unpitying, unforgiving; unmitigable, inflexible, unbending, resisting, grudging; hard, imperious, obdurate, adamant, intransigent; uncompassionate, unfeeling, unsympathetic, intolerant.

The next letter was delivered on a windy Saturday night when Lesley was out on a date with somebody else. It was sitting there in the mailbox when she got home at midnight. The weather had turned cold and her driveway was filling up suddenly with crispy yellow leaves. When she opened the back door, dozens of them swirled around her ankles and slipped inside. She imagined Cliff crunching through them on his way to the mailbox, worrying about the noise, which was amplified by the hour and the wind, then noticing that her car wasn't in the garage, and then worrying about that, too.

In this letter, Cliff said:

I love you like ten thousand freight trains.

Lesley thought she rather liked this one, but then she wasn't sure. She thought she'd better think about it. She hung up her coat, poured herself a glass of white wine, and sat down in the dark kitchen to think. The oval of her face reflected in the window was distorted by the glass, so that her skin was pale, her eyes were holes, and her cheeks were sunken. She did not feel pale, hollow, or sunken. She felt just fine.

I love you like ten thousand freight trains.

This was like saying:

I love you to little bits.

Who wants to be loved to *little bits*?

This was like saying:

I love you to death.

Who wants to be loved to *death*?

I love you like ten thousand freight trains.

Who wants to be loved like or by *a freight train*?

The more she thought about it, the more she realized that she knew a thing or two about trains; railroading; relentlessness.

DREAM TRAIN

As a young girl growing up in Winnipeg, Lesley lived in an Insul-brick bungalow three doors down from the train tracks, a spur line leading to Genstar Feeds. Trains travelled the spur line so seldom that when one passed in the night, it would usually wake her up with its switching and shunting, its steel wheels squealing on the frozen rails. She would lie awake listening in her little trundle bed (it wasn't really a trundle bed, it was just an ordinary twin bed, but every night at eight o'clock her mother, Amelia, would say, "Come on, little one, time to tuck you into your little trundle bed").

Lesley liked to imagine that the train outside was not a freight train but a *real* train, a passenger train: the Super Continental, carrying dignified wealthy people as carefully as if they were eggs clear across the country in its plush coaches, the conductors in their serious uniforms graciously bringing around drinks, pillows, and magazines. She imagined the silver coaches cruising slowly past, all lit up, the people inside riding backwards, eating, sleeping, playing cards with just their heads showing, laughing as if this were the most natural thing in the world. She imagined that the Super Continental could go all the way from Vancouver to St. John's (never mind the Gulf of St. Lawrence—there must be a way around it) without stopping once.

If the train on the spur line did not actually wake Lesley up, then it slid instead into her dreams, disguised as a shaggy behemoth with red eyes and silver hooves, shaking the snow from its curly brown fur as it pawed the rails and snorted steam.

TRAIN TRACKS

As a teenager, Lesley walked along the train tracks every morning to Glengarry Heights High School. On the way, she usually met up with a boy named Eric Henderson, who was two grades older and dressed all year round in faded blue jeans, a teeshirt, and a black leather jacket with studs. Occasionally he condescended to the cold weather by wearing a pair of black gloves.

After a couple of weeks, Eric took to waiting for Lesley on the tracks where they crossed her street. He would be leaning against the signal lights smoking when she came out her front door. They never walked home together at four o'clock because, even though Lesley sometimes loitered at her locker hoping, Eric was never around at that time, having, she assumed, other more interesting, more grown-up things to do after school.

Every morning Lesley and Eric practised balancing on the rails with their arms outstretched, and they complained about the way the tar-coated ties were never spaced quite right for walking on. Lesley kept her ears open, looking over her shoulder every few minutes, just in case. Her mother, Amelia, had often warned her, "Don't get too close to a moving train or you'll get *sucked under*."

Sometimes Eric would line up bright pennies on the silver rails so the train would come and flatten them. Lesley would watch for the pennies on her way home from school, would gather them up and save them, thin as tinfoil, in a cigar box she kept under the bed. She never put pennies on the tracks herself because she was secretly afraid that they would cause a derailment and the train would come toppling off the tracks, exploding as it rolled down the embankment, demolishing her house and her neighbours' houses and everything in them. It was okay though when Eric did it, because somehow he could be both dangerous and charmed at the same time.

Every morning Eric told Lesley about what he'd done the night before. Lesley was not expected to reciprocate, which was just as well, since all she ever did in the evening was homework and dishes and talk on the phone.

One Monday morning Eric said he'd gone to the Gardens on Saturday night to see the Ike and Tina Turner Revue. He said Tina Turner was the sexiest woman in the world and the way she sang was like making love to the microphone right there on stage. He said he thought he'd die just watching her, and all the other guys went crazy too.

On the phone every night after supper, Lesley told her new best friend, Audrey, every little thing Eric had said to her that morning, especially the way he'd said, "I like your new haircut a lot," and then the way he'd winked at her in the hall between History and French.

"Do you think he likes me?" she asked Audrey over and over again.

"Of course he likes you, silly! He *adores* you!"

This went on all fall, all winter, all spring, until the raging crush which Lesley had on Eric Henderson could be nothing, it seemed, but true true love.

The week before final exams, Eric asked Audrey to the last school dance.

Lesley spent the night of the dance barricaded in her bedroom, lying on the floor with the record player blasting Tina Turner at top volume. She propped a chair against the door and would not let her parents in. She was mad at them too: at her father, Edward, because he'd laughed and said, "You'll get over it, pumpkin!" and at her mother, Amelia, because she was old and married, probably happy, probably didn't even remember what love was *really* like, probably hadn't explained things properly in the first place, should have warned her about more than freight trains.

She would, Lesley promised herself savagely, spend the entire summer in her room, learning all the lyrics to Tina Turner's songs, and reading fat Russian novels which were all so satisfyingly melancholy, so clotted with complications and despair, and the characters had so many different, difficult names. Especially she would read *Anna Karenina* and memorize the signal passage where Anna decides to take her own life:

> . . . And all at once she thought of the man crushed by the train the day she had first met Vronsky, and she knew what she had to do . . . .
>
> " . . . And I will punish him and escape from everyone and from myself . . . ."
>
> . . . And exactly at the moment when the space between the wheels came opposite her, she dropped the red bag, and

drawing her head back into her shoulders, fell on her hands under the carriage, and lightly, as though she would rise again at once, dropped on to her knees . . . .

. . . She tried to get up, to drop backwards: but something huge and merciless struck her on the head and rolled her on her back . . . .

. . . And the light by which she had read the book filled with troubles, falsehoods, sorrow, and evil, flared up more brightly than ever before, lighted up for her all that had been in darkness, flickered, began to grow dim, and was quenched forever.

And she would probably carve Eric Henderson's initials into her thigh with a ballpoint pen, and she would probably not eat anything either, except maybe unsalted soda crackers, and she would not wash her hair more than once a week, and she would stay in her pyjamas all day long. Yes she would. She would *languish*. And for sure she would never ever ever ever fall in love or have a best friend ever again so long as she lived, so help her.

NIGHT TRAIN

When Lesley moved away from home at the age of twenty-one, she took the train because there was an air strike that summer. Her parents put her on the train in Winnipeg with a brown paper bag full of tuna sandwiches and chocolate chip cookies, with the three-piece luggage set they'd bought her as a going-away present, and a book of crossword puzzles to do on the way. They were all weeping lightly, the three of them: her parents, Lesley assumed, out of a simple sadness, and herself, out of an intoxicating combination of excitement and anticipation, of new-found freedom, and, with it, fear. She was, she felt, on the brink of everything important. She was moving west to Alberta, which was booming.

Seated across the aisle of Coach Number 3003 (a good omen,

Lesley thought, as she had long ago decided that three was her lucky number) was, by sheer coincidence, a young man named Arthur Hoop who'd given a lecture at the university in Winnipeg the night before. His topic was nuclear disarmament and Lesley had attended because peace was one of her most enduring interests.

After an hour or so, Lesley worked up enough courage to cross over to the empty seat beside him and say, "I really loved your lecture." Arthur Hoop seemed genuinely pleased and invited her to join him for lunch in the club car. Lesley stashed the brown-bag lunch under the seat in front of hers and followed Arthur, swaying and bobbing and grinning, down the whole length of the train.

Arthur Hoop, up close, was interesting, amiable, and affectionate, and his eyes were two different colours, the left one blue and the right one brown. Arthur was on his way back to Vancouver, where he lived with a woman named Laura who was sleeping with his best friend and he, Arthur, didn't know what he was going to do next. Whenever the train stopped at a station for more than five minutes, Arthur would get off and phone ahead to Vancouver, where Laura, on the other end, would either cry, yell, or hang up on him.

By the time the train pulled into Regina, Lesley and Arthur were holding hands, hugging, and having another beer in the club car, where the waiter said, "You two look so happy, you must be on your honeymoon!"

Lesley and Arthur giggled and giggled, and then, like fools or like children playing house, they shyly agreed. The next thing they knew, there was a red rose in a silver vase on their table and everyone in the car was buying them drinks and calling out, "Congratulations!" over the clicking of the train. Arthur kept hugging Lesley against him and winking, first with the brown eye, then with the blue.

They spent the dark hours back in Arthur's coach seat,

snuggling under a scratchy grey blanket, kissing and touching and curling around each other like cats. Lesley was so wrapped up in her fantasy of how Arthur would get off the train with her in Calgary or how she would stay on the train with him all the way to Vancouver, and how, either way, her real life was about to begin, that she hardly noticed how brazen they were being until Arthur actually put it in, shuddered, and clutched her to him.

Lesley wept when she got off the train in Calgary, and Arthur Hoop wept too, but he stayed on.

From her hotel room, Lesley wrote Arthur long sad letters and ordered up hamburgers and Chinese food from room service at odd hours of the day and night. On the fourth night, she called her mother collect in Winnipeg and cried into the phone because she felt afraid of everything and she wanted to come home. Her mother, wise Amelia, said, "Give it two weeks before you decide. You know we'll always take you back, pumpkin."

By the end of the two weeks, Lesley had a basement apartment in a small town called Ventura, just outside the city. She also had two job interviews, a kitten named Calypso, and a whole new outlook on life. She never did hear from Arthur Hoop and she wondered for a while what it was about trains, about men, the hypnotic rhythm of them, relentless, unremitting, and irresistible, the way they would go straight to your head, and when would she ever learn?

It wasn't long before she was laughing to herself over what Arthur must have told the other passengers when she left him flat like that, on their honeymoon no less.

TRAIN TICKET

All the way home to Winnipeg to spend Christmas with her parents, Lesley drank lukewarm coffee out of Styrofoam cups, ate expensive dried-out pressed-chicken sandwiches, and tried to get comfortable in her maroon-upholstered seat with her purse as a pillow or her parka as a blanket. She tried to read but could not concentrate for long, could not keep herself from staring out the window at the passing scenery, which was as distracting as a flickering television set at the far end of the room. All the way across Saskatchewan, the train seemed to be miraculously ploughing its way through one endless snowbank, throwing up walls of white on either side of the tracks.

She didn't feel like talking to anyone and closed her eyes whenever the handsome young man across the rocking aisle looked her way hopefully. She had just started dating a man named Bruce back in Ventura and she did not like leaving him for Christmas. But this was her first Christmas since she'd moved away from home and the trip back for the holidays had been planned months ago. Once set in motion, the trip, it seemed, like the train once she had boarded it, could not be deflected. She was travelling now with a sorrowful but self-righteous sense of daughterly obligation that carried her inexorably eastward. For a time she'd believed that moving away from her parents' home would turn her instantly into a free, adult woman. But of course she was wrong.

She kept reaching for her purse, checking for her ticket. She memorized the messages printed on the back of it, as if they were a poem or a prayer:

RESERVATIONS: The enclosed ticket is of value. If your plans are altered, the ticket must be returned with the receipt coupon intact, for refund or credit. If you do not make the trip, please cancel your reservations.

ALCOHOLIC BEVERAGES: Alcoholic beverages purchased on board must be consumed in the premises where served. Provincial liquor laws prohibit the consumption of personal liquor on trains except in the confines of a bedroom or roomette.

BAGGAGE: Personal effects consisting of wearing apparel, toilet articles, and similar effects for the passenger's use, comfort, and convenience (except liquids and breakables) are accepted as baggage. Explosive, combustible, corrosive, and inflammable materials are prohibited by law.

The train trip took sixteen hours. The inside of Lesley's mouth, after thirteen hundred kilometres, tasted like a toxic combination of diesel fuel and indoor-outdoor carpeting.

Her parents were there to meet her at the Winnipeg station, her father, Edward, smiling and smiling, his shy kiss landing somewhere near her left ear; her mother, Amelia, looking small in her big winter coat with a Christmas corsage of plastic mistletoe and tiny silver bells pinned to the lapel. The train pulled away effortlessly in a cloud of steam and snow.

FREIGHT TRAIN

They had a saying in Ventura—when Lesley was still living there with Bruce—a saying that was applied, with much laughter and lip-smacking, to people, usually women, who were less than attractive.

"She looks like she's been kissing freight trains," one of the boys in the bar would say, and the rest of them round the table would howl and nod and slap their knees. Lesley would laugh with them, even though she felt guilty for it, and sometimes, calling up within herself noble notions of sisterhood, sympathy, and such, she would sputter uselessly something in defence of the poor woman they were picking on.

But she would always laugh too in the end, because she knew she was pretty, she knew she was loved, she knew she was exempt from their disgust and the disfiguring, inexorable advent of trains.

RUNAWAY TRAIN

There was a story they told in Ventura—when Lesley was still living there with Bruce—about the time Old Jim Jacobs stole the train. It was back in the winter of 1972. Old Jim was a retired engineer who'd turned to drink in his later years. He sat in the Ventura Hotel day after day, night after night, ordering draft beer by the jug with two glasses, one for himself and one for his invisible friend. He would chat amiably for hours in an unintelligible language with the empty chair across from him, politely topping up the two glasses evenly and then drinking them both.

"At least he's never lonely," Bruce would always say.

On toward closing time, however, Old Jim, or his invisible friend, or both, would start to get a little surly, and soon Old Jim would be jumping and cursing (in English), flinging himself around in the smoke-blue air of the bar.

"I hate you! I hate you!" he would cry.

"Let's step outside and settle this like men!" he would roar, hitching up his baggy pants and boxing in the air.

"So what, then," Bruce would wonder, "is the point of having invisible friends, if you can't get along with them?"

Lesley knew Old Jim from when she worked in the grocery store and he'd be standing in the lineup in his old railway cap with a loaf of bread, a package of baloney, and some Kraft cheese slices. By the time he got to the cash register, he'd have made himself a sandwich and, wouldn't you know it, he must have left his wallet in his other pants—as if he even owned another pair of pants.

When he wasn't drinking or shopping, Old Jim was sitting in the long grass beside the CPR main line, counting boxcars, and waving at the engineers.

At the time of the great train robbery, he'd been bingeing, so they said, for eight days straight (this number could be adjusted, at the storyteller's discretion, up to as many as ten days but never down to less than six) in Hawkesville, a nearby town twelve miles west of Ventura. He'd been barred for two weeks from the Ventura Hotel for sleeping on the pool table, which explained why he was drinking in Hawkesville in the first place. So Old Jim was getting to be a little homesick after all that time away from his old stomping grounds, and on the Friday night he decided it was high time to get back, seeing as how his two weeks were up on Saturday. But he was flat broke after his binge, pension cheque long gone, no money for a cab, and it was too damn cold to hitchhike. So he decided to take the train.

So he hopped right in, so they said, to the first engine he found in the yard, fired her up, and off he went, hauling forty-seven empty boxcars behind him (this number too could be adjusted, interminably up, it seemed, because, after all, who was counting?). He made it back to Ventura without mishap, parked her up on the siding behind the Ventura Hotel so he'd be good and ready when they opened in the morning and he knew they'd give him credit for a day or two. He curled up in the caboose and went to sleep. Which was where the railway police and the RCMP found him when they surrounded the runaway train, guns drawn, sirens screaming, at 5:36 a.m. (the time of his legendary capture was unalterable, a part of the town's history which could not be tampered with).

"But what, then," Bruce would wonder whenever he heard the story again, "is the point of stealing a train, when you can never take it off the tracks, when you can only go back and forth, back and forth, back and forth, and you can never really get away?"

EXPRESS TRAIN

One summer Lesley and Bruce took the train up to Edmonton where his brother was getting married. Halfway there, they were stopped on a siding in the middle of nowhere, waiting for a freight train to pass. Bruce was getting impatient, sighing huge conspicuous sighs as he fidgeted and fussed in his seat, while Lesley beside him read on peacefully.

Spotting a white horse from the window, he said, "Sometimes simple things glimpsed in the distance can bring great comfort."

TRAIN TRIP EAST

All the way back to Winnipeg for her Uncle Mel's funeral, Lesley drank beer out of cans and wrote postcards to Bruce in Ventura. She bought the cards at various train stations along the way and then she mailed them at the next stop. She suspected that Bruce was on the brink of having an affair with a French-Canadian woman named Analise who was spending the summer in Ventura with her sister. All of this suspicion, sticky and time-consuming as it was, had left Lesley feeling sick and tired, a little bit crazy too. On the back of a green lake, she wrote:

I tried to take pictures from the train, of a tree and some water, some sky, but they wouldn't hold still long enough.

On the back of a red maple tree:

I saw a coyote running from the train, also white horses, brown cows, black birds, and a little girl in Maple Creek wearing a pink sunsuit with polka dots, running. All of them running away from the train.

Black city spotted with blue and white lights:

There was a station wagon stopped at a crossing. It was filled with suitcases, babies, and basketballs. For a minute, I wanted to scream: "Stop! Stop! There's a train coming! We'll all be killed!" Then I remembered that I was the train and I didn't have to stop for anything. Trains are so safe from the inside.

Yellow field of wheat:

What else is there to do on a train anymore but remember? I thought of a witchy woman who lived on the corner of Cross Street and Vine, in a wooden shack with pigeons on the roof and chickens in the porch. She watched me through the window when I walked by to Sunday school. The winter I was eight she got hit by a train. For a time I had nightmares . . .

Here she ran out of room on the card and finished up her message on the next one. Purple mountain:

. . . about arms and legs broken off like icicles, about a head rolling down a snowbank wearing a turquoise toque just like mine. Then I forgot all about her till now. I remember rocking my cousin, Gary, in his cradle, the way he couldn't hold his head up yet, and now he's the chef at a fancy French restaurant.

Sitting at her Aunt Helen's kitchen table in Winnipeg, surrounded by relatives, neighbours, warm casseroles, and frozen pound cakes, she wrote on the back of a sympathy card:

I've still got the sound of the train in my head. It makes it hard to think of anything but songs. Tomorrow.

WAR TRAIN

In Lesley's parents' photo album, there was a picture of her mother and her Aunt Helen seeing her father and her Uncle Mel off at the train station. The women were waving and blowing kisses from the platform, stylish in their broad-shouldered coats and little square hats with veils. The men were grinning and walking away, handsome in their sleek uniforms and jaunty caps. They were all very young then, and splendid. The silver train was waiting behind them, its windows filled with the faces of many other young men. They went away to the war and then some of them came back again.

After her Uncle Mel's funeral, Lesley's father told her about the time he'd ridden the train all across France with Mel's head in his lap, Mel nearly dying of ptomaine poisoning from a Christmas turkey, but he didn't.

TRAIN TRIP WEST

All the way back to Ventura after her Uncle Mel's funeral, Lesley slept fitfully or looked out the train window and thought about how everything looks different when you're passing through it in the opposite direction. On this return journey, she was riding backwards, facing where she'd come from, as if she had eyes in the back of her head.

The train whistled through the backsides of a hundred anonymous towns, past old hotels of pink or beige stucco, past slaughterhouses, gas stations, trailer parks, and warehouses. Children and old men waved. Dogs barked, soundless, powerless, strangling themselves straining at their chains. White sheets tangled on backyard clotheslines and red tractors idled at unmarked crossings.

Lesley never knew where she was exactly: there are no mileage signs beside the train tracks the way there are on the highway. There is no way of knowing how far from, how far to. No way, on train time, of locating yourself accurately inside the continuum. You just have to keep on moving, forward and forward and forward, or back, trusting that wherever you are heading is still out there somewhere.

HORSE AND TRAIN

One year for her birthday in Ventura (or could it have been
Christmas . . . could it have been that same year when Lesley
bought Bruce the guitar he'd been aching after, the Fender Stra-
tocaster, and when she couldn't take the suspense a minute
longer, she gave it to him on Christmas Eve instead of in the
morning, just to see the look on his face, and then they stayed up
all night playing music and singing, drinking eggnog till dawn . . .
when Bruce took the guitar to bed with him and Lesley took a
picture of him cuddling it under the puffy pink quilt her mother
had sent, and then she kept him awake even longer, telling her
theory that if men were the ones who had babies, then there
would be no more war . . . the best Christmas ever, it could have
been then), Bruce gave Lesley a framed reproduction of the Alex
Colville painting *Horse and Train.*

In the painting, a purple-black horse on the right is running
headlong down the tracks toward an oncoming train on the left.
The landscape around them is gravel and brown prairie grass.
The ears of the horse are flattened, its tail is extended, and the
white smoke from the black train is drifting across the brown
prairie sky at dusk.

Bruce hung the painting over the couch in the tiny living room
of their basement apartment and Lesley admired it every time
she walked into the room.

After Bruce left Lesley and moved to Montreal with Analise,
Lesley took the painting off the wall and smashed it on the
cement floor, so that she was vacuuming up glass for an hour
afterwards, weeping.

When Lesley moved back to Winnipeg a few months later and
rented the little stucco bungalow on Harris Street, she had the
painting reframed with new glass and hung it on her bedroom
wall. She liked to look at it before she went to sleep at night.

She looked at it when she was lying in bed with Cliff, who had his hands behind his head and the ashtray balanced on his bare chest, who was talking and smoking and talking, so happy to be spending the night. She looked at it as she tried to concentrate and follow Cliff's train of thought, but really she was thinking about how they'd been seeing each other for three months now and it wasn't working out.

But really she was thinking about an article she'd read in a women's magazine years ago, and the writer, a marriage counsellor, said that in every romantic relationship there was one person who loved less and one who loved more. The important question then, which a person must face, was: Which would you rather be: the one who loves less or the one who loves more?

When Lesley asked Cliff this question, she already knew what his answer would be.

Which would you rather be: the one who loves less or the one who loves more?

This was like saying:

Which would you rather be: the horse or the train?

It should have been simple.

The Look of the Lightning, The Sound of the Birds (1989)

You, who have lived your whole life believing
if you made enough plans
you wouldn't need to be afraid . . .

—Bronwen Wallace, "Into the Midst of It," in *Common Magic*

Fear is the general term for the anxiety and agitation felt at the presence of danger; **dread** refers to the fear or depression felt in anticipating something dangerous or disagreeable (to live in *dread* of poverty); **fright** applies to a sudden, shocking, usually momentary fear (the mouse gave her a *fright*); **alarm** implies the fright felt at the sudden realization of danger (he felt *alarm* at the sight of the pistol); **terror** applies to an overwhelming, often paralyzing fear (the *terror* of soldiers in combat); **panic** refers to a frantic, unreasoning fear, often one that spreads quickly and leads to irrational, aimless action (the cry of "fire!" created a *panic*).

—*Webster's New World Dictionary*

An excessive secretion of adrenalin arising out of fear eventually produces shock, a constriction of small arterioles in the body, lowered blood pressure, loss of blood fluid to the tissues, dehydration, increased heart beat, and ultimate death.

—Kimble and Garmezy, *Principles of General Psychology*

If a story is not to be about love, then I think it must be about fear.

I am meeting my friend Melody at Van's for lunch around noon. It's Friday and the relative humidity is 100 percent, so that upon waking, I find the sheets wadded in a damp ball at the foot of my bed. On the clock radio, the weatherman is cheerfully promising another unbearably hot day and then they play "Summertime." I groan and try to remember how snowflakes feel, falling on my face.

Melody and I made these arrangements earlier in the week on the telephone. I noted them in my appointment book and also on the calendar on the kitchen wall. I am fond of calendars and like to have one in every room. The one in the kitchen, under the clock, features, predictably, milk recipes. The one in the bathroom, over the white wicker clothes hamper, features classic cars in well-polished poses struck upon black asphalt, wet cobblestones, or circular driveways in front of cathedrals, wheat fields, or stately white mansions. The one in my bedroom, next to the vanity, features contemporary female artists, their paintings with names like *Cabbage in Bloom, Chernobyl and Navajo Medicine,* and *Apple Blossoms, 1987.*

Melody and I have lunch together at least once a month and we always meet at Van's on a Friday around noon. Melody, who is once again (or still) trying to lose that ten pounds she gained over the winter, will order the soup of the day and a small Caesar salad. I will have the chicken pasta and a side order of cheese and garlic bread. We will drink black coffee before, during, and after the meal.

When I have lunch with my other friends, we go to different places on different days. Ellen and I always go to the White Spot on a Wednesday. We both have the steak sandwich and a beer. Janie and I always go to the Burger King on a Saturday with our kids: my son, Andrew, and her twin daughters, Ashley and Kate.

All of our children are three. At the Burger King, I have a Whopper, a large order of fries with gravy, and a chocolate milkshake. Andrew only eats the onion rings.

What I mean is: I cannot imagine being at the Burger King on Saturday afternoon on Princess Street with Melody.

At one time, close to ten years ago now, Melody and I were roommates. We were best friends then. Now we are close, but no longer a conspiracy or a cartel.

At that time, Melody and I were both single and spent all of our evenings in bars. For three solid years we were drinking and partying like mad fiends. We were good-natured and resilient enough then to have hangovers which lasted for fifteen minutes at the most, rather than for two whole days the way they do now. We were going through a phase together: that was how I thought of it then. We were in disguise, playing at self-destruction. Or we had a new hobby. Or we had spring fever. We were generally pleased with ourselves, especially when we walked into our favourite tavern at The Belvedere Hotel and Billy, the bartender, would tease us, saying, "Here comes trouble!" We didn't even have to order, he knew what we wanted. He would let us write cheques if we got carried away and ran short of cash.

We sat around The Belvedere night after night, drinks and cigarettes in hand, talking about the time to come when we wouldn't be doing this anymore. The bar would be filling up around us: there was a country and western band on stage, people dancing by themselves, minor altercations around the pool table, somebody sending us another pitcher of beer, and, over the twanging guitars, we could talk glibly about the future because the end of the pointless present was always firmly in sight. We were just waiting to get tired of it. We were going through our mid-life crises early or our adolescent rebellions late.

We were never in real danger, or so we thought. There was

always a part of us that didn't enter into it, that didn't get drunk.
Much as I liked to drink, I always assumed that I would be sober
when the time came: sober when my real life began. And now
here we are.

Melody has no children. She does have a husband (his name is
Ted) whereas I don't: this, however, is not a reason for anything
and can hardly be construed as her fault. I did have one once, for
a little while, and now I have Andrew.

Sometimes along about midnight or later on a Friday or Saturday night, I catch myself longing for those irresponsible old days,
longing for a blast of loud brainless music, an elongated bloated
beer drunk, a party all night with Richard falling into the stereo
three times, Evelyn spilling a fish bowl full of strawberry
daiquiris into the piano, Donny dancing naked like he always did,
his underwear like a bunny hat on his head. Then breakfast in
the morning, the birds are already singing and we're all down at
Smitty's at six a.m. where they were tolerant, the waitress was
benign or blessed, the coffee pots were bottomless, and Melody,
yelping at the sunrise coming pink all over the sky, said, "Wow!
Wow! Wow! WOW!", and the construction workers ate bacon and
eggs in their yellow hard hats silently and Melody said, "Think of
it, just think of it, all of these guys have been home, been to bed,
been to sleep already and everything, and here we are!" I was
poking at Hugh, who was falling asleep with his dreadlocks resting against the plate-glass window as if he were riding cross-
country on a Greyhound in the rain.

I am no longer the woman who does these things. Perhaps I am
no longer the woman who did them. I have become the woman
who can always find, fix, or reach things.

This is from the hard-drinking days when new friendships
were frequent, instant, emotional, and brief. I have no idea what
became of those people who seemed so important, so bright, or
so clever at the time, those people that I bought beer for, whose

terrors and troubles I listened to, then decanted a few of my own, and sometimes the woman weeping by the window was me. They wouldn't know me if they knew me now. They are like the young dead, never changing, struck like statues back in time. I imagine them still drinking, still partying, in some other bar now, as if nothing ever happened, nothing ever changed. I think of them as witnesses, waiting and watching a woman who used to be me.

There were often near-strangers sleeping in our living room on Saturday morning: a man on the couch snoring, still wearing his jacket, his sunglasses, his pointy-toed shoes, or a woman fully clothed face down on the carpet with her right elbow resting in an ashtray and her long red hair spread around her like a peacock's tail.

The residue of the night before would be spread through the entire apartment: beer bottles, caps, and cans covering the kitchen table, dirty ashtrays, empty album covers, and somebody's socks strewn around the living room, a dirty handprint on the bathroom wall, and long black hairs in the sink.

Even then, as I cleaned up the butts and the bottles while Melody vacuumed, I knew better than to mention the other residue, the disquieting dread which clung to me all the next day, which had something to do with staying up so late, then crawling to my bed while the party continued downstairs, the stereo raging, the bass notes crashing, the conversation flapping drunkenly around the room, me not drunk enough to stay awake, but not sober enough to sleep either, or was it the other way around? The anxiety hummed through me all day, striking a honed high note upon hearing, for instance, the news that a small plane had crashed into a bookstore in Atlanta, Georgia, and everyone on board was killed, everyone in the store, too, those patient browsers swiftly incinerated while fondling crisp copies of *The Shining, The Velveteen Rabbit,* or *Six Memos for the*

Next Millennium. I was certain then, in my spike-edged angst, that I too was bound to suffer heartbreak, loneliness, and terror forever, bound to be the victim of a random, ridiculous death, someday, somehow, soon.

The only thing to do then, it seemed to Melody and me, was to head back down to the bar where, if you got there early enough and helped put out the ashtrays, they'd give you the first round free. In the morning, we drank Bloody Caesars, which we called "seizures," our stomachs queasy, our furry tongues stinging with black pepper and Tabasco sauce, my spirits lifting by increments until by noon it appeared that another day might actually be passed without panic or punishment. I was once again cushioned by that false sense of security, that expansive illusion of well-being you get on your third drink and then you have ten more trying to recapture the feeling and end up wondering why you're crying in your beer at three a.m.

It was there, at The Belvedere, that I met Andrew's father, who appeared to be a brown-eyed handsome man, gentle, polite, olive-skinned in a pink striped shirt. He was only unusual in the sense that he was nothing like the men I usually went for: the scruffy disreputable ones, unemployed, with a propensity for alcohol in large quantities. It was also there that Melody met Ted, who, unlike most men you meet in bars, turned out to be exactly what he seemed to be: kind, generous, and sane. The Belvedere is closed down now, bankrupt, scheduled for demolition in the fall.

That was a long time ago and now I understand about the comfort to be found in fear, also the power. Sometimes now I think it is the fear that keeps me safe; sometimes now I think the fear is *all* that keeps me safe. When I am scared of everything, the fear becomes a gauze bandage around me and I am convinced that if I stop being afraid, if I let my guard down for just one minute, all hell will break loose and fly apart in my face like a shattered windshield. On airplanes, I am so scared that I think if I relax and let myself enjoy the flight, the movie, the drinks, the conversation of the interesting woman beside me, we will crash for sure. It is my fear alone that keeps us airborne. All the other passengers can do whatever they damn well please: they have no responsibility and so no power. I realize there is a pumped-up kind of vanity in this, a perverse delusion of grandeur in the belief that I could single-handedly avert disaster and save these smug, stupid strangers, not to mention myself.

The power of fear lies in its conceit or the conceit of fear lies in its presumption of power.

Even as a child, I never thought that terrible tragedies could only happen to other people. I never acquired or accomplished this particular form of delusory armour with which most people gird themselves. I was a nervous child. I was quite confident that disasters could only happen, naturally enough, to me. Maybe it was selfish to be so afraid, but at a very young age I had stopped believing in protection, no longer expected to become safe, grown-up, or immortal. There were too many things to worry about: car accidents, plane crashes, kidnapping, fire, explosions, cancer, burglars, guns, knives, the bomb. The other girls at my school in their pastel angora sweaters and their A-line skirts, they didn't worry, I was sure of it. They didn't worry their pretty little heads about anything except their hair.

My flagrant fear, I figured, must single me out as the conspicuous choice for a catastrophe. The persistence of my fear was like a song stuck in your head first thing in the morning and it won't go away all day.

I did not tell this to anyone, knowing instinctively that fear was something to be ashamed of.

I was not afraid of monsters or magic: it was, I had decided early on, only people and thunderstorms that were seriously dangerous. One night at supper my mother was telling, with great amusement, the story of how her boss at the bank, Mr. E. Ingram, was on the toilet Tuesday night reading *Reader's Digest* in a thunderstorm when the lightning came in through the window and danced all around the sink while he just sat there, what else could he do? It was attracted by the water, my mother said.

This was the same summer that lightning struck the chimney of the Hatleys' house across the back lane and their television exploded. When the fire trucks arrived, Mrs. Hatley was standing in our backyard with the heads of her three children buried in her white nightgown, all of them crying. Water and chimneys, my mother said, electricity, lightning conductors.

After supper, she and my father went out (a rare occurrence in itself and I can't think now where they might have gone) and I was left in charge of cleaning up. The minute they left the house, another storm blew in and the thunder began. I roamed through the rooms of our suddenly flimsy frame house, unplugging the electrical appliances, and avoiding the windows. I imagined my face flung down into the hot soapy dishwater when the lightning came out of the ceiling and struck the sink straight through the back of my head. I sat at the kitchen table with my eyes closed for an hour, praying.

When my parents came home and found the dishes not done, my mother slapped me across the face because I was too big to spank. The humiliation of fear was inexcusable.

In my bed that night, I could not sleep and I lay there contemplating my dolls, which were hung by their necks from a pegboard on the far wall, me being too old to play with them anymore but not ready yet to give them away. Their plastic eyes in the half-light were like those of an animal caught in the headlights of a car on the highway. Their boneless legs were still pink but useless. I could hear my father snoring wisely in the next room but could no longer convince myself that he would be, at any given moment, braver than me. He was afraid of snakes and Ferris wheels: this was not comforting at all.

I used to know a woman who was afraid of moths, the powdery-winged white ones my mother called "dusty millers," and this woman had nightmares in which the moths flew up her nose and suffocated her with their twitching trembling wings.

Andrew's father was afraid of horses and pigs, although he lied to me about this (he lied to me about many things, most of them equally irrelevant) and said he loved animals of all kinds, especially horses with their handsome legs and pigs with their pink snuffling snouts.

In order to understand, it is not necessary to know that I am afraid of snowmobiles, needles, caterpillars (especially the furry black and yellow ones), down escalators, short blonde men with beards, and other people's mothers. (And—not many people know this about me—I am also afraid of libraries.) It is only necessary to know that I am more afraid of pain than of death and sometimes this seems sensible.

Melody says she is not afraid of anything and I believe her. Melody does not think about things the way I do, which is probably why we were best friends then and are still close now. She is unsuspecting, unquestioning, and her conscience is clear. She has not heard that the unexamined life is not worth living and she thinks the aphorism, *There is nothing to fear but fear itself,* is actually true. Her clarity is contagious, and when I am with her, I too feel weightless.

While I have black coffee for breakfast and read last night's paper, Andrew is once again refusing to eat the meal I've made for him (oat bran, raisins, yogurt, cantaloupe, healthy, healthy, healthy: he'd rather have red licorice and a hot dog).

The newspaper headlines this morning are still about the pair of human legs discovered last week in a green garbage bag on the highway west of town. The severed legs were discovered at seven a.m. Thursday by a man on his way to work who saw a foot lying in the middle of the road. Despite the fact that the limbs had been badly mutilated by predators, it has now been determined that they belonged to a twenty-five-year-old local woman named Donna Dafoe who had been missing for a week. They are looking for her estranged husband, Stuart Steven Dafoe, and for other body parts. The sergeant on the case has commented that it's like putting together a jigsaw puzzle.

Almost everyone I know is disturbed by this story in one way or another. It undermines the imagination. On the street, in the grocery store, the drugstore, the bank, everywhere I go all week, I overhear strangers discussing it. Their voices are soft, frightened, or outraged. They are all shaking their heads.

Two nights ago my boyfriend, Joe, came over after Andrew had gone to bed. We played three games of Scrabble and then we were watching the news and I said, "It's so sick," and Joe said, "Everybody's sick."

"Well, yes, probably," I said, "but not like that."

Joe said, "Yes, you're right."

But am I?

Right after the news, we got ready for bed and, while Joe was brushing his teeth, I put pot lids over all the ashtrays like I do every night.

Curled into his back in the bed, I said, "I smell something burning. Do you smell something burning?"

"You always think you smell something burning," he said, but not unkindly.

"I can't help it, I'm afraid of fire."

"I don't smell anything," he said. "There's nothing burning but your imagination."

"When I was a child, I always thought I could smell the gas," I started to say, but Joe was making that deflating endearing little sigh he always makes just as he's falling asleep, so I wrapped my arms and legs around him and hung on.

Now, as I get up for more coffee, Andrew dumps his breakfast on the floor. Feeling too defeated for the moment to be angry, I say, "You hurt my feelings when you do that," and he says, "Do you have feelings, Mommy?"

In the bathroom, putting on my makeup and trying to tame my hair which has gone completely out of control in this humidity, I see by my face there is no way of knowing. The black eye is long gone and the broken finger on my left hand, the one that had to be mended with a metal pin, only hurts now when I knit or the weather in winter turns damp. There is no way of knowing that, in what I think of as my former life, I was once thrown to the floor by a man I loved, and while he kicked me in the head, I made a sound like a small animal with soft brown fur and beady eyes.

By the time I've located a clean pair of pantyhose without a run and Andrew has spilled his milk twice, we are both bitchy in the heat and I am yelling indiscriminately about the toys scattered everywhere and I keep tripping over them, about the cracker crumbs all over the floor and they are sticking to the bottoms of my bare feet, about his fear of flying insects which I think is foolish because he screams his head off every time we go out to work in the garden and I'm afraid of bumblebees but I haven't let it ruin my life and now there's no more milk.

Andrew says seriously, "I'm a person too you know."

I take him on my lap in the sticky morning and his hair smells like sleepy trees. His damp eyelashes on my naked neck flutter like butterfly wings or a baby bird scooped off the sidewalk, fallen out of its nest, and you hold it in your palm like a heart and you know it will die no matter what you do.

I want him so much that I weep.

I take him to daycare and then drive downtown. Going along Johnson Street, I see a pretty red-haired woman in a black jacket and grey pants coming out of the funeral home smiling as she steps around the hearse which is running. Her immunity is evident, even from across the street.

I get to work on time as usual. I am co-owner of an arts and crafts store called Hobby Heaven. We sell paint-by-number kits, model airplanes and cars, embroidery hoops, and the like. There is a large market for this sort of thing these days and the business is flourishing.

This morning I am unpacking three cartons of rug-hooking kits. As I stock the shelves, I hear a female voice behind me saying, "And then he pulled a gun on me." A second female voice sighs.

Looking around as discreetly as I can manage, I see two elderly women with carefully curled hair wearing polyester dresses, one beige and one navy blue, with matching square plastic purses hooked over their arms as they riffle through racks of knitting patterns for baby clothes. The woman in the beige dress has in her shopping basket several balls of baby-blue wool and a pair of size twelve needles. As I turn back to my rug-hooking kits, she is telling the woman in the navy dress about her new grandchild, her sixth, a boy who was breech, nine pounds, nine ounces, and they named him Hamish, of all things.

The morning passes slowly.

As usual, I am the first to arrive at the restaurant. Melody, who is a medical secretary, has the day off and so is coming from the other side of town where she and Ted have recently rented a two-bedroom apartment in a building on Driscoll Street. It is the kind of squat flat-topped yellow-brick building with black iron balconies deemed modern by builders in the fifties. But Melody has a flair for decorating and so, inside, their apartment is strikingly cluttered with coloured cushions, wicker baskets, and fresh-cut flowers.

Eighteen months ago, a woman was murdered in that apartment. This is not the sort of thing that would bother Melody, but every time I go over there, I think I can see faint brownish stains on the carpet in the hallway leading to the bathroom. This is where, according to the newspaper reports, the murder took place, the woman stabbed twenty-seven times by her husband while her two children slept. The police took the children out past the body with blankets over their heads. The woman's name was Janice Labelle. Why do I remember her age, the date, the number of wounds? Why did I cut the articles out of the newspaper and save them in a big brown envelope? I didn't even know her.

I imagine Melody and Ted living out their lives in that apartment, cooking meals, reading magazines, listening to music, making love, taking a bath, and they would never notice how even the fresh-cut flowers smell sinister sometimes.

Van's is always busy on Friday but I have arrived early enough to get a table by the window overlooking Lewis Avenue. The restaurant, with its white furniture, pale green walls, and the air conditioning on full-blast, is an oasis. I order a coffee, with lemonade on the side. It is fresh-squeezed and comes with a pink umbrella in a frosted glass.

I've brought along some new product information pamphlets to read while I wait for Melody, who would be late even if she lived next door—I am both irritated by and envious of this because it seems to me to embody a carefree attitude which I know I will never be able to muster.

I pretend to be reading while I watch the people going in and out of the building across the street, a high-rise with copper-tinted windows which houses the offices of various insurance companies, lawyers, travel agents, and architects. Most of these people are women, stylishly dressed in pastel summer suits and white sandals. They come out of the building in confident clumps, chatting and smiling, making their lunch-time plans. Even from across the street, I can see how clear-eyed and fresh-faced they are—there is no way of knowing anything else about them.

The people at the next table, two women and a man, are talking about the severed legs. The one woman, it seems, the one wearing the diamond jewellery, knows someone who knows someone who knew the Dafoes when they were still married. There were signs, she is saying, there were signs all along. Someone turns the music up and I cannot hear her clearly anymore. She is saying something about jealousy, alcohol, arguments, death threats, jail. The other woman and the man are nodding seriously, satisfied somehow, ordering another coffee, another glass of wine. Is this how it is done then—sorting through the past to find premonitions, portents, and signs, until you have convinced yourself that you knew what was going to happen all along, until you can say, *I knew it, I just knew it*. But then of course you didn't really know it, couldn't, were too far away, too busy, too tired, asleep.

I feel the fear come winding around me again. Maybe there *were* signs, maybe I just wasn't paying attention at the time, maybe there were signs all along and I missed them.

Melody arrives at 12:17 p.m. and does not apologize. She has brought me a bouquet of daisies. The waitress brings us a big glass of water to put them in.

Melody orders the soup of the day, which is cucumber with yogurt, and a small Caesar salad. I order the chicken pasta with cheese and garlic bread.

I am feeling jumpy, but try to match my mood to hers. We talk about her husband, Ted, and his promotion at the lumberyard. We talk about my boyfriend, Joe, and how good he is with Andrew. We talk about the new words Andrew is learning and how he is almost tall enough now to pee standing up.

I try to remember Melody drinking beer at The Belvedere, dancing and flirting with strangers, one time climbing up on a table to sing the national anthem just for fun. But it does not seem possible that she ever did those things. She is attended now by a blissful aura of amnesia which renders the past innocuous and the future bright.

When the food arrives, we fall silent except for occasional sighs and murmurs of appreciation. The people at the next table are leaving now, laughing and flashing their charge cards around in the cheerful argument over who will pay the bill this week.

After the coffee arrives, I try to talk to Melody about the severed legs. She's not sure at first what I mean. I tell her the whole story as far as I know it, including what the woman with the diamonds said about signs, there were signs all along.

Melody says, "Don't think about it. You just can't think about things like that."

I want to say, *How can you not, how can I stop*? But she has already launched into the story of a woman named Martha, a patient at the clinic where she works. Martha is a young woman, pregnant with her first child and also dying of cancer. She does not cry. She goes out and buys baby clothes, a crib, a teddy bear named Tex. She is knitting a yellow baby blanket and a green sweater set, which she works on in the waiting room until her turn comes. There is no way of knowing if she will live long enough to deliver, but, to look at her, there is no way of knowing that she is dying either. She does not cry but sometimes, as she's leaving the office after her weekly examination, she grins and shakes her fist at the sky.

Saying goodbye in the parking lot, Melody and I make plans to

get together next weekend. Joe and I will go over to their apartment for a game of Scrabble and a pizza. Then she hugs me and
brushes her soft cheek against mine and I too am weightless
again.

The afternoon passes quickly and I am friendly to all the
customers, even the ones who will not look me in the eye.

After work I pick Andrew up at daycare. He has had a pretty good
day, having only had to stand in the corner once, for calling one of
the other kids "shithead," one of his new words.

We are both in good spirits and, as I wind through the rush-
hour traffic along Montreal Street, I am humming "Summertime"
and Andrew too is singing in fits and starts: "Old MacDonald had
a farm," or his own version, "Old MacDonald had a hamburger."
We are pointing out the passing sights to each other: "truck,"
"bus," "dog," "smoke." I tell him that tomorrow we are going to
meet Janie and the twins at Burger King. I imagine that he too
likes to have something to look forward to.

We idle briefly at the red light at Railway Street and the man in
the silver BMW in front of us is talking on his car phone, waving
his hands, and picking his nose as if he were invisible. He's not
paying attention when the light turns green and all the horns
behind me start to honk.

A flock of fat glossy pigeons flies up from the roof of a yellow-
brick apartment building. Through my open car window, the
sound of their wings is like sheets on a clothesline, drying in the
wind.

Andrew, excited, cries, "Birds, birds, birds!", reaching his arms
up as if to catch them.

I drive around a running shoe lying like a dead animal in the
middle of the intersection and I think about those severed legs
and pray that Andrew will never be hurt or unhappy. There is no
way of knowing, there is nothing I can do. For the first time I fully

understand that having given birth to him guarantees nothing, gives me no power, no shelter, no peace save that to be found in the sound of the birds.

If a story is not to be about love or fear, then I think it must be about anger.

Mastering Effective English (A Linguistic Fable)

(1989)

You tell me to close my mouth when we kiss. Think "man" in English, you say. In your language, it starts with the lips together and opens slowly the way love should begin.

—Linda Rogers, "Devouring"

Words describe features of the world judged stable. Something that appears to be a slice of cheese for a split part of a second, the tone of a violin for the next, then a prairie dog, a painting, a toothache, then the smell of garlic could not be given a name.

—J. T. Fraser, *Time, The Familiar Stranger*

A. PRONOUNS

1. She

The woman is named Naomi Smith, after her mother, her mother's mother, her great-aunt, her third cousin twice-removed, and so on. In fact, there are so many Naomis in her family that, in order to keep track of themselves, they call each other things like Big Naomi, Little Naomi, Old Naomi, New Naomi, Naomi the Pianist, Naomi the Nurse, Naomi the Mani-curist, and so on. This Naomi is Naomi the Teacher. She is young and strong, intelligent and honest, but she has never been very attractive to men. She has puzzled over this repeatedly. It must be her mouth, she thinks sometimes, which is too big and always open so that her silver fillings show. Or it could be her eyes, which are too small, too close together, and colourless, like the white eyes of those dogs which give many people the creeps. Either way, she is still a virgin. She suspects that's what the other Naomis call her behind her back, some saying it with pride, others with pity: "Here she comes, Naomi the Virgin!" Privately, she thinks of herself as Naomi the Anachronism.

She teaches Grade Ten English at an inner city high school with concrete-block walls and a barbed wire fence around it. Every September she faces a new room full of thirty potential juvenile delinquents and warns them about the dangers of dangling participles, split infinitives, and the unforgivable incorrect usage of those tricky little words *which, that,* and *who.* Even while she asks the class to write two pages, double-spaced, one side, on one of the following topics: butterflies, nuclear war, submarines, the etymology of the word *word,* or "How I Spent My Summer Holidays," she is wondering why nobody ever falls madly in love with her.

At the age of thirty-two, she has had a sum total of two boyfriends. Neither of these romances was officially consummated. (When thinking along these lines, Naomi often mixes up the words *consummated* and *conjugated,* and then she discovers that they really do amount to essentially the same thing.)

First there was Hector Addison, who was temporary head of her department for six months in 1983 when the regular head was away on maternity leave. The trouble with Hector, it turned out, was that he was just no fun. What attracted Hector to Naomi in the first place (her free spirit, he said, her liveliness, her sense of humour, her penchant for wild dancing and imported beer) was exactly what he tried to knock out of her in the end. She should not dress so casually, he said. She should not be so friendly. She should not drink, talk, or laugh so much. She should not listen to that rock and roll music anymore because it was puerile and would probably damage her morals, not to mention her eardrums. He was always correcting her grammar, the more so when she said "Youse guys" on purpose just to annoy him. Hector was, Naomi decided, too smart for his own good.

And so her second boyfriend, two years later, was Billy Lyons, a dump truck driver she met in the laundromat. The trouble with Billy, it turned out, was that he was just not serious enough. And what attracted Billy to Naomi in the first place (her brains, he said, her education, her good job, her informed opinions on everything) was exactly what he tried to knock out of her in the end. She read too much, he said. She didn't know how to *live,* really *live.* She shouldn't think so much. She should just *lighten up.* Naomi was always correcting his colourful speech, especially when he said, "Right on, fuckin' A!" Naomi was, Billy decided, too damn smart for her own damn good.

Modern men, Naomi decided then and there, were a bunch of malcontents. They wanted too much or too little, or they wanted somebody else altogether. They thought women were like empty rooms, just waiting to be redecorated. The wonderful women they had in their heads had little or nothing to do with the ones they took to their beds. It was hardly her fault that all she wanted, all she really wanted, was to be *adored,* to be *swept away* by a man who thought she was perfect. She decided she was tired of being disappointed. She would rather be a cynic. She would rather give up on men than give in. And they would all be sorry in the end.

Now, every summer, once school is out, Naomi takes herself on an expensive vacation. She goes for a month or six weeks to somewhere warm and exotic, tropical, preferably an island. She has already worked her way through the more popular tourist attractions: Hawaii, Barbados, Majorca, Jamaica, and the Virgin Islands (she's always had a good sense of humour, even in reference to herself, and is especially fond of irony). She now favours more remote destinations: tiny primitive islands which are difficult to get to, where the natives resemble those bare-breasted women and loin-clothed men frequently featured in *National Geographic*. These islands are the well-kept secrets of a certain travel agent who specializes in, as he puts it, offbeat vacations for unusual people and vice versa. Naomi likes to think of these islands as uncharted and unnamed, although she knows this is no longer possible in our shrinking world. But still, she finds comfort in putting herself in a place where no one would ever think to look for her, where no one will ever find her.

2. He

The man is named Iquito Hermes Honda Plato Mariscal Estigar-ribia. "Iquito," he says to everyone, "you can call me Iquito." But the truth is that he calls himself by different names on different days, depending on the weather, a whim, or a voice in a dream. On the day he met Naomi, he was thinking of himself as "Honda," but said, automatically, "Iquito, you can call me Iquito." So she does, and sometimes he doesn't know who she's talking about.

Iquito has lived on this small island for his entire life, fishing mostly, and sleeping in the sun. He is, in English years, almost seventeen, but the island calculations for such quantitative defi-nitions are complicated, akin to figuring a dog's real age by multi-plying its people-years times seven or to converting Celsius to Fahrenheit by doubling and adding thirty-two. Chronological age, to the islanders, is either an approximation or a popular misconception.

Iquito works as a courier, delivering the island mail which arrives by boat every other Monday. His brown feet are muscular and sinewy from all the running around he must do. As part of his training for the courier job, Iquito has been to the missionary school to learn how to read, write, and speak English. When he delivers a letter, he reads it aloud to the recipient, who then dictates the response, which Iquito skillfully translates and transcribes and then carries back to the boat. Like most colonials, Iquito speaks English with a stilted precision, better than Naomi speaks it herself, so that he sounds thoughtful and genteel at all times, even when he is telling jokes or talking dirty. Iquito knows everything about everyone on the island and they all depend on him, with collective good faith and great respect. The grateful islanders reward him regularly with food, liquor, sex, and more secrets. On this island anyway, no one would dream of shooting the messenger.

The day he met Naomi, Iquito had just returned from a run to the eastern side of the island. He was feeling loose-limbed and nimble after all that exercise, and he was pumped up with pride, having just delivered and deciphered a complex letter from a lawyer on the mainland to a woman who was about to inherit a small fortune from a distant uncle she'd never heard of. The letter was dense with words and phrases like *forthwith, hereto, whereof,* and *the party of the first part.* The woman was so pleased with the good news (once Iquito had figured out that it was indeed good news) that she rewarded him with a bottle of homemade wine and a blow job.

Naomi, who had arrived on the island just three days before, was lying on the beach, her bare stomach flat on the hot white sand, her bathing suit top unhooked so she wouldn't end up with tan-lines across her back. She was half asleep, listening to the water lapping at the sand like a tongue. Iquito squatted down beside her and kissed the small of her back, where the sweat was gathering in a salty pool. Startled, she rolled over quickly and her bathing suit top fell right off so that she lay there bare-breasted and blinking her little white eyes at him. "Iquito," he said, "you can call me Iquito."

In the language of love, as Naomi had learned it from her high school students, Iquito was "hot stuff." Much to her own surprise, she realized that she wanted nothing more or less than to lie him down and fuck his brains out for a whole week straight.

3. They

Naomi and Iquito have now known each other for three weeks and five days. They have been married for six and a half hours. For their honeymoon, they have travelled on horseback to the northern end of the island where there is a luxury hotel with one hundred air-conditioned rooms, two heated swimming pools in the shape of kidneys, and a restaurant specializing in French cuisine. It rises out of the humid green jungle like an oasis or a mirage, its copper-coated windows reflecting circling seagulls and clouds banked up in thunderheads to the west. Iquito and Naomi are the only visible guests. A uniformed valet leads the thirsty horse away and ties him up out back.

Iquito takes the unlikely presence of such a structure in such a place totally for granted. He cannot tell Naomi when it was built or why or by whom. He lives in a world of such perpetual wonderment that nothing surprises him. He never has got a grip on words like *incredible, incongruous,* or *imagine.*

4. I

"I can hear what you're saying," Naomi says, "but I don't know what you mean." She is not exactly complaining.

5. You

"You must listen," Iquito says in his elegant English, "to the water instead of the words."

Naomi still doesn't know exactly what he means, but she's willing to give it a try. She figures it should be simple enough, something like listening to the ocean inside a seashell. She has to admit she's been getting a little fed up with words lately anyway, having spent her whole life (or so it seems in retrospect) surrounded by them, struggling with them, up to her ears in syllables and syntax. (Iquito, she has observed, has unusual ears, which remind her of gills. Maybe he is from the lost continent of Atlantis, washed up here by accident, waiting.)

She has suspected all along that there is a trick to words that she hasn't figured out yet: if you can just find the right ones and then string them together in the right order, it will all make sense. But there are so many of them, arbitrary and constantly shifting like sand beneath her feet. Sometimes she is overwhelmed by the sheer number of words in the world, by the sheer number of people flinging them around so freely, so certain that their words can mean something, *do* something, *change* something: so that silence is no longer significant or socially acceptable.

6. It

It is a question of mind over matter.

B. NOUNS

1. Water

After a pretentious but delicious supper in the French restaurant, Naomi and Iquito take a stroll along the shoreline. They drag their bare feet through the wet sand and let the warm water wash them clean again. Naomi has never learned how to swim because she is afraid of the water. For somebody who spends so much time on islands, she realizes this is slightly ridiculous but she can't help herself. Mostly she is afraid to get her face wet. She is afraid of the way when you open your eyes underwater, everything around you is colourless, including the other swimmers, who look then like corpses, their stringy hair like seaweed, their arms and legs like driftwood. When they open their mouths, they look like bloated fish and only bubbles come out.

Iquito, who cannot imagine a world without water all around it, wades out deeper and deeper, until he is swimming parallel to Naomi who is still walking in the sand. She thinks of the time when she was twelve and her best friend, Lucy, nearly drowned. Lucy couldn't swim either, Lucy couldn't even float, and when she tried it, she sank silently out of sight into the water so deep it looked black. Naomi, who was perched on a rock on the shore, could do nothing but watch as the other girls, screaming and crying, dragged Lucy out by her hair and then pounded on her until the water and the mucus streamed like fish guts out of her mouth and her nose. Afterwards, they went back to the cottage where their unsuspecting parents were and they sat outside in the lawn chairs eating a whole watermelon, smearing the juice and the seeds all over each other, laughing hysterically, and flirting outrageously with Lucy's older brother and his friends, until finally somebody's mother turned the hose on them to calm them down and clean them off.

If Iquito drowns now, Naomi thinks, she will be a widow in her widow's weeds. She is not exactly sure what this phrase is supposed to mean but she imagines herself on this beach with green-black strings of seaweed draped over her face and bare shoulders like a veil, while the water-logged body of her new husband is plucked by the fishermen out of the sea.

If she was going to get wet at all, she would rather be in one of the kidney-shaped pools back at the hotel, where there is a lifeguard and blue water wings. But swimming in a heated pool while in sight of the actual ocean strikes even her as an absurd thing to do, so she doesn't suggest it. She lets Iquito coax her out to him bit by bit until suddenly she is in past her waist. She is proud of herself for not panicking. Iquito swims slowly away just beneath the surface. When Naomi isn't looking, he circles back and grabs her from behind. He holds her head under the water with both hands.

She has always been afraid that once her head was under, the water would rush in through her ears and her nostrils, filling up her whole head, which would then either burst or stay like that, leaving her with water on the brain like her cousin who was born that way.

She remains absolutely still and nothing happens. Iquito lets go and she stays under for a few more seconds of her own free will. Her lungs are beginning to ache as she opens her eyes and there to the left is a car, a white car with the trunk, the hood, and all the windows open. A golden fish with large blue fins swims through it, undulating and unconcerned. Its gills seem to throb and its iridescent scales flicker through the milky sea like laughter or tiny hands in motion.

If the Eskimos have twenty different words for snow (and everybody says they do, although nobody seems to know what they are), the islanders have at least that many for water. So that a glass of water, a body of water, and water under the bridge have virtually nothing to do with each other. There is even a different word for water when you are in it as opposed to water when you are only looking at it, thinking about it, or wishing for it. Naomi is coming to understand that this dislocation makes more sense than a lot of other things. Iquito has never had any reason to think otherwise.

2. Angel

Back on the beach, Naomi lies down to dry off in the sinking sunlight. Her white cotton shirt and shorts stick to her skin like warm plastic. Iquito squats by her head and braids her long blonde hair which is stringy and gritty with sand.

She stretches out her arms and legs, moves them slowly back and forth, making an angel in the fine white sand. Iquito finds this hilarious and lies down beside her and makes one too. She tells him how the children in her country do this in the winter in the snow, how she used to do it too, in her red snowsuit with the bunny ears, flat on her back in the front yard at five o'clock on a January Saturday afternoon when it was already dark and the houses of her friends up and down the street were already receding into the night which was pressing down on her face like a pillow. She tells him how the tricky part is getting up again and jumping out of your angel without messing it up or leaving a trail of footprints which will give you away.

Iquito does it again and again all around her, until he can do it perfectly and there are sandy angels everywhere. He heard about angels at missionary school, but he thought they had to be ethereal, airborne, and self-righteous. They were also chubby, and probably irritating, hanging around, as they did, at all the wrong times. He decided then and there that angels weren't for him. But he likes these ones better.

He has also heard about snow but has never been able to get it clear in his mind. He would like more information.

"What does it taste like?" he asks Naomi.

"Water," she says, which is not quite true.

"What does it smell like?" he asks.

"Nothing," she says, which is not true either. Snow smells like snow. There is no way around it.

They jump out of their angels and walk slowly on.

Iquito is no angel. He is an innocent, Naomi thinks, a reckless and remorseless innocent, who has no sense of sin and so no sense of the guilt which animates the remains of the real world.

3. Monkey

As they walk beneath the smooth-faced cliffs, they meet a man with a monkey named Atimbo. The man is also named Atimbo. Both the man and the monkey are wizened, with leathery brown skin and no eyelashes.

"What a nice monkey," Naomi says politely.

"She is not just any monkey," the old man informs them proudly. "She is a talking monkey."

Iquito is very rude to the monkey, turns his face away and will not look the animal in the eye. The monkey snorts and spits at him. Iquito spits back at her. The old man doesn't seem to mind. "Say hello to the nice white lady," he tells the monkey, who makes a series of quick graceful motions with her black fingers, as if she were a magician about to pull a dove out of a handkerchief. She is talking with her hands. The old man rewards her with a kiss on the lips and a chocolate.

Iquito says to Naomi, "You're not white, you're pink."

The monkey squats square in front of him and makes the signs again, with a slight variation this time, poking herself in the chest with her right index finger. "I am nice white lady," the old man translates, laughing. "She is one funny monkey," he says.

"You're not white, you're brown," Iquito says scornfully.

"So are you," the monkey signs back.

Iquito stomps away. (Stomping away in bare feet, Naomi notes, is much less effective than stomping away in stiletto high heels or hiking boots.)

Iquito hates monkeys. He is convinced that they are really just funny-looking people who are only pretending they can't talk. He says they are evil incarnate. He swears by the story that his older sister, Komatsu, was kidnapped by a big black monkey who had stalked her for weeks and then this monkey forced her to live with him in a banana tree and bear his little black monkey babies. He swears by the story that, when these monkey babies grew up, they formed a gang and killed his sister and then they ate her all up.

Naomi thinks this sounds like a story straight out of the weekly tabloids back home: WOMAN GIVES BIRTH TO MONKEYS or MONKEYS EAT THE HANDS THAT FEED THEM. But she

manages to be serious and reassuring for Iquito's sake. She tells
him that in her country all the monkeys live in zoos or circuses,
where they are kept on leashes, dressed in little red jackets and
hats, forced to dance while an organ-grinder plays music for the
audience which then drops pennies into the monkey's little silver
cup. "Good idea," Iquito grumbles.

Naomi doesn't tell him that when all her friends were wanting
ponies, she was longing for a cute little monkey of her very own.
She would dress it up in doll clothes, she thought, with pink
ruffles and a bonnet, and she would push it around town in a
baby carriage. She would even teach it to talk, with its mouth, not
its hands, and they would be best friends forever. But her parents
wouldn't go for it and they got her a goldfish instead.

Naomi just nods now as Iquito tells her again about his stolen
sister. She has never seen him angry about anything else and she
doesn't know what to think.

4. Fish

Goldfish, sunfish, swordfish, jellyfish, angelfish, devilfish, fish
story, fishwife.

His tongue in her mouth flickers like a fish: tickling. The taste
of her later on his lips is like fish: salty. His hands upon her face
smell like fish: familiar. The major (indeed, the only) export of
the island is fish: indispensable.

But even in the utopian ocean the fish must eat each other to
survive.

5. Time

Time passes. All time passes in its own good time.

Iquito does not think in hours.

At first, Naomi is always asking, "What time is it? What time is
it now?"

Iquito gives her answers like, "It is time to eat. It is time to sleep. It is time to make love. The sun is shining. It is raining. It is dark. I am hungry. It is time to make love." Naomi would rather have a nice simple number to go by but Iquito cannot figure out how or when the number six might mean supper and what difference does it make if the sun comes up at seven, eight, or nine: it comes up anyway.

Eventually he teaches Naomi how to tell time by the sun and the stars, by the tides of the sea and of her own body. She stops asking stupid questions. She will also learn to navigate eventually.

No matter how you figure it, time is always passing and proving that everything changes, everything must move forward and forward and on. It is only when you think of it that time stands still.

C. VERBS

1. To Love

Iquito loves everything (except monkeys). He is always saying, "I love you. I love the sun. I love your left nipple. I love red bicycles. I love your yellow hair. I love all the stars and the full moon too. I love your teeth and your great big mouth. I love bananas. I love the way your belly button sticks out. I love raw meat."

Teasing him gently, Naomi says, "I love the way you love me and I love pizza too."

Iquito, who has never seen, let alone eaten, a pizza in his life, says, "Ah yes, that too."

2. To Laugh

They laugh at each other with their eyes squeezed shut, their mouths wide open and round. Their laughter is delicious, like that of mischievous children stuffed to bursting with secrets and plans.

3. To Rain

Iquito wants to sleep on the beach. He does not trust the hotel. To him, all enclosures are an aberration. Naomi can suddenly see what he means.

They lie down in the sand with their legs entwined. Naomi nestles her head into the curving bowl below Iquito's left shoulder. She presses her ear to his moist brown skin. She can hear the blood inside of him (or is it her own blood?) like the ocean inside a seashell. The sound of the surf seems to come not from the sea but from the stars speckled above them. While they sleep, the clouds come in like ghost ships. The rain drops down on their skin like cool silver coins.

4. To Sleep

The little green island feels like a boat, sealed up and salty, on the verge of becoming gladly and forever lost at sea. There is no telling what has become of the rest of the world.

In the dream, he asks, "What do you want?"

She says, "I want you to grovel." And in the dream he does it. With great delight. Prostrating himself before her on the sand, winding around her ankles, and whimpering like a slippery well-fed cat. She loves him so much in her sleep that she wakes up in the morning exhausted and covered with fine white sand and Iquito's elfin face sleeps on softly beside her.

D. CONJUNCTIONS

1. And

And the rain still falls silently into the sea.

2. Because

Because there is nothing to be said, there is nothing to be remembered or regretted.

In the dream there is no word for love.

In the silence, Iquito and Naomi are jumping out of their angels and swimming sleekly away.

3. But

But there is always the rest of the world out there, waiting to be acknowledged and appeased.

E. INTERJECTIONS

1. Oh

Oh never mind about that.

2. O

O to lie down in your arms and laugh.

Nothing Happens (1990)

Somehow the realization that nothing was to be hoped for had a salutary effect on me. For weeks and months, for years, in fact, all my life I have been looking forward to something happening, some extrinsic event that would alter my life, and now suddenly, inspired by the absolute hopelessness of everything, I felt relieved, felt as though a great burden had been lifted from my shoulders.

—Henry Miller, *Tropic of Cancer*

To the anxious (ardent, eager, anguished, or tormented) lover embedded (immersed, marooned, sunk, or stuck) in unrequited (uncertain, unreliable, undeclared, or unrealistic) love, the simple but eloquent phrase "I love you" becomes charged with a divine potential power. In such circumstances one is inclined to believe that if only one can say those three words often enough, then something will happen.

I love you.

I love you.

I love you.

(Do something.)

The phrase, in repetition, assumes an incantatory quality, becomes like the mystical chant of a sorcerer which, if administered with the appropriate number of abracadabras while sprinkling the beloved's beautiful head with just the right kind of magic dust, will make something happen.

It is perhaps a self-delusory trick of all human natures to believe that if only one can make oneself clear (perfectly, fervently, exquisitely, heart-wrenchingly clear), *then* something will happen, *then* what one wants to happen *will* happen.

When does one acquire the maturity to stop trying to make things happen? How does one arrive at the wisdom of knowing how and when to just *let it go*?

Didn't our mothers always tell us that where there's a will, there's a way? Didn't we always believe them?

When are we going to realize that whenever we say, It didn't work out, what we really mean is, It didn't work out the way I wanted it to?

When are we going to accept the fact that for at least sixty-five (seventy-five, eighty-five, ninety-five?) percent of the time our hands are tied? Tied perhaps with golden bracelets fine as angel hair, with white satin ribbons slippery as skin. Tied perhaps by a benevolent assemblage of family, friends, and distant relatives, by a bank of memories accumulating compound interest daily, a shared history rich and complex as a Latin American tapestry, unusual icons woven in vivid colours on a black background against a white wall.

Tied pleasantly enough perhaps, but tied nonetheless.

It is important to come to the conclusion that while strong people have strength, less strong people—I am reluctant to use the word *weak* here because of its negative connotations which bring to mind newborn mewling children or purblind suckling kittens, infirm old people, or the kind of tea you want when you're sick—less strong people have power. Strength is like a box, a straight-edged sharp-cornered protective packaging around the one who possesses it. Strong people are like monoliths on legs and other people automatically assume they are invincible, never needing anyone or anything. Power, on the other hand, is like a web, elastic, a little sticky perhaps, expanding in all directions, taking everyone in and keeping them there. Strength gives a person the means to survive. Power gives a person the means to make things happen.

My lover always tells me that I am a strong person and that is one of the things he loves about me most. He says, You are a survivor. Which is supposed to be a compliment but sometimes sends me into a ridiculous rage, for which I am later embarrassed and apologetic. Sometimes these arguments send us out to a bar late at night when nobody knows us, a diversion which is meant to be relaxing and distracting, but in the morning I have a round bruise the size of a silver dollar on my right wrist-bone from banging my fist on the table while trying to make myself clear.

His wife, he says, is not strong. Not *as* strong. He says he loves her but he admits (to me anyway) that he knew marrying her was a mistake in the first place. Not a fatal mistake, he says, but a mistake nonetheless. Once, in anger, he said, I made a mistake. Why can't you just accept that? I made a mistake. All right?

When is he going to realize that the danger of mistakes lies not in making them (for everyone alive must do that) but in feeling bound forever after to perpetuate them?

When is he going to realize that the only *right* reason for being (or staying) with someone is because you want to?

There are, in my opinion and experience, a great many possible *wrong* reasons—some of them noble, honourable, or decent perhaps, but wrong nonetheless.

These wrong reasons may include (this is akin to those ingredient listings on food packages which say *may include* as if they can't remember now, can't really say for sure what the hell they put in the stuff) staying because your family will disown you, because her family (who loves you like blood) will disown you, because you have a nice house with a big mortgage and a good garden, because maybe in fifteen years you will both have turned back into who you were when you first met and then you will be happy again, because the other person is a good person and does not deserve to be hurt, because you have always thought of yourself as a good person and do not want to hurt anyone ever.

When is he going to see it my way?

One of the things my lover and I have in common is our proclivity for complicating every single thing beyond recognition (beyond resolution, beyond hope, beyond belief).

Sometimes I say, Some things *are* simple.

I do not mean simple/easy, I mean simple/straightforward. Who is it that he cannot live the rest of his life without? I do not ask this question out loud because even when I'm angry I am afraid of the answer.

Sometimes he says, I'm a monster. He says this with his eyes closed, with his head in his hands. I am quick to assure him that he is *not* a monster, that *I* don't think he is a monster, that I would not *love* him if he was a monster. But there is little real consolation to be found for either of us in this because within it there is also always a lingering doubt: maybe he *is* a monster and maybe I am just plain stupid. His wife is a good person and we do not try to pretend otherwise—our powers of self-delusion are not that well developed. We cannot find any reason to dislike her at all. So maybe we are *both* monsters, maybe we are not decent people after all, maybe we are detestable, evil, and damned.

Sometimes we joke that if something doesn't happen soon, we will end up in adjoining rooms at the psychiatric hospital (or, I say, at the detox centre). Do we really mean that we will end up in adjoining catacombs in hell with the flames licking at our treacherous unfaithful feet?

Usually he calls in the morning around eleven o'clock, every morning except Saturday and Sunday. We seldom get to see each other on weekends. Sometimes on Saturday I am possessed by a compensatory frenetic energy so that I spend the whole day rushing around doing errands and chores I've been putting off for six months, vacuuming, washing floors, polishing silver, and rearranging the kitchen cupboards. Sometimes by Sunday I am so worn down and depressed that I stay in bed till noon and then spend the rest of the day pacing around the clean rooms of my house in my sweat pants, drinking coffee, smoking too much, and mumbling to myself, rehearsing aloud the It's-all-over-this-is-killing-me-I-can't-take-it-anymore-I-deserve-better-than-this-I-never-want-to-see-you-again speech which I will never give.

On weekday mornings I go about my business nonchalantly, pretending that I am not waiting for the phone to ring. But I *am* waiting, always waiting, waiting just the same, and usually hating myself for it. This is like having an itchy spot on your back in the middle of the night and you try to ignore it, you try not to scratch it because somehow scratching seems like giving in to things beyond your control. But after a while you can't help it and before you know it, you've got your arm twisted around at an impossible angle beneath you and you are scratching so hard that your fingernails leave long red welts on your skin. It is an involuntary response as is my anticipation. So for a while I'm not waiting and then all of a sudden I am. The difference is that waiting does not bring with it the relief that scratching does. It is only an admission, not a release.

When he is late calling, I start to worry. I imagine that something has happened, something *big, The Big Thing.*

I imagine that the shit has hit the fan.

I have the feeling then that we are poised upon the proverbial fence (a whitewashed fence with uncomfortably pointy pickets which we are gingerly straddling). This is the fence between nothing happening and all of our (my) dreams coming true.

When he finally does call, I am both relieved and disappointed to discover that he was late for some silly reason—friends dropped by for coffee, the toilet backed up, he had to take the dog to the vet—for some silly reason that has nothing do with me, her, or us.

When he finally does call, I cannot picture his face.

Sometimes he calls from a phone booth on a busy downtown street and I can hear the heavy morning traffic, the passersby laughing, a baby crying, a dog barking, sirens, brakes squealing, once the sound of breaking glass.

But usually there is only silence in the background and I imagine him calling me out of some vacant lunar landscape dotted with boulders and craters, foggy and unfathomable. I cannot bring his face into focus but his voice comes to me out of this opaque moonscape like a lantern or a buoy on a dark lake in the cool north.

When he finally does call, the first thing he says is, Are you all right?

He is always calling, calling, always asking, asking, Are you all right? Are you all right?

And I am always saying, I'm better, yes, I'm much better now.

But I'm not and sometimes when I hang up the phone, I find myself crying, crying for no reason, crying for all the reason in the world (too damn much reason in the world). I am always saying, I'm fine, just fine, don't worry about me, I'll be fine. But what if I'm not? And still I cannot picture his face.

The only time I can see him clearly is when we are making love and his face above me is illuminated and when I come he whispers my name and I close my eyes but he is still there and afterwards he rests his head on my shoulder and I can feel his breath on my neck and I can still see his face.

But then he has to go home again and before he gets to the end of my driveway, once again I cannot picture his face, can think only of how his back looks out there in the real world, walking away.

Sometimes when we are together we talk about ordinary things and I love to hear about the movie he saw last night, the dull dinner party he went to, the dream he had about pumpkins. I love to tell him about the great book I read, the fabulous dinner I cooked for myself, the erotic dream I had about him, making love on a mountain with the gods all around.

Other times we talk about "the situation." This is what we have taken to calling it—"the situation"—as if what is happening, or not happening, between us has assumed a life of its own, has become greater than the sum of its parts and is now a free-floating entity in its own right. This way, when we get angry (mostly I'm the one who gets angry), we can say we are angry at "the situation" instead of at each other. What this really means is that I rant and rave and he understands and nothing happens.

Once he said there is a part of himself that he always holds back, even in this situation, even though he loves me more than anything, anyone, ever. Maybe that is why he can always afford to understand me, even when I'm crazy. On a rainy evening alone again (drinking draft beer in a downtown bar, sitting in a booth by the window watching the headlights of the cars coming down the wet street like stars, the seat across from me empty and enlarging moment by moment with the absence of anyone to make myself clear to, drinking and dreaming that he is out there in the storm searching, the rain on his face and my name on the frantic tip of his tongue), I realize that this is the part of him I will always love the best: this part of him that I can never have. This is the part of him that his wife can never have either.

Sometimes I say reckless things when I'm angry, things like:

I think I'll go to Vancouver for a while.

I think I'll go out with Leonard who has been calling twice a week for a month.

I think I'll move away forever.

But I say these things and then I regret them. I don't say them because I mean them. They are just recklessness trying to get a reaction, trying to make something happen, searching for that key which will throw our lives back into motion. Sometimes I crave action the way other people crave a drink or a good thick steak, medium rare.

Sometimes I wish I had a gun. I have always been afraid of guns but sometimes now I wish I had one. I would carry it outside carefully on a warm and fragrant August night. I would stand in my white nightgown in the middle of my front yard between the two giant fir trees which would be black in the dark, their tops gone out of sight. I would stand in front of my little white house with the gun in my hands over my head and I would shoot blanks at the sky. The red shutters would be the colour of blood. The moon would be full or absent altogether.

My neighbours, who are respectable peace-loving people, would call the police in a panic, of course.

By the time they arrived, I would be sitting on the front step in my nightgown, resting my back against the black iron railing, resting my head on my knees. The gun then could be anywhere: invisible, lost, a figment of all imagination.

By the time they arrived, I would be innocent.

A Change is as Good as a Rest

(1990)

> What it all comes down to is that we are the sum of our efforts to change
> who we are. Identity is no museum piece sitting stock-still in a display
> case but rather the endlessly astonishing synthesis of the contradictions
> of everyday life.
>
> —Eduardo Galeano, *The Book of Embraces*

On Monday I decided to change my life.

Granted, I've made this decision before. In fact, when I told my alleged friend, Laurie, that I was going to turn over a new leaf, she snorted and said, "Cynthia, you've already turned over every leaf in the forest. What more can you do?" But this was the first time I had any real inkling as to how to go about it.

What precipitated my decision was nothing spectacular. It was simply that the night before I had a dream: a blatant but brilliant dream in which I had just achieved perfection and been crowned Absolute High Priestess of the Modern World. This impressive title was emblazoned in white letters on a black satin banner draped diagonally across my breasts. I was sitting naked on an elaborate throne, a cross between a peacock wicker chair and a flower-festooned dentist's chair. Ranged around me, cross-legged and humble on the cold stone floor, were all the people (including Laurie) who had ever hurt, insulted, ignored, demeaned, dismissed, degraded, or laughed at me in my entire life. While they bowed their heads before my consummate beauty and wept at their hitherto wicked ways, words of wisdom were plopping out of my mouth and rolling around their dirty suppliant feet like pearls. When I arose and waved a limp royal hand over their heads, they fell to their knees, scrabbling like seagulls for the shimmering pulsating pearls, scooping them up with their long pink tongues and swallowing them whole. I levitated briefly and then dissolved right before their adoring apologetic beady little eyes.

This dream was in the nature of an epiphany and I woke from it saying, "Of course, yes, of course, now I see, yes."

I knew better than to tell this dream to skeptical negative Laurie, so after I said I had to hang up because there was someone at the door (there wasn't), I called in sick from my job at the delicatessen and then I called my better friend, Brenda.

Brenda said she'd just had a call from Bruce, the man who has been wanting to marry her for over a year and a half. Brenda doesn't know whether she wants to marry Bruce or not. They do love each other but whenever they spend more than two days together, they end up arguing about absolutely everything. Then they break up and Brenda is sure that she wouldn't marry Bruce if he were the last available man on earth. But after a week or two Brenda gets lonely: it begins to look more and more like Bruce *is* the last available man on earth. So then they get back together and Brenda thinks she might as well marry him after all.

This Monday morning Bruce had called Brenda and said, "I just wanted to tell you all the things I love about you." He told her that he loved her eyes, hair, lips, heart, belly button, breasts, arms, legs, fingers, nose, ears, toes, lungs, liver, her neck, her stretch marks, her leopard-skin underwear, her quirky sense of humour, and the hairy little mole in the middle of her back.

So now Brenda and Bruce might be getting married in August.

I could hardly blame her: who could resist a man who loves the hairy mole in the middle of your back, not to mention your stretch marks?

All of this fit right in with my decision to change my life. I was at the tail end (or so I hoped) of a long series of misguided, unpleasant, and ultimately unsuccessful romances. There was a time in my life when I had actually found myself in danger of being happy but that was a long time ago, I was much younger then, and perhaps my ideas of happiness were rather stunted. It was, to coin a phrase, a humbling experience. Since then I've had nothing but bad luck and after a while I pretty well gave up on men altogether. I just couldn't seem to get it right. But I had to admit that without a man in my life, I felt old, ugly, undesirable, and totally uninteresting. I felt nigh unto invisible. Without a man in my life, I barely recognized myself. The life, it seemed, had gone out of my life.

Listening to Brenda, I realized that all I really wanted was a man who would tell me all the things he loved about me every single day of my life, at least once a day, preferably three or four times if necessary. I realized that I had been looking for years for a man who would tell me all day long that I was wonderful.

I also realized that at my age the only men who are willing to do this are married to other women. So far all the other men of my dreams have been unwilling or unable to comply with my hyperactive expectations.

After I told Brenda my fabulous dream, we pondered briefly and without resolution the reasons why we are so incapable of convincing ourselves of all our wonderful attributes on our own. It has something to do with seeing our reflections in another pair of eyes. Admittedly, those eyes must be masculine, for the reflective properties of other women's eyes are not nearly as effective. Other women's eyes, we conceded, are likely to be clouded by a murky and ambivalent combination of sheer envy, the need to be nice, and a set of self-esteem problems all their own.

It was only in a man's eyes, we decided, that we could really see ourselves. I fantasized about a world where all men wore mirrored sunglasses in which I could see myself in all my splendour, twirling on my tiptoes like the tiny pink ballerina in my first jewellery box.

If I could not find a man to reflect me, perhaps it was time to concentrate on other reflective surfaces. Finally I had a plan.

Brenda and I knew we liked each other a lot but we had to admit that we didn't much like ourselves. This, according to all the pop-psychology books I've been reading, is the root of all evil. I have studied these best-selling books in some detail. I have done all the quizzes to determine exactly how low my self-esteem really is:

A. I feel that I am not as happy/smart/attractive/funny/
   successful/good as other people.
   1. rarely
   2. sometimes
   3. often
   4. always
B. I feel hopeless, helpless, and out of control of my own life.
   1. sometimes
   2. often
   3. always
C. I feel defeated and pessimistic about the future.
   1. often
   2. always
D. I feel disgusted, depressed, and dissatisfied.
   1. always

I have tried the exercises guaranteed to improve my wilted self-esteem once and for all. I have tried, for instance, to generate feelings of control and accomplishment by:

1. planting a garden (but I hate gardening and do not see the point of all that dirty work when you can buy perfectly good vegetables downtown at the market three days a week, cheap)

2. organizing my photo album (which I hadn't touched in years because it always makes me depressed to see how much my life has or hasn't changed since 1973)

3. alphabetizing my spices (this proved more difficult than you might imagine: does Sweet Basil, for instance, belong under S for Sweet or B for Basil?)

I have tried replacing my negative thoughts about myself with positive ones so that I was walking around all day chanting silently: *I am good. I am beautiful. I am kind. I am strong. I am damn near perfect. I am a bloody miracle.* I was not convinced.

In the end, these books just made me feel like I was a lost cause and the only thing I could do now was kill myself or turn into somebody else altogether.

So on Monday I decided to make myself over. Brenda thought this was a great idea. We agreed though that we wouldn't call each other for the rest of the week because I did not want to be consulted, advised, or otherwise interfered with until my transformation was complete.

After talking to Brenda, I got right down to business and spent the rest of Monday making a list. In the middle of the afternoon, my mother called for our weekly chat, but I said, "Not now, Mom, I'm changing my life," and she said, "Good, it's about time. Call me when you're done," and I said, "Yes, I'll call you back on Sunday night."

As for the make-over, I would begin with the basics. First, it would be in the nature of those full-colour Before-and-After spreads featured in women's magazines:

BAMBI GETS A NEW LOOK

*Meet Bambi Bird, thirty-two, mother of six, skydiver, gourmet
cook, award-winning quilter, and Children's Hospital Volunteer
of the Year. Bambi's hair was too long, her skin was too oily, her
lips too thin, her nose too big, her cheekbones too low, and her
absolutely colourless eyes were set too close together. See how
ugly Bambi was! With just a little help from a battalion of
beauticians (and no major surgery whatsoever!), see Bambi
become a cover girl! See Bambi become the most beautiful
woman in the world!*

The trouble, I have always thought, with these magazine
make-overs is that they never go far enough. I, on the other
hand, was going to change the whole picture. I was going to
change my life.

Tuesday morning I got my hair cut short to show off the graceful bones of my skull. I had what was left tinted a deep and
dramatic shade of black. This, my hairdresser assured me, was
the look I was lacking: the look of a strong, independent, confident, socially correct woman who knew how to take charge of her
own imminent life. "It's you, it's you!" he cried. "Thank you," I said
smugly and let him sell me a bottle of jojoba shampoo with
matching aloe vera conditioner (guaranteed no animal testing).

I went to the dentist and got my front teeth fixed. I got green
contact lenses. I had a facial to slough all the dead cells off my
face. I had a full-body massage to relax and rejuvenate my tired
muscles. I signed up for aerobics three mornings a week plus a
one-week crash course in water ballet.

I dropped by the delicatessen and handed in a formal letter of
resignation in which I explained that it was against my new principles to be up to my elbows all day in so much dead meat, not to
mention the preservatives, the artificial colouring, and all those
other chemical additives.

Having quit my job, I became a painter. I went to the art supply store and bought an easel, two dozen prestretched canvases, a set of oil paints in forty-eight different colours including Basic Flesh, one of every paintbrush they had in stock, a twenty-volume set of hardcover books called *Painting Through the Ages*, and a case of rectified turpentine. I also bought a cotton painter's smock, smoky blue. I held off on the matching beret though, as I suspected such a time-honoured symbol of artistic inclination had lately become passé.

The salesman told me I was bound to be brilliant. He said he could tell just by looking at me. He also asked me out for a cappuccino but I said I was too busy, I was changing my life, maybe next week when I was more myself.

That evening I set up my new easel, put on my blue painter's smock, and created my first masterpiece. It was a still life of red and green apples in a yellow bowl on a wooden table in a shack located somewhere in a Third World country.

On Wednesday I went to the government offices and put in my application to change my name from Cynthia to Xochiquetzal who was the Mexican equivalent to the Greek Aphrodite. I liked the idea of being a many-faceted Love Goddess, Moon Virgin, Fairy Queen, and Madonna. I had done my homework and discovered she was also the patroness of marriage and sacred harlots, of dancing, singing, spinning, weaving, magic, and art. Best of all, Xochiquetzal was in charge of all change and trans-formation.

The woman at the desk said it was a great name but warned me it could take up to three months to process my application. I told her that simply would not do: I did not have all the time in the world. When I explained that I was changing my life, she said she'd put a rush on it. She said she'd speed up the bureaucratic machinery so it would get through by the end of the week for sure. I could see that changing my life was already changing the world. I could see that I was already becoming a significant and powerful person.

Wednesday evening I went back to my easel and my blue smock (which was now aesthetically spotted and charmingly smeared with red, green, and yellow paint) and whipped up another creation. I painted a Mexican child eating a burrito and refried beans, holding a broken doll, wearing a serape and a big sombrero. I resisted the urge to give her big brown tear-filled eyes and simply closed them instead.

On Thursday I stopped smoking, drinking, and biting my nails. I stopped watching game shows and listening to AM radio. I cancelled my lifetime subscription to *People* magazine. I also stopped plucking my eyebrows, shaving my legs, and picking my nose. I went through my photo album and ripped out the pictures of all my old lovers. I rewrote my entire romantic history, renounced all former folly, and became a virgin again. Since I had faithfully practised all these nasty habits for years, they were deeply ingrained and most difficult to eradicate. It took me all day to master them.

Thursday evening I painted a blue recycling box filled with pretty green wine bottles, old newspapers, a TV set, and a VCR.

Friday morning I threw out every single thing in my clothes closet. I was especially relieved to be rid of my red and black deli uniform. I knew I was on the path to true freedom when I cut my high school graduation dress (peach satin, Empire waistline, a bulging bow at the back) into ribbons and tossed them out the window, watching the satin strips waft down like something out of a tickertape parade. I laughed gaily as I bundled up my blue jeans, my brushed nylon nighties, and my pantyhose. I contemplated giving up underwear altogether but decided that in this climate, replacing all my nylon panties with pure cotton was a more reasonable compromise.

Friday afternoon I went downtown in my burlap sack and

bought myself a whole new wardrobe. I bought embroidered vests, flowing gauzy floor-length skirts with matching scarves, flowered 100% cotton pants, Birkenstock sandals in four different styles, six new colours, and a shopping cart full of 100% virgin wool sweaters. No more of this halfway stuff for me: I wanted to go all the way: 100% pure or nothing. I was making a fashion statement. I also bought a lot of black, which sartorially speaks for itself.

I left the burlap sack in the fitting room and walked back onto the street. Catching sight of myself in a plate-glass window, for once I did not cringe at my own reflection. Crossing the next intersection, I was sure I spotted envy in the tired eyes of the woman trudging along beside me. Yes, there it was: pure glittering envy so green her eyes were like flies.

Friday evening I painted a naked woman wearing a string of 100% cultured pearls.

Saturday morning, dressed in my new diaphanous duds, I tackled the kitchen. I threw out every scrap of food I could lay my lusty hands on. I put the Twinkies, the Crunchy Cheez Doodles, the Oreo Ice Cream Sandwiches, and the Schneiders Spicy Pepperettes in a double plastic bag so that not even the garbage-man would get wind of my former secret shameful ways. I also tossed my microwave oven, my aluminum pots, and my ridiculously primitive coffee percolator.

Then I went downtown and started from scratch. At the health food store, I stocked up on wheat germ, lentils, oat bran, millet, sprouted wheat berries, soy grits, buckwheat groats, extra-virgin olive oil, ten pounds of unsulphured dried apricots, and a case of carrot juice. I also bought all five flavours of tofu and a book on how to make Tofu Cheesecake, Tofu Pizza, Tofu Croquettes, and Hot Tofu Sandwiches with Miso Gravy.

Waiting in the checkout line, I chatted amiably with an intensely friendly woman about the relative merits of torula versus brewer's yeast. This woman, whose name was Nirvana, said, "I've never seen you here before, you must be new in town," and I said, humbly, "Yes, brand new." Even as we spoke, I could feel my blood being purified, my colon being cleansed, and my karma, like that turpentine, being rectified.

I thought fondly of my former self crouched not a week before over a quarter-pound bacon burger with fries and gravy on a Styrofoam plate in Eddy's Eats across the street. From Eddy's window I had watched the granola girls passing in and out of the health food store as if it were a church. They sported Birkenstock sandals, prettily hairy legs, and 100% cotton string grocery bags. I was so intimidated that I ordered more gravy and a double Coke float. Now here I was: already one of them, reborn as a sister with the whole wide world of health at my empowered fingertips. I knew I would never see the inside of Eddy's Eats again.

At the hardware store on my way home, I picked up a yogurt maker and a cappuccino machine.

That night I soaked for an hour in a hot baking soda bath, dreaming up my future and sponging off my past. This took longer than I'd bargained on so there was little time left for my painting. I didn't get to my easel until nearly midnight and then all I could come up with was a Jackson Pollock derivative of multicoloured splotches on a plain white ground. The splatters on my smock, I had to admit, were more aesthetic than that. However, I did not despair. By this time I was thoroughly convinced that come tomorrow I would be a whole new person. I would be the woman I had always meant to be.

On Sunday I rested and spent the whole day sitting around relaxing in my nice new self. Come Monday I would tackle my whole apartment. My belongings, I figured, should be like accessories to the new me, accessories after the fact. Not only would I replace my cheap tattered posters, my fuzzy pink toilet seat cover, and my cute kitten calendar, but I would also throw out all my tacky furniture, my juvenile record collection, and my sadly unenlightened and generally misinformed library. What I wanted first and foremost was one of those intricate handmade dried flower arrangements to put in the centre of my new coffee table, which would of course be natural genuine 100% knotty pine.

At six o'clock I called my mom but she wasn't home. Then I called Brenda but all I got was her answering machine. Since I no longer believed in modern technology (except for my yogurt maker and my cappuccino machine), I couldn't leave a message and hung up politely in its electronic ear. Succumbing temporarily to a wave of nostalgic generosity, I called my unsympathetic friend, Laurie, but she wasn't home either. It occurred to me that not only was I going to have to find new friends, but probably new parents too.

After a delicious and nutritious supper of broiled teriyaki tofu with buckwheat groats, I put on my blue smock, which was hardly blue at all anymore, covered as it was with splatters and splashes of the rainbow in forty-eight different colours including Basic Flesh. I stood in front of the pure white canvas on my easel. I concentrated. I squinted. I held one sturdy thumb up at arm's length, wiggled it around, and peered at it meaningfully with my right eye screwed shut.

But the canvas would not cooperate. It seemed to have developed a mind of its own. Before my very eyes it transformed itself and took on a silvery mirror-like sheen in which I could see nothing save my own sweet face.

I would have known it anywhere.

The Antonyms of Fiction (1991)

FACT

The facts of the matter are these:

When I was twenty-one years old, I met and fell in love with a man named Jonathan Wright. We met at a Christmas party given by a mutual friend and two months later he moved in with me. We made a lot of jokes about him being Mr. Right. Two years later he moved out. After a brief but intensely unpleasant period of accusations, hysterics, and the odd suicide threat, it became what is fondly referred to as "an amicable separation" and then we made a lot of jokes about him being Mr. Not-So-Right-After-All. We remained (or should I say, we *became*) friends, suggesting that maybe someday, maybe ten years from now, who knows, maybe then we would get back together again and get it right. This led to another batch of bad jokes about him being Mr. Not-Right-Now. All of this happened ten years ago.

Sometime later I moved away, two thousand miles away in fact, back to the city I'd come from in the first place. For a while Jonathan and I kept in touch with birthday cards, Christmas cards, and the occasional phone call for no good reason. Neither one of us was much good at writing real letters.

Eventually, as so often happens over distance and the passage of time, our sporadic attempts at maintaining communication petered out and we lost track of each other's lives. I can't remember now the last time I heard from Jonathan. I also can't remember the last time Jonathan and I made love. I can remember the first time very clearly but not the last because, as so often happens, I didn't know it was to be the last time at the time and so I was not paying as much poignant attention as I might have been.

Last Sunday morning at ten o'clock, I had a phone call from a woman named Madeline Kane, a woman I hadn't heard from in years and who was, in fact, the mutual friend who'd given the Christmas party at which Jonathan and I first met. Madeline was calling Sunday morning to tell me that Jonathan was dead. She said she thought I would want to know. She said she thought I would want to know the truth. But as it turned out, she knew nothing, nothing but the facts.

TRUTH

According to *The Concise Oxford Dictionary of Current English*, truth is *the quality or state of being true or accurate or honest or sincere or loyal or accurately shaped or adjusted.*

There were at least forty people at Madeline Kane's Christmas party that year. It was a small friendly town and many of the residents, like myself, had moved there from other places and so did not have family handy for such festive occasions. We tended to gather frequently for these pot-luck parties, bearing from one house to another hearty steaming casseroles, salad in wooden bowls the size of wagon wheels, and many jumbo bottles of cheap wine.

At Madeline Kane's Christmas party, there was a big Scotch pine tied to the wall so it wouldn't topple over and we all helped decorate it before dinner, stringing popcorn and cranberries, arguing amiably about the proper way to put on the tinsel: the one-strand-at-a-time advocates versus the heave-a-whole-handful-with-your-eyes-closed contingent.

After dinner, we brought out the guitars and sang for hours.

Jonathan Wright sang that Kenny Rogers song, "Don't Fall In Love With A Dreamer." And so of course I did.

After the party, he came home with me. After we got undressed and climbed into my bed, I said, "I just want to sleep with you, I don't want to make love," and he said, "That's okay, I just want to be close to you tonight."

In the morning we made love for a long time. In fact, we stayed in bed all day which was something I had never done before.

Jonathan Wright and I loved each other suddenly and, in reality, we were very happy for a while.

REALITY

According to *The Concise Oxford Dictionary of Current English*, reality is *the property of being real*. According to *The Concise Oxford Dictionary of Current English*, real is *actually existing as a thing or occurring in fact, objective, genuine, rightly so called, natural, sincere, not merely apparent or nominal or supposed or pretended or artificial or hypocritical or affected.*

In fiction, we are accustomed to encountering people driven to extremes, people brought to their proverbial knees by love and loss and other such earth-shaking heart-stopping soul-shifting events, people who are thrashing around inside their lives instead of just living them. In reality, these extremes are merely the end points of the continuum. In reality, it is all the points in between, cumulative and connected, if not downright boring, which are the important part. In real life, it is all the points in between which comprise the real life we are really living. In real life, people driven repeatedly to the limit are very hard to take. The friends of such people (if they have any friends left) suspect they are crazy, emotionally disturbed, mentally unbalanced, manic-depressive, but mostly just plain foolish. In reality, people who go from one extreme to the other (and back again) on a regular basis are more fun to read about than to know.

Jonathan Wright and I loved each other suddenly and, in reality, we were very unhappy after a while.

NON-FICTION

On the phone last Sunday morning, Madeline Kane took down my current address and sent me the newspaper clipping and the obituary, which arrived in the mail today. It was unlikely that Jonathan's death would be noted in the newspaper here two thousand miles away. It would be considered local news.

Both these versions of the story are very short and to the point. As if there was a point. As if the truth could really be known.

The newspaper clipping said:

Jonathan Wright, 38, was shot to death in his apartment on Saturday night. An eyewitness, unidentified for her own protection, told police that when Mr. Wright answered a knock at the door at approximately 3 a.m., a lone gunman shot him twice in the head and then fled on foot. Police have neither confirmed nor denied the many rumours surrounding the case. Investigation continues.

The obituary said:

WRIGHT, Jonathan Lawrence—Suddenly at his residence on Sunday, August 5, 1991, Jonathan Lawrence Wright in his 38th year, beloved son of David and Elizabeth Wright, dear brother of Patricia and Susan, sadly missed by several aunts and uncles. Resting at Goodman Funeral Home. Friends will be received on Wednesday, 7–9 p.m. Funeral Service will be held in the Chapel, Thursday, August 9 at 2 p.m. Interment Landsmere Cemetery.

POETRY

I never expected to see you again / but I never expected you to
die either. / I hadn't seen you in so many years: / it was as if you
were already dead / or / it was as if you would never die / would
just go on living somewhere else / two thousand miles away /
while I was still here / going on about my business / never giving
you a second thought. / Unless a stranger in the street happened
to have / a jacket, a walk, a smile, / or a receding hairline just like
yours. / Unless I happened to be cooking your favourite meal /
for another lover (pork chops, green beans, mashed/you called
them "smashed" / potatoes) and it turned out he didn't like pork. /
Unless I surprised myself / looking through the old photo album
/ and weeping. / If this were a poem / I would have had a premo-
nition / a cold-sweat shiver down my spine / at the very moment
you died. / If this were a poem / I would still be able to see your
face / your real face / not your other face, shot to pieces / exploding all over the wall / like the time we were splitting up / I was
crying / you were drunk and raging / threw a whole plate of
spaghetti across the room / and nobody cleaned it up for a week.
/ If this were a poem / I would be able to remember everything /
including the weight of your body on mine / and how it felt to
love you. / If this were a poem / the truth would be known.

FICTION

But the truth of the matter is: this is fiction.

Pure fiction.

Pure: *mere, simple, sheer, not corrupt, morally undefiled, guilt-
less, sincere, chaste.*

Fiction: *feigning, invention, conventionally accepted falsehood.*

Pure fiction: a convenient literary device which allows me to
say that I never knew a man named Jonathan Wright, there was
no Christmas party at Madeline Kane's house ten years ago, no

Scotch pine, no tinsel, no Kenny Rogers song, no dreamers falling fast into love, and no bad jokes. Which allows me to say that I never cried into your angry arms, there was no spaghetti splattered on the wall, and I never ever missed you.

If the truth were known, this is fiction, a valuable revisionist device which allows me to say there was no man at the door with a gun.

Weights and Measures

(1993)

It is the question the writer asks when writing a book: Shall I fill in all the details? Or shall I let the reader imagine them all? . . . What if I give you dots and numbers and you draw in the lines?

—Kristjana Gunnars, *The Substance of Forgetting*

1. On the dining room table in my parents' house, there is a shallow crystal bowl filled with 10 ceramic balls. They are like billiard balls without the weight, Christmas baubles without the hooks. They are perfect and useless, bright globes of pure colour. I am forbidden to touch them and, being a good girl, I don't. Only my mother handles them. I suppose my father could too if he wanted but he doesn't. Once a week my mother removes the balls one by one from the bowl and polishes them with a soft rag, a piece of my old nightie with ducks and bunnies on it. She lines the polished balls up like beads at the edge of the table against the wall. They make my heart ache.

Occasionally she lets me hold one: the red one, the green one, just for a minute now, the blue one is my favourite, be careful. This is how I know the balls are nearly weightless. Occasionally I imagine smashing them one by one against the wall. More often I imagine juggling them in slow motion, a luminous halo of colours suspended over my head.

In 1989, Anthony Gatto of the United States juggled 5 clubs

without a drop for 45 minutes and 2 seconds. That same year, Jas Angelo of Great Britain juggled 3 objects without a drop for 8 hours, 57 minutes, and 31 seconds. In 1990, in Seattle, Washington, 821 jugglers kept 2,463 objects in the air simultaneously. Each person juggled at least 3 objects. The nature of these objects is not noted, nor how high or how long they were airborne.

I try to learn how to juggle from a book but I can't get the hang of it. I take up baton twirling instead.

2. When my mother is happy, she bakes. She gets up before my father and me and ties an apron over her nightgown. She rattles and hums in the warm yellow kitchen while it's still dark outside. If I get up early enough, she lets me measure the flour, the butter, the brown sugar which must be tightly packed into the measuring cup. If I sleep later, entering the dining room is like coming downstairs on Christmas morning. The bowl of ceramic balls on the perfectly polished table is surrounded by hot pies with flaky lattice crusts and multi-layered cakes with white or chocolate icing in delicate swirls on top. Sometimes I am allowed to have a piece of cake or pie after breakfast. All morning at school I walk around with the weight of it in the bottom of my stomach, the taste of it still sweet on the back of my tongue.

The largest apple pie ever baked was made by Chef Glynn Christian in a 40×23 foot dish in Chelsfield, Great Britain, in August 1982. The pie weighed 30,115 pounds and was cut by Rear-Admiral Sir John Woodward. The largest cake ever baked weighed 128,238 pounds and 8 ounces, including 16,209 pounds of icing. Created in the shape of the state of Alabama, the cake was made to celebrate the centenary of Fort Payne. Prepared by a local bakery called EarthGrains, it was cut by 100-year-old resident, Ed Henderson, on October 18, 1989. The flavour of the cake is not noted, nor how much longer Ed Henderson lived.

When my mother is unhappy, we go without dessert. But even when she is in her bedroom crying with the door shut, the rest of the house is still filled with the fragrance of her baking and my father is still smiling. On my birthday, whether my mother is happy or not, she bakes me a special chocolate cake with nickels in it.

3. My diary is a small pink book with gilt-edged pages and a tiny gold lock and key. In it, I am allotted one page per day, one tissue-thin page covered with fine blue lines. No matter what does or doesn't happen on any given day, I feel obliged to fill each page. I briefly note the events of home and school: The math test was hard. My mother made me clean my room. My true love kissed me after school behind the little kids' slide.

On boring days, I pay cursory attention to world events: Canada celebrates its centennial. The world's first successful heart transplant is performed in South Africa. Martin Luther King, Jr. is shot and killed in Memphis. Robert Kennedy is shot and killed in Los Angeles. Jackie Kennedy marries Aristotle Onassis. The U.S. death toll in Vietnam passes 30,000.

Mostly though I write about the future. I describe in detail the man I will marry. I choose names for our 3 perfect children and our dog. Sometimes I draw pictures of the house we will live in, the car we will drive, the dress I will wear on our wedding day. If the present is frequently confusing, at least the future and the exquisite weight of its abundant possibilities are always clear. Even from this distance, I can see the colour of his eyes, the smile on my lips, the never-ending song in my heart.

The largest mirage ever recorded was sighted in the Arctic at 83°N 103°W by Donald B. Macmillan in 1913. It included hills, valleys, and snow-capped peaks extending through at least 120° of the horizon. It was the type of mirage known as the "Fata

Morgana," so called because such visions were formerly believed to be the nasty work of Morgan le Fay, King Arthur's evil fairy half-sister. The technique used to measure and record a mirage is not described.

I have all the confidence in the world. I wear the key to my diary on a chain around my neck like a locket. Being a good girl, I naturally assume that I will eventually be the recipient of an appropriate measure of eternal happiness. The future will be my just reward.

4. I fall in love every time I turn around. I am supposed to be studying Philosophy and the great works of Literature but I am drinking coffee in the university cafeteria and falling in love instead. Even Plato had a theory of desire. I am always ready to be swept off my feet, even when I'm sitting down. I fall in love with a wrist on a table, a thigh in blue denim, a lock of black hair, the tickle of a moustache, the tender angle of a manly neck bent toward me. I pick up the electricity in the air, the force fields of handsome men who mill around me, until my stomach feels charred and my hands are shaking. This could be from all that caffeine but I take it to be another symptom of love.

The only person in the world to be struck by lightning 7 times was ex-park ranger Roy C. Sullivan of Virginia, U.S.A. His attraction for lightning began when he was struck in 1942 and lost his big toenail. In July 1969 he lost his eyebrows. In July 1970 his left shoulder was seared. In April 1972 his hair was set on fire. In August 1973 his hair was set on fire again and his legs were seared. In June 1976 his ankle was injured. In June 1977, struck while fishing, he suffered burns to his stomach and chest. In September 1983 he died by his own hand, reportedly after being rejected by the woman he loved. The method of Roy Sullivan's suicide is not noted.

My best friend tells me I'm addicted to love. I say, At least it's more harmless than heroin. She says, Are you sure?

5. The men I love don't love me back. I sleep with them anyway. The men I don't love call me in the middle of the night, crying or cursing because I won't sleep with them. I feel like I'm banging my head against a wall, one of those stucco walls with bits of coloured ground glass embedded in it.

The beak of the red-headed woodpecker, *Melanerpes erythro-cephalus*, hits the bark of a tree with an impact velocity of 13 mph. This means that when the head snaps back, the brain is subject to a deceleration of approximately 10 g. The type of tree is not noted, nor the possible long-term effects of this activity.

I decide I will marry the next man who asks me. In the meantime, I try on the notion of celibacy the way other women try on a new coat. It doesn't fit. I try learning to live without desire but I can't get the hang of it. Years pass.

6. My husband is a poet. His poetry is epic, anguished, and rhyming. Although no one will publish his work, he refuses to compromise his artistic integrity by catering to the marketplace. He is sure he will be famous someday, perhaps posthumously. In the meantime, he drives a taxi to pay the bills. He also spends a lot of time lying on the couch watching TV, eating potato chips, and thinking great thoughts. He hasn't written a poem in 6 months. In that time he has gained 10 pounds from all those chips and I have gained 20 because I am pregnant. His depression grows in direct proportion to the size of my belly. He eats more chips and changes the channel. His shirt is covered with crumbs. At least he's dressed. The living room is filled with his misery. I read baby name books in the kitchen. Sometimes I think that the couch with the weight of him and his depression on it

will eventually crash through the floor and plummet directly to the centre of the earth.

The deepest depression so far discovered is the bedrock of the Bentley Subglacial Trench in Antarctica at 8,326 feet below sea level. The greatest submarine depression is an area of the Northwest Pacific floor that has an average depth of 15,000 feet. The deepest exposed depression on land is the shore surrounding the Dead Sea, now 1,310 feet below sea level. The rate of fall in the lake surface has been 13 3/4 inches per year since 1948.

My husband says he cannot possibly be a poet and a parent at the same time. He reads *Paradise Lost* and sometimes speaks in iambic pentameter. I borrow books on childbirth and breast-feeding from the library. I go to prenatal classes and practice the breathing alone.

7. We talk and we talk and we talk. We cry. He makes up his mind and then changes it back again. Finally he goes out, ostensibly to buy a bag of chips. He returns an hour later with a 3-piece set of matching luggage, soft-sided in royal blue with locks and tiny keys like the one I had for my diary in Grade 8. He fills the biggest suitcase with books. It is so heavy he cannot lift it. He rearranges the contents of the suitcases to achieve a more even distribution of weight. He sets them on the back porch and calls a taxi. He kisses me goodbye. We do not discuss where he is going. We are all talked out.

In 1988, students at University College, Dublin, debated the notion that "Every Dog Should Have Its Day" for 503 hours and 45 minutes. This record was broken in April 1992 by students at St. Andrews Presbyterian College in Laurinburg, North Carolina, who debated the idea that "There's No Place Like Home" for 517 hours and 45 minutes. The winners of these debates are not noted.

My daughter is born 12 days later. I am in labour for 18 hours and 45 minutes, with my best friend as my coach. My daughter weighs 7 pounds, 6 1/2 ounces and is 20 inches long. I should be afraid, but I'm not.

8. My best friend and I find babysitters so we can go downtown on Friday night. We are giddy with freedom while our beautiful babies sleep. We cruise the shiny streets arm in arm laughing with our heads thrown back. We go inside and stand at the bar. We order Scotch and water which after 3 sips tastes like apple juice to me. We flirt with 2 young men in tight jeans and bandanas. They wear silk vests with nothing underneath. Their pectorals are hairless, shiny, and distinct. We flick our long hair, our slim hips, our little pointy tongues. We tell them we are tourists. When they become obnoxious, we hold hands and tell them we are gay. We do not tell them we are mothers in disguise. We tease them till they sulk. We snort and snicker and order more Scotch. We speculate as to the exact nature of the male ego, this allegedly natural phenomenon which gets so much attention. Where is it located? In the head, the heart, the penis? What colour is it? Blood red, royal blue, deep purple, black? How big is it really, this marvellous chimera which we have spent so much of our lives tending to, massaging, tippy-toeing around?

The largest living organism on earth was discovered in a forest in Northern Michigan on April 2, 1992. This fungus, a member of the species *Armillaria bulbosa*, covered at least 37 acres and weighed over 100 tons. Only a month later, this discovery was dwarfed by yet another fungus, the closely related *Armillaria ostoyae*, reported to be covering 1,500 acres in Washington State. Its weight has yet to be determined.

We go home to our babies happy and self-satisfied. This is

more than can be said for the men, who go home drunk and alone, shaking their heads, bearing their big wounded egos in their heavily muscled outstretched arms.

9. My daughter crawls with determination. Her little hands and knees thump all over the hardwood floors. All the knees of all her clothes are worn through. She is fast and curious. She gets into everything. She empties the toy box, the bottom dresser drawers, the lower kitchen cupboards and bookshelves. I follow her from room to room cleaning up the mess, fearful for her safety. I remember reading in the newspaper about a little girl who pulled a bookcase down on top of herself and was crushed to death beneath its weight. Childproofing the house, I keep moving things up and up and up until eventually, I imagine, everything I own will be suspended from the ceiling by invisible strings. She never stops moving.

The longest continuous voluntary crawl on record is 31.5 miles by Peter McKinley and John Murrie, who covered 115 laps of an athletic track at Falkirk, Great Britain, on March 28 to 29, 1992. Over a space of 15 months ending March 9, 1985, Jagdish Chander crawled 870 miles from Aligarh to Jamma, India, to appease his revered Hindu Goddess, Mata. What sin or crime he may have committed to so offend her is not specified.

On the advice of the parenting books, I get down on my hands and knees and crawl along beside my daughter to see the world from her angle, to scout out dangerous objects within her reach. She laughs at me and claps her hands. She thinks I'm playing. Little does she know. I am doing my best to protect her. It will be years yet before she falls in love and flies away.

10. The crystal bowl of ceramic balls sits on my table now. My mother passed them on to me after my daughter was born. I guess she figures that, having proven my ability to handle a baby without damaging it, I'm old enough now to juggle these balls without breaking them. Next thing you know I'll be baking.

After my daughter is safely sleeping, I remove the balls one by one from the bowl and admire them carefully. They are as light as the brush of my daughter's eyelash against my cheek. I imagine I am the woman in Vermeer's painting, the woman weighing pearls on a balance. She stands before a wooden table in the corner of a room. The light comes through the window and illuminates her right hand, the balance, the pearls, and the white fur on her blue morning jacket. Intent upon her task and the attainment of equilibrium, the woman's eyes are downcast and her forehead is smooth. She looks to be several months pregnant. On the wall behind her is a large dark painting of The Last Judgement. To weigh is to judge. Recent microscopic examination has revealed that the pans of the balance contain neither pearls nor gold but are empty. The woman nevertheless is suffused with serenity.

The ceramic balls glow in the moonlight cast through my window. The picture on the wall behind me is not a painting, but an enlarged photograph of my best friend and me and our little girls in the park. The girls are strapped safely into the baby swings. We push them as high as we dare. Breaking free of gravity, they squeal on the upswing and kick their little legs. My best friend and I commandeered a passing stranger to take this picture. His shadow falls just to the left of me. I am looking past him.

I've been hearing rumours lately about a scientist who has measured the weight of the human soul. People talk about it at parties, at work, even at the hairdresser's. Invariably they laugh.

Apparently the scientist set up a delicate system of scales and balances beneath the bodies of the dying. Everyone has read the newspaper report but they cannot remember the details and none of them can find it now. Someone at work says the scientist was German. Others say the experiments were performed in Switzerland, Italy, Paris, France. Someone says this scientist has determined that at the moment of death, a person's body weight decreases by exactly 21 grams. This, he has concluded, is the weight of the human soul which exits the body at death. Where it goes after that has yet to be determined.

Apparently the contents of a soul do not alter its weight. Good or evil, souls are all the same. It is only the weight of the world upon each soul that varies, not to mention the miracles or atrocities which issue from it.

I have tried to learn the metric system but cannot get the hang of it. In the back of my *Better Homes and Gardens New Cookbook* there is a section called "Putting Metric In Perspective." It says that 1 gram is the weight of a paper clip. I put the ceramic balls back in the bowl and hold 21 paper clips in my left hand instead. If I had a balance like the Vermeer woman, what would I put on the other side? A ballpoint pen? A letter from my ex-husband? My daughter's first rattle, a purple plastic hippopotamus? One of the ceramic balls? The red one, the green one, just for a minute now, the blue one is my favourite, be careful.

Someone at work says 21 grams is too light. Someone else says it's too heavy. But to me, the weight of these paper clips as I pass them from hand to hand by the window in the moonlight feels exactly right. As I contemplate them, I imagine my face is expectant but serene. My forehead is smooth.

Years pass. The future becomes the present which then becomes the past. This transformation is inevitable. All events must first occur in the present tense. Before the fact, they are mirages; after the fact, memories. Through it all, the weight of my soul remains unchanged. A stable still point of reference, it continues, constant, motionless, and invisible. The exact nature of its contents has yet to be revealed.

The longest a person has continuously remained motionless is

24 hours, by William Fuqua at Glendale, California, on May 17 to 18, 1985 while sitting on a motorcycle. On July 30, 1988, António Gomes dos Santos of Zare, Portugal, stood motionless for 15 hours, 2 minutes, and 55 seconds at the Amoreiras Shopping Centre in Lisbon.

Forms of Devotion (1994)

Strangely enough we are all seeking a form of devotion which fits our sense of wonder.

—J. Marks, *Transition*

I. FAITH

The faithful are everywhere. They climb into their cars each morning and drive undaunted into the day. They sail off to work, perfectly confident that they will indeed get there: on time, intact. It does not occur to them that they could just as well be broadsided by a Coca-Cola delivery truck running the red light at the corner of Johnson and Main. They do not imagine the bottles exploding, the windshield shattering, their chests collapsing, the blood spurting out of their ears. They just drive. The same route every day, stop and go, back and forth, and yes, they get there: safe and sound. In the same unremarkable manner, they get home again too. Then they start supper without ever once marvelling at the fact that they have survived. It does not occur to them that the can of tuna they are using in the casserole might be tainted and they could all be dead of botulism by midnight.

They are armed with faith. They trust, if not in God exactly, then in the steadfast notion of everyday life. They do not expect to live forever of course, but they would not be entirely surprised if they did. On a daily basis, death strikes them mostly as a calamity which befalls other people, people who are probably evil, care-less, or unlucky: just in the wrong place at the wrong time.

On weekend mornings, the faithful take their children to the park and assume they will not be abducted or fondled behind the climber by a pervert in a trench coat. In the afternoons, they work in their gardens, quite confident that those tiny seeds will eventually produce more tomatoes, zucchini, and green beans than they will know what to do with. They dig in the dirt and believe in the future. They put up preserves, save for retirement, and look forward to being grandparents. After they retire, they plan to buy a motorhome and travel.

When they go to bed at night, they assume that their white houses will stay standing, their green gardens will keep growing, their pink babies will keep breathing, and the yellow sun will rise in the morning just as it always does. Many of the faithful are women, giving birth being, after all, the ultimate act of pure faith. When their sons and daughters (whose as yet embryonic faith may temporarily fail them) wake sobbing from nightmares and wail, "Mommy, I dreamed you were dead. You won't die, will you?" these faithful mothers say, in all honesty, "Don't worry, I won't." The faithful sleep soundly.

If ever they find themselves feeling unhappy or afraid (as sometimes they do because, although faithful, they are also still human), they assume this too shall pass. They expect to be safe. They expect to be saved in the long run. They are devoted to the discharge of their daily lives. It does not occur to them that the meaning of life may be open to question.

II. MEMORY

Remember to put out the garbage, pick up the dry cleaning, defrost the pork chops (the ground beef, the chicken thighs, the fillet of sole). Remember to feed the dog (the cat, the hamster, the goldfish, the canary). Remember the first smile, the first step, the first crush, the first kiss. Remember the bright morning, the long hot afternoon, the quiet evening, the soft bed, gentle rain in the night. Also remember the pain, the disappointments, the humiliations, the broken hearts, and an eclectic assortment of other sorrows. Take these tragedies in stride and with dignity. Do not tear your hair out. Forgive and forget and get on with it. The faithful look back fondly.

They are only passingly familiar with shame, guilt, torment, chaos, existentialism, and metaphysics. The consciences of the faithful are clear. They are not the ones spending millions of dollars on self-help books and exercise videos. They know they've done the best they could. If and when the faithful make mistakes, they know how to forgive themselves without requiring years of expensive therapy in the process.

In the summer, remember the winter: snow sparkling in clear sunlight, children in puffy snowsuits building snowmen and sucking icicles. Remember hockey rinks, rosy cheeks, Christmas carols, wool socks, and hot chocolate with marshmallows. In the winter, remember the summer: tidy green grass beneath big blue sky, long-limbed children playing hide-and-go-seek and running through sprinklers. Remember barbecues, sailboats, flowers, strawberries, and pink lemonade. The faithful can always find something to look forward to. The faithful never confuse the future with the past.

III. KNOWLEDGE

The knowledge of the faithful is vast. They know how to change a tire on a deserted highway in the middle of the night without getting dirty or killed. They know how to bake a birthday cake in the shape of a bunny rabbit with gumdrop eyes and a pink peppermint nose. They know how to unplug a clogged drain with baking soda and vinegar.

They know how to paint the hallway, refinish the hardwood

floors, wallpaper the bedroom, insulate the attic, reshingle the roof, and install a new toilet. They know how to build a campfire and pitch a tent single-handedly. They know how to tune up the car, repair the furnace, and seal the storm windows to prevent those nasty and expensive winter drafts.

They know how to prepare dinner for eight in an hour and a half for less than twenty dollars. They know how to sew, knit, crochet, and cut hair. They know how to keep themselves, their houses, their cars, and their children clean, very clean. They do not resent having to perform the domestic duties of family life. They may even enjoy doing the laundry, washing the walls, cleaning the oven, and grocery shopping.

They know how to make love to the same person for twenty years without either of them getting bored. They know how to administer CPR and the Heimlich manoeuvre. They know how and when to have fun.

The faithful know exactly what to say at funerals, weddings, and cocktail parties. They know when to laugh and when to cry and they never get these two expressions of emotion mixed up. The faithful know they are normal and they're damn proud of it. What they don't know won't hurt them.

IV. INNOCENCE

The faithful are so innocent. Despite all evidence to the contrary, they believe that deep down everybody is just like them, or could be. They believe in benevolence, their own and other people's. They think that, given half a chance, even hardened criminals and manic-depressives can change. They are willing to give everyone a second chance. For the faithful, shaking off doubt is as easy as shaking a rug.

The faithful believe in law and order. They still look up to policemen, lawyers, teachers, doctors, and priests. They believe every word these people say. They even believe what the radio weatherman says in the forecast right after the morning news. It does not occur to them that these authority figures could be wrong, corrupt, or just plain stupid. Mind you, even the faithful are beginning to have serious reservations about politicians.

The faithful take many miraculous things for granted. Things like skin, electricity, trees, water, fidelity, the dogged revolution of the earth around the sun. They believe in beauty as a birthright and surround themselves with it whenever they can. They believe in interior decorating and makeup. They never underestimate the degree of happiness to be engendered by renovating the kitchen, placing fresh-cut flowers on the table, purchasing a set of fine silver, a mink coat, a minivan, or miscellaneous precious jewels. The faithful still believe you get what you pay for.

The faithful take things at face value. They do not search for hidden meanings or agendas. They are not skeptical, cynical, or suspicious. They are not often ironic. The faithful are the angels among us.

V. STRENGTH

The faithless say the faithful are fools. Obviously it must be getting more and more difficult to keep the faith these days. Read the paper. Watch the news. Wonder what the world is coming to. All things considered, it has become harder to believe than to despair.

The faithless say the faithful are missing the point. But secretly the faithless must admit that if indeed, as they allege, there is no point (no purpose, no reason, no hope), then the faithful aren't missing a thing.

The faithless say the faithful are living minor lives, trivial, mundane, frivolous, blind. But secretly the faithless must envy the faithful, wondering if they themselves are simply too faint-hearted for faith.

While the faithless gaze into the abyss, fretting, moaning, and brooding, the faithful are busy getting on with their lives: labouring, rejoicing, carving Hallowe'en pumpkins, roasting Christmas and Thanksgiving turkeys, blowing out birthday candles year after year, and kissing each other wetly at midnight on New Year's Eve.

No matter what, the faithful know how to persevere. They are masters of the rituals that protect them. To the faithful, despair is a foreign language which they have neither the time nor the inclination to learn. The faithful frequently sing in the shower.

The faithful understand the value of fortitude. They carry always with them the courage of their convictions. They do not go to extremes but they could perform miracles if they had to. The faithful will not be crushed by the weight of the world. The faithful are sturdy and brave.

VI. IMAGINATION

The faithful have their imaginations well in hand. They do not lie awake at night imagining earthquakes, tornadoes, flash floods, or nuclear war. They do not deal in cataclysms. They do not entertain the possibility of being axed to death in their beds by a psychokiller on the loose from the psychiatric hospital on the eastern edge of town. They do not lie there wide-eyed for hours picturing malignant cells galloping through their uteruses, their intestines, their prostate glands, or their brains. To the faithful, a headache is a headache, not a brain tumour. They do not imagine themselves rotting away from the inside out. They do not have detailed sexual fantasies about the mailman, the aerobics instructor, or their children's Grade Two teacher. The nights of the faithful are peaceful. Even their nightmares have happy endings. The faithful wake up smiling. Their subconsciouses are clear.

Imagine perfect health, financial security, your mortgage paid off, a new car every second year. Imagine mowing the lawn on Sunday afternoon and enjoying it. Imagine raking leaves in the fall without having to contemplate the futility of daily life. Imagine your grandchildren sitting at your knee while you tell them the story of your life.

The faithful are seldom haunted by a pesky sense of impending doom. They imagine that their lives are unfolding as they were meant to. They imagine that they are free. They imagine finding their feet planted squarely on the road to heaven. The faithful are prepared to live happily ever after.

Imagine laughing in the face of the future.

Imagine belonging to the fine fierce tribe of the faithful.

VII. PRAYER

Pray for sunshine, pray for rain. Pray for peace. Pray for an end to the suffering of the unfortunate. Pray silently in a language simple enough for a child to understand. It is not necessary to get down on your knees with your eyes closed, your hands clasped. It is not necessary to hold your breath. Pray while you are cooking dinner, doing the dishes, washing the floor, holding your sleeping child in your arms. Pray with your heart, not just your mouth.

The faithful know how to pray to whatever gods they may worship. The faithful are praying all the time, every step of the way. Their prayers are not the sort that begin with the word *Please*. They do not bargain with their gods for personal favours. They do not make promises they can't keep, to their gods or anyone else. They do not beg for money, power, easy answers, or a yellow Porsche. They do not beseech, petition, implore, solicit, entreat, adjure, or snivel. They do not throw themselves upon the unreliable mercy of the pantheon. They are not dramatic zealots. The faithful are dignified, stalwart, and patient. All things come to them who will but wait. They are committed to simply enduring in a perpetual state of grace. Their faith itself is a never-ending benediction. The faithful may or may not go to church on Sunday. Their faith is their business.

The prayers of the faithful are mostly wordless forms of devotion. Actions speak louder than language. The faithful are reverent, humble, blessed. They are always busy having a religious experience. The faithful are seldom alarmed or afraid. The faithful barely have time to notice that all their prayers have been answered.

VIII. ABUNDANCE

The faithful have more than enough of everything. They are never stingy. They believe in abundance and they know how to share the wealth. They give regularly to local and international charities and to most panhandlers. They give their old clothes and toys to the poor. The faithful are always generous. Of course they can afford to be. Of course there's more where that came from.

Every evening at dinner the faithful cry, "More, more, let's have some more!" The table is completely covered with heavy oval platters of meat and giant bowls of mashed potatoes and garden salad. They always have dessert. They prefer their children soft and plump. The faithful never bite off more than they can chew.

The days of the faithful are as full as their stomachs. They have energy to burn. They never whine about having too much to do. They like to be busy. They do not need time to think. Their bounty abounds. Their homes and their hearts are always full. Full of exuberance or solemnity, whichever current circumstances may require. The cups of the faithful frequently runneth over.

The arms of the faithful are always open. They have time for everyone. The faithful know how to share both the triumphs and the sorrows of others. They've always got the coffee on, blueberry muffins in the oven, a box of Kleenex handy just in case. The faithful know how to listen and they only offer advice when they're asked.

The faithful know how to count their blessings, even if it takes all day. They have all the time in the world. They know when to thank their lucky stars. The faithful are privileged but they are not smug.

IX. WISDOM

The faithful are uncommonly wise. They are indefatigably glad to be alive. To the faithful everything matters. It does not occur to them that their whole lives may well end up having been nothing but a waste of time. The faithful are always paying attention. They know how to revel in the remarkable treasures of the everyday: a pink rose blooming below the window, a ham and cheese omelette steaming on the plate, a white cat washing her face in the sun, a new baby with eyes the colour of sand, a double rainbow in the western sky after a long hard rain. The faithful love rainbows and pots of gold. They know how to take pleasure wherever they can find it. The faithful are always exclaiming, "Look, look, look at that!" To the faithful nothing is mundane.

The faithful are everywhere. See if you can spot them: in the bank lineup on Friday afternoon, at McDonald's having hamburgers and chocolate milkshakes with their children, in the park walking the dog at seven o'clock on a January morning, at the hardware store shopping for a socket wrench and a rake. The faithful may be right in your own backyard.

The faithful are thankful for small pleasures and small mercies.

The faithful are earnest.

The faithful are easily amused.

The faithful do or do not know how lucky they are.

The faithful frequently cry at parades.

The faithful are not afraid of the dark because they have seen the light.

Nothing is lost on the faithful. As far as they are concerned, wonders will never cease. The faithful are convinced that the best is yet to come.

X. HOPE

The hope of the faithful is a tonic. Their eyes are bright, their skin is clear, their hair is shiny, and their blood flows vigorously through all of their veins. Even in times of adversity, the faithful know how to take heart. At the tiniest tingle of possibility, the faithful are not afraid to get their hopes up. They believe in divine providence. It all depends on how you define *divine*. The faithful are not fools. Although the faithless would dispute this, the faithful live in the real world just as much as anyone. They know all about hoping against hope. But they are not troubled by paradox. They are immune to those fits of despair which can cripple and dumbfound.

Concerning matters both big and small, the faithful have always got hope. Their whole lives are forms of perpetual devotion to the promise which hope extends. The faithful breathe hope like air, drink it like water, eat it like popcorn. Once they start, they can't stop.

Hope for world peace. Hope for a drop in the crime rate, shelter for the homeless, food for the hungry, rehabilitation for the deranged. Hope your son does well on his spelling test. Hope your team wins the World Series. Hope your mother does not have cancer. Hope the pork chops are not undercooked. Hope your best friend's husband is not having an affair with his secretary. Hope you win the lottery. Hope the rain stops tomorrow. Hope this story has a happy ending.

The hope of the faithful is infinite, ever expanding to fill the space available. Faith begets hope. Hope begets faith. Faith and hope beget power.

The faithful lean steadily into the wind.

How Deep is the River? (1996)

Train A and Train B are travelling toward the same bridge from opposite directions. The bridge spans a wide deep river in which three young women drowned two years ago in the spring. Train A is 77 miles west of the bridge, travelling due east at a speed of 86 miles per hour. Train B is 62 miles east of the bridge, travelling due west at a speed of 74 miles per hour. Which train will reach the bridge first?

(Assume that Trains A and B are travelling on a double track so there is no danger of a head-on collision. Assume that both Trains A and B are mechanically sound, that both engineers are well trained, well rested, and have not been drinking. Assume the bridge is well constructed and meets all federal safety standards. Assume it is August.

Assume that if any of the passengers on Trains A and B are in danger, it has nothing to do with their presence here on the shining steel rails approaching the bridge. Assume that nothing bad will happen to any of them during the course of this trip.)

This is like those word problems in high school math, the ones where bits and pieces of supposedly relevant information were given and then a mysterious question was posed.

An elephant's eye is 10.36 feet above ground level. The angle of elevation from a mouse on the ground to the elephant's eye is 46°. How far is the mouse from the elephant?

These knotty problems could only be solved by manipulating the information, making qualified assumptions, and then performing agile feats of arithmetical magic.

A bird is perched at the top of a tree. A cat sits on the ground below. The angle of depression from the bird to the cat is 58°. The cat is 39.67 feet from the base of the tree. How high is the tree?

These problems either caused the mind to go blank or else filled it with other questions, unasked, unanswerable, irrelevant but no less compelling for that. Are elephants really afraid of mice? How hungry is the cat?

Some of these problems were constructed around everyday situations to which high school students were supposed to be able to relate.

When Melanie is shopping, her heart beats about 100 times per minute and she takes 21 breaths per minutes. During a trip to the mall that lasts 130 minutes, how many times will Melanie's heart beat? How many breaths will she take?

How fast will Melanie's heart beat when she finally finds the perfect shirt which she has been dreaming of for the past three months? (Assume that Melanie has enough money to buy the shirt. Assume the shirt is blue.) How many breaths will Melanie hold while trying on the shirt, praying that it will look as good on her in real life as it does in her dreams?

The solutions to these problems were always in the back of the book. But no explanation was ever given as to how the answers were arrived at, why the questions had been asked in the first place, or what good the solutions could possibly do you once you had them.

Julie is walking west down Markham Street. She stops to wave to her friend, Karen, who is leaning out the window of her sixth-floor apartment. The vertical distance between Julie and Karen is 92 feet. The angle of elevation from Julie to Karen is 79°. How far is Julie from the apartment building?

(Assume that Julie and Karen are sixteen and seventeen years old respectively. Assume that Karen will not fall out the window. Assume that Julie is wearing her favourite red cowboy boots.

Assume it is Saturday morning.) Will Karen invite Julie up for a visit? Will Julie then tell Karen a secret told to her the night before by their mutual friend, Melanie, a secret which Karen promised Melanie she would never ever tell? (Assume that Julie crossed her heart and hoped to die. Assume that Melanie was wearing her new blue shirt.)

Of these three girls, Julie, Karen, and Melanie, which one will get pregnant and drop out of school? Which one will become a veterinarian? Which one will eventually find herself on Train B, 62 miles east of the bridge, travelling due west at a speed of 74 miles per hour?

Train A is full of Friday afternoon travellers. They have all left behind their more or less comfortable homes in City X and are now well on their way to City Y. The population of City X is twenty times greater than the population of City Y. Some of the residents of City X think it is the centre of the universe. They are no longer completely convinced that the rest of the country still exists. If it does, they feel sorry for the people who have to live there. They are certain that nothing significant, interesting, or memorable ever happens in the backward barrens beyond the limits of City X. They have never been to City Y. They are not among the passengers aboard Train A as it now approaches the bridge.

Other residents of City X are constantly longing to move away but they are tied there by their jobs, their spouses, their spouses' jobs, or their own inertia. City X suffers from all the social problems indigenous to a metropolis of its size. These problems are now called *issues* and they are running rampant through the streets of City X. Besides all that, the streets of City X are smelly in the August heat and the smog hovers, trapped by a low-lying bank of humidity currently stalled over the city. It is because of these and other more personal issues that some residents of City X are chronically discontent. It is from this portion of the population that most of the passengers on Train A have come. They are so glad to be escaping, if only for the weekend.

What is the ratio of people who love City X to those who don't? (Assume that some people are ambivalent, moody, and unpredictable, loving the city one day while hating it the next. Assume that some people are just never satisfied.) What proportion of those who now love City X will eventually change their minds after one or more of those endemic social issues has impacted directly upon their own lives? What proportion of those who now hate City X will eventually muster enough gumption to leave?

The atmosphere aboard Train A is undeniably festive. Each of its six full cars fairly hums with anticipation and high holiday spirits. Strangers strike up animated conversations, share newspapers, and point out interesting features of the passing landscape: cows, barns, ducks on a pond, once a white-tailed deer bolting gracefully into the bush at the sound of the train. Now this is more like it: no high-rises, no traffic jams, no pollution, no neon, no issues. They are travelling through wilderness now, or at least what passes for wilderness in this overly civilized part of the country. Occasionally their idyll is interrupted by the appearance of the highway, four lanes of blacktop running parallel to the train tracks. The traffic is heavy in both directions, shiny cars and dirty trucks skimming along beside them like little windup toys. Soon enough the highway veers away again and disappears.

On the other side of the wilderness, City Y awaits. Hardly a city at all in comparison to City X, its downtown streets are clean and safe, frequently closed to traffic to allow for buskers' festivals, street dances, and miscellaneous parades. (Assume that if City Y suffers from any of the social issues which plague City X, they are well hidden and so need not concern the carefree weekend visitor.) City Y rests on the shores of a large lake and much of its summer activity revolves around the water. There are sailing regattas, fish derbies, and free boat rides around the harbour.

There is even a beach where the water is still clean enough to swim in. In the waterfront park there are craft fairs, dog shows, jugglers and mimes, hot dog stands, ice cream carts, and bands playing all day long, some with bagpipes, some without.

None of the passengers on Train A are currently thinking about the bridge, how far they are from it, how soon they will reach it, or about the river, how those poor young women drowned, how the current caught them up and carried them away. The passengers on Train A will simply cross that bridge when they come to it.

Right now the passengers on Train A are thinking about lunch. The food service porter has just begun to make his way down the aisle with his wheeled metal cart. All up and down the car, the passengers are pulling out their plastic trays from where they have been quietly nestled inside the padded arms between the seats. Although they are all well aware of the fact that train food is nothing to get excited about, still they smile expectantly at the approaching porter. He skillfully hands out food, drinks, plastic knives and forks, and little packets of condiments from side to side down the swaying aisle.

The porter offers three varieties of pre-packaged sandwiches: pressed turkey on brown, ham and cheese on a bagel, and egg salad on white. The beverages available include seven varieties of soda pop, three kinds of juice, three brands of beer, four types of hard liquor, and two kinds of bottled water.

Those who have not travelled by train in some time are surprised to discover that, although these sandwiches used to be a "complimentary light meal," now they must be paid for. What remains complimentary are the non-alcoholic beverages and a small package of either salted peanuts or two chocolate chip cookies. How many passengers will now settle for a package of peanuts when they would have ham and cheese on a bagel if it were still free? (Assume that by the time the porter is two-thirds of the way down the car he will have run out of ham and cheese anyway. Assume that a free dry pre-packaged sandwich of any type is much more appetizing than one that costs $3.25. Assume that the porter is pretty well fed up with listening to people complain about the prices.) If twenty-seven people in this car had ham and cheese on a bagel and seventeen people had pressed turkey on brown, how many people had egg salad on white? Why are there always six egg salad sandwiches left over?

After the basically unsatisfying distraction of lunch, the porter comes around again and collects the garbage in a big black plastic bag. The passengers drop their trays back into their hiding places. Some people order another beer. There is congestion at the very back of the car as people line up for the bathrooms. They stand in the tiny vestibule and look through the glass door at the tracks unrolling hypnotically beneath them. Some of those people staring at the tracks with their bladders full experience a distinct urge to jump. (Assume that everyone successfully suppresses this impulse.) What are the odds that, once any given passenger is finally inside the bathroom and comfortably installed upon the plastic toilet seat, Train A will then encounter a particularly bumpy stretch of track or a sharp curve to the right?

Once the passengers have settled themselves in their seats again, they can get back to contemplating the weekend ahead of them. While visiting City Y, the passengers of Train A will do many different things. Some of them will enjoy shopping for souvenir teeshirts, key chains, and coffee mugs. Others will spend all day in the park eating junk food, while still others will go sailing, waterskiing, fishing, or swimming. They will all enjoy themselves immensely.

(Assume that no one from City X will be mugged, raped, stabbed, hit by a car, bitten by a dog, or spit on by a panhandler while visiting City Y. Assume that no one will be struck down by food poisoning, appendicitis, a heart attack, a cerebral aneurysm, or a severe allergic reaction to seafood. Assume that no one will choke to death on a fish bone. Assume that no one will drown, not in the lake, the bathtub, or a puddle of tears.)

Train B is just as full of festive weekend travellers as Train A. The passengers on Train B are just as happy to be going to City X as the passengers on Train A are to be leaving it. (Assume that this apparent paradox is a manifestation of the notion that the grass is always greener on the other side. Assume that the shortage of grass in many areas of City X is not prohibitive to the exercise of this notion.) Although most of those aboard Train B genuinely enjoy living in City Y, still sometimes they get restless. City Y is so quiet, so safe, so boring, so *parochial.* Some of its residents long for the bustle of the big city, the pulse, the vigour, the culture, the *grit.* While visiting City X, they feel alive again.

Other residents of City Y are not the least bit impressed by City X. These people are utterly convinced that should they ever venture into its congested malodorous streets, some ferocious urban evil would immediately befall them and they might or might not be lucky enough to escape with their lives. What proportion of these people are right?

The passengers on Train B have just been served exactly the same lunch as the passengers on Train A. Their porter has been around to collect the garbage and has scolded several people for changing seats when he wasn't looking. Now the passengers are settling themselves in for the rest of the ride. They are wiggling into more comfortable positions, dozing, or pulling out newspapers, crossword puzzle books, and fat paperback novels by Stephen King and Danielle Steel. Many stare vacantly out the windows, searching still in vain for incipient signs of civilization.

Nothing yet: just fields and trees, cows and birds, a cloudless August sky. They sigh impatiently and resume making plans for the weekend ahead.

Depending on their particular predilections, they will partake liberally of the many amenities which City X has to offer. Some of them will shop in malls as big as airports until they are exhausted and broke. Confronted with such a vast array of merchandise, some of them will become overstimulated. Their hearts will beat too fast and they will hyperventilate while running all their credit cards up to the limit. Others, paralyzed by indecision, will walk away empty-handed, sulky and tearful in a fit of frustrated consumerism.

Some people will spend all day long in museums and art galleries, soaking up culture like sponges. In the evening they will dine in expensive restaurants and then go to the theatre, the opera, the ballet, or a poetry reading. How many of these people don't really like poetry? How many of them would rather be at a baseball game, a strip club, or an X-rated movie?

Families with young children will go to the zoo, an amusement park, an afternoon show featuring six-foot-tall cat puppets and a man dressed as an elephant playing the violin. How many of these children will pee their pants or throw up while waiting in line to have their faces painted?

The passengers aboard both Trains A and B come from all across the demographic spectrum. This, after all, is one of the beauties of train travel. While in transit, people are held in temporary suspension, free for the moment from all the obligations and inhibitions normally imposed upon them by class, race, religion, gender, and by all the doubts they may usually harbour about the rest of humanity. While in transit, people often find themselves telling total strangers things they have not told their best friends.

On Train A, for instance, an elderly woman with blue hair finds herself sitting beside a teenager with green spiked hair and three rings in her nose. They are discussing their favourite brands of hair dye and how hard it is to find a hairdresser you can really trust. (Assume that, although the teenager may eventually dye her hair blue, the elderly woman is not ever going to dye hers green. Assume also that the elderly woman will never have her nose, her tongue, or her nipples pierced.)

Across the aisle, a born-again Christian with a Bible in her purse is assuring an unhappy-looking young man with severe acne and bad teeth that if only he will give himself over to the Lord, all his problems will be solved. How many years will pass before this young man's acne clears up, suddenly, miraculously, without leaving a single scar? How many years will pass before he wins the lottery and uses some of the money to get his teeth fixed and then gives the rest anonymously to the Divine Temple of Supreme Virtue? (Assume that God works in mysterious ways.)

Similarly, on Train B, a grey-haired man in a three-piece suit is listening avidly to an attractive buxom woman with a husky voice describing in great detail her now-estranged husband's reaction to her belated revelation that she had begun her life as a man. (Assume that after years of intensive therapy, the husband will get over it. Assume that the grey-haired man in the suit will not. Assume that he will have erotic dreams about this woman for the rest of his natural life.)

Across the aisle and three rows down, a pale woman in a green dress is pretending to sleep in an attempt to avoid any further conversation with the woman in the mauve blouse beside her. Let the woman in the green dress be Woman A. Let the woman in the mauve blouse be Woman B. Ever since they both boarded Train B at the station in City Y, Woman B has been talking. She is ten years older than Woman A who is the same age now as Woman B was when her youngest child was born. Woman A is five years older now than Woman B was when she got married.

How old is Woman A? How long has Woman B been married? Why is Woman A so unfriendly? (Assume that the oldest child of Woman B is the same age now as Woman A was when she lost her virginity. Assume that Woman A was very much in love with the boy who deflowered her. Assume they got married four years later. Assume that this husband of Woman A does not know that she is now aboard Train B on her way to City X. Assume that he thinks she has gone shopping at the mall and will be home in time to make his supper. Assume that until now Woman A has always done what was expected of her.)

While Train B has been steadily approaching the bridge, the river, and City X, Woman B has told Woman A all about the shag carpeting she has just had installed in her living room, the many interesting ways she has found to use cream of mushroom soup, and the colours she intends to repaint the bedrooms in the fall. She has gone on at great length about her husband's mid-life crisis two years ago during which he had an affair with his secretary—let the secretary be Woman C—and she, Woman B, pretended she never knew a thing about it until finally her husband got it out of his system and fired Woman C and now their marriage is stronger than ever and they are going to Bermuda at Christmas.

Now Woman A is wishing she had the nerve to tell Woman B to shut up. She can feel the details of Woman B's life bubbling into her ears, filling up her nose, her mouth, her throat, her lungs. She is afraid that if she listens to Woman B long enough, she will either scream or be swept away by the torrent and turn into her. What are the odds that she is right? (Assume that Woman B represents everything Woman A is running away from. Assume that Woman C has her own problems.)

Woman A, the one in the green dress, is Karen, who once waved to her friend, Julie, from her sixth-floor apartment on Markham

Street in City Y. (Assume that years have passed since then. Assume it was Melanie who got pregnant and dropped not only out of school but out of sight as well. Assume the secret Melanie told Julie, who then told it to Karen, was that she had finally gone all the way with her boyfriend, Joe.

Assume this story played itself out in a predictable way: Melanie pregnant, Joe gone, Melanie's parents horrified but anti-abortion, Melanie sent away to a home for unwed mothers, intending to give the baby up for adoption but changing her mind at the last minute, Melanie's parents disowning her, Melanie and her baby never heard from by Karen or Julie again.

Assume that Julie finished high school with good grades, went on to university, moved far away from City Y, and became a veterinarian. Assume that Julie always loved animals.)

Now Karen aboard Train B en route to City X feigns sleep until her garrulous seatmate nods off herself, snoring lightly with her mouth ajar. Karen opens her eyes and looks out the window. The sky is beginning to cloud over. They are still in the middle of nowhere. If nowhere has a middle, does it also have a beginning and an end? What formula must be used to measure the dimensions of nowhere? What other properties of nowhere can be accurately ascertained? Is nowhere vegetable, animal, or mineral; a solid, a liquid, or a gas? (Assume that nowhere is probably most like water: a shape-shifting liquid which can also disguise itself as a solid or a gas. Assume that no matter in which form it is encountered, nowhere, like water, can be fatal.

Assume it is Karen's penchant for the contemplation of this and other metaphysical questions which has led, at least in part, to her growing dissatisfaction with her quiet normal life in City Y and, subsequently, to her purchase of a one-way train ticket to City X. Assume that her recent realization that her husband is a stupid, boring, insensitive man who is as selfish in bed as anywhere else is also a contributing factor to her defection.)

Karen sits perfectly still and lets Train B carry her forward. She lets all possibility, all promise, all freedom and the future wash gently over her. Ever since those high school days when she lived with her parents on Markham Street in City Y, Karen has been waiting for her real life to begin. Now she imagines that in City X she will find a whole new life and live it, happily ever after. She thinks she will never be bored, lost, or lonely again. She thinks she is going to finally find herself in City X.

(Assume that once Train B crosses the bridge, Karen will imagine it and all other bridges like it bursting into jubilant flames behind her. Assume that Karen will never look back.)

In fact, it is Train A that reaches the bridge first. On the right bank of the river there are four small boys with fishing rods. Considering the heat, the season, and the time of day, how many fish are they likely to catch? (Assume that not one of these boys has ever heard about the three young women who drowned in this river two years ago in the spring. Assume that, as far as these small boys are concerned, there is nothing beneath the surface of the water but many elusive, tantalizing fish and several old tractor tires illegally dumped there by the owner of a nearby farm. Assume that when the boys' fishing lines get snagged, it is on one of these tires, on a rock or a branch, not on a long-dead body still waiting to be raised from the depths.)

Many of the people aboard Train A admire the river, the boys, the quaint and nostalgic picture they make. The boys on the bank wave at the train. The passengers smile and think beatific watery thoughts. They think of floating on their backs with their eyes closed for hours, of warm waves lapping sandy beaches, blue lakes still and clear as windows, aquariums filled with graceful multicoloured tropical fish. They think of brooks babbling, a raging thirst quenched, mermaids, sailboats, the sea.

It is only the born-again Christian with the Bible in her purse who thinks about the drownings. She crosses herself and thinks of the four rivers of paradise, the four rivers of hell, the purifying sacrament of baptism, and of how in the olden days those accused of witchcraft were immersed in water and if they floated they were deemed guilty but if they sank they were declared innocent and saved. She imagines the souls of the innocent flying up to the waiting arms of the Lord. (Assume that someday this woman will be one of them. Assume that even now she can feel her wings beginning to grow.)

After Train A has crossed the bridge, it passes Train B, which has stopped briefly to allow Train A to safely proceed. Then Train B continues on to the bridge. The boys on the riverbank are still fishing. Again they look up and wave at the train. What are the odds that any of the passengers on Train B are having exactly the same watery thoughts while crossing the bridge as did the passengers on Train A just minutes before? (Assume the observation that you can never step into the same river twice is still true.) What percentage of the passengers on Train B find themselves thinking about sharks, sewage, tidal waves, floods, water on the brain, water on the knee, too much water under the bridge?

Woman B, the garrulous seatmate of Karen, Woman A, has been awakened by the stopping and starting of the train. The minute her eyes are open, she starts talking again. Why is it not surprising that Woman B knows all about the three young women who drowned? Karen does not want to think about them. Karen wants to think about how, when floating in still water of just the right temperature, you cannot feel your body anymore. Woman B keeps talking, apparently angry at the three young victims for having been so careless, so foolish, so selfish as to go out and drown themselves like that. What were they doing out in that little boat anyway when the river was obviously dangerous, what with the spring runoff, heavy rains the week before, warning signs posted all over the place? Why weren't they wearing life jackets at least? What, she wants to know, what on earth were they thinking of?

(Assume they were not thinking of death. Assume they were thinking of fish, sun, sex, shopping, school, the case of beer in the bottom of the boat. Assume they were not thinking of water as a symbol of both fertility and oblivion, of water as both the source of all life and the end of it, or of the river as the point of transition from one life to the next. Assume that they, like Karen, were thinking they still had their whole lives ahead of them.)

A small boat floats upside down in the middle of a wide deep river which is spanned by a concrete railway bridge. (Assume that someone has spray-painted a crude drawing of a naked woman on the side of the bridge. Assume the drawing is visible only from the river, not from any train crossing over the bridge.) *How high is the bridge?*

The boat is wooden, white. (Assume that on both sides of the bow are the words JESUS SAVES painted in red block letters.) *How big is the boat?*

On the left bank of the river, Body A is caught in the roots of a tree 33.75 feet from the boat. (Assume this tree in the middle of nowhere is a weeping willow. Assume that Body A will be found first, bobbing face down in the reeds.) *How old is the tree?*

On the bottom of the river lies Body B. The angle of depression from the boat to this body is 53°. (Assume that soon enough the river will spit out Body B which will then be carted away in a large black bag.) *How many men will it take to lift the bag?*

Body C is nowhere in sight. (Assume that by the time she is found, her hair will have turned into seaweed, her eye sockets will be filled with shells, and her feet will have sprouted silver-green fins. Assume that by the time she is found, there will be no one left to identify her.) *How many miles downstream has Body C travelled?*

The surface of the river sparkles in the sun. (Assume it is disturbed only by fish jumping, ducks diving, the gentle shudder of the wind.)

How deep is the river?

Five Small Rooms
(A Murder Mystery)

(1996)

I have learned not to underestimate the power of rooms, especially a small room with unequivocal corners, exemplary walls, and well-mannered windows, divided into many rectangular panes. I like a small room without curtains, carpets, misgivings, or ghosts.

I. SMALL ROOM WITH PEARS

I like a room painted in a confident full-bodied colour. I steer clear of pastels because they are, generally speaking, capricious, irresolute, and frequently coy. Blue is a good colour for a small room, especially if it is of a shade called Tidal Pool, Tropical Sea, Azure, Atoll, or Night Swim.

I once painted a room a shade of blue called Rainy Day. I find a rainy day to be a fine thing on occasion, particularly after an unmitigated stretch of gratuitous sunshine. In that blue room, I kept a stock of umbrellas ready at hand just in case. This was the first room I ever painted all by myself. For years I had believed that painting a room was a task I could never master, a task better left to professionals or men. After I finished painting this room, I was as proud of myself as if I had discovered the Northwest Passage.

This room had many outstanding features including lots of large cupboards and a counter ample enough to perform surgery on if necessary. In the cupboards I kept all kinds of things:

dresses that no longer fit or flattered me, a bird's nest I'd found in the park when I was six, a red and white lace negligee, the program from a musical version of *Macbeth,* several single socks and earrings, instruction manuals for a radio, a blow-dryer, and a lawn mower that I no longer owned, a package of love letters tied up with a black satin ribbon. No matter how many secrets I stowed in these cupboards, they never filled up.

Often I found myself wandering into the blue room in the middle of the night. I would stand naked staring into the refrigerator at three in the morning, until the cold air gave me goose-bumps and my nipples got hard. It was a very old refrigerator which sometimes chirped like a distant melancholy cricket. I was searching not for food so much as for memories, motives, an alibi: how it looked, how it happened, when.

I would reach into the refrigerator and pull out a chunk of ham, a chicken leg, a slice of cheese, or some fruit. Pears were my favourite. Imagine the feel of the sweet gritty flesh on your tongue, the voluptuous juice on your chin. Pears are so delicate. My fingertips made bruises on their thin mottled skin.

This was nothing like "The Love Song of J. Alfred Prufrock": *Shall I part my hair behind? Do I dare to eat a peach? / I shall wear white flannel trousers, and walk upon the beach. / I have heard the mermaids singing, each to each.* Peaches I am not fond of. Their fuzz gives me shivers like fingernails on a chalkboard. The colour of their flesh close to the pit is too much like that of meat close to the bone. My consumption of pears had nothing to do with daring or indecision. It was strictly a matter of pure pleasure, which always comes as a great relief. At that point in my life, I'd had no dealings with mermaids and did not expect to. I am tone-deaf and, much as I admire a good body of water, I have never learned to swim.

As for the women who come and go, they are not likely to be talking of Michelangelo.

II. SMALL ROOM WITH SEASHELLS

Later there was another small blue room, this one painted in a shade called Atlantis because it was situated on the very edge of the ocean. In this room I enjoyed the omnipresent odour of salt water and the ubiquitous sound of the surf. These struck me as two things I would never grow tired of.

This room was very sturdy, with support beams as substantial and steadfast as tree trunks. The windows were recessed deep into the thick outer walls. These walls were solid straight through, not hollow in the middle like most. They put me in mind of chocolate Easter bunnies, how the best bunnies are the solid ones, how cheated you feel when biting into a hollow one only to discover that it is just a thin shell of chocolate around a rabbit-shaped pocket of sweet empty air.

Here I often wandered out to the beach in the middle of the night. I did not wear white flannel trousers and I never heard the mermaids singing. I had no desire to disturb the universe. I simply stood there with my toes in the ocean and my head in the sky. The hair on my arms stood up in the moonlight. I studied the constellations and thought about words like *firmament, nebula,* and *galactic cannibalism.* I had to keep reminding myself that some of the stars I was seeing were already dead. I had trouble at first with the whole notion of light-years, with time as a function of distance, speed, and illumination, rather than as simply the conduit from then to now.

On cloudy nights, when I could not pursue the perfection of my theory of stars, I turned instead to collecting the miscellaneous offerings which the ocean so munificently deposited at my feet.

I gathered seashells by the fistful, listened for the ocean in each of them, and it was always there, like the same moon seen from every continent, the same God petitioned in every prayer. From the sand I plucked moon shells, harp shells, angel wings, helmets, goblets, butterflies, cockles, and tusks. Less plentiful and so of course more desirable were the sundial and chambered nautilus shells. I'd read somewhere once how the young cephalopod at first lives in the centre of its shell but as it grows larger, it must move forward, sealing off each chamber behind itself. This would be like shutting a door and having it permanently locked behind you.

The seashells, like the stars, were long dead, the beautiful cast-off husks of the ugly mollusks that had made them. Only these pretty skeletons had survived, just as it was only the light of the stars that could still reach me. I thought long and hard about chambers, skeletons, a series of small rooms, the missing bodies of seashells and stars.

There were other things too offered up by the sea: tangled balls of fishing line, plastic bags, a bracelet, a knife. A pair of pantyhose, a set of keys, a bathing suit, and several used condoms. Pieces of driftwood like bones, coils of seaweed like entrails. One night I found a water-bloated copy of a murder mystery called *Dead Dead Double Dead*. The last five pages were missing. This, I could not help but think, was hitting a little too close to home.

Apparently the ocean, in addition to being a weighty and ambivalent symbol of dynamic forces, transitional states, the collective unconscious, chaos, creation, and universal womanhood in all its benevolent and heinous incarnations, was also the repository of all lost things. I had long wondered what happened to those socks that went into the washing machine and never came out.

At this time I still believed that I could summon up my former self whenever I was ready, that I could gather up my innocence and step back into it like an old pair of shoes. Now I began to see this was no longer true. Eventually I realized that in this small room I was forever in danger of drowning or being swallowed by a sea monster. This epiphany marked the end of my blue period.

III. SMALL ROOM WITH CATS

Various shades of brown are good for small rooms too. Brown imparts a sense of serenity, solidity, and security. Imagine lying down on a bed of warm soil. Imagine being buried alive and liking it. I am partial to any colour of brown that looks like coffee with milk in it or any shade that is named after food: Honey Nut, Bran Muffin, Caramel Chip, or Indian Corn. In a small room painted a colour called Pumpkin Loaf, I always felt full. Sometimes in the morning I thought I could smell the sweet bread baking.

In this room there were tables but no chairs. Clearly the importance of chairs has been overestimated. I quickly got over my atavistic longings for them. Soon enough I could hardly imagine what I'd ever deemed to be indispensable about chairs. Like so many other things I once thought I could never live without, chairs, once I got used to their absence, proved to be just another habit, a knee-jerk reflex like flinching, apologizing, or falling in love. The only time I seriously missed them was when I wanted to sit down and tie my shoes. This was like wishing for a man when you want to clean out the eavestrough or open a new jar of pickles.

There were also many shelves in this brown room, tidy well-spaced shelves like boxes built right into the wall. Some of them still bore items left behind by some former fugitive tenant. There was a pink lampshade which, in a happier time, I might have put on my head. There were some pale yellow bedsheets, soft from many washings, stained with the bodily fluids of long-gone strangers. No matter where you go, you are always leaving incriminating tidbits of evidence behind you.

There was a stack of old *National Geographic* magazines. Everyone has a pile of these stashed away somewhere. There were also several empty picture frames propped up on the shelves and hammered to the walls. I carefully cut photographs from the magazines and stuck them in these frames. I selected several panoramic views of jungles, mountains, fields of wheat. I chose skies without clouds, seas without boats, landscapes without figures. I changed these pictures often so as not to feel that I was just treading water or running in place.

Here I kept cats for company. I like the look of a small room with two cats in it. I tried to emulate the way they can settle themselves anywhere like boneless shape-shifting pillows and how, when falling from a great height, they will almost always land on their feet. I was impressed too by their apparently infinite ability to adapt, the way they can live well anywhere: in an alley, a barn, a palace, or a small brown room with tables and shelves, no chairs.

I told my cats stories of other cats, famous cats, tenacious cats, heroic cats, miraculous cats who found their way home again after travelling through endless miles of wilderness, fording rivers, scaling canyons, leaping tall buildings with a single bound. My cats curled around me and purred. It is not true that cats only purr when they're happy. They also do it when they're worried or in pain.

In my time I have been accused of many things: jealousy, arrogance, selfishness, viciousness, laziness, bitterness, and lust. Also infidelity, inclemency, insanity, immorality, and pride. I have been called reckless, heartless, shameless, malicious, sarcastic, demanding, domineering, cold-blooded, and cruel. The cats, of course, knew none of this and did not care to ask. They were well aware of the perils of curiosity, the trials and tribulations of being misunderstood. There is always someone who will be offended by a cat's enthusiasm for killing. Think of the way they play with their prey and then, once it is sufficiently dead, how they always eat the head first, often swallowing it whole. Think of the way they leave the hearts behind, those slimy little lumps drawing flies in the driveway. Myself, I do not find this distasteful. There is always someone who will tell you that your instincts are wrong. Outside, the sweet yellow fog pressed against the windowpanes.

IV. SMALL ROOM WITH MOTH

Most kinds of green paint, as you would expect, are named after pastoral scenes and growing things: Meadow, Pasture, Orchard, Leaf, Broccoli, Asparagus, Spinach, and Dill. In a small room painted a shade called Forest Lane, the air was always moist, emitting an intimate odour of new growth and decay. The light was leafy and diffuse, like a green glaze on my skin. The ceiling was done in Maiden of the Mist, a humid colour much like that of the sky on a hazy August afternoon. If I stared at this ceiling for too long, I found I could not catch my breath.

Where the walls met the ceiling, there were curves instead of straight lines and angles. The tops of the windows and doorway were vaulted too. I enjoyed these arches the way you enjoy a symphony, your whole body thrilling at the crescendo's inevitable approach. I like a good old-fashioned symphony, the way it stirs the blood. At this point in my life I knew I was ripe for a transformation.

In this room there were many solid wooden benches, the purpose of which was never clear. Perhaps the room had once been the meeting place of a secret cult whose members would sit on these benches in rows of black cloaks and hoods, worshipping their various devils and gods, planning their next move. Arranged upon these mysterious benches was an impressive assortment of cookware, metal pots and bowls of many sizes, some battered, some smooth. Perhaps these had been used to boil the sacrificial virgins or lambs. My desires both to cook and to eat having been dislodged by the heat and my overactive imagination, I filled these vessels with flowers instead of stew, sacrificial or otherwise. In this green room I ate only raw green things: lettuce, celery, sweet peppers, and limes.

Here I did not wander at night. I still went to bed not knowing what I had been accused of but this uncertainty no longer tormented me. I had only two bad dreams during my sojourn in this green room. The first was of having my head shrivelled to the size of a small sweet pepper, then sliced in half and served upon a big green platter. The second was of having my body covered with a fine white powder and then pinned still wriggling to the wall. It was not a green wall. It was a red wall. I slept flat on my back with the windows open and a candle burning on the floor beside me.

Moths flew in through the open windows, misguided emissaries from the unbridled night. The patterns on their wings were written in a language I did not yet understand. They came from miles around, unable to resist the sweet deadly pull of the flame any more than I could ever resist a ripe pear, a good murder mystery, or a man who said he could save me. Moths, like humans, engage in complicated courtship rituals which involve elaborate dances and sudden dazzling flights. It was hard to determine whether they were courting each other or the promise of a hot dramatic death. I could have reached up from my bed and touched them. But as a child I was told you must never touch a moth because if that fine powder is rubbed off its wings, it will die. Outside, I thought I heard voices but I was mistaken.

I did not touch the moths. They died anyway. In the morning I would find their corpses littering the floor around my guttered candle. Their beautiful wings were scorched, their feathery antennae fried, that magic powder turned to ash. There was a lesson to be learned here, something about fortitude and the purification of the soul by fire. Either that or the moths were simply too stupid to survive. Some people believe that white moths are actually the souls of the dead and that if a black moth flies into a house, it means that someone who lives there will die within the year.

Looking back on my own life, it is hard to determine which was the moth and which was the flame. In these matters, there is no such thing as black and white.

V. SMALL ROOM WITH CLOCKS

I have learned to be wary of the purples which have names like Dazzle, Delusion, Charade, Mirage, and Masquerade. When I first painted this small room a shade of purple called New Year's Eve, it was easy to fool myself into believing that here I could make time stand still. I imagined myself poised in the middle of the countdown to midnight. All around me expectant voices chanted: *Ten nine eight seven six five.* Then they stopped. Thousands of upturned faces gaped incredulously as the silver ball hung there and dropped no farther. Like the boy with his finger in the dike, I believed I could hold back time by the sheer forces of will, desire, and good intentions. I was encouraged by the knowledge that ancient sailors without clocks had navigated solely by instinct and fortuity.

This room, like the others, has large windows divided into many rectangular panes, thick walls solid straight through, built-in shelves filled with an efficient array of cookware, several sturdy tables, and no chairs. I see now that I am beginning to repeat myself.

In an old barrel with wooden slats and rusted iron bands I found two large clocks, identical in every way. Under normal circumstances I appreciate an accurate clock, but here I tried not to dwell on the fact that these two clocks kept impeccable time.

It was winter. Christmas was coming. I hung clusters of purple glass baubles from the ceiling on strands of invisible thread. This was meant to be festive. Outside, it should have been snowing. But in this part of the world at this time of the year it rains instead.

Each night as dusk fell, I liked to sit on the edge of the table closest to the windows. I would roll up my shirt sleeves, eat my toast, and sip my sweet milky tea. Sometimes it was raining, cold drops on black asphalt. On Christmas Eve, children sang carols in the street, their faces and their voices cherubic under red and green umbrellas in the rain. I was smug, thinking myself exempt from the passage of time, the wretched welter of loneliness, the annoying need to question, insist, or explain. Despite all the evidence against me, I was not afraid. It was easy enough to be brave with these purple walls wrapped like the robes of royalty around me.

On New Year's morning I awoke to the sound of a million calendars turning their pages in the wind. I was forced to acknowledge the unbearable sweetness of being. You can run but you can't hide.

Now I find myself watching the clocks instead of the rain-sprinkled street. Their faces are impassive but their hands are always in motion. All mechanical clocks depend on the slow controlled release of power. Like the ticking of the clocks, there is a refrain in my head all day long now: *Be careful. Be careful. Be careful.* Sometimes it is only background noise and I am not actually hearing it. But then, if I pay attention to it even for an instant, it drives everything else right out of my head. This is like the way mothers are always warning their rambunctious children: *Be careful, don't fall. Be careful, don't bump your head. Be careful, it's hot. Be careful, it's sharp. Be careful, it's dark.*

When I need to hear a human voice instead of this carnivorous ticking of my brain and the clocks, I talk to the walls. Talking to the walls is not necessarily a bad thing, not if they are good strong walls, perfectly perpendicular, freshly painted, cool and smooth when you press your fevered lips against them. Purple walls in particular can convince you that everything you are telling them is brilliant, witty, and profound.

Time, they say, heals all wounds. Unless of course the wounds were fatal in the first place. He is not Lazarus. He will not rise from the dead. Even time has its limits. Do not expect that your life will follow the orderly unfolding of beginning, middle, and end. Once upon a time our hearts were innocent, generous, and sweet, oh so sweet, sweethearts. It is time to make it clear that, although hell indeed hath no fury like a woman scorned, still I did not leave his heart to draw flies in the driveway. I did not eat his head first. I did not swallow it whole.

It is time to turn my back on the seduction of these small rooms. It is time to address the issues and answer the charges. It is time to go home: home, where the walls are white and the hearts are black. Oh, do not ask, "Where is it?" *Let us go and make our visit.*

It is time to make it clear that I did not kill him. But yes, oh yes, I wanted to.

Publishing History and Notes

The date given after the title of each story is the year in which it was written. The publishing history of the stories is as follows:

"Losing Ground": *Event,* December 1981; *The Man of My Dreams,* Macmillan of Canada, 1990.

"This Town": *NeWest Review* (as "Our Town"), February 1981; *Banff Crag and Canyon,* December 1983; *Coming Attractions 2,* Oberon Press, 1984; *Hockey Night in Canada,* Quarry Press, 1987; *Hockey Night in Canada and Other Stories,* Quarry Press, 1991; *Under NeWest Eyes: Stories from the NeWest Review,* Thistledown Press, 1996.

"Frogs": *Quarry Magazine,* April 1983; *Coming Attractions 2,* Oberon Press, 1984; *Frogs and Other Stories,* Quarry Press, 1986; *Hockey Night in Canada and Other Stories,* Quarry Press, 1991.

"Hockey Night in Canada": *Western Living Magazine,* Vancouver Edition, August 1985; *Western Living Magazine,* Calgary Edition, March 1986; *Hockey Night in Canada,* Quarry Press, 1987; *The Rocket, The Flower, The Hammer and Me,* Polestar Press, 1988; *Hockey Night in Canada and Other Stories,* Quarry Press, 1991.

"Clues": *Alberta Bound: Thirty Stories by Alberta Writers,* NeWest Press, 1986; *Hockey Night in Canada,* Quarry Press, 1987; *Hockey Night in Canada and Other Stories,* Quarry Press, 1991.

"Tickets to Spain": *The Fiddlehead,* May 1986; *87 Best Canadian Stories,* Oberon Press, 1987; *Hockey Night in Canada,* Quarry Press, 1987; *The Man of My Dreams,* Macmillan of Canada, 1990. The sections about Spain in this story are from a number of sources including *Spain: The Land and its People* by Carmen Irizarry, Macdonald Educational Ltd., 1974; and *Spain* by Hugh Thomas and the Editors of *LIFE,* Time Inc., 1962, 1966. The Spanish sentences are from *Spanish in Three Months: Hugo's Simplified System,* Hugo's Language Books Ltd., 1959.

"A Simple Story": *Hockey Night in Canada,* Quarry Press, 1987; *The Macmillan Anthology 1,* Macmillan of Canada, 1988; *The Fiddlehead,* May 1988; *Hockey Night in Canada and Other Stories,* Quarry Press, 1991; *The New Story Writers,* Quarry Press, June 1992.

"The Man of My Dreams": *The Macmillan Anthology 1,* Macmillan of Canada, 1988; *The Man of My Dreams,* Macmillan of Canada, 1991. The sections about dream interpretations in this story are from *The Dictionary of Dreams: 10,000 Dreams Interpreted* by Gustavus Hindman Miller, Prentice Hall Press, 1986. This volume is a facsimile reprint of the original 1909 publication.

"In a Dark Season": *Mademoiselle* (as "The Wrong Men"), February 1990; *You (The Mail on Sunday),* April 1997.

"Red Plaid Shirt": *Saturday Night,* December 1989; *The Man of My Dreams,* Macmillan of Canada, 1990; *Canadian Short Stories,* Fifth Series, Oxford University Press, 1991; *The New Story Writers,* Quarry Press, 1992; *The New Oxford Book of Canadian Short Stories,* Oxford University Press, 1995; *The Writer's Path: An Introduction to Short Fiction,* ITP Nelson, 1998.

"Stranger Than Fiction": *The Malahat Review,* December 1989; *The Man of My Dreams,* Macmillan of Canada, 1990; *Meltwater: Fiction and Poetry from the Banff Centre for the Arts,* Banff Centre Press, 1999. John Berger's essay "The Credible Word" appeared in *Harper's Magazine,* July 1988, as did the items from the "Harper's Index" mentioned in this story.

"Railroading or: Twelve Small Stories with the Word *Train* in the Title": Excerpt in *Books in Canada,* October 1989; *The Man of My Dreams,* Macmillan of Canada, 1990; *And Other Stories,* Talonbooks, 2001.

"The Look of the Lightning, The Sound of the Birds": *The Third Macmillan Anthology,* Macmillan of Canada, April 1990; *The Man of My Dreams,* Macmillan of Canada, 1990.

"Mastering Effective English (A Linguistic Fable)": *The Man of My Dreams,* Macmillan of Canada, 1990. My Grade Twelve English textbook was *Mastering Effective English*, Third Edition, by J. C. Tressler and C. E. Lewis, Copp Clark Publishing Co. Ltd., 1961.

"Nothing Happens": *The New Quarterly,* October 1990.

"A Change is as Good as a Rest": *The Malahat Review,* October 1992.

"The Antonyms of Fiction": *Parallel Voices/Voix Paralleles,* Quarry Press/xyz, 1993.

"Weights and Measures": *Queen's Quarterly,* November 1994. The facts and figures in this story are from *The Guinness Book of World Records 1993,* Bantam Books, 1993.

"Forms of Devotion": *Saturday Night,* April 1996; *Forms of Devotion: Stories and Pictures,* A Phyllis Bruce Book, HarperCollins Canada, 1998.

"How Deep is the River?": *Forms of Devotion: Stories and Pictures,* A Phyllis Bruce Book, HarperCollins Canada, 1998. Some of the math questions in this story are from *Math Matters, Book 1* by Frank Ebos and Paul Zolis, Nelson Canada Ltd., 1981; and *Math in Action 2* by P. Pogue, S. Coombs, R. Graham, and W. Morrison, Copp Clark Pitman, 1982.

"Five Small Rooms (A Murder Mystery)": *Forms of Devotion: Stories and Pictures,* A Phyllis Bruce Book, HarperCollins Canada, 1998; *The Oxford Book of Stories by Canadian Women in English,* Oxford University Press, 1999. The names of the paint colours in this story are from the series of paint chips available at Canadian Tire.

Permissions

A special thanks to Zal Yanovsky and Rose Richardson, owners of Kingston's wonderful restaurant, Chez Piggy, for letting me borrow back my red plaid shirt which they bought several years ago at a Celebrity Auction for Kingston Literacy.

FOR THE BEST IN PAPERBACKS, LOOK FOR THE

In every corner of the world, on every subject under the sun, Penguin represents quality and variety—the very best in publishing today.

For complete information about books available from Penguin—including Penguin Classics, Penguin Compass, and Puffins—and how to order them, write to us at the appropriate address below. Please note that for copyright reasons the selection of books varies from country to country.

In the United States: Please write to *Penguin Group (USA), P.O. Box 12289 Dept. B, Newark, New Jersey 07101-5289* or call 1-800-788-6262.

In the United Kingdom: Please write to *Dept. EP, Penguin Books Ltd, Bath Road, Harmondsworth, West Drayton, Middlesex UB7 0DA.*

In Canada: Please write to *Penguin Books Canada Ltd, 10 Alcorn Avenue, Suite 300, Toronto, Ontario M4V 3B2.*

In Australia: Please write to *Penguin Books Australia Ltd, P.O. Box 257, Ringwood, Victoria 3134.*

In New Zealand: Please write to *Penguin Books (NZ) Ltd, Private Bag 102902, North Shore Mail Centre, Auckland 10.*

In India: Please write to *Penguin Books India Pvt Ltd, 11 Panchsheel Shopping Centre, Panchsheel Park, New Delhi 110 017.*

In the Netherlands: Please write to *Penguin Books Netherlands bv, Postbus 3507, NL-1001 AH Amsterdam.*

In Germany: Please write to *Penguin Books Deutschland GmbH, Metzlerstrasse 26, 60594 Frankfurt am Main.*

In Spain: Please write to *Penguin Books S. A., Bravo Murillo 19, 1° B, 28015 Madrid.*

In Italy: Please write to *Penguin Italia s.r.l., Via Benedetto Croce 2, 20094 Corsico, Milano.*

In France: Please write to *Penguin France, Le Carré Wilson, 62 rue Benjamin Baillaud, 31500 Toulouse.*

In Japan: Please write to *Penguin Books Japan Ltd, Kaneko Building, 2-3-25 Koraku, Bunkyo-Ku, Tokyo 112.*

In South Africa: Please write to *Penguin Books South Africa (Pty) Ltd, Private Bag X14, Parkview, 2122 Johannesburg.*